ANGUS, THONGS AND FULL-FRONTAL SNOGGING
Confessions of Georgia Nicolson:

"A younger Bridget Jones – but funnier." **Sunday Telegraph**

"A delicious diary which pinpoints exactly the large and small emotions of a teenager. Don't miss this gem." **The Guardian**

"[Georgia] recounts these traumas with a sense of irony and a deadpan hilarity Bridget Jones could only dream of, and it's one of the funniest books of the year."
Terence Blacker, Independent on Sunday

"This is the Bridget Jones diary for young teenagers and it really is hilarious." **The Irish Times**

"This is very funny – very, very funny. It really is very funny." **Alan Davies, comedian**

"The perfectly-observed catalogue of anxieties – from shaming school uniforms and plucked eyebrows to first kisses and (maybe) true love." **Time Out**

"This very funny book perfectly captures the agony of being a teenager." **Book of the Week, Sunday Mirror**

"I laughed like a drain." **John Peel**

"Suppose you combined two modern British diarists, Adrian Mole and Bridget Jones. Here's what you'd get. A little raunchy and very funny." **The New York Times Book Review**

IT's OK, I'm WEARING REALLY BIG KNICKERS!
Further Confessions of Georgia Nicolson:

"Seriously funny – so be careful about reading it in public."
Daily Telegraph

"This is laugh-out-loud stuff for adolescent girls and for anyone
worn down by adult life who needs reminding that being young
isn't all good fun. Except in this book." **Sunday Mirror**

"Hurray! She's back! Georgia, the muddle-headed, angst-ridden
drama queen of Angus, Thongs and Full-frontal Snogging reveals
all again in a diary full of thrills, spills and hilarious escapades."
Time Out

KNOCKED OUT BY MY NUNGA-NUNGAS
Further, Further Confessions of Georgia Nicolson:

"This (the third delicious chronicle of her adventures) is as fast,
furious and funny as ever, and we love her even more every time
she pens another agonised diary entry." **Time Out**

"Readers who became addicted to Georgia's hilarious reflections
on adolescence will identify with Georgia's competing emotions
even as they laugh their way through every situation."
Publishers Weekly

"Louise Rennison has swept all before her with her dazzlingly
titled diaries of Georgia Nicolson." **TES**

DANCING IN MY NUDDY-PANTS
More Confessions of Georgia Nicolson:

"Reading it on a train or plane will make a giggling idiot of you
in public." **Sunday Times**

"As addictive as the first three." **Sunday Telegraph**

"Wickedly funny." **The Bookseller**

Confessions of Georgia Nicolson

Louise Rennison

Piccadilly Press • London

Printed and bound in Great Britain by MPG Books Ltd, Bodmin for the publishers Piccadilly Press Ltd., 5 Castle Road, London NW1 8PR

A catalogue record for this book is available from the British Library

ISBN 1 85340 753 4

3 5 7 9 10 8 6 4

Text design by Judith Robertson
Cover design by Fielding Design

Louise Rennison spends her waking hours in a whirlpool . . . er . . . wind of excitement and glamour. Often up at the crack of midday in her seafront flat in Brighton, she fills her day with swimming, dancing (quite often in the semi nuddy-pants) and, of course, exercising her creativosity.

She is petless at the moment (unbeknownst to the hugely fat cat next door, who had to be removed from Louise's redundant but normal sized cat flap by the fire brigade).

Future plans include a film and (alarmingly) a live musical version of the Georgia series, featuring the Stiff Dylans.

This fat book (and I am not being fattist, merely factual) is
dedicated to my lovely family and all of my chums. Even those
who border on the criminally insane (and I think you know who
you are, you girls who wore "Och aye Jimmy" wigs and
tam-o'-shanters on your school trip to Belgium).
I love you all.
Yes I do.
Don't argue; it just cheapens my love for you all.

A word from the author

"Blimey."

Lots of love,

Georgia xxxxx

<u>There are six things very wrong with my
life:</u>

1) I have one of those under-the-skin
   spots that will never come to a head
   but lurk in a red way for the next
   two years.

2) It is on my nose.

3) I have a three-year-old sister who
   may have peed somewhere in my room.

4) In fourteen days the summer hols
   will be over and then it will be back
   to Stalag 14 and Oberführer Frau
   Simpson and her bunch of sadistic
   "teachers".

5) I am very ugly and need to go into
   an ugly home.

6) I went to a party dressed as a stuffed
   olive.

ANGUS, THONGS AND FULL-FRONTAL SNOGGING

Confessions of Georgia Nicolson

august

la marche avec mystery

sunday august 23rd

my bedroom
raining

10.00 a.m. Dad had Uncle Eddie round so naturally they had to come and nose around and see what I was up to. If Uncle Eddie (who is bald as a coot – two coots, in fact) says to me one more time, "Should bald heads be buttered?" I may kill myself. He doesn't seem to realise that I no longer wear romper-suits. I feel like yelling at him, "I am fourteen years old, Uncle Eddie! I am bursting with womanhood, I wear a bra! OK, it's a bit on the loose side and does ride up round my neck if I run for the bus . . . but the womanly potential is there, you bald coot!"

Talking of breasts, I'm worried that I may end up like the rest of the women in my family, with just the one bust, like a sort of shelf affair. Mum can balance things on hers when her hands are full – at parties, and so on, she can have a sandwich and drink and save a snack for later by putting it on her shelf. It's very unattractive. I would like a proper amount of breastiness but not go too far with it, like Melanie Andrews, for instance. I got the most awful shock in the showers after hockey last term.

3

Her bra looks like two shopping bags. I suspect she is a bit unbalanced hormonally. She certainly is when she tries to run for the ball. I thought she'd run right through the fence with the momentum of her "bosoomers" as Jas so amusingly calls them.

still in my room
still raining
still sunday

11.30 a.m. I don't see why I can't have a lock on my bedroom door. I have no privacy; it's like *Noel's House Party* in my room. Every time I suggest anything around this place people start shaking their heads and tutting. It's like living in a house full of chickens dressed in frocks and trousers. Or a house full of those nodding dogs, or a house full of . . . anyway . . . I can't have a lock on my door is the short and short of it.

"Why not?" I asked Mum reasonably (catching her in one of the rare minutes when she's not at Italian evening class or at another party).

"Because you might have an accident and we couldn't get in," she said.

"An accident like what?" I persisted.

"Well . . . you might faint," she said.

Then Dad joined in, "You might set fire to your bed and be overcome with fumes."

What is the matter with people? I know why they don't want me to have a lock on my door, it's because it would be a first sign of my path to adulthood and they can't bear the idea of that, because it would mean they might have to get on with their own lives and leave me alone.

4

still sunday

11.35 a.m. There are six things very wrong with my life:

1 I have one of those under-the-skin spots that will never come to a head but lurk in a red way for the next two years.
2 It is on my nose.
3 I have a three-year-old sister who may have peed somewhere in my room.
4 In fourteen days the summer hols will be over and then it will be back to Stalag 14 and Oberführer Frau Simpson and her bunch of sadistic "teachers".
5 I am very ugly and need to go into an ugly home.
6 I went to a party dressed as a stuffed olive.

11.40 a.m. OK, that's it. I'm turning over a new leaf. I found an article in Mum's *Cosmo* about how to be happy if you are very unhappy (which I am). The article is called "Emotional Confidence". What you have to do is *Recall . . . Experience . . . and HEAL.* So you think of a painful incident and you remember all the ghastly detail of it . . . this is the Recall bit, then you experience the emotions and acknowledge them and then you JUST LET IT GO.

2.00 p.m. Uncle Eddie has gone, thank the Lord. He actually asked me if I'd like to ride in the sidecar on his motorbike. Are all adults from Planet Xenon? What should I have said? "Yes, certainly, Uncle Eddie, I would like to go in your pre-war sidecar and with a bit of luck all of my friends will see me with some mad, bald bloke and that will be the end of my life. Thank you."

Jas came round. She said it took her ages to get out of her catsuit after the fancy dress party. I wasn't very interested but I asked her why out of politeness.

She said, "Well, the boy behind the counter in the hire shop was really good-looking."

"Yes, so?"

"Well, so I lied about my size – I got a size ten catsuit instead of twelve."

She showed me the marks around her neck and waist; they are quite deep. I said, "Your head looks a bit swollen up."

"No, that's just Sunday."

I told her about the *Cosmo* article and so we spent a few hours recalling the fancy dress party (i.e. the painful incident) and experiencing the emotions in order to heal them.

I blame Jas entirely. It may have been my idea to go as a stuffed olive but she didn't stop me like a pal should do. In fact, she encouraged me. We made the stuffed olive costume out of chicken wire and green crêpe paper – that was for the "olive" bit. It had little shoulder straps to keep it up and I wore a green T-shirt and green tights underneath. It was the "stuffed" bit that Jas helped with mostly. As I recall, it was she that suggested I use crazy colour to dye my hair and head and face and neck red . . . like a sort of pimento. It was, I have to say, quite funny at the time. Well, when we were in my room. The difficulty came when I tried to get out of my room. I had to go down the stairs sideways.

When I did get to the door I had to go back and change my tights because my cat Angus had one of his "Call of the Wild" episodes.

He really is completely bonkers. We got him when we went

6

on holiday to Loch Lomond. On the last day I found him wandering around the garden of the guest-house we were staying in. Tarry-a-Wee-While, it was called. That should give you some idea of what the holiday was like.

I should have guessed all was not entirely well in the cat department when I picked him up and he began savaging my cardigan. But he was such a lovely looking kitten, all tabby and long-haired, with huge yellow eyes. Even as a kitten he looked like small dog. I begged and pleaded to take him home.

"He'll die here, he has no mummy or daddy," I said plaintively.

My dad said, "He's probably eaten them." Honestly, he can be callous. I worked on Mum and in the end I brought him home. The Scottish landlady did say she thought he was probably mixed breed, half domestic tabby and half Scottish wildcat. I remember thinking, Oh, that will be exotic. I didn't realise that he would grow to the size of a small Labrador only mad. I used to drag him around on a lead but, as I explained to Mrs Next Door, he ate it.

Anyway, sometimes he hears the call of the Scottish Highlands. So, as I was passing by as a stuffed olive he leaped out from his concealed hiding-place behind the curtains (or his lair, as I suppose he imagined it in his cat brain) and attacked my tights or "prey". I couldn't break his hold by banging his head because he was darting from side to side. In the end I managed to reach the outdoor brush by the door and beat him off with it.

Then I couldn't get in Dad's Volvo. Dad said, "Why don't you take off the olive bit and we'll stick it in the boot."

Honestly, what is the point? I said, "Dad, if you think I am sitting next to you in a green T-shirt and tights, you're mad."

7

He got all shirty like parents do as soon as you point out how stupid and useless they are. "Well, you'll have to walk, then . . . I'll drive along really slowly with Jas and you walk alongside."

I couldn't believe it. "If I have to walk, why don't Jas and I both walk there and forget about the car?"

He got that stupid, tight-lipped look that dads get when they think they are being reasonable. "Because I want to be sure of where you are going. I don't want you out wandering the streets at night."

Unbelievable! I said, "What would I be doing walking the streets at night as a stuffed olive . . . gatecrashing cocktail parties?"

Jas smirked but Dad got all outraged parenty. "Don't you speak to me like that, otherwise you won't go out at all."

What is the point?

When we did eventually get to the party (me walking next to Dad's Volvo driving at five miles an hour), I had a horrible time. Everyone laughed at first but then more or less ignored me. In a mood of defiant stuffed oliveness I did have a dance by myself but things kept crashing to the floor around me. The host asked me if I would sit down. I had a go at that but it was useless. In the end I was at the gate for about an hour before Dad arrived, and I did stick the olive bit in the boot. We didn't speak on the way home.

Jas, on the other hand, had a great time. She said she was surrounded by Tarzans and Robin Hoods and James Bonds. (Boys have very vivid imaginations . . . not.)

I was feeling a bit moody as we did the "recall" bit. I said bitterly, "Well, I could have been surrounded by boys if I hadn't been dressed as an olive."

8

Jas said, "Georgia, you thought it was funny and I thought it was funny but you have to remember that boys don't think girls are for funniness."

She looked annoyingly "wise" and "mature". What the hell did she know about boys? God, she had an annoying fringe. Shut up, fringey.

I said, "Oh yeah, so that's what they want, is it? Boys? They want simpering girly-wirlys in catsuits?"

Through my bedroom window I could see next door's poodle leaping up and down at our fence, yapping. It would be trying to scare off our cat Angus . . . fat chance.

Jas was going on and on wisely, "Yes they do, I think they do like girls who are a bit soft and not so, well . . . you know."

She was zipping up her rucksack. I looked at her. "Not so what?" I asked.

She said, "I have to go, we have an early supper."

As she left my room I knew I should shut up. But you know when you should shut up because you really should just shut up . . . but you keep on and on anyway? Well, I had that.

"Go on . . . not so what?" I insisted.

She mumbled something as she went down the stairs.

I yelled at her as she went through the door, "Not so like me you mean, don't you?!!!"

11.00 p.m. I can already feel myself getting fed up with boys and I haven't had anything to do with them yet.

midnight Oh God, please, please don't make me have to be a lesbian like Hairy Kate or Miss Stamp.

9

12.10 a.m. What do lesbians do, anyway?

monday august 24th

5.00 p.m. Absolutely no phonecalls from anyone. I may as well be dead. I'm going to have an early night.

5.30 p.m. Libby came in and squiggled into bed with me, saying, "Hahahahaha!" for so long I had to get up. She's so nice, although a bit smelly. At least she likes me and doesn't mind if I have a sense of humour.

7.00 p.m. Ellen and Julia rang from a phonebox. They took turns to speak in French accents. We're going for a mystery walk tomorrow. Or *La marche avec mystery*.

10.30 p.m. Have put on a face-mask made from egg yolk just in case we see any *les garçons* gorgeous on our walk.

tuesday august 25th

9.00 a.m. Woke up and thought my face was paralysed. It was quite scary – my skin was all tight and stiff and I couldn't open my eyes properly. Then I remembered the egg yolk mask. I must have fallen asleep reading. I don't think I'll go to bed early again, it makes my eyes go all puffy. I look like there is a touch of the Oriental in my family. Sadly not the case. The nearest we have to any exotic influence is Auntie Kath, who can sing in Chinese, but only after a couple of pints of wine.

11.00 a.m. Arranged to rendezvous with Ellen and Julia at Whiteleys so we can start our *La marche avec mystery*. We agreed we would dress "sports casual", so I'm wearing ski trousers, ankle boots and a black top with a roll neck, with a PVC jacket. I'm going for the young Brigitte Bardot look which is a shame as, a) – I am nothing like her and b) – I haven't got blonde hair, which is, as we all know, her trademark. I would have blonde hair if I was allowed but it honestly is like *Playschool* at my house. My dad has got the mentality of a Teletubby only not so developed. I said to Mum, "I'm going to dye my hair blonde, what product would you recommend?" She pretended not to hear me and went on dressing Libby. But Dad went ballistic.

"You're fourteen years old, you've only had that hair for fourteen years and you want to change it already! How bored are you going to be with it by the time you are thirty? What colour will you be up to by then?"

Honestly, he makes little real sense these days. I said to Mum, "Oh, I thought I could hear a voice squeaking and making peculiar noises, but I was mistaken. TTFN."

As I ran for the door I heard him shouting, "I suppose you think being sarcastic and applying eyeliner in a straight line will get you some O-levels!!!"

O-levels, I ask you. He's a living reminder of the Stone Age.

noon *La marche avec mystery*. We walked up and down the High Street, only speaking

11

French. I asked passers-by for directions, *"Où est la gare, s'il vous plaît?"* and *"Au secours, j'oublie ma tête, aidez-moi, s'il vous plaît."*

Then . . . this really dishy bloke came along . . . Julia and Ellen wouldn't go up to him but I did. I don't know why, but I developed a limp as well as being French. He had really nice eyes . . . he must have been about nineteen, anyway I hobbled up to him and said, *"Excusez-moi. Je suis Française. Je ne parle pas l'Anglais. Parlez-vous Français?"*

Fortunately he looked puzzled, it was quite dreamy. I pouted my mouth a bit. Cindy Crawford said that if you put your tongue behind your back teeth when you smile, it makes your smile really sexy. Impossible to talk, of course, unless you like sounding like a loony.

Anyway, dreamboat said, "Are you lost? I don't speak French."

I looked puzzled (and pouty). *"Au secours, monsieur,"* I breathed.

He took my arm. "Look, don't be frightened, come with me."

Ellen and Jools looked amazed: he was bloody gorgeous and he was taking me somewhere. I hobbled along attractively by his side. Not for very long, though, just into a French pâtisserie where the lady behind the counter was French.

8.00 p.m. In bed. The French woman talked French at me for about forty years. I nodded for as long as humanly possible then just ran out of the shop and into the street. The gorgeous boy looked surprised that my limp had cured itself so quickly.

I really will have to dye my hair now if I ever want to go shopping in this town again.

11.00 a.m. I have no friends. Not one single friend. No one has rung, no one has come round. Mum and Dad have gone to work, Libby is at playschool. I may as well be dead.

Perhaps I am dead. I wonder how you would know? If you died in your sleep and woke up dead. Who would let you know?

It could be like in that film where you can see everyone but they can't see you because you are dead. Oh, I've really given myself the creeps now . . . I'm going to put on a really loud CD and dance about.

noon Now I am still freaked out but also tired. If I did die I wonder if anyone would really care. Who would come to my funeral? Mum and Dad, I suppose . . . they'd have to as it's mostly their fault that I was depressed enough to commit suicide in the first place.

Why couldn't I have a normal family like Julia and Ellen? They've got normal brothers and sisters. Their dads have got beards and sheds. My mum won't let my dad have a shed since he left his fishing maggots in there and it became bluebottle headquarters.

When the electrician came because the fridge had blown up he said to Mum, "What madman wired up this fridge? Is there someone you know who really doesn't like you?" And Dad had done the wiring. Instead of DIY he talks about feelings and stuff. Why can't he be a real dad? It's pathetic in a grown man.

I don't mean I want to be like an old-fashioned woman –

you know, all lacy and the man is all tight-lipped and never says anything even if he has got a brain tumour. I want my boyfriend (provided, God willing, I am not a lesbian) to be emotional . . . but only about me. I want him to be like Darcy in *Pride and Prejudice* (although, having said that, I've seen him in other things like *Fever Pitch* and he's not so sexy out of frilly shirts and tights). Anyway, I'll never have a boyfriend because I am too ugly.

2.00 p.m. Looking through the old family albums . . . I'm not really surprised I'm ugly, the photos of Dad as a child are terrifying. His nose is huge . . . it takes up half of his face. In fact, he is literally just a nose with legs and arms attached.

10.00 p.m. Libby has woken up and insists on sleeping in my bed. It's quite nice, although she does smell a bit on the hamsterish side.

midnight The tunnel of love dream I've just had, where this gorgey bloke is carrying me through the warm waters of the Caribbean, turns out to be Libby's wet pyjamas on my legs.

Change bed. Libby not a bit bothered and in fact slaps my hand and calls me "Bad boy" when I change her pyjamas.

thursday august 27th

11.00 a.m. I've started worrying about what to wear for first day back at school. It's only eleven days away now. I wonder how much "natural" make-up

I can get away with? Concealer is OK – I wonder about mascara? Maybe I should just dye my eyelashes? I hate my eyebrows. I say eyebrows but in fact it's just the one eyebrow right along my forehead. I may have to do some radical plucking if I can find Mum's tweezers. She hides things from me now because she says that I never replace anything. I'll have to rummage around in her bedroom.

1.00 p.m. Prepared a light lunch of sandwich spread and milky coffee. There's never anything to eat in this house. No wonder my elbows stick out so much.

2.00 p.m. Found the tweezers eventually. Why Mum would think I wouldn't find them in Dad's tie drawer I really don't know. I did find something very strange in the tie drawer as well as the tweezers. It was a sort of apron thing in a special box. I hope against hope that my dad is not a transvestite. It would be more than flesh and blood could stand if I had to "understand" his feminine side. And me and Mum and Libby have to watch whilst he clatters around in one of Mum's nighties and fluffy mules . . . We'll probably have to start calling him Daphne.

God, it's painful plucking. I'll have to have a little lie down. The pain is awful, it's made my eyes water like mad.

2.30 p.m. I can't bear this. I've only taken about five hairs out and my eyes are swollen to twice their normal size.

4.00 p.m. Cracked it. I'll use Dad's razor.

4.05 p.m. Sharper than I thought. It's taken off a lot of hair just on one stroke. I'll have to even up the other one.

4.16 p.m. Bugger it. It looks all right, I think, but I look very surprised in one eye. I'll have to even up the other one now.

6.00 p.m. Mum nearly dropped Libby when she saw me. Her exact words were, "What in the name of God have you done to yourself, you stupid girl?"

God I hate parents! Me stupid?? They're so stupid. She wishes I was still Libby's age so she could dress me in ridiculous hats with earflaps and ducks on. God, God, God!!!

7.00 p.m. When Dad came in I could hear them talking about me.

"Mumble mumble . . . she looks like . . . mumble mumble," from Mum, then I heard Dad, "She WHAT??? Well . . . mumble . . . mumble . . . grumble . . ." Stamp, stamp, bang, bang on the door.

"Georgia, what have you done now?"

I shouted from under the blankets – he couldn't get in because I had put a chest of drawers in front of the door – "At least I'm a real woman!!!"

He said through the door, "What in the name of arse is that supposed to mean?"

Honestly, he can be so crude.

10.00 p.m. Maybe they'll grow back overnight. How long does it take for eyebrows to grow?

16

friday august 28th

11.00 a.m.

Eyebrows haven't grown back.

11.15 a.m.

Jas phoned and wanted to go shopping – there's some new make-up range that looks so natural you can't tell you have got any on.

I said, "Do they do eyebrows?"

She said, "Why? What do you mean? Do you mean false eyelashes?"

I said, "No, I mean eyebrows. You know, the hairy bits above your eyes." Honestly friends can be thick.

"Of course they don't do eyebrows. Everyone's got eyebrows, why would you need a spare pair?"

I said, "I haven't got any any more. I shaved them off by mistake."

She said, "I'm coming round now, don't do anything until I get there."

noon

When I open the door Jas just looks at me like I'm a Klingon. "You look like a Klingon," she says. She really is a dim friend. It's more like having a dog than a friend, actually.

6.00 p.m.

Jas has gone. Her idea of help was to draw some eyebrows on with eyeliner pencil.

Obviously I have to stay in now for ever.

7.00 p.m.

Dad is annoying me so much. He just comes to the door, looks in and laughs, and then he goes away . . . for a bit. He brought Uncle Eddie upstairs for a look. What am I? A daughter or a fairground attraction? Uncle Eddie said, "Never mind, if they don't grow back you and I can go into showbiz. We can do a double act doing impressions of billiard balls." Oh how I laughed. Not.

8.00 p.m. The only nice person is Libby. She was stroking where my eyebrows used to be and then she went off and brought me a lump of cheese. Great, I have become ratwoman.

I wonder who our form teacher will be?

Pray God it's not Hawkeye Heaton. I don't want her to be constantly reminded of the unfortunate locust incident. Who would have thought a few locusts could eat so much in so little time? When I let them out into the Biology lab for a bit of a fly round I wouldn't have expected them to eat the curtains.

Strikes me that Hawkeye has very little sense of humour. She is also about a hundred and a Miss – which speaks volumes in my book. Mind you, as ratwoman I'll probably end up as a teacher of Biology in some poxy girls' school. Like her. Having cats and warm milk. Wearing huge knickers. Listening to the radio. Being interested in things.

I may as well kill myself. I would if I could be bothered but I'm too depressed.

saturday august 29th

10.00 a.m. M and D went out to town to buy stuff. Mum said did I want her to buy some school shoes for me? I glanced meaningfully at her shoes. It's sad that someone of her mature years tries to keep up with us young ones. You'd think she'd be ashamed to be mutton dressed as lamb, but no. I could see her knickers when she sat down the other day (and I wasn't the only one).

11.00 a.m. Phone rang. Ellen and Julia and Jas are coming round after they've been to town. Apparently Jas has seen someone in a shop that she really likes. I suppose this is what life will be like for me – never having a boyfriend, always just living through others.

noon I was glancing through *Just 17* and it listed kissing techniques. What I don't understand is how do you know when to do it, and how do you know which side to go to? You don't want to be bobbing around like pigeons for hours but I couldn't tell much from the photos. I wish I had never read it, it has made me more nervous and confused than I was before. Still, why should I care? I am going to be staying in for the rest of my life. Unless some gorgeous boy loses his way and wanders into my street and then finds his way up the stairs into my bedroom with a blindfold on I am stuck between these four walls for ever.

12.15 p.m. Perhaps as I can't go out I can use my time wisely. I may tidy my room and put all my dresses in one part of my wardrobe, and so on.

12.17 p.m. I hate housework.

12.18 p.m. If I marry or, as is more likely, become a high-flying executive lesbian, I am never going to do housework. I will have to have an assistant. I have no talent for tidying. Mum thinks that I deliberately ignore the obvious things but the truth is I can't tell the difference between tidy and not tidy. When Mum says, "Will you just tidy up the kitchen?" I look around and I think, Well, there's a few pans on the side, and so on, but I think it looks OK. And then the row begins.

2.00 p.m. Putting the coffee on for the girls. It's instant but if you mix the coffee with sugar in the cup for ages it goes into a sort of paste, then you add water and it's like espresso. It makes your arms ache like billy-o, though.

7.00 p.m. Brilliant afternoon! We tried all different make-ups. I've been Sellotaping my fringe to make it longer and straighter and to cover up the space where my eyebrows were. Jas said, "It makes you look like you've escaped from the funny lads' home." Ellen says if I emphasise my mouth and eyes then attention will be drawn away from my nose. So it's heavy lippy for me from now on.

We were all lolling about on my bed, listening to the Top Forty and Jas told us about the gorgeous boy in the shop. She knows he is called Tom because someone called him Tom in the shop he works in. Supersleuth! We all pledged that we would wait until I can go out again and then we will go and look at him.

Talk then turned to kissing. Ellen said, "I went to a

20

Christmas party at my cousin's last year and this boy from Liverpool was there. I think he was a sailor. Anyway, he was nineteen or something, and he brought some mistletoe over and he kissed me."

We were full-on, attention wise. I said, "What was it like?"

Ellen said, "A bit on the wet side, like a sort of warm jelly feeling."

Jas said, "Did he have his lips closed or open?"

Ellen thought. "A bit open."

I asked, "Did his tongue pop out?"

Ellen said, "No, just his lips."

I wanted to know what she did with her tongue.

"Well, I just left it where it normally is."

I persisted, "What about your teeth?"

Ellen was a bit exasperated. "Oh, yeah, I took those out."

I looked a bit hurt. You know, like, I was only asking . . .

She said, "I can't really remember. It was a bit tickly and it didn't last long, but I liked it, I think. He was quite nice but he had a girlfriend and I suppose he thought I was just a little thirteen-year-old who hadn't been around much."

I said, "He was right."

10.00 p.m. My sister Libby kisses me on the mouth quite a lot, but I don't think sisters count. Unless I am a lesbian, in which case it's all good practice probably.

11.00 p.m. Through my curtains I can see a big yellow moon. I'm thinking of all the people in the world who will be looking at that same moon.

I wonder how many of them haven't got any eyebrows?

21

11.00 a.m. Thank God they're all actually going out. At last. What is all this happy family nonsense? All this "we should do things as a family"?

As I pointed out to Dad, "We are four people who, through great misfortune, happen to be stuck in the same house. Why make it worse by hanging around in garden centres or going for a walk together?"

Anyway, ratwoman does not go out. She just hangs around in her bedroom for the next forty years to avoid being laughed at by strangers.

I will never ever have a boyfriend. It's not fair, there are some really stupid people and they get boyfriends. Zoe Ball gets really nice boyfriends and she has got sticky-out ears.

1.00 p.m. I still haven't tackled Dad about his apron.

1.15 p.m. God I'm bored. I can see Mr and Mrs Next Door in their greenhouse. What do people do in them? If I end up with someone like Mr Next Door I will definitely kill myself. He has the largest bottom I have ever seen. It amazes me he can get in the greenhouse. One day his bottom will be so large he will have to live in the greenhouse and have bits of chop passed to him, and so on. *O quel dommage! Sacré bleu!! Le gros monsieur dans la maison de glass!!!*

1.20 p.m. I may start a neighbourhood newspaper.

1.22 p.m. Oh dear. I have just seen Angus hunkering down in the long grass. He's stalking their poodle. I'll have to intervene to avert a massacre. Oh, it's OK, Mrs Next Door has thrown a brick at him.

11.00 p.m. What a long, boring day. I hate Sundays, they are deliberately invented by people who have no life and no friends. On the plus side, I've got six o'clock shadow on the eyebrow front.

september

operation sausage

tuesday september 1st

10.00 a.m. Six days to school and counting. I wish my mum could be emancipated, a feminist, a working mother etc. and manage to do my ironing.

I thought I'd wear my pencil line skirt the first day back, with hold-up stockings and my ankle boots. I'm still not really resolved in the make-up department because if I do run into Hawkeye she'll make me take it off if she spots it. Then I'll get that shiny red face look which is so popular with PE teachers. On the other hand, I cannot possibly risk walking to school without make-up on. No matter how much I stick to sidestreets, sooner or later I will be bound to bump into the Foxwood lads. The biggest worry of all is the bloody beret. I must consult with the gang to see what our plan is.

5.00 p.m. We're having an emergency Beret and Other Forms of Torture meeting tomorrow, at my place again. I have got eyebrows now but still look a bit on the startled earwig side.

7.00 p.m. After tea, when Dad was doing the washing-up, I said casually, "Why don't you wear your special apron, Dad?"

He went ballistic and said I shouldn't be prying through his drawers. I said, "I think I've got a right to know if my dad is a transvestite."

Mum laughed, which made him even madder. "You encourage her, Connie. You show no respect, so how can she?"

Mum said, "Calm down, Bob, of course I respect you, it's just that it is quite funny to think of you as a transvestite." Then she started laughing again. Dad went off to the pub, thank goodness.

Mum said, "It's his Masonic apron. You know, that huddly duddly, pulling up one sock, I'll scratch your back if you scratch mine sort of thing."

I smiled and nodded but I haven't the remotest idea what she is talking about.

11.30 p.m. Why couldn't I be adopted? I wonder if it's too late. Am I too old to ring Esther Rantzen's helpline? I might get Esther. Good grief.

wednesday september 2nd

five days to purgatory

10.00 a.m. Oh. No, it's here already. As a special "treat" my cousin James is coming to stay with us overnight.

I mean, I used to like him and we were quite close as kids and everything, but he's so goofy now. His voice is all peculiar and he's got a funny smell. Not hamsterish like Libby but sort of doggy/cheesy. I don't think all boys smell like that, perhaps it's because he's my cousin.

2.00 p.m. James actually not such bad fun; he seems much younger than me and still wants to do mad dancing to old records like we used to. We worked out some dance routines to old soul records of Mum's. "Reach Out I'll Be There" by the Four Tops was quite dramatic. It was two pointy points, one hand on heart, one hand on head, a shimmy and a full turn around. Sadly there's not much room in my bedroom and James trod on Angus who, as usual, went berserk.

Actually, it would be more unusual to say "Angus went calm". Anyway, he ran up the curtains and finally got on top of the door and crouched there, hissing (Angus, that is, not James). We tried to get him down and also we tried to get to the bathroom but he wouldn't let us. If we tried to get through the door he'd strike out with his huge paw. I think he is part cat, part cobra. In the end Mum got him down with some sardines.

7.00 p.m. After "tea" James and I were listening to records and talking about what we were going to do after we ditch The Olds (as we call our parents). I'm going to be a comedy actress or someone like those "it" girls who don't actually do anything except be "it". The newspapers follow them all day and the headlines say, *Oh, look, there is Tara Pompeii Too-Booby going out to buy some biscuits!!* or *Tamsin Snaggle-Tooth Polyplops goes skiing in fur bikini.* And they just make money from that. That is me, that is.

James wants to do something electronic (whatever that means, I didn't encourage him to explain because I felt a coma coming on). He wants to travel first, though. I said, "Oh, do you, where?" Thinking . . . Himalayas, yak butter, opium dens, and he said, "Well, the Scilly Isles in particular."

11.00 p.m. Something a bit weird happened. We went to bed – James slept in a sleeping bag on some cushions on the floor, and we were chatting about Pulp, and so on, and then I felt this pressure on my leg. He had reached out and held my leg. I didn't know what to do so I kept really still, so that he might think he'd just got hold of a piece of the bed or something. I stayed still for ages but then I think I must have dropped off.

thursday september 3rd

9.00 a.m. At last the eyebrows are starting to look normal.

2.00 p.m. James went home. The "leg" incident was not mentioned. Boys are truly weird.

5.00 p.m. Libby has the flu. She was all pale and miserable. I let her sleep in my bed and she was snuffling, poor thing. Poor little thing, I really love my little sister.

8.30 p.m. Took Libbs some hot milk and thought she might like me to read *The Magic Faraway Tree*. She said, "Yes, now, more please," and sat herself up in my bed. Then, as I opened the book, she took my duvet cover and blew her nose on it. It's absolutely covered in green snot. Who

27

would have thought such a tiny girl could produce a bucket of snot?

10.00 p.m. I had to sleep in the sleeping bag. What a life.

friday september 4th

11.00 a.m. Emergency Beret and Other Forms of Torture meeting to be held this afternoon. I've decided that my eyebrows have recovered enough to venture out (obviously not on their own). I feel like one of those blokes who have been held in solitary in a cellar and come out into the daylight blinking.

We go to Costa Ricos for cappuccino. I hate cappuccino but everyone drinks it so you can't say no. I haven't been out for weeks – well, five days. Town looks great. Like New York . . . but without the skyscrapers and Americans. We decide we'll have the meeting and then go and sneak a look at the boy that Jas likes, Tom. He works in Jennings. I said, "What, the grocers?"

Jas said, "It's a greengrocer-cum-delicatessen," and I said, "Yes, well it sells houmus." And she said, "And yoghurt," and I said, "*Quel dommage*, I forgot the yoghurt. Yes, it's like going to Paris going into that shop, apart from the turnips."

Jas sort of went red, so I thought I would shut up. Jas doesn't get angry very often but she has a hefty kick.

Jools said, "Shall we talk beret plan?" At our stupid school you have to wear a beret with your outdoor uniform. It's a real pain because, as we know, everyone – and especially the French who invented it – looks like a stupid prat in a beret. And they flatten your hair. Last term we perfected a way of

28

wearing it like a pancake. You flatten it out and then pin it with hair grips right at the back of your head. Still a pain, but you can't see it from the front. Ellen said she had made up a different method, called "the sausage". She showed us how to do it. She rolled her beret up really tight like a little sausage and then pinned it with hair grips right at the back in the centre of her head. You could hardly see it at all. It was brilliant. We decided to instigate Operation Sausage at the beginning of the term.

It has been a constant battle about these berets. The so-called grown-ups will not negotiate with us. We sent a deputation to the headmistress Slim (so-called because she weighs twenty-five stone . . . at least. Her feet cascade out of her shoes). At the deputation we asked why we had to wear berets. She said it was to keep standards up, and to enhance the image of the school in the community. I said, "But the boys from Foxwood call out, 'Have you got any onions?' I don't think they do respect us, I think they make a mock and a sham of us."

Slim shook herself. It was a sort of habit that she had when she was irritated with us (i.e. all the time). It made her look like a jelly with shoes on.

"Georgia, you have had my last word on this, berets are to be worn to and from school. Why not think about something a bit more important, like perhaps getting less than twenty-one poor conduct marks next term?"

Oh, go on, play the old record again. Just because I am lively.

We did have another campaign last year, which was If You Want Us to Wear Our Berets, Let's Really Wear Our Berets.

This involved the whole of our year pulling their berets right down over their heads with just their ears showing. It was very

29

stunning, seeing one hundred girls at the bus stop with just their ears showing. We stopped eventually (even though it really infuriated Slim and Hawkeye) because it was terribly hot and you couldn't see where you were going and it played havoc with your hair.

Meeting over and time for boy-stalking. Jas was a bit nervous about us all going into the shop. She's not actually spoken to Tom – well, apart from saying "Two pounds of greens".

We decided that we'd lurk casually outside and then, when she went in to be served, we'd sort of accidentally spot her and pop into the shop and say "Hi". This would be casual and give us the chance to give him the once-over and also give the (wrong) impression that Jas is a very popular person.

Jas popped to the loos to make herself look natural with panstick, etc. Then she went into Jennings. I gave it five minutes and then I was the first one to walk by the shop doorway. Jas was talking to a tall, dark-haired boy in black jeans. He was smiling as he handed over some onions. Jas was a bit flushed and was twiddling with her fringe. It was a very irritating habit she had. Anyway, I stopped in my tracks and said in a tone of delight and surprise (which convinced even me), "Jas! . . . hi! What are you doing here?" And I gave her a really warm hug (managing to say in her ear, "Leave your bloody fringe alone!").

When I stopped hugging her she said, "Hi, Georgie, I was just buying some onions," and I laughed and said, "Well, you know your onions, don't you, Jas?"

Then Ellen and Jools came in with arms outstretched and shrieking with excitement, "Jas! Jas! How lovely! Gosh, we haven't seen you for ages. How are you?"

Meanwhile, the boy Tom stood there. Jas said to him, "Oh,

30

I'm really sorry to keep you waiting," and he just went, "It's cool," and Jas asked him how much she owed him and then she said, "Bye then, thanks," and he said, "See you later." And we were outside. When we got a few metres away we didn't say anything but sort of spontaneously all started running as fast as we could and laughing.

7.00 p.m. Just spoken to Jas on the phone. She thinks Tom is even more gorgeous but she doesn't know whether he likes her, so we have to go through the whole thing.

I could hear Jas's dad in the background, saying, "If you are seeing each other tomorrow can't you wait and not add to my phone bill?"

Parents are all the same – all skinflints. Anyway, Jas said, "He said, 'See you later.' "

I agreed but added thoughtfully, "But he might say that to everyone, like a sort of 'See you later' sort of thing."

That upset her. "You mean you don't think he likes me?"

I said, "I didn't say that. He might never say 'See you later' unless he means, 'See you later'."

That cheered her up. "So you think he might mean 'See you later', then?"

I said, "Yes."

She was quiet for a bit; I could hear her chewing her chewing-gum. Then she started again, "When is 'later', though?"

Honestly, we could be here all night. I said, "Jas, I DON'T KNOW. Why don't you decide when 'later' is?"

She stopped chewing then. "You mean I should ask him out?"

I could see my book sort of beckoning to me, saying, "Come and read me, come and read me, you know you want to." So

I was firm but fair. "It's up to you, Jas, but I know what Sharon Stone would do. Goodnight."

saturday september 5th

10.00 a.m. Same bat time. Same bat place.

10.15 a.m. Jas called. She wants to launch Operation Get Tom. We're going to go to Costas for more detailed planning.

10.30 a.m. Lalalalala. Life is so fab. Lalala. I even managed to put mascara on without sticking the brush in my eye. Also I tried out my new lipliner and I think the effect definitely makes my nose look smaller. In a rare moment I shared my nose anxiety with Mum. She said, "We used to use 'shaders'. You know, light highlights and darker bits to create shadow – you could put a light line of foundation down the middle and then darker bits at the sides to sort of narrow it down." Wrong answer, Mum, the correct answer is "You are gorgeous, Georgia, and there is nothing wrong with your nose."

I didn't say that, I didn't give her the satisfaction. Instead I said, through some toast so I could deny it if I had to, "Mum, I don't want to look like you and your friends did, I've seen the photos and no one wants to look like Abba any more."

11.30 a.m. Mrs Next Door complained about Angus again. He's been frightening their poodle. She says Angus stalks it. I explained, "Well, he's a Scottish

32

wildcat, that's what they do. They stalk their prey."

She said, "I don't really think it should be a household pet, in that case."

I said, "He's not a household pet, believe me. I have tried to train him but he ate his lead. There is only so much you can do with Angus."

Honestly, is it really my job to deal with hysterical neighbours? Why doesn't she get a bigger dog? The stupid yappy thing annoys Angus.

1.00 p.m. I'd better be nice though, otherwise I'll be accused of being a "moody teenager" and the next thing you know it will be tap tap tap on my door and Mum saying, "Is there anything you want to talk about?" Adults are so nosy.

1.30 p.m. Went next door and asked Mrs Fussy Knickers if she wanted anything from the shops as I was going. She sort of hid behind the door. I must be nicer. I start out being nice and then it's like someone else takes over. Am I schizophrenic as well as a lesbian?

2.00 p.m. Jas phoned. She wants me to help her with part two of her plan to get Tom. The plan is subtle. Jas and I will pass by Jennings, and as we pass the door I will pause and then say, "Oh, Jas, I just remembered I said I'd get some apples. Hang on a minute." Then I go into the shop and buy the apples. Jas stands behind me looking attractively casual. I smile as Tom hands over the grannies (Granny Smiths) and then – and here is the masterstroke (or actually, as it was my idea, the mistress-stroke) – I say, "School in two days. Back to Stalag 14. Which centre of boredom and torture do you go to?" (Meaning, which school do you go to, do you see?) Then he tells me and then we know how to accidentally bump into him.

4.00 p.m. Well, we got to Jennings and Tom was in there – Jas went a bit swoony. He is nice-looking, I must say, with sort of crinkly hair and great shoulders. I said my "Hang on, Jas, I promised I'd get some apples," and we went in, so she could lurk attractively behind me, as planned.

When he saw her Tom looked and smiled. I asked for my grannies and he said, "Sure. Are you looking forward to going back to school?"

(Hang on a minute, those were my lines. Still, I've done drama for four years so I improvised.) I rejoined, "Does the Pope hate Catholics?"

He smiled but I didn't really mean to say anything about the Pope, it just popped out. Tom went on, "Which school do you two go to?" I was just about to tell him (even though in our plan it wasn't really his turn) . . . when a Sex God came out of the back room.

I swear he was so gorgeous it made you blink and open your mouth like a goldfish. He was very tall and had long, black hair and really intense, dark blue eyes and a big mouth and was dressed all in black. (And that's all I remember, officer.) He came over to Tom and handed him a cup of tea. Tom said, "Thanks," and the Sex God spoke. "Can't let my little brother slave away, serving apples to good-looking girls without even a cup of tea." Then he WINKED at Tom and SMILED at me, then he went out the back.

I just stood there, looking at the space where SG had been. Clutching my apples. Tom said, "That's forty pence. Did you tell me what school you both go to?"

I came out of my trance and hoped I hadn't been dribbling. "Er . . . I . . ." and I couldn't remember.

Jas looked at me as if I had gone mad and said, "Oh, it's only the one we've been at for four years, Latimer and Ridgley. Which one do you go to?"

7.00 p.m. I am still in a state of shock. I have just met Mr Gorgeous. And he is Tom's brother. And he is gorgeous. He saw me with my mouth open. But, fortunately, not without eyebrows. Oh God! Quick, nurse, the screens!!

7.05 p.m. I tried opening my mouth in the mirror like I imagine it looked like in the shop. It doesn't make me look very intelligent but it also doesn't make my nose look any bigger, which is a plus (of sorts).

1.00 a.m. I wonder how old he is? I must become more mature quickly. I'll start tomorrow.

sunday september 6th

8.00 a.m. When I walked into the kitchen Dad dropped his cup in an hilarious (not) display of surprise that I was up so early. "What has happened, George, has your bed caught fire? Are you feverish? It's not midday yet, why are you up?"

I said, "I came down for a cup of hot water, if that's OK."

(Very cleansing for the system, I must avoid a spot attack at all costs.)

Mum said, "Well, I'm off. Libby, give your big sister a kiss before we go." Libby gave me a big smacking kiss which was nice but a bit on the porridgey side. Still, I must get on.

10.00 a.m. I have completed the *Cosmo* yoga plan for inner peace and confidence. I vow to get up an hour before school and go through the twelve positions of "Sun worship". I feel great and two or three foot taller. The Sex God will not be able to resist the new, confident, radiant, womanly me.

2.00 p.m. Face-pack done and milk bath taken. I must try and get the milk stains off the bath towel somehow, it already smells a bit sour.

Jas rang. She thinks we should track Tom tomorrow after school. Tom – what is he to me?

4.00 p.m. Just discovered that Libby has used the last of my sanitary towels to make hammocks for her dolls.

4.30 p.m. She has also used all of my Starkers foundation cream on her panda; its head is entirely beige now.

5.00 p.m. I have no other foundation or money. I may have to kill her.

5.15 p.m. No. Peace. Ohm. Inner peace.

8.00 p.m. Aahhhh. Early to bed, early to rise.

9.30 p.m. Woke with a start. Thought it might be time to get up.

midnight Should I wear my pencil skirt or not tomorrow?

monday september 7th

8.30 a.m. Overslept and had to race to get a lift to Jas's with my dad. No time for yoga or make-up. Oh well, I'll start tomorrow. God alone knows how the Dalai Lama copes on a daily basis. He must get up at dawn. Actually, I read somewhere that he does get up at dawn.

8.45 a.m. Jas and I running like loonies up the hill to the school gate. I thought my head was going to explode I was so red, and also I just remembered I hadn't got my beret on. I could see Hawkeye at the school gate so no time for the sausage method. I just rammed it on my head. Bugger bugger, pant pant. As we ran up to the gate I catapulted into . . . the Sex God. He looked DIVINE in his uniform. He was with his mates, having a laugh and just strolling coolly along. He looked at me and said, "You're keen." I could have died.

9.00 a.m. My only hope is that a) – he didn't recognise me and b) – if he did recognise me he likes the "flushed, stupid idiot" look in a girl.

9.35 a.m. After assembly I popped into the loos and looked in the mirror. Worst fears confirmed – I am Mrs Ugly. Small, swollen eyes, hair plastered to my skull, HUGE red nose. I look like a tomato in a school uniform. Well, that is that then.

4.00 p.m. The bell. Thank God, now I can go home and kill myself.

7.00 p.m. In bed. Uncle Eddie says there is an unseen force at work of which we have no comprehension . . . Well, if there is, why is it picking on me?

tuesday september 8th

8.00 a.m. Still no time to do my yoga. Not that it matters any more. I did manage to do the sausage beret and the lip-gloss and the concealer. Nothing like shutting the stable door and tarting up the horse after it's bolted.

8.20 a.m. Nice and early with Jas. This time we are both ready. We walked up the hill really chatting and laughing. Waving at friends (well actually, waving at anyone, just to give the impression that we are really popular). We walked slowly at the end bit leading up to the gate and although there was the usual crush of Foxwood boys ogling, there was no sign of Tom or SG.

9.30 a.m. I'd forgotten how utterly crap school is.

In assembly there was a bit of chatting going on before Slim took the stage, and do you know what she said? She said, "Settle, girls, settle." Like we were a bunch of pigeons or doves or something. She's already started her fascist regime by saying she has been told that some girls were not wearing their berets as they arrived at school. She would like the older girls to set an example to the younger ones, rather than the other way round. Is this what my life is now? Talking about berets? Whilst a Sex God strolls around on the planet? I felt like shouting out, in front of assembly, "Get a life, Slim!! In fact, get two . . . there's enough of you!!"

But Hawkeye was looking at me. I know she was thinking about the locusts. She's always watching me. She's like a stoat. I don't think I can stand much more of this and it's only nine thirty.

5.00 p.m. What a nightmare! Jas, Ellen, Jools and I are NOT ALLOWED to sit together at the back. I CANNOT BELIEVE IT. Instead, I have been placed next to Nauseating Pamela Green. It is more than flesh and blood can stand. Nauseating P. Green is so boring it makes you want to slit your wrists just looking at her. Plus Hawkeye is our form mistress. *Quelle horreur* and triple *merde*. And it's Physics last thing Friday afternoon. What is the point?

wednesday september 9th

8.40 a.m. I have perfected putting a little bit of mascara on so that you can't tell I have got any on.

No sign of the lads.

39

After lunch Alison Peters and Jackie Mathews came by. They were smoking and I must say they are common girls, but obviously I must not say it to them as I do not want a duffing up, or chewing-gum in my tennis shoes.

Jackie said, "We're doing a new thing tomorrow, it's a sort of Aleister Crowley thing, so you can all come and meet us in 5C form room tomorrow after second lunch."

Cheers, thanks a lot. Good night. It is, of course, strictly forbidden to be in school after second lunch. I sense something . . . what is it? Oh yes, it's my first poor conduct mark coming along.

6.00 p.m. Is my life over? Is this all there is? Downstairs my parents are laughing at something and in the other room Libby is playing with her dolls, I can hear her talking to them. It's so sad, that she is so young and she doesn't know the sadness that lies ahead. That is what is so sad. I can hear her little voice murmuring . . . what is she saying . . . ?

Oh, it's "Poor Georgia, poor Georgia."

thursday september 10th

5.00 p.m. Boring day at school, then home to my even more boring home life. I wanted to debrief with Jas but she had to go to the dentist. Jackie and Alison's proposed Aleister Crowley extravaganza was put off this lunch-time, thank the Lord. The message got passed along at assembly that Jackie was off sick. She has started taking sickies very early on in term. Anyway, we are spared whatever they had in mind for a few days. I think they take drugs. Horse tranquillizers, probably.

tuesday september 15th

4.30 p.m. Absolutely no sign of SG. However, I have found out some gossip because Katie Steadman's parents know SG's parents from some naff card club the really old go to. Apparently he's called Robbie Jennings – his parents, Mr and Mrs Jennings, own the shop – the so-called greengrocer-cum-delicatessen, according to Jas. I don't normally like Katie Steadman that much. She's OK but I get the impression she thinks I am a bit on the superficial side.

She's bloody tall, I'll say that for her, and her hair is nice, but she sort of tries too hard. She puts her hand up in class, for instance. Properly, I mean. She doesn't do the putting your hand up but leaving it all floppy at the end of your arm, so it just flaps around. That is the sign of someone who is obliged to put their hand up because that is the fascist way, but isn't really putting their hand up. I have taken to putting my hand up and pointing one finger forward – you know, like at football matches when everyone points at a chubby player and chants, "Who ate all the pies?" But as usual any sign of humour is stamped down in this place. Hawkeye said, "Georgia, if you are too tired to put your hand up properly perhaps you should go to bed earlier . . . or perhaps a few thousand lines might strengthen your wrist?"

I may try it out on Herr Kamyer – we have him for German and Physics, which is the only bright spot in this hell-hole. He has the double comedy value of being both German and the only male teacher in an all girls' school.

41

8.00 p.m. Listening to classical music, I thought it might be soothing, but it's really irritating and has no proper tune.

8.05 p.m. I love life!!! Jas has just phoned to say we've been invited to a party at Katie Steadman's and . . . Katie has asked Tom and Robbie. YESSSSS!!!! I must have done a good job of being nice to Katie. WHAT ON EARTH CAN I WEAR??? Emergency, emergency! It's only a couple of weeks away.

8.10 p.m. I'd better do my yoga.

8.15 p.m. I'd better start applying face-masks now.

8.20 p.m. I wonder if I slept with a peg on my nose, like Amy in *Little Women*, if it would make it smaller? Why couldn't Mum choose someone with a normal sized hooter to marry?

8.30 p.m. I asked Mum why she married Dad (he was bowling with Uncle Eddie – I ask you). She thought for a bit and then she said, "He makes me laugh." He makes her laugh. He makes her laugh. Well, Bart Simpson makes me laugh, but I'm not going to marry him.

midnight Hahahahahahahaha.

monday september 21st

8.00 a.m.

Eleven days to the party.

tuesday september 22nd

9.30 a.m.

Someone farted in assembly this morning (I suspect Nauseating P. Green). Whoever it was, it was really loud and during the silence we were having to think about all the poor people. And it wasn't just a quick one, it was a knee-trembler. Jas, Ellen, Julia and me were shaking with laughter, well everyone was. I was laughing for most of the day and now my stomach hurts.

thursday september 24th

5.30 p.m.

In bed. I'm absolutely frozen. I may have TB. Honestly, Miss Stamp is obviously a sex pervert as well as clearly being a lesbian. Why else would anyone make girls run around in sports knickers hitting a ball with sticks? She calls it hockey – I call it the sick wanderings of a sick mind. If I miss this party because of lesbian lust Miss Stamp WILL DIE. SHE WILL DIE.

friday september 25th

10.00 a.m.

A sighting at last!! On the way to school we saw Tom. He actually stopped to chat, he said, "Hi, having fun?"

I said, "Yes, what could be more fun than being with

sadistic loonies for eight hours every day?"

He laughed and said, directly to Jas, "Are you going to Katie's party?"

Jas went all pink and white, then sort of pinky-white apart from the tip of her nose which remained red. I must remember to tell her what she looked like. She managed to reply and he said, "Well, I look forward to seeing you there."

Jas was ecstatic. "Did you hear what he said?"

"Yes."

"He said, 'Are you going to Katie's party?' "

"Yes."

"He said, 'Well, I look forward to seeing you there.' "

"Yes."

"He said, 'I look forward to seeing you there.' "

"We've been through this."

"He said, 'I look forward to seeing you there,' . . . to me. He said 'you' because he meant me."

"Er, Jas."

"Yes?"

"Will you shut up now?"

5.00 p.m. She didn't though.

Herr Kamyer didn't take us for Physics as he has a cold. Double damn. When am I going to have any fun? *Sacré bleu.*

saturday september 26th

10.00 a.m. Went for a moody autumn walk with Libby in her pushchair. She was singing, "I am the Queen, oh, I am the Queen." She wouldn't take off

44

the fairy wings that I had made for her. It was a nightmare getting her into the pushchair. The clouds were scudding across the sky but it was quite sunny and crisp. I cheered up enough to join in the singing with Libby. We were both yelling, "I am the Queen, oh, I am the Queen!" and that's when he got out of a red mini. Robbie. The SG. He saw me and said, "Oh hello, we've met before, haven't we?"

I smiled brilliantly, trying to do it without making my nose spread out over all my face. It's a question of relaxing the mouth, putting the tongue behind the back teeth but slightly flaring the nostrils so that they don't go wild. He looked at me a bit oddly.

"Apples," I said wittily.

"Oh yeah," he said, "the shop, you and your friend."

He smiled again. He was dreamy when he smiled. Then he bent down to Libby who, true to form, gave him one of her scary "I am a crazy child" looks. She said, "I am the Queen," and he said, "Are you?" (Ooohhh, he's so lovely to children.)

Then Libby said, "Yes, I am the Queen and Georgia did a big poo this morning."

I couldn't believe it. He could not believe it. Nobody could believe it. It was unbelievable, that's why. He stood up quickly and I said, "Er, well, I'd better be going."

And he said, "Yes, see you later."

And I thought, Think Sharon Stone, think Sharon Stone. So I said, "Yes, well I'll probably see you at Katie's party," and he said, "No, I'm not going, I'm doing something else that night."

7.00 p.m.   "Georgia did a big poo . . ."

45

7.05 p.m. "No, I'm not going, I'm doing something else that night."

7.06 p.m. Does life get any worse?

8.00 p.m. Yes it does. Dad has just put his head round the door to say, "James is popping over tomorrow. We thought we'd all go to Stanmer Park for the day."

sunday september 27th

10.00 p.m. James tried to kiss me!!!

It was disgusting. He's my cousin. It's incest. I can't even think about it or I'll be sick. Erlack erlack.

10.05 p.m. It was in my room after a *horriblement* day spent tramping around a bloody park. How old do they think I am? They made me go on a see-saw. I, of course, snagged my new tights.

So a summary of my lovely day out is . . . I snagged my tights, then I was attacked by my cousin. *Perfectamondo*. In my room!!!

10.07 p.m. When we got back James and me were listening to records and reading old joke books and suddenly he switched off the light and said, "Shall we play tickly bears?" Tickly bears!! We used to play that when we were about five. One person would be the tickly bear and they would chase the other person and tickle them and, er . . .

that's it. I was so shocked (and also couldn't see a thing in the dark) that I just sort of went "Nnnnnn-nnnn". And then he said, "Grr gotcha!" and started tickling me. It was the most embarrassing thing. But it didn't end there – a sort of wet thing touched my face near my nose. I leaped up like a salmon and stumbled for the light. James sort of stood up and then he picked up a joke book and started reading it. So I did as well. Then he got taken home by my dad. The wet thing on the nose incident was never mentioned. Like the leg.

I don't think I can stand much more of this.

monday september 28th

11.00 a.m. At break I told Jas and Jools everything. They went, "Ergghhhlack, that's truly disgusting. Your cousin? That is sad." Jools said that she had actually seen her brother's "how's your father" quite often. She said, "It's quite nice, really, like a mouse." She lives in a world of her own (thank God). Well bless us, Tiny Tim, one and all, I say.

4.15 p.m. On the way home. I could kill Jas. She's all excited about the party and I might as well not go now. Jackie and Alison caught up with us on the way home. Jackie had so much make-up on. And her hair was all done. As we passed the loos in the park she made us stand lookout whilst she changed out of her school uniform.

"I'm off clubbing," she said from inside the loos, mistaking me for someone who was remotely interested in what she did.

"I didn't think that clubs opened at four thirty," I said.

She called out, "Don't be dim, Ringo." (I hate her, I hate her.) "I'm off to my mate's first to get ready, put my make-up on and everything." Put her make-up on? If she put any more make-up on she'd hardly be able to hold her head up because of the weight.

She emerged in a sort of satin crop top and tight trousers; she looked about twenty-five.

"I've got a date with the DJ at Loveculture – he's so cool. I think he's about thirty but I like mature men."

After they'd gone I walked on with Jas. "Do you think that Jackie has 'done it'?" I asked her. Jas said, "Well, put it this way . . . is the Queen Mother really, really old?" Sometimes Jas is quite exceptionally mad. Just to prove my point she went on, "Gemma Crawford was telling me that she knows a boy who gives kissing lessons. Do you think we should go before the party?"

I just looked at her. "Jas, are you suggesting that we go to a male prostitute?"

Jas went on, "He only does kissing and you don't pay."

I just tutted.

10.00 p.m. I lay on my arm until it went numb and then I lifted it (with the non-numb arm) on to my breasts. I wanted to see what it felt like to have a strange hand on them. It was quite nice, but what do I know? I'm too full of strange urges to think properly. Should I wear my bra to the party?

10.05 p.m. Urgh, it's horrible when the feeling starts coming back into your arm when it's been numb.

11.07 p.m. Kissing the back of your hand is no good because you can't tell which is which – which is lip and which is hand – so you don't get a proper sensation from either. Do boys have this trouble or do they just know how to do stuff?

11.15 p.m. No, is the answer, if the "tickly bear" incident is anything to go by.

tuesday september 29th

8.30 a.m. Biology, Dble maths, Froggie and Geoggers. *Qu'est ce que le point?*

in my room

6.00 p.m. What a fiasco. Jackie and Alison decided that today was the day for the Aleister Crowley fandango in the 5C form room.

It's amazing how few people stand up to them, including the teachers.

We all trooped up to 5C after second lunch. This in itself is a fiasco – you have to lurk outside the main door until the coast is clear, then dart to the downstairs loo, check if the coast is clear, then leap up the stairs to floor one and so on, up to the fifth floor.

I was shattered by the time I got up there. There were seven of us all in peak condition – i.e. spluttering and coughing. Jackie said we were going to do a black art act of levitation, calling on the dark forces to help us. Oh goodie, we're summoning the devil. What larks.

Why, I thought, oh why am I here? Maybe if we are going to be forced to commune with the devil I could strike some sort of bargain with him, swap my dad's soul in exchange for bigger breasts for the party on Friday.

Abby Nicols "volunteered" to be the sacrificed one and she had to lie down on a desk. Jackie went at her head and Alison at her feet and then the rest of us spread out evenly around her. Jackie said, "Please be very quiet and concentrate, we are summoning dark forces. Put one finger of each hand underneath Abby's body and then we will begin."

We all did as we were told. Then Jackie shut her eyes and started chanting in a low, husky voice, "She's looking poorly. She's looking poorly," and we all had to repeat it after her one by one round the desk. Then she said, "She's looking worse. She's looking worse. She's looking ill. She's looking ill."

Actually, she was looking a bit peaky by this time. It went on for about five minutes as Abby's condition deteriorated. Finally Jackie whispered, "She's dying. She's dying . . ." We all repeated it. "She's dead. She's dead." She certainly did not look at all well and she was as stiff as a board, I couldn't see her breathing.

Then Jackie said, "Help us, oh Master, to send Abby Nicols upwards." And then she said, "Lift her up," and it was really freaky-deaky because I just slightly lifted with my two fingers and she sort of rose up really easily as if she was light as a feather. She was right above our heads. It was weird.

After a couple of minutes we all simultaneously got the jitters and let her down really heavily on to the desk. This seemed to perk her up a bit, because as we ran out I heard her saying, "I think I've broken my bottom."

11.00 p.m. I woke up with a start because I heard the bedroom door open. It just opened by itself . . .

wednesday september 30th

7.30 a.m. I can't move my head from side to side because I sat up in bed all night and I have cricked it now.

1.00 p.m. Gemma said her friend Peter Dyer, the professional kisser, is going to be around tomorrow after school. All you have to do is go to his house and knock on the door after four thirty and before six thirty when his parents get home. Apparently it's first come first served. Has it come to this? No it has not.

9.30 p.m. Had to discuss again with Jas what she is going to wear on Friday. She can go in the nuddy-pants for all I care.

october

tainted love

thursday october 1st

4.30 p.m. For some reason I found myself outside Peter Dyer's house and knocking on his door. Ellen and Jas, Jools, Patty, Sarah and Mabs were all hiding behind the hedge at the bottom of the garden. What is the matter with me? I am DESPERATE – that's what the matter is.

I didn't know whether to wear lipstick or not. I don't know what the point would be if it was just going to come off . . . What am I saying?

4.31 p.m. Peter opened the door. He's about seventeen and blond, sort of sleepy-looking, not unattractive in a sort of Boyzone way. I notice he is chewing gum. I hope he takes it out, otherwise I might choke to death. There is muffled giggling from behind the hedge. Peter hears it but doesn't seem fazed.

"Do you want to come in – er – what's your name?"

I say, "Georgia," (damn, I meant to say a false name) and we go into his house.

He has tight blue jeans on and there are those tinkly things that the Japanese have outside the doors. (Not on his jeans,

52

obviously – on the door.) You know . . . wind chimes. Why do they do that? It's such an annoying noise and do you really need to know that the wind is blowing? We're doing Japan in Geography and to annoy Hawkeye I have memorised the islands. Hokkaido, Honshu . . . er, well, I nearly have. I did it last year with Northern Ireland and reciting the counties (you remember them by the mnemonic FAT LAD – Fermanagh, Antrim, Tyrone, Londonderry, Armagh, Down) – can be very impressive to trot out when you are accused of not concentrating.

Oh-oh, we are going up the stairs to Peter's room. He hasn't said a word. His room is much tidier than mine. He has made his bed, for a start. On the walls are posters of Denise van Outen and Miss December, and so on. On my walls there's a poster of Reeves and Mortimer showing their bottoms and a group shot of the cast of *Dad's Army*. Is this the big difference between girls and boys? Is this . . . oh-oh, Peter is sitting on his bed.

"Do you want to sit down?" he says, patting the bed.

I think, No thanks, I would rather put my head in a bag of eels, but I say, "OK," and sit down.

He puts his arm round me. I think of putting my arm round him like an hilarious Morecambe and Wise joke but I don't because I remember the stuffed olive incident. Then, with his other hand, Peter turns my face towards his. It's a good job he didn't try that yesterday when I had rigor mortis of the head. Then he says, "Close your eyes and relax."

9.00 p.m. Phew, I suppose I am a woman now. Libby doesn't seem to realise as she has made me wear her deely-boppers to bed. She is insisting I

53

am a huge bee. If I say, "Look, it's your bedtime now," she just goes, "Bzzzz bzzz," and looks cross.

I have to say, "Bz bz bzzy buzz buzz," and point at her bed with my feelers before she will go.

9.20 p.m. When I got home neither Mum nor Dad seemed to notice the change in me. Mind you, I'd have to walk in with my head under my arm before Dad would get out of his chair. He's getting very chunky. I may mention it in a caring way. Anyway, as I said, phew.

When I closed my eyes Peter said, "We're going to do an ordinary kiss first." Then he kissed me. We started off with number one kissing, which is just lips, not moving. He said I was a natural, not too "firm" or toothy, which is apparently very common.

He told me how to know which side to go to (you sort of watch where the boy is going and then you fit in). Then we did a bit of movement and he told me what to do with my hands (waist is safest).

Oh, we got through a lot in half an hour. We did a bit of tongues, which was the bit I was most scared of, but actually it wasn't too bad, a bit like a little lizard tongue darting about. Cute really, in a bizarre way. The main thing to do is to strike a happy balance between "yielding" and "giving". Peter says you can take a horse to water but you can't make it kiss properly.

At the end of the session (he had a little alarm clock) he shook my hand and saw me to the door. I passed Mabs on the way out – it was her turn. I was glad that I had gone first. Jools and Ellen and Jas tried to pump me on the way home but I said, in a dignified sort of way, "I think I'd just like to think about this for a while, if you don't mind. *Bon soir.*"

10.45 p.m. Hahahahahahahaha, I'm a natural.

friday october 2nd

4.00 p.m. Party time!!! I don't know why I'm so excited as SG is not even going to be there. But maybe I'll be able to try out my new snogging skills.

Jackie Mathews has got a huge lovebite on her neck. She's put about six centimetres of concealer on it and is wearing a scarf . . . how inconspicuoso!! It's HUGE! What has she been snogging with – a calf? I think it is so common. Why would you let someone bite you?

The day dragged by. I really am going to complain about Miss Stamp – she should be working in a prison. I'm sure she has done before. Even though it was icy outside she insisted that in our games period we ran round the hockey pitch. You could see your breath. She found Jackie and Alison hiding in the showers having a fag and made them change into their sports knickers and do the circuit twice. Which is almost a reason to have her as a teacher. It was hilarious! Jackie might look OK when she's all dolled up in some dark nightclub, but you should see her from behind in big navy knickers!!

4.15 p.m. Only three hours to get ready and made up before I meet Jas, Jools and Ellen and the gang at the clock tower. We're going to arrive together. Dad is insisting on picking me up at midnight. It's useless arguing with him, he'll only say, "You're lucky, in my day . . . blah blah blah," and then we'll be back in the Middle Ages, or the seventies as he calls it.

7.30 p.m. Meet the gang. We look like a group of funeral directors going out for a drink. Black is our new black. Katie Steadman's house is quite posh – she has her own room as well as a bedroom. Shagpile carpets all rolled up round the walls, for dancing.

When we arrived there were about thirty people there already, including Tom. Cue Jas going all dithery and daft. He was in a group but he came over to talk to us straight away. I left Jas to it and circulated. It was good fun. I had a mad dancing phase for about an hour. I suppose I was vaguely looking for substitute snoggers for SG, but all the boys seemed a bit on the nice but goofy side. There were one or two most unfortunate skin complaints. I feel lucky just getting the odd lurker – some people looked like they had mountain ranges of spots on their faces . . . and some down their backs too . . . *Au secours!!!!*

Then I saw Peter Dyer. I waved at him and he came over. He had been talking to Katie Steadman and she seemed a bit miffed when he came over to me. Peter said, "Hi!" and I said, "Hi . . . er . . . thanks for the other day. It was really . . . er . . . great. I learned a lot. Thanks."

He looked at me sideways and stood quite close. "There was something I didn't have time to show you, come with me." And he took hold of my hand and led me out of the room. We hadn't done hand-holding but I improvised . . . not too floppy but not too gripping. I don't think anyone besides Katie saw us go, they were too busy dancing stupidly to a Slade record.

We went outside into the garden and went behind a big tree just by the path. Peter started kissing me (he didn't seem to be a big talker).

There was a lot more tongue business. It was all right but it was making my jaw ache a bit. Peter seemed to like it quite a lot more than I did because he sort of moaned and pushed me against the tree. Then Peter started nuzzling my neck and I thought, Oh, we haven't done necks before, he's branching out a bit, and then I nearly choked to death trying not to laugh (up against a tree . . . branching out, do you get it?) . . . but I stopped myself. You have to keep reminding yourself about boys not liking a laugh. Then I heard a car door slam and people crunching up the drive towards us.

I stepped backwards but Peter was still attached to my neck. I tripped over a root and fell on to my bottom. Peter lost his balance and fell over on top of me and made us both go "Ooofff!". From upside-down I found myself looking up at a tall, blonde girl I recognised from the sixth form and, next to her . . . SG. He was all in black and looked really annoyed.

He said, all tight-lipped, "Don't you think it's about time you two went inside to the party?" I remembered the blonde's name, it was Lindsay, a notorious wet. She was looking at my legs. Probably envying them. I looked down, and noticed that my skirt had all ridden up and you could see my knickers. I wriggled it down in a "dignity at all times" sort of way, but she still smirked.

Peter said quite calmly, "Hi, Robbie, I thought you had a gig tonight."

Robbie said, "I have, but Tom forgot his key so I'm just dropping it off for him."

He didn't even glance at me or say goodbye or anything.

midnight I bloody hate him. Big, full-of-himself type thing. Bugger bugger, double *ordure* and *merde*. What business is it of his what I do behind trees?

tuesday october 6th

3.00 p.m. Peter phoned me over the weekend. I don't know how he got the number because I just left in a hurry from the party. Gemma must have given it to him. Dad answered the phone, which is the end of life as we know it because HE WILL NOT LET IT LIE. He thinks it is funny and calls Peter "Your fancy man."

Peter wanted to know if I would go to the pictures next week. I said that would be great. So it looks like I have sort of got a boyfriend. Why do I feel so depressed then?

Jas is unbearable since the party. She sent me notes all through Maths.

Dear Gee-gee,

Tom is sooooo cool. He walked me home and then, when we got to the door, he gave me a really nice kiss on the cheek. His lips are really soft and he smells nice, not like my brother. He asked for my phone number – do you think he will call? What day do you think he will call?

It's Monday today and I saw him on Friday so that is three days already. I'd call tonight if I was him, wouldn't you? Should I say yes to any day he says for a date? Or if he says Friday should I say, "Oh, sorry, I'm busy that night," and then when he says "What about Saturday?" I can say, "Oh, yeah, Saturday would be cool." What do you think? Or do you think he might think I'm putting him off if I say I'm busy on Friday, so I should

58

say yes to any day he says? Please reply quickly. TTFN.

I've given her my worst look but she keeps sending things. I am not interested in any of the prat family Jennings.

4.00 p.m. Sadly it makes no difference to Jas whether I am interested or not. All the way home she was telling me what Tom said or did. The more I hear about him the less I think Jas should have to do with him. All right, maybe I am being unfair and bitter, but she is my best friend and should do everything I say . . .

Tom wants to go into the fruit and veg business. Oh, how fascinating . . . Jas thinks it is.

"I think it's great that he's young but he knows where he is going."

I said brightly, "Yes, you'd never be short of potatoes."

Eventually even Jas noticed that I wasn't so keen. She looked a bit confused and said, "I thought you liked him."

I didn't say anything. All I could think of was his brother looking down at me and sort of sneering. Jas went on, "Don't you think I should go out with him?"

I still didn't say anything.

She said it again. "So you don't think I should go out with him?"

I was all enigmatic, which is not easy in a beret.

11.30 p.m. I am a facsimile of a sham of a fax of a person. And I have a date with a professional snogger.

midnight Angus has eaten some of Mum's knickers.

59

She says he'll have to go. Why can't she go, and Dad go? Or am I being unreasonable?

thursday october 15th

noon Slim has put a ban on levitation. She made an announcement in assembly this morning. She was all shaky and jelly-like, her jowls were bouncing around like anything. Anyway, she said, "This school is like the back streets of Haiti. It must stop forthwith. Any girl found practising levitation will face the gravest consequences. I, for one, would not like to be in that girl's shoes."

I whispered to Ellen, "She wouldn't get in any girl's shoes. How much do you think each leg weighs? Imagine the size of her knickers . . . you could probably get two duvets out of them."

Then we got the eagle eye from Hawkeye for giggling.

2.00 p.m. I feel like killing something. If I was that sort of person I'd scare a first former, as it is I will have to content myself with hiding Nauseating P. Green's pencil-case.

3.00 p.m. On my way to the Science block I saw Lindsay. How wet can you be? She really is Mrs Wet. She has the wettest haircut known to humanity – all curled under at the bottom. I saw her legs in hockey and they are really spindly. Little spindly legs like she has been in a wheelchair and not been walking for years, and also when she is concentrating she wears big goggly glasses like Deirdre Barlow. I bet she keeps those well-hidden when she goes out with Pratboy. Oh, hell's teeth, it's my "date" in four hours. The horrible thing is that I don't want to go. I just don't. There's nothing wrong with him or anything, I just can't be bothered somehow.

my bedroom

midnight I wish I'd never started this snogging business. I feel like I've been attacked by whelks. I can't see Peter any more. Why is he so keen on me, anyway? I haven't had chance to say more than, "Er, what are you doing at GCSE . . . ?" before I'm attacked by the whelks again. I can't go out with him any more. How can I tell him, though?

1.00 a.m. I'll make Jas do it.

friday october 16th

9.00 p.m. What a week!
I got Jas to dump Peter for me. I said for her to let him down gently, so she told him that I had a personal problem. He asked what, and she said that I thought I was a lesbian. Cheers, Jas.

monday october 19th

4.00 p.m. It's all round school that I'm a lesbian. In games we were in the changing-room and Miss Stamp came in to change out of her gear. Suddenly everyone had disappeared, leaving me on my own with her. She really has got a moustache. Does she not notice?

friday october 23rd

8.00 p.m. Tom phoned Jas and they're going on a "date" to watch Robbie's band. The band is called The Stiff Dylans. I bet it's crap. I bet it's *merde*. I bet it's double *merde*.

Mum and Dad were talking in the kitchen and when I came in they stopped and looked all shifty. Don't get me wrong, I like it when they shut up when I come in, well I would like it if it had ever happened before. Mum said, "Have you ever thought you'd like to see a bit more of the world, Gee?" and I said, "If you're thinking of trying to persuade me to visit Auntie Kath in Blackpool for Christmas, you can forget it."

I can be hilariously cutting when I try.

10.00 p.m. No matter from what angle you look at it, I do have a huge, squishy nose.

I wonder if Mum would pay for me to have plastic surgery . . . ? If I went to the doctor and said it was psychologically damaging, to the extent that I couldn't go out or do my homework, I wonder if I could have it done on the NHS?

Then I remember to have a reality check . . . I don't have the George Clooney-type doctor from *ER* – the caring, incredibly good-looking face of medicine. I've got Dr Wallace, the incredibly fat, red, uncaring face of medicine. It's hard enough getting an aspirin out of him when you've got flu.

11.00 p.m. Jas rang. She had a great time with Tom.

"Did he bring you a present, a bunch of leeks or something?" I asked meanly but Jas refused to come down from cloud nine.

She said, "No, but he's a brilliant dancer. The Stiff Dylans were ace. Robbie is a cool singer."

I had to ask in a masochistic way, "Was Lindsay there?"

Jas said, "Yes, she was, she's quite nice really, she had her hair up."

I was furious with Jas for being so disloyal and said, "Oh, it's nice that you've made new friends. I can't help thinking though, that as Lindsay's BEST friend you could advise her that people with massive ears should not wear their hair up."

I put the phone down on her.

midnight *Qu'est ce que le point?*

monday october 26th

7.00 p.m. I've been ignoring Jas. It's tiring, but someone has to do it.

thursday october 29th

5.00 p.m. In Slim's office today for a bit of a talking-to. Honestly, she has no sense of humour whatsoever.

The main difficulty is that she imagines we are at school to learn stuff and we know we are at school to fill in the idle hours before we go home and hang around with our mates doing important things. Life skills, like make-up and playing records and trapping boys.

Anyway, it was just one more little, trivial thing.

We had to have our school photo taken, all of the fourth form and the teachers together. Even including Herr Kamyer, the rogue male. Ellen and Jas, Jools and Rosie Mees and me were all in the back row because we are the tallest. Well, we've started this new craze which is based around those old TV puppet shows *Stingray* and *Supercar*. Rosie has all the old videos which we watch. We know all the key phrases like "Fire retro rockets" and "Calling International Rescue". And we walk around all stiffly like we are being worked (badly) by puppeteers. At the moment we are concentrating on Marina Aquamarina. She was part of an underwater kingdom, well her dad was the king of it, but they were being threatened by these horrible fish people (no they didn't wear codpieces but it would have been excellent if they did).

Anyway, Marina Aquamarina floated around underwater with her blonde hair trailing behind her and her arms all flopping by her side. All the boys really liked her, especially because she was dumb – when anyone spoke to her she just blinked in an appealingly dumb way. So anyway, when we are being Marina Aquamarina, as well as floating around with our arms by our sides we are not allowed to speak, just shake our heads and blink. So, for instance, if a prefect said, "Where is your beret?" you could only blink and stare and then float off quickly.

But then there is phase two, which is pretending to be a little boy in *Supercar* called Jimmy. Jimmy has a very upturned nose with freckles on it. Obviously you could just put your finger on your nose and force the tip back to get the snub nose

64

effect but a more sophisticated method is to use egg-boxes. You take one of the bits that the egg fits in and paint some nostrils on it, and some freckles, and Bob's your uncle. Pop it on some elastic and put it over your own nose. *Voilà l'enfant* Jimmy!!

So, when we had the school photo done, Rosie, Ellen, Julia, Jas and me all had our Jimmy noses on. When you see the photo you don't actually notice at first, but then, when you look closely, you can see that five girls at the back all have snub noses with freckles. Bloody funny in anyone's language. Not Slim's, though. She was all of a quiver.

"Do you know how costly it is to have these photographs done? No you do not, you silly girls. Do you know how ridiculous you make yourselves and the school seem? No, you seem not to know these obvious things."

Forty years later we got let out. Our punishment is that we have to pick up all the litter in the school grounds. That should please Mr Attwood, the school caretaker. Revenge on us because we call him Elvis. He's only about one hundred and nine, and the most boring, bad-tempered man in the universe, apart from my dad. I really don't know what is the matter with him lately (my dad), he's always hanging around, looking at me. Oh well, incest seems to run in my family. (That's quite a good joke, actually.)

november

a bit of rough

thursday november 5th

7.00 p.m. I hate November the fifth. On the way to school it was a nightmare of jumping-jacks and bangers. Boys are obsessed with loud noises and frightening people. I saw Peter Dyer (whelk boy) but he ignored me and also said something to his mate. He's going out with Katie Steadman now – she's welcome. I wonder if he will be my first and last boyfriend? Jas and I are talking again, which is a shame because all she wants to do is talk about Tom. She's miffed because he has to work in the shop all weekend. I said, "Well, that's what happens in the fruit and veg trade, Jas. You will always be second fiddle to his *légumes.*" For once, she didn't argue back.

7.30 p.m. Angus loves Bonfire Night. The dog next door has to be locked in a padded cell it's so frightened, but Angus loves it. He chases the rockets – he probably thinks they are grouse on fire. There's a big bonfire out on the back fields, all the street is going. I'm not, though, because I know that firelight emphasises my nose. I could wear a hat, I suppose. Is that my life, then, going around wearing a hat? No, I'll just stay in my bedroom and watch other people having fun through the window.

10.00 p.m. Brilliant bonfire!!! I love Bonfire Night. I had baked potatoes and got chatted up by a boy from up the street. He looks a bit like Mick Jagger (although not, of course, eighty). He said, "See you around," when I left to come home. I think he might go to the thick boys' school but, hey ho, he can be my bit of rough. Snigger snigger.

Angus is curled up on my bed, which means I can't straighten my legs, but I daren't move him. He's got a singed ear and his whiskers are burnt off but he's purring.

wednesday november 11th

4.20 p.m. Jas comes round for a bit of a "talk" after school. I make her my special milky coffee drink. She starts to moan on, "Tom is going to be working again this weekend."

I said, "Well, I told you, it's a family business." I felt like a very wise person and also I seemed to have turned into a Jewess. I've never said "family business" in my life. *Oy vey.*

Jas didn't seem to notice my sudden Jewishness, she just raved on, "I don't know, I mean, I really, really like him but I want to have fun . . . I don't want to have to be all serious and think about the future and never go out."

I'd really got into the swing of my new role now. "Look, Jas, you're intelligent (see what I mean? I could say these things without any hint of sarcasm), you're a good-looking young girl, the world is at your feet. Do you want to end up with a fruit and veg man? Stay with him and the next thing you know you'll have five children and be up at dawn arguing about cabbages. Look what happened to my mum,' I said meaningfully.

Jas had been following me up until that point but then she said, "What did happen to your mum?" and I said, "She got Dad."

Jas said, "I see what you mean."

monday november 16th

4.10 p.m. Jas has finished with Tom. She came in all ashen-faced and swollen-eyed this morning. I had to wait until break to talk to her.

We went to the tennis courts even though it was bloody freezing. I refuse to wear a vest, though. I'm going to persevere with my bra, even if it does bunch up. I think my breasts are definitely growing. Fondling is supposed to make them bigger. Melanie Griffith must do nothing but fondle hers, they're gigantic. Anyway, Jas told me the whole thing about Tom and how she has now become a dumper.

(Verb to dump: I dump, you dump, he/she/it dumps etc.)

Jas said, "He was upset and angry at the same time. He said he thought we were good together."

Jas looked as if she was about to cry again so I put my arm round her. Then I took it away quickly – I don't want to start the lesbian rumour again. I said, "Jas, there's plenty of other boys. You deserve better than a greengrocer with a horrible bigger brother."

10.00 p.m. Oh dear God, Jas on the phone again. Has she done the right thing? etc. etc. etc . . . I must get her interested in someone else.

8.00 p.m. Drama drama!!!

We had a substitute teacher today for Biology. No, I don't mean substitute, I mean reserve, no, I don't mean that, I mean . . . oh anyway, a student teacher. She was very nervous and very short-sighted and we'd all got that mad bug that you get some days and we couldn't stop laughing. The student teacher, Miss Idris, asked me to hand out pipettes or something and I tried to get up, only to find that Ellen and Jools had tied my Science overall tapes to the drawer handles.

They were helpless with laughter and so couldn't undo them. It took me ages to get free. Then Rosie wrote a note: *This is the plan – Operation Movio Deskio. Whenever Miss Idris writes on the board we all shift our desks back a couple of centimetres, really quietly.*

By the end of the lesson when she looked round from the board we were all squashed up against the back wall and there was a three metre gap in front of her. We were speechless with laughing. She just blinked through her glasses and didn't say anything.

Then it happened. Jas and I got to the school gate and Robbie was there. For one moment I thought he had realised that it was ME ME ME he wanted and not old dumbo, but he gave me a HORRIBLE look as I passed by. I said to Jas, "Did you see that? What's he got against me? All right, he's seen my knickers, but it's not a hanging offence."

Jas went a bit red. I said, "Do you know something I don't?"

And she said nervously, in a rush, "Well, erm, maybe. I think he's a bit cross, because Tom's upset we're not going out

69

and I said it was partly because I'd spoken to you and you had said I really shouldn't go out with someone in a fruit and veg shop because it was not really good enough for me. Well, you did say that."

I got hold of her by her tie. "You said *what*????!!!"

She just blinked and went pink and white.

midnight I CANNOT BELIEVE IT. Stabbed in the back by my so-called best friend. It was never like this in the Famous Five books. No wonder Robbie is so moody and stroppy with me.

monday november 23rd

4.15 p.m. Terrible day. Jackie "suggested" that we do something to pass the time in German, whilst Herr Kamyer amused himself declining verbs on the blackboard. (What a stupid language German is, you have to wait until the end of the sentence to find out what the verb is. But my attitude by then is, Who cares?? I think I might start calling my father Vater and my mum Mutter just for a change. Vati and Mutti, for short.)

Anyway, Jackie said we should mark each other out of ten for physical attractiveness. The list was skin, hair, eyes, nose, figure, mouth, teeth. You had to write out the list and put your name on the top of the paper and then pass it round to everyone to give you a mark. It was Jackie, Alison, Jas, Rosie, Jules, Ellen and Beth Morgan. I didn't want to do it but you don't say no to Jackie. I more or less gave everyone near top marks for everything . . . even in the face of obvious evidence to the contrary. For instance, I gave Beth seven for her teeth – my logic

70

was that they might be nice when the front ones grow back in, you never know. All the marks were given anonymously. Then we got our papers back with the marks listed.

My list was:

skin	7 8 8 7 8 8 7
hair	8 8 8 8 8 8 8
eyes	7 8 8 8 8 8 8
nose	4 3 3 0 4 4¼ 4
figure	7 6 7 7 7 7½ 7
mouth	6 6 6 6 5 6⅓ 6
teeth	8 8 9 9 8 9 9

Someone gave me a nought for my nose!!! I got the lowest marks out of anyone. My best feature was my teeth! Jas had got mostly eights for all of her features and so she was in that really annoying mood when you've done quite well in an exam and it makes you sort of "kind" to people who haven't done as well. We compared marks on the way home.

"You've got more marks for your mouth than me, Jas. What's wrong with mine? Why is yours so much better? Did you give me six and a third? That looks like your handwriting."

She was squirming a bit by now. "Does it? . . . No, I don't think it is."

Then I had her. "Well, if it's not that one you must have given me even less than that."

She backed down. "Oh yes, actually, yes, that is my writing, yes. I was livid. "What is wrong with my mouth?"

71

"Nothing, that's why I've given you six and a third."

"But that's only average."

"Well, I know I would have given you more, because I think that it's definitely seven or even an eight when it's closed."

"When it's closed," I said dangerously.

Jas was as red as two beetroots. "Well, I had to consider things overall. You see, it's your smile."

"What about my smile?"

"Well, when you smile, because your mouth is so big . . ."

"Yes, do go on . . ."

"Well, it sort of splits your face in half and it, well, it spreads your nose out more."

7.00 p.m. In my room in front of the mirror. Practising smiling without making my nose spread. It's impossible. I must never smile again.

8.00 p.m. Phoned Jas.

"Jas, you only gave me seven and a half for my figure, and I gave you eight for yours."

"Well?"

"Well I only gave you eight because you are my friend."

"Well I only gave you seven and a half because you are my friend. I was going to give you seven."

midnight How dare Jas only give me – what was it? – eight for my eyes? I gave her eight for hers and she has got stupid brown eyes.

1.00 a.m. That Beth stupid Morgan can only have given me four, three or nought for my nose. I gave her six and a half for hers and I was being very bloody generous when I did.

What is the point of being a nice person?

thursday november 26th

9.00 p.m. Vati dropped a bombshell today – he is going on a trip to NEW ZEALAND because M and D are thinking of going to live there! I don't know why they bother to tell me. I don't really see what it has to do with me. It was just as I was on the dash to school and Vati said, "Georgia, I don't know if you have heard any-thing but there's been a lot of redundancies at my place."

I said, "Vati, don't tell me you are going to have to go on the dole with students, and so on. You could always sell your apron if we get too short of money."

monday november 30th

4.20 p.m. Jas still moping about Tom. We have to avoid "his" part of town now. I hope I'm not going mad but Rosie told me that she draws stuff on the roof of her mouth with her tongue. Like a heart or a little house. I said she was bonkers but now I've started doing it.

5.00 p.m. Bumped into the boy up the street I met at Bonfire Night. We sat on our wall for a bit. It's funny, he's one of the only lads I don't feel like I should rush off and cover myself in make-up for. I don't even flick my hair so that it covers half my face (and therefore half my nose). Dad says if I keep doing it I will go blind in one eye, and also

73

that it makes me look like a Pekinese, but what does he know? And anyway, it won't bother him in New Zealand.

Bonfire Boy is called Mark and I suppose the reason I'm not too self-conscious in front of him is that he has a HUGE mouth. I mean it, like Mick Jagger. He is about seventeen and he goes to Parkway, the rough school. He's mad about football and he and his mates go play on the park. I think I've seen them when I've "accidentally" taken Angus for a walk up there. He's sort of quite attractive (Mark, not Angus), despite the mouth. He wants to be a footballer and has got a trial somewhere. When I left he said, "See you later." Oh no, here we go again, on the "See you later" trail.

9.00 p.m. Saw Mark walking down the street with his mates. He looked round and up at my bedroom window so I had to bob down quickly. I hope he didn't see me because I had an avocado mask on and my hair Sellotaped down to keep my fringe straight. I wonder where he is going? He had trainers and joggerbums on.

10.30 p.m. Heard Mutti and Vati arguing. Oh perfect, now they'll split up and they'll both want custody of me.

10.40 p.m. If I go with Mum I will have access to make-up, clothes, and so on, and I can usually persuade her to let me stay out later. She laughs at my jokes and goes out a lot. On the other hand, there is Vati.

10.42 p.m. Ah well, bye bye, Vati . . .

december

the stiff dylans gig

tuesday december 1st

11.00 a.m. *Mucho excitemondo!* There is going to be a Christmas dance at Foxwood school. Slim announced it in assembly.

"Girls, there is to be a dance at Foxwood school, to celebrate Christmas, on December 12th, commencing at seven thirty."

It was like something out of *Upper Fourth at Malory Towers*. Me and Rosie and Jas and Ellen went "Oooohhhhhhhhhhhhhhh ooohhhhhhh!" for so long that Slim had to say "Settle, girls". At last she went on, "To add to the festivities there will be a . . . band." We started doing our "ooohhhing" again but Hawkeye glared at us so viciously we stopped.

I had thought of shouting "Three cheers for the Headmaster of Foxwood, and three for Merry England!" but I didn't.

Slim still hadn't finished. "The band will be The Stiff Dylans."

lunch-time

12.30 p.m. Jas and me had a confab by the vending machine. Jas said, "Do you think we

75

should go? I mean, Lindsay will be there, and Tom might . . . well, he might go with someone else and then we'd be like . . ."

"Two spare whatsits at a wedding?" I suggested.

4.00 p.m. The most cringe-making thing in the Universe of Cringe-making Things happened this afternoon in RE. It was with Miss Wilson, who is not what you might call normal (still, who would be – teaching RE?). She is a very unfortunate person, with ginger hair in a sad bob, her tights are always wrinkly, plus she wears tragic cardigans, usually done up the wrong way. She is not blessed in the looks department, but worse than this, she has not got a personality – at all – none.

Mostly she just talks and we get on with writing notes to each other or filing our nails. Last summer Rosie was so relaxed that she started moisturising her legs during RE. It was so hot that we hadn't been wearing stockings and Rosie put her legs on the desk and started putting cream on them. Well, even Miss Wilson noticed that. I remember she said, "Rosie, you'd better buck up your ideas and buck them up fast." Which struck us as very funny indeed – we were still laughing hours later.

Anyway, this afternoon, for some reason, Miss Wilson got talking about personal hygiene. I swear I don't know how she got there from religious education, maybe people in ancient Hebrew times cast someone out for being a smelly leper. I don't know.

We just heard her say, "Yes, girls, I know how that person felt because when I was younger I had a BO problem myself and people used to avoid me. I never used to wash because I was an orphan and depressed . . ." We just sat there staring at our desks

76

whilst she went on and on about her body odour . . . it was AWFUL. I have never been so glad to get up and go to PE.

We all ran screaming into the showers and washed ourselves like loonies. Miss Stamp was amazed, she usually has to prod us and shout at us to get us to change at all in winter. She came and looked at us in the shower in amazement. Then we remembered she is a lesbian. So we ran screaming out of the shower.

It's a bloody nightmare of pervs, this school. You'd be safer in Borstal.

8.00 p.m. Jas came over for the night. We yattered on about a plan for the school dance.

9.00 p.m. Looking through my bedroom window to see if we could see into next door's bedroom window because I wanted to know what Mr Next Door wore to bed. Jas thought jimjams but I thought shortie nightshirt.

Then as we were looking we saw Mark (Bonfire Boy) coming up the street with a girl. They stopped under a lamp-post but I couldn't see what she looked like as they were kissing. Not in the shadows or anything, but under the lamp. We couldn't stop watching and to get a better view we got up on to the window ledge. It was a tight squeeze but you could see everything. Then I heard tip tap tip tap and Libby came in, carrying her blanket (or "blankin" as she calls it – it's not actually a blanket, it's an old bra of Mum's but she likes it and won't let it go. It must have been white once but now it's a horrible grey colour).

She spotted us on the window ledge and said, "Libby see."

I said, "No, Libby, I'm coming down," but then she started

77

saying, "No, no, bad boy, bad boy . . . me see," and hitting me with her "blankin" so that I had to lift her up. Honestly, I'm bullied by a three-year-old and a Scottish wildcat.

I lifted her up and she snuggled down in between me and Jas. She spotted the couple under the lamppost. "Oohh, look! Manlady manlady!!! Hahahaha." It was a bit difficult knowing where Mark ended and the girl began but all was revealed when Mark stopped kissing and looked over her shoulder. Right up at my window. I don't know if he could see us in the dark but we got down from the window ledge so quickly we fell on to my bed. Libby said, "More bouncy now!!!"

Pray God Mark didn't see us spying.

wednesday december 2nd

8.30 a.m. Dashing out of the house, Jas and I almost fell into Mark, waiting by the corner. Jas (big pal) said she had to run to her house first and she would see me at school. I went a bit red and walked on with him walking beside me. He said, "Have you got a boyfriend?"

I was speechless. What is the right answer to that question? I tell you what the right answer is . . . a lie, that's the right answer. So I said, "I've just come out of a heavy thing and I'm giving myself a bit of space."

He looked at me. He really did have the biggest gob I have ever seen. "So is that no?"

And I just stood there and then this really weird thing happened . . . he touched my breast!!! I don't mean he ripped my blouse off, he just rested his hand on the front of my breast. Just for a second, before he turned and went off to school.

12.30 p.m. What does it mean when a boy rests his hand on your breast? Does it mean he has the mega-horn? Or was his hand just tired?

4.30 p.m. Why am I even thinking about this? No sign of Mark (the breast molester) when I got home, thank goodness.

4.45 p.m. Still, you would think if a boy rests his hand on your breast he might bother to see you sometime.

5.00 p.m. Up in my bedroom "doing my home-work" when the doorbell rang. I put down my magazine and answered it. It was Mark. He said, "I've dumped Ella, do you want to go to The Stiff Dylans gig?"

I said, "Er, well, er, yes thanks."

He said, "OK, see you later."

6.00 p.m. On the phone to Jas, telling her about Mark, I said, "So then I said, 'Er, yes,' and he said, 'OK, see you later.'"

Jas said, "See you later – what does that mean?"

I said, "I don't know – who does know? . . . See me later tonight, or at the gig, or what?"

Jas said, "Well, do you like him?"

I thought about it. "I don't really know. He makes me feel like a cobra, you know, all sort of funny and paralysed when the bloke starts playing the bugle thing."

Jas said, "What do you mean? Your head starts bobbing around when he plays his instrument?"

I said, "Don't start, Jas. Anyway, what do you think of him?"

Jas thought. "He's got a very big mouth."

I said, "Yes, I know," and then she said, "But then so have you."

midnight Oh-oh. What to do. Why is life so complicated? Do I like Mark? Why did I say yes? Why can't Robbie realise that Lindsay is a drippy git? Ohhhhhhh. *Quel dommage!!! Merde*. Poo.

monday december 7th

5.00 p.m. Mark sent a note, which is quite sweet, except that it is very badly written: *Dear Georgia, Away training till Saturday. Meet you at 8 at clock tower on Saturday. Mark*.

That's it, then, I have no choice. I have to go with him.

9.00 p.m. Mum comes into my room and says will I come down for a "talk"? I pray it's nothing to do with personal hygiene or her and Dad's relationship problems. Dad seems a bit nervous and he's growing a moustache, how ridiculous, it looks like some small animal is just having a bit of a sleep on his top lip. He says, "Look, Georgie, you're a young woman now [what was I before? a young horse?] and I don't think there should be any secrets in our house [on the contrary, Vati, you will never know about the hand on the breast scenario even if hell freezes over], which is why I need to tell you that as work is so hard to find here in England I am flying off to Auckland straight after Christmas. I'll be staying there for a month or two to get a feel for the place and to try a new job opening there. Then, when I get settled, your mum and you and Libbs can come out and see what you think."

I said, "I know what I think of New Zealand, I have seen *Neighbours*."

Mum said, "Well, that's set in Australia."

What is this, a family crisis or a geography test? I went on patiently, "My point is, Mutti and Vati, that it is very far away, I'm not from there, all my friends are here. Or to put it another way: I would rather let Noel Edmonds adopt me than set foot on New Zealand soil."

We argued for ages – even Libby came down and joined in. She had dressed Angus up in her pyjamas and he had a bonnet on and a dummy in. I don't know how she gets away with it, if I went anywhere near him with a bonnet he would have my hand off.

midnight   So Vati is off to New Zealand. But that still doesn't solve what I am going to be wearing for The Stiff Dylans gig.

friday december 11th

2.50 p.m.   Christmas fever has set in at school. We all wore silver antlers in Physics this afternoon. Herr Kamyer tried to join in with the joke by saying, "Oh ja, jingle bells, jingle bells." It's pathetic really. Also, why are his trousers so short? You can see acres of pale, hairy ankle between his trousers and his plaid socks. (Yes, I did say plaid socks, now that is not just sad, it's double sad.)

8.00 p.m. Mutti and Vati strangely quiet and nice to each other. I saw Dad put his arms round Mum in the kitchen. Also Libby was singing, "Dingle balls, dingle balls, dingle on the way," and Dad got all sort of wet round the eyes. Honestly, I thought he was going to cry, which would have been horrific. He picked her up and hugged her really hard. Libby was furious, she called him, "Bad, big uggy, bad," and stuck her finger in his eye which made him cry properly.

saturday december 12th

the stiff dylans!

7.00 a.m. Damn, I didn't mean to wake up so early. Still, it gives me lots of time to get ready for tonight. I thought first of all I would do my yoga, which I haven't been able to fit into my busy schedule.

7.20 a.m. Now I know why I don't bother with yoga, it's too hard, that's why. When I did "dog pose" I thought I'd never be able to get up again. I'll just have a lie down and relax with an uplifting book for a few minutes.

7.40 a.m. I'm not reading the *Tibetan Book of Living and Dying* ever again. I'm not going to become a Buddhist if I might come back reincarnated as a stick insect.

7.50 a.m. Cup of milky coffee and toast, yum yum yum. Mum has got a new *Cosmo*.

8.10 a.m. Back in bed for a few minutes' read. Hmmm . . . "What men say and what they mean".

9.30 a.m. If a boy says "See you later" it might mean, "Leave me alone, it was great while it lasted but I am not ready for anything more serious" or "See you later".

9.40 a.m. I am going to become a writer for *Cosmo* – you don't have to make any sense at all. Or maybe I'll be a bloke, they don't have to make any sense either.

10.00 a.m. I am going to wear my short black Lycra dress. Jas has already phoned five times and changed her mind about what to wear each time.

1.00 p.m. Rosie has asked the foreign exchange guest student who is staying next door to come to The Stiff Dylans. I said, "Are you sure that's a good idea?" and she said, "He's called Sven," and I said, "Well, that's what I mean."

Rosie says he's a "laugh", whatever that means. She said, "He doesn't speak any English but he is very tall."

When I asked where he was from she said, "I don't know, Denmark, I think. He's blond."

Apparently she asked him to go to The Stiff Dylans by pointing at him, pointing at herself and doing a bit of a dance. She's bonkers. We arranged to go to Boots because we needed to have perfume for tonight and we can use the samples whilst we pretend we might buy them.

4.30 p.m. Back home, covered in Paloma – I hope it wears off a bit as it's making my eyes water. Also, I've got some new lip-gloss which is supposed to plump up your lips. I'm not sure that this is such a good idea in my case, especially going with Mark. I wonder if the same rule applies to lips as does to breasts? I mean, if you use them more, I wonder if they get bigger?

5.00 p.m. If using your lips does make your lips bigger, what on earth has Mark been up to? Am I going to let him kiss me? What does the hand on the breast mean? Do I want him to be my boyfriend? I don't think he's very bright but he might turn out to be a brilliant footballer like Beckham and then I could marry him and be kept in luxury.

5.10 p.m. But then I'd be in all the papers. I'd have to have my nose done. I would have to be careful not to smile . . . what if I forgot? What if I got caught by the paparazzi smiling and my nose spreading all over my face . . . in the *Daily Express*?

5.15 p.m. I can't marry him, the pressure is just too much. I am losing my own self-esteem whilst he gets all the attention. I'll have to explain to him tonight that it is all over.

6.00 p.m. I feel a bit sick. I've got a bit of hair that will NOT go right, in a minute I am going to cut it off. Also, I think I have got knobbly knees. Maybe when I am Mark's wife I could have fat injected into them (possibly taken from my nose, so it would be a two-in-one operation . . . smaller nose and fatter knees all in one swift plunge of the huge, hypodermic, fat-extractor needle . . . er, I really do feel sick . . .).

7.30 p.m. I wish I had gone with Jas and Rosie, all in a big gang, now it means I'll have to walk in with Mark and everyone will look at me and think he's my boyfriend.

midnight I cannot BELIEVE my life. Well, if you could call it a life . . . When I think about tonight I feel like staying in bed for the rest of it.

Mark was at the clock tower, smoking a fag . . . he looked sort of OK. When I got near him he grabbed me and gave me a kiss right on the mouth, no messing about. I was surprised and also a bit worried . . . maybe the hand would sneak up to the breast for a bit of a rest . . . but no.

Mark doesn't seem to say much – after the kiss he took my hand and we started walking to the gig. It was a bit awkward because I am actually bigger than him, so I had to sort of let my shoulder down on one side like Quasimodo.

As soon as we got there Mark went to say hello to a few of his mates. Rosie's Sven was a GIANT – about eight foot tall, with a crewcut. Jas was all moony and looked a bit pale. She said, "I wanted that anorexic model look, like I've been up partying all night. I want Tom to think I've not been thinking about him."

The gig was packed, mostly boys on one side and girls on the other. Jas said, "Aren't you going to talk to your boyfriend?"

Which is when Tom and Robbie walked in. They saw us and Robbie caught my eye and he smiled . . . I'd forgotten what a Sex God he is. He's all muscly and dark and oooh-hhhh. I smiled back, a proper smile because I'd forgotten about my nose for the moment. Then from behind me came Lindsay and crossed over to Robbie. He had been smiling at her!!! My face was so red you could fry an egg on it. Robbie kissed Lindsay on the cheek. She had her hair up and was quite literally all ears. Yukko.

Robbie went up on stage and Tom was left by himself as wet Lindsay chatted to some of her stupid, sixth-form mates. Jas said, "Do you think I should go over and say something to him?"

I said, "Have some pride, Jas, he chose vegetables over you." At that moment a dark-haired girl came out of the loos and went over to Tom. She put her hand on his arm and they went off together.

And it got worse.

The Stiff Dylans started playing and Mark came across to me, got hold of my hand and pulled me on to the dance floor. His Mick Jagger impersonation did not stop at the lips. He was a lunatic on the dance floor, strutting around with his hands on his hips. I nearly died. Then Sven joined in, dragging Rosie with him. His style of dancing was more Cossack, a lot of going down into a squat position and kicking his legs out. Then he lifted Rosie up above his head!!! He was whirling her around, going, "Oh ja, oh ja," and Rosie was trying to keep people from seeing up her skirt.

And that is when I lost it. It was just too funny . . . Jas, Ellen and Jools and I were laughing like hyenas. I had a coughing fit and had to rush to the loos to try and recover. I'd just calm myself down and then poke my head round the door to see Sven dancing around and it started me off again.

Then Mark wanted to slow dance. I knew because he grabbed me and pulled me up against him. He was all lumpy, if you know what I mean, and had his mouth against my neck. It was even more difficult dancing with him than it was holding hands. I had to sort of bend my knees and sag a bit in order to "fit in". At one stage I found myself looking straight at Robbie. He looked so cool. Oh bloody *sacré bleu*. Even though I hate him and he is a pompous pratboy, I think I may love him.

Then the band stopped playing for a break but Mark yelled, "Play more." Some of his mates started joining in, then they sort of rushed the stage and Mark grabbed the microphone from Robbie. He was "singing" – I think it may have been "Jumpin' Jack Flash". Robbie put his hand on his shoulder and then a massive fight broke out. All Mark's thick friends got stuck into the band and then the band's mates got stuck into them. All us girls were screaming.

Sven lifted two boys up at once and tossed them outside into the street and that's when Ellen, Jas, Jools and I decided to do a runner.

So, a gorgeous night. I am tucked up in bed, my "boyfriend" is a hooligan, before him I had another "boyfriend" called whelk boy. The boy I like hates me and prefers a wet weed with sticky-out ears . . .

PS My so-called "pet" spat at me when I walked in all upset.

PPS I have found my sister's secret used nappy at the bottom of my bed.

sunday december 13th

5.00 p.m. No sign of Mark, thank goodness. I stayed in reading all day. Mum and Dad are having a night out – they suddenly want to do things together, it's so unnatural! – so I have to babysit Libby. I don't mind as I never want to go out again.

6.00 p.m. Libby cheered me up by pretending to be Angus. She curled up in his basket and hid behind the curtains, growling. I had to stop her when she started eating his dinner.

6.15 p.m. Jas on the phone. "I'll never get a boyfriend. I may become a vet."

6.20 p.m. Jas phoned again. "Do you think I am really ugly?"

6.30 p.m. Rosie phoned. "I managed to get Sven home before the police arrived. He has given me a bit of holly."
I said, "Why?" and she said, "I don't know, maybe it's a Danish tradition."

7.15 p.m. Jools phoned. "Someone said they noticed that Lindsay wears an engagement ring when she's at school."

8.00 p.m. Perfect. The doorbell rang but I made Libby be really quiet and pretend we weren't in. No note or anything.

Fed up, depressed, hungry.

9.00 p.m. Fed up, depressed, feel sick.

Had:

2 Mars bars;

toast;

milky coffee;

Ribena;

Coke;

toast;

cornflakes and

Pop-Tarts.

10.00 p.m. Going to bed. Hope I never wake up.

monday december 14th

8.30 a.m. Nearly bumped into Mark on the way to school. Got round the corner just in time, thank goodness.

9.45 a.m. Slim was livid about The Stiff Dylans gig; she was trembling like a loon.

"I sincerely hope none of my girls were in any way associated with the hooligans who behaved like animals at the dance . . ."

Rosie looked up at me and put her teeth in front of her bottom lip like a hamster. I don't know why but it really made me laugh so much I thought I would choke. I had to pretend to have a coughing fit and get my hankie out.

Jas wasn't in school. I wonder where she is. Maybe the

"painters are in", if you know what I mean. Rosie was full of Sven this and Sven that. I said, "Is he your boyfriend, then?" and she went a bit red and said, "Look, I don't think we're going out or anything. He's only given me a bit of holly." But as I said, that could mean anything in Denmark.

Oh bloody hell, Jackie and Alison, the Bummer twins, are back with a vengeance. They sent a note round saying they want us all to meet by the canteen on Thursday lunch for, as they call it, "the latest".

4.30 p.m. Note from Mark when I got in from school: *Georgia, I looked for you after the other night. Meet me at 10 at the phone box tonight. Mark*

9.50 p.m. If I don't go I'll only see him in the street anyway . . .

I shouted to M and D (spending time together AGAIN), "I'm just taking Angus out for a walk."

Dad yelled, "Don't let him near that poodle."

I had to drag Angus away from Next Door's, he wants to eat that poodle. He has about four cans of petfood a day as it is, if he gets any bigger Mum says she is going to give him to a zoo, as if they would want him.

10.00 p.m. Mark smoking by the phone box. He didn't see me coming – hardly surprising as Angus had dragged me behind a hedge, chasing a cat. In the end I tied him to the gatepost. From behind the hedge I could see Mark, and you know when you have one of those moments when you know what you have to do? No, well neither do I . . . but I did think, I must come clean

90

with Mark, it is not fair on him, I'm going to say, "Look, Mark, I like you and you mustn't think it's you, it's me really, I just think I could never make you happy, we're so different. I think it is best that we stop right here and now before anyone gets hurt."

So I went up to him. He was half in the shadows and he threw his cigarette down when he saw me. I opened my mouth to speak and he just kissed me right on the open mouth. What if I had been sucking a Polo mint? I could have choked to death!! Also, he put his tongue in my mouth, which was a bit of a surprise . . . but then he did it again!!! He put his hand on my breast! What was I supposed to do? I hadn't gone to breast classes. My arms were sort of hanging by my sides like an orang-utan when I remembered what whelk boy had said about putting your hands on someone's waist, so I did that. He had one hand on my breast and one on my bottom. But just when I was thinking, What next? in the hand department, he stopped kissing me.

Was this a good moment to say he was dumped?

He said, "Look, Georgia, this is not personal or anything, but er . . . I think you are too young for me. I'm going back out with Ella because she lets me do things to her. Sorry, see you later."

midnight See you later? Mark has had the cheek to dump me just as I was about to dump him! I'm never getting up again. Ella lets him do things to her . . . what things? Two hands on her breasts?

tuesday december 15th

8.10 a.m. Told Mum I was not going to school or, in fact, getting out of bed. She said, "Why not?"

91

And, against my better judgement, I told her, "I've been dumped by someone I didn't even like. I was going to dump him but I didn't even get the chance."

She sat on my bed. "That is bad. It's never nice to be dumped. But look at it this way . . . you are in exactly the place you wanted to be – you're single and free again. And you have ten pounds to spend."

I grumbled on, "Yeah, well, you would say that. You don't know how sensitive I am, and how I really get hurt and it really takes me ages to get over things and . . . what did you say about the tenner?"

Mad Auntie Kath had come up trumps with a belated birthday present . . . hurrah!!!

3.30 p.m. I didn't even bother to put make-up on today, it doesn't matter – I'm not trying to impress boys any more. No more "See you later" for me. I'm just going to take my time to grow up and concentrate on my work so I can get a good job, and so on.

4.18 p.m. Hell's bells! Robbie was at the gate . . . probably waiting for his fiancée. I walked by, sort of pretending I hadn't even noticed he was there. But he spoke to me. "Nice company you keep."

I had to stop then. I was livid, I wanted to say something really clever and cutting and witty. Something that would let him know I was someone to be careful with. So I said, "I think you are mistaking me for someone who is interested in what you have to say." And I walked on.

5.30 p.m. Yessssss!!!! Ha!!! Three times ha and a

yessss!!! Double ha with a hyphen!!!!

10.00 p.m. Vati showed me a map of where he is going. Apparently the area has the most violent geothermal activity in the world. Earthquakes and volcanoes and lava shooting out of the earth and geysers and hot-water rivers. It makes you question his sanity (not for the first time). My vati is not even the outdoors type here, he gets exhausted getting out of his chair or grooming his moustache. It will all end in tears . . . his. Mutti is draping herself all over him. It is grotesque. The next thing you know I'll have another little sister or little brother. Ugh. I don't even want to think about it.

wednesday december 16th

1.30 p.m. Jas still not back. I'll visit her after school.

4.15 p.m. No reply at Jas's house.

6.30 p.m. Phoned Jas. Her mum said she couldn't get to the phone as she is not very well. I said, "Is it the flu?" and her mum said, "Well, I don't know, but she's not eating."

Not eating. Jas. Jas not eating. Things are bad. I said, "What, not even Pop-Tarts?" and her mum said, "No."

Things are much worse than I thought.

10.00 a.m. Still no Jas. This is getting ridiculous.

1.30 p.m. Jackie and Alison's "latest thing" turns out to be so bonkers it is not even in the bonkers universe. We all had to go out into the freezing cold at the back of the tennis courts . . . I was surprised that Jackie knew where they were, I don't think she's ever been near the sports area before. Then Jackie told us what it was all about. "OK, this is what you do. You crouch down like this, then you start panting really hard and then you stand up and start running forward."

I said, "Why?" and she looked at me and lit a fag. Tarty or what? She had a huge spot on her chin, it looked like a second nose. I'm not surprised her skin is so bad, it's probably been covered in make-up since she was five.

She blew the smoke in my face and said, "When you run forward it makes you faint."

Even Rosie, who usually doesn't say much to Jackie, had to repeat this. "You faint?"

Jackie drew on her fag like she was dealing with the very, very stupid. She didn't say anything, so eventually Rosie said, "Then what?"

Jackie totally lost it, then. "Look, four-eyes, think about how useful it can be to just faint when you want to . . . in assembly – faint, get taken out. In Physics, when you haven't done your homework – faint, get taken out . . . games . . . anything."

Rosie is nothing if not stupid, so she kept going on, "Don't you think someone might notice if we crouched down in assembly or Physics and started panting and then ran forward?"

Jackie walked over to Rosie, and she is quite a big girl. Her breasts are sturdy-looking and she's got big arms.

11.00 p.m. I still feel a bit odd. I'm not going to be doing anything that Jackie and Alison say ever again. That is it. This stupid fainting thing is it. That is it. I did the panting and then stood up and started running and I did feel very faint, but not as faint as when I ran into Mr Attwood coming out of his hut. I may have broken my shin. Sadly Elvis was OK.

friday december 18th

7.30 p.m. Jas off all week. I'm worried about her now, she won't even speak to me on the phone. Even when I pretended I was Santa Claus.

friday december 25th

10.00 a.m. Happy St Nicholas Day, one and all!!!

My fun-filled day started at five fifteen a.m. when Libby came in to give me my present, something made out of Playdough that had horrible, suspicious-looking brown bits in it. She said, "Tosser's baby . . . ahhh," and tucked it up into bed with me.

As we are "a bit strapped for cash" as Vati puts it (due to his inability to hold down a job in my opinion, but I didn't say in case I spoiled Christmas even more) we could not have expensive presents. Mum and Dad got me CDs and make-up and leggings and trainers and undies and perfume, and I made Dad a lovely moustache holder which I think he will treasure.

I made Mum some home-made cosmetics out of egg yolks and stuff. She tried on the face-pack and it gave her a bit of a rash, but on the whole livened up her complexion.

I made Libby a fairy costume, which was a big mistake as she spent the rest of the day changing us into things by wacking us with her wand. I had to be a "nice porky piggy" for about an hour. I never want to see a sausage again.

Jas phoned, but still isn't venturing out – so no escaping "merry" Christmas with the family.

Angus looked nice in his tinsel crown until it annoyed him and he ate it. When we had lunch Mum made him a special mouse-shaped lunch in his bowl out of Katto-meat. He ate its head and then sat in it. Heaven knows what goes on in his cat brain.

I think I may become a New Age person next year and celebrate the winter solstice by leaving my family and going to Stonehenge to dance with Druids. It couldn't be more boring than watching my dad trying to make his new electric toothbrush work. However, there was a bright moment when he got it tangled up in his moustache.

saturday december 26th

noon *Quel dommage!!* M and D have selfishly asked me to babysit Libby whilst they have "a last night out together". Dad leaves for Whangamata on the 29th . . . sob, sob . . . and so as a brilliant treat he is taking Mum . . . to the pub!! With Uncle Eddie!!

If I was Mum I would have faked an accident, or if necessary had a real accident. A broken ankle would be a small price to pay to avoid Uncle Eddie's version of "Agadoo".

11.30 p.m. Mum and Dad came crashing in, giggling. They were drunk. I was in bed TRYING to sleep but they have no consideration. I could hear them dancing around to "The Birdy Song". They are sad.

Then they crept upstairs saying "Ssshhhh" really loudly. Mum gave a bit of a gasp when she came into my room because Libby was in bed with me but she had gone to sleep upside-down so her feet were on the pillow next to me. Mum put her in her own bed, but then horror of horrors DAD RUFFLED MY HAIR. I pretended even harder to be asleep.

sunday december 27th

11.00 a.m. M and D still in bed. I will take their lovely young daughter Liberty in to them to chat.

2.00 p.m. Going out. Dad's given me a fiver to look after Libby.

tuesday december 29th

8.00 p.m. Vati left today. I must say even I had a bit of a cry. He went off in Uncle Eddie's sidecar. We all waved him off. He says that he'll ring when he gets to Whangamata. It takes two days to fly there – imagine that. I suppose it is the other side of the world. Mum is all glum and snivelling, so I bought her some Milk Tray. That made her cry more, so I don't think I'll do it again. Libby got her Angus's bowl to cry into.

january

exploding knickers

friday january 1st

11.00 a.m. Resolutions:

I will be a much nicer person, to people who deserve it.

I will be interested in my future.

I will speak nicely to Mr and Mrs Next Door.

I will be less superficial and vain.

I will concentrate on my positive and not my negative,

e.g. I will think less about my nose and more about my quite attractive teeth.

saturday january 2nd

11.30 a.m. At last! News of Jas. It seems that she might have glandular fever. I'm wearing a scarf over my mouth and nose when I visit her, just in case. Apparently you get glandular fever from kissing. It's a night-mare, this kissing business – if it's not a mysterious hand on the breast it's huge swollen glands. Celibacy or a huge fat neck, that is the stark choice. I wonder if Slim has got big fat feet from too much kissing in the foot area? Uuurgghh, now I feel

98

really sick. I'm far too ill to visit the sick. I must go home to bed.

No . . . Jas needs me. I'll just try not to breathe the same air as her.

4.00 p.m. Jas has finally let me see her. She's all pale and thin, just lying in bed. Her bedroom is tidy, which is a bad sign and she has turned her mirror to the wall. She didn't even open her eyes when I came in. I sat on her bed.

"Jas, what are you doing? What's the matter? Come on, tell me, your best pal."

Silence.

"Come on, Jas, whatever it is, you can trust me."

Silence.

"I know what it is, you think that just because everyone else besides Nauseating P. Green and Hairy Kate the lezzo have got boyfriends – or have kissed someone properly – there is something really wrong with you, don't you?"

Silence. I was getting a bit irritated. I was trying to help and I had problems of my own. I was practically an orphan, for instance . . . and a substitute parent. It was all, "Will you babysit Libby?" since Dad had selfishly gone to the other side of the world. What did Jas know of trouble? Had she taken her little sister to the swimming pool? No, she didn't even have a little sister. Had her little sister's swimming knickers exploded at the top of the toddlers' water slide? No. Is there ever any point in trying to tell Mum that Libby always has bottom trouble after baked beans? No, there is not. The swimming knickers could not contain

Libby's poo explosion and it was all over the slide and nearby toddlers. Did Jas know what it was to see a pool being cleared of sobbing toddlers, dragged out by their water wings? No. Did she know what it was like to sluice her little sister down and then have to walk the gamut of shame past all the mothers and toddlers and swimming-pool attendants in masks with scrubbing brushes? I think not. I had to take it on the chin like a taking-it-on-the-chin person, so why couldn't Jas?

I didn't say any of this to Jas but I took a tough line. "Come on, Jas, what can be so bad about swollen up glands?"

Jas spoke in a quiet voice so I had to bend down to hear her, "I haven't got swollen up glands. I don't think I'll ever get a boyfriend, no one asked me to dance even. Tom was my only chance and even he preferred his onions."

Aha, time for all that stuff I read in Mum's *Feel the Fear and Do It Anyway* book. I got Jas's mirror from the wall and held it in front of her face. "Look into that mirror, Jas, and love the person that you see. Say, I love you."

Jas looked in the mirror – she couldn't help it, it was about three centimetres away from her nose. She was almost sick. "Uuurggghhhh, I look hideous."

She wasn't really getting it. I said, "Jas, Jas, love yourself, love the beauty that is there, look at that lovely face, look at that lovely mouth. The mouth that your friend marked eight out of ten. Think of that, Jas. Think of all the poor people who only got six and a third . . . and you have an eight for a mouth . . ." (I can be like an elephant for remembering things that annoy me, sadly I can remember nothing to do with French, History, Maths or Biology.)

Jas was definitely perking up. She was puckering her mouth

and trying for a half smile. "Do you really think I have got a nice mouth?"

"Yes, yes, but look at the rest of you, look at those eyes, look at the spot-free skin . . ."

Jas sat up. "I know, it's good, isn't it? I've been drinking lemon and hot water first thing."

monday january 4th

7.00 a.m. Woke up and felt happy for a minute until I realised I had to go back to loony headquarters (school) today.

2.30 p.m. Gym. Discovered Angus had stored his afternoon snack in my rucksack. There are hedgehog quills in my sports knickers.

tuesday january 12th

noon Victory. Victory.

Madame Slack has been on my case about being lazy in French and I have just got eighty-five per cent in a test. Hahahaha. *Fermez la bouche*, Madame Slack. I did it by learning twenty-five words and then making sure I answered every question by using only those words. So to question one – "In French, what is your favourite food?" my answer was "*Lapin*" (rabbit).

For my essay, "What did you do on a sunny day?" I made sure I played with a rabbit.

Describe a favourite book – *Watership Down* – lots of *lapins* in that.

1.00 p.m. In line with my new resolution to concentrate on school and not boys I went to do my yoga in the gym at lunch-time. My yoga routine is called the Sun Salute and you stretch up to welcome the sun and then you bend down as if to say "I am not worthy." Then you do cobra pose and dog pose . . . it's all very flowing and soothing.

1.15 p.m. Miss Stamp came in just as I was doing dog pose. She said, "Oh, don't let me disturb you. I'm glad you're taking an interest in yoga, it's one of the best exercises for the body. It will be really good for your tennis in summer. Don't mind me, I'm just getting ready for this afternoon." Well, I was upside-down with my bottom sticking up in the air. Not something you want to do in front of a lesbian. So I quickly went into cobra but that made it look like I was sticking my breasts out at her. I think she may now be growing a beard as well as a moustache.

Honestly, there is no bloody peace in this place.

1.30 p.m. I tried my yoga outside, even though it was hard to do it with my gloves and coat on. Again I'd just got into dog pose when Elvis appeared round the corner. He's a grumpy old nutcase. "What are you up to?" he shouted at me.

I said, from upside-down, "Nnn doing nmy nyoga."

He pulled down his cap. "I don't care if you're doing nuclear physics, you're not doing it in my yard. Clear off before I report you."

As I went, I said, "Did you know that Elvis is dead?"

4.30 p.m. Saw Mark on my way home. I smiled in a mature way at him. He just said, "All right?"

6.00 p.m. Mum has gone mental in Vati's absence. When I asked her if she would pay for my nose reduction surgery she came out with the old "We can barely afford to feed Angus" line. As if he needs feeding anyway, there's never a day goes by that I don't find something decomposing in the airing cupboard. Anyway, she can't afford to invest in the happiness of her daughter but she can afford to have the lounge decorated, apparently, because the decorator is coming next week.

9.30 p.m. Watching TV Mum said, "Do you miss your dad?" and I said, "Who?"

monday january 18th

biology

2.40 p.m. I can do a great impression of a lockjaw germ. Rosie passed me a note: *Dear G. You know we have a double free period on Thursday? Well, do you fancy bunking off and going down town? Rrrrrrrrrxxxxx*

4.30 p.m. Walking home with Jas. I think she is well on the way to recovery. "What do you think of this lip-gloss? Do you think it makes me look a bit like Claudia Schiffer? My mouth is the same shape, I think." I wish I hadn't started this. Still, if she wants to live in a fantasy wonderland and it cheers her up . . . We went to her house and up to her room. Oh, the bliss of a normal household, no mad mum, no strange sister, no wild animals. Jas's mum asked us if we would like some Ribena and sandwiches. Imagine my mum doing that? . . . Imagine my mum being in! I suppose she is a good role model . . . if you want to be a hospital administrator – but couldn't she make the odd sandwich as well?

In Jas's bedroom we did our vital statistics with her tape measure. I am thirty-two, twenty-three, thirty-two and Jas is thirty, twenty three, thirty-three. I think she was breathing in for the twenty-three myself. Also my legs are two inches longer than hers. (I didn't mention it to Jas but one of my legs is two inches longer and the other one is only one and a half inches longer. How can you develop a limp at my age? It might be because I carry my bag on one shoulder and it's making that side longer. I must remember to swap sides. Nobody likes a lopsided girl.)

thursday january 28th

3.30 p.m. Rosie got up first and left the room. Miss Wilson came in as we were working, to "supervise", but we asked her who invented God and she left pretty quickly. We were busy making a list of all the qualities we want in a boyfriend – sense of humour, good dancer, good kisser, nice smile, six-pack, etc. Rosie sent her list and it just said, *HUGE*. I wrote back, *Huge what?* and she wrote back, *Huge everything*. Then I wrote back, *Huge teeth, you mean?* and she replied, *Yes*. Sven has begun to infect her with his Danishness, I think.

104

Anyway, Rosie, Jools and Ellen went out first, and then me and Jas. We met up in the ground floor loos and put our boots and skinny tops and make-up on. We made sure the coast was clear and then went out of the back doors. We had to crouch down beneath the Science block windows – Hawkeye was teaching in there and she could smell a girl at twenty paces. Once past the Science block it was a quick dash behind Elvis's hut. He was in there, reading his newspaper, and as we crept by we heard him fart loudly and say "Pardon". I started giggling and then every-one caught it. We had to run like mad. All afternoon if anyone did anything we'd say "Pardon".

Great in Boots. We tried all the testers, and this stuff that you put on your hair, like a wand and it puts a streak of colour into your own hair. I tried all of them but blonde looked really brilliant. Just a streak across the front, I knew it would look good. I'm going to get Mum to let me dye my hair blonde now that Vati's safely in Whangamata.

midnight Brilliant day!!! Jas and I sung "Respect" by Aretha Franklin on the way home.

february

jas must die

saturday february 6th

11.00 a.m. The doorbell rang. Mum was in the loo debagging Libby; it was not a pretty sight. At the weekend Mum wears these awful dungarees that only lesbians or people on *Blue Peter* in the sixties wear. Libby was singing "Three bag bears, three bag bears, see how they run, see how they run . . ." ("Three Blind Mice" to other people). Libby was as happy as a mad sandbag but Mum was all flustered. "Will you answer that, Georgie? It will be this builder called Jem I phoned up to look at the lounge. Let him in and make a cup of coffee while I finish with this."

When I opened the door I got an impression of blond hair and denims but then there was this awful squealing from next door's garden. Mrs Next Door was screeching, "Get him, get him! Oh oh oh!" She was dashing around the garden with a broom. I thought that Angus had got the poodle at last, but when I looked over the fence he had a little brown thing in his mouth.

Mrs Next Door yelled at me, "I'm going to call the police! It's my niece's guinea pig, we're looking after it. And now this, this . . . THING has got it."

Angus crouched down not very far away. I said, in my

sternest voice, "Drop it, now drop it, Angus."

Due to my training he recognised my voice and let the guinea pig drop out of his mouth. I started to go over to get it and the guinea pig started scampering away. After it had got a few centimetres Angus put his huge paw out and just let it rest on the end of its bottom. It squiggled and squiggled and Angus yawned and took his paw off again. The guinea pig streaked off and Angus lumbered to his feet and ambled after it. He biffed it on to its back and then he sat on it and closed his eyes for a little doze. I said to Mrs Next Door, "Sorry, he can be very annoying, he's having a game with it." She was very unreasonable. I managed to lure Angus away from his little playmate with a kipper. Mrs N D says she is going to complain to someone official. I wonder who? Cat patrol, I suppose.

Jem had been watching from the doorstep. He had a nice, crinkly smile. He said, "He's big for a cat, isn't he?"

I sighed, "Come in, Mum's in the bathroom, she'll be out in a minute." Jem came into the front room and I gave him some of my coffee. He's quite good-looking for an older man.

Mum came rushing in in her dungarees. Then she saw Jem and went all weird and even redder. She said, "Nnnnghhhh!" and then just left the room.

I shrugged my shoulders at Jem. He said, "Are you doing your GCSEs?" (Good, he thought I was at least sixteen . . . hahahahaha) . . . I went "Nnngghhh" as well. Then Mum came back with LIPSTICK on and proper clothes. I left them to it.

sunday february 7th

11.00 a.m. Got dressed in a short skirt, then me and Jas walked up and down to the main road. We wanted to see how many cars with boys in them hooted at us. Ten!! (We had to walk up and down for four hours . . . still, ten is ten!!!)

monday february 22nd

4.15 p.m. Something really odd happened today when Jas and I left school. Robbie was at the school gate in his mini. He was leaning against it. I wish my legs didn't go all jelloid when I see him. How do you make yourself not like someone? I think you're supposed to concentrate on some of their bad points. Maybe he's got horrible hands? I looked at his hands . . . they are lovely – all strong-looking but quite artistic too. Like he could put up a shelf and also take you to a plateau of sensual pleasure at the same time. I bet he doesn't rest his hand on your breast . . . I wish he would. Shut up!!!!! Anyway, I was getting ready to put on my coolest look and he said, "Hello, Jas, how are you?"

Jas flushed and said, "Oh, hi, Robbie, yeah fine thanks, and you?"

He said, "Cool." Then he said, "Jas, could I have a . . . could I speak to you sometime? Maybe you would come for a coffee next Wednesday after school?"

And Jas went, "Er . . . well . . . er . . . yes. Fine. See you then."

I was quite literally speechless.

When we got to Jas's house I just walked in through the

gate, through the door and straight up the stairs into her bed-room. It was like I had a furball in my throat. I thought I was going to choke and explode and poo myself all at the same time.

Jas sat down on her bed and just went "Foof".

I said, "What do you mean by 'Foof'?"

And she said, "Just that . . . 'Foof'."

I said, "Well, what does he want to see you about?"

And she looked at her nails in a very annoying way. "I don't know."

I said, "Well, you won't go, will you?"

And she said, "He asked me to go for a coffee and I said I would."

I went on, "Yes, but you won't go, will you?"

She looked at me. "Why shouldn't I go? He said he wanted to talk to me."

I couldn't believe it. "But you know he's my sworn enemy."

Jas went all reasonable. "Yes, but he's not my sworn enemy, he seems to really like me."

I was beyond the valley of the livid. "Jas, if you are my friend you will not go and meet Robbie."

She just went silent and tight-lipped. I slammed out of her house.

tuesday february 23rd

11.00 p.m. I left the house ten minutes early today and walked on the other side of the road. Jas usually hangs about outside her gate between eight thirty-five and eight forty-five and then she walks on if I don't turn up. I ran like mad past her house, keeping to cover, and arrived ten minutes before assembly.

Hawkeye stopped me. "I've never seen you early for anything, what's going on? I'll be keeping my eye on you." Honestly, she is so suspicious. I don't suppose she's got anything else to do, no real life of her own. When I went into the assembly hall I didn't stand in my usual place, I went and talked to Rosie. Jas came in to where we stand together, she caught my eye and gave a half smile but I gave her my worst look.

I didn't see her again until lunch when she came into the loos. I was sort of trapped because I was drying my fringe under the hand dryer. I'd slept on it funny and it was all sticking up. My head was upside-down and she said, "Look, this is really silly, we can't fall out over some bloke."

I said, "Nyot snum bluk."

She said, "Pardon?"

I stood up and faced her. "Jas, you know what I've been through with Robbie, he is not just 'some bloke'."

She was being Mrs Reasonable Knickers. "What are you so bothered about? It's just coffee . . . at the moment."

I pounced on that like a rat on a biscuit. "What do you mean, 'at the moment'?"

She was putting chapstick on, pouting in the mirror . . . she really has snapped, she thinks she looks like Claudia Schiffer. "I'm just saying, it's only coffee at the moment, if anything else happens of course I will let you know first." That's when I kicked her on the shin. HOW DARE SHE? That is it!!! I'm never speaking to her again.

saturday february 27th

10.00 a.m. Mum up and humming in the kitchen like a happy person, whatever that is.

110

I've made a list of my friends:

I have 12 "close casuals';

20 "social only" and

6 "inner circle" (you know, the kind of friends who would cry properly at your funeral).

Libby is too small to be a chum, although she's a better chum than some, if you know what I mean. Jas is not on my list.

10.30 a.m. I wonder if I have got enough friends? I worry that if British Telecom asks me for ten friends and family for my list of cheap calls I would have to count the astrological phone line for Librans which I ring more often than not.

11.00 a.m. Doorbell went. Mum shouted, "Will you get that?" It was Jem, he really is quite cool and fit-looking. He was wearing a T-shirt and you could see his muscly arms. I smiled at him. Maybe I need an older man to teach me the ways of love . . .

11.05 a.m. Mum came rushing out of the bedroom with Libbs. "Take Libby for a walk, love, will you? Thanks. Now, Jem, would you like a cup of coffee?"

He said, "I wouldn't say no, I've got a bit of a hangover."

She giggled (yes, she giggled), and said, "Honestly, what are you like? Did you have a good time?"

They went off into the kitchen. He said, "Yeah, we went to this club, it's a laugh, you should come one night."

She giggled and said, "Be careful, I might take you up on that."

I couldn't hear what happened after that because Libby hit me with her monkey. "Out now," she said, so I had to go.

What next? My mum goes off with a builder whilst my vati is trying to build a new life for her in the Antipodes?

Actually, when put like that, it seems fair enough . . .

Vati sent a letter and some photos from Whangamata. In his letter he said, *The village has the most geothermal activity in the world. When I had lunch in the garden the other day, the table was heaving and lurching around . . . I could hardly eat my steak. The ground lurches and heaves around because underneath the earth's crust thousands of billions of tons of molten steam is trying to get out. The trees go backwards and forwards, the sheep go up and down . . .*

Oh, very good, Vati, I'll be over there on the next flight. Not. And he sent some photos of his New Zealand mates . . . they were all heavily bearded like the Rolf Harris quadruplets.

Still, he is my vati, I will have to have a word with Mum in order to save the family.

12.05 p.m.   Can't be bothered.

march

my dad has become rolf harris

monday march 1st

10.30 a.m. Still not speaking to Jas, but things have gone horribly wrong in that she is not speaking to me either. I don't know how this has happened as I was supposed to be in charge. It's bloody difficult coming to school because if she gets ahead of me I have to walk really, really slowly behind her because my legs are longer.

wednesday march 3rd

9.00 a.m. Today is the day that Jas is to meet Robbie after school for a "coffee". I wonder if Lindsay knows about this? I wonder if I have a duty to tell her?

3.00 p.m. I can't help myself – I have been trailing Jas around all day. I notice she has her very short skirt on and she's done her hair. Perhaps I could leap on her as she comes out of the loo and duff her up, or I could pay Jackie and Alison to do it.

113

3.15 p.m. Rosie, Ellen and Jools are not taking sides in this, which I hate . . . how dare they be so fair-minded? Rosie said, "He's only asked her for a coffee to talk . . . you don't know what about," and Jools said, "It's a free world, you know, you can't make people do anything."

How dim and thick can you be? I'd stop speaking to them but then I wouldn't have anyone to talk to at all.

4.05 p.m. He's there in his mini!! Where is Lindsay? Perhaps there will be a fight at the gates. There was a fight once before but that was Mr Attwood and an ice-cream man. Elvis had gone to see him off. He went up to the van and said, "Clear off!" and the ice-cream man said, "Make me, short arse."

Elvis took off his glasses and his cap and said, "Come out of that van and I will."

So the ice-cream man did come out of his van and he was about twenty-five foot tall and Elvis said, "Right, well, I've told you. That's my final word . . . As soon as you have sold as many ice-creams as you want, you must leave the school boundaries."

4.08 p.m. No sign of Lindsay. I said to Rosie and Jools and Ellen, "Where is Lindsay?" and Rosie said, "She's playing badminton." For heaven's sake, she is so wet – some snivelling, scheming snot takes her fiancée/boyfriend and all she can do is run around in sports knickers, hitting a ping-pong ball with some feathers stuck in it.

4.10 p.m. Jas came out in boots. Suede boots, knee-length, with heels!! She'll get offered money if she hangs around in the streets looking like that.

4.12 p.m. She has reached the gates. Robbie has opened the door of his mini and gone round the other side and driven off.

home

4.38 p.m. I'm going mad. What are they doing now?

5.00 p.m. Ring Rosie. "Have you heard anything?"
Rosie: "No."
I said, "Well, call me if you do."

5.20 p.m. I've called everyone and nobody has heard anything yet. It's like being in one of those crap plays we have to study. I'll be left lonely and looking out to sea at the end . . . possibly with a beard.

5.30 p.m. I've just found I've got hairs growing out of my armpits. How did they get there? They weren't there yesterday.

5.40 p.m. I've got some on my legs as well. I'd better distract myself by getting rid of them with Mum's razor.

6.00 p.m. Oh God! Oh God! I'm haemorrhaging. My legs are running with blood – I had to staunch the flow with Mum's dressing-gown. She'll kill me if she finds out. I'd better wash it.

6.10 p.m. Put it in the washing-machine with some other stuff before she gets home.

6.30 p.m. Phone rings. It's only Mum. She and Libby are round at Uncle Eddie's and won't be home until later and I've got to get my own tea. *Quelle surprise!*

Go to the fridge.

6.32 p.m. I wonder what I'll have? Hmmm . . . oh, I know, I'll have this mouldy old tin of beans that is the only thing in there . . .

7.00 p.m. Phone rings.

I fell over the cord getting to it, legs started bleeding again. It was Rosie. "Jas just phoned."

I almost screamed at her, "And???"

"Well, they had coffee, she says he really is fantastic-looking and also very funny."

"And?"

"Well, he wanted to talk to her about Tom."

I started laughing. "Hahahahahha . . . and she wore her boots. Hahaha."

Rosie went on, "Yes, he wanted to know if she still likes Tom because he still likes her."

I put the phone down. Tom. Who cares? Hahahaha.

Life is fabby fab fab fabbity fab fab.

7.30 p.m. La lalalalalalala. Fabbity fab fab.

7.40 p.m. Yum yum, beans. Lovely lovely beans.

10.00 p.m. Oh dear, slight problem. Mum's dressing-gown has shrunk to the size of a doll's dressing-gown. It might fit Libby, I suppose.

Hmmm.

Still. Fabbity fab fab. I'll think about it tomorrow. For now I must just dance about a bit to a loud tune.

11.00 p.m. Heard Mum come in but I pretended I was asleep. I've hidden the dressing-gown at the bottom of my wardrobe.

thursday march 4th

8.30 a.m. Jas was waiting for me at her gate. I saw her and started walking really slowly and pretending to be looking through my bag for something. Then I acted like I'd forgotten something and had to go home for it. I walked back and waited behind a hedge for about four minutes and then walked back again. Hurrah, she was gone, my plan worked. But just as I passed her gate she popped up from behind her hedge. She walked alongside me and didn't say anything and neither did I. It's funny being silent – you have to be careful to not make any noise. You can't belch or anything or even clear your throat in case the other person thinks you are going to speak first. When we got to school she handed me a letter. I wouldn't take it at first but I quite wanted to read it so I did eventually put it in my bag.

1.00 p.m. First opportunity I've had to read the letter because I didn't want Jas to know that I was keen to read any stupid thing she had to say.

Dear Georgie,
I am sorry that a boy has come between us, it will never happen again. I was stupid and didn't think of your feelings even though you are my best friend. If there is anything I can do to be your friend again, I will do it.
Jas   PS He isn't engaged to Lindsay.

1.15 p.m. So Jas thinks she can just forget the whole affair – drop it just like that. Well, it will take more than a note to make me change my mind about her.

1.20 p.m. Jas found me by the vending machine and she was a bit nervous. Let her suffer.

1.21 p.m. Jas went "Er . . ." and I said, "What do you mean he's not engaged to Lindsay?"

in my room

5.00 p.m. Jas is helping me to stretch Mum's dressing-gown. As a punishment for her appalling behaviour she's promised that she will say it was her who put it in the washing-machine. Mum won't get cross with Jas.

5.15 p.m. The dressing-gown is exactly the same doll size except that now it has very long arms like an orang-utan.

5.25 p.m. Apparently Robbie was very surprised that he was supposed to be engaged. When he asked Jas why she thought that, she had to pretend that someone had told her.

5.30 p.m. Jas is plucking my eyebrows. She said, "So what do you think I should do about Tom? Robbie says he still likes me, and that the girl at the dance was his cousin."

I said, "Oh, does that mean he can't get a girlfriend, then?"

Jas said (mid-pluck), "Georgie, don't start again. Do you think I should give him another chance?"

I thought, What am I, an agony aunt? But I said, "Well, maybe, but I'd play a bit hard to get. Don't kiss him on your first date . . . well, unless he really wants to."

midnight Got away surprisingly easily with the "It was Jas – I'm innocent!" plan re the dressing-gown. Mum seems even more mad than ever. And how long can it take to decorate one room? Jem is taking for ever. I'm not really surprised – he spends most of his time sitting around giggling with Mum. Libby called him "Dad" the other day.

Ho hum.

1.00 a.m. Looking up at the sky from my bed I can hear an owl hooting and all is well with the world. Robbie is not engaged!!! Thank you, Baby Jesus.

tuesday march 16th

3.00 p.m. Miss Stamp says I show "promise" at

tennis. It is very nice slamming the ball across the court past people. Or not past them, in Rosie's case, when it hit her in the face this afternoon. Her glasses went all sideways like Eric Morecambe which I thought was very funny. I couldn't serve for ages because of laughing so much.

10.45 p.m. Woke up from a dream of winning Wimbledon. I think I may be becoming sexually active, as the dream only really got interesting in the dressing-room. First there was the usual stuff – you know, the final ace, the crowd going mad, going up for my trophy, Princess Margaret handing it over and saying, "Absolutely first class, most thrilling. It made me wish I still played."

Me saying, "Hahaha, I find it hard to believe you've ever played anything, Ma'am – except gin rummy." Then a quick wave and into the dressing-room.

Once in the privacy of the changing-room I began to get undressed for a well-deserved shower. When I had got down to my (well-filled D-cup) bra and knickers I was startled to find someone had come in the room. It was Leo DiCaprio. He said, "I'm sorry, did I startle you?" Then he started covering my quivering (but extremely fit and tanned) body with kisses. Just then someone else came in. I pulled away from Leo but Leo said, "It's OK, it's only Brad," and Brad Pitt came and joined us.

monday march 22nd

2.00 p.m. It's almost embarrassing how friendly Jas is being. A few days without my hilarious and witty conversation has reminded her of how much she likes me. In a roundabout way I suggested this to her on the way to school.

"Jas, I suppose a few days without my hilarious and witty conversation has reminded you of how much you like me."

She said, "Hahahaha . . ." but then saw my face and said, "Oh yes, how true. That will be it."

wednesday march 31st

assembly

9.08 a.m. I nearly passed out with laughing this morning. As we were praying Rosie whispered, "Have a look at Jackie's nose, pass it on . . ." so the word passed right along the line. I couldn't see anything at first because Jackie had her head down and her hair was hanging over her face.

Then, as we were shuffling around to start the hymn, I went, "Jackie! Pssstt!" She looked up and round at me. The end of her nose was completely black!!! She looked like a panda in a wig. I almost wet myself it was so funny. Our whole line was shaking.

Jackie looked daggers at us but that only made it worse. There's nothing funnier than a really cross panda!! We staggered into the loos and were bent over the sinks, crying with laughter. At last, when I could speak, I said, "What . . . what . . . happened?"

Ellen said, "You know that DJ she was raving about? Well, he got drunk with his mates, came to meet Jackie and thought it would be very funny to give her a lovebite on the end of her nose."

Happy days.

april

the snogging report

tuesday april 6th

5.00 p.m. Had a game of tennis against Lucy Doyle from the fifth form and I beat her!!! I am a genius!!!

6.30 p.m. Practising tennis against our wall at home but it's hopeless. Angus gets the ball and then takes it a few feet away from me and guards it. I go to get it and he waits until I can nearly get it and then he walks off with it again. I managed to hit him on the head with my tennis racquet but he doesn't seem to feel pain.

7.00 p.m. Phoned Jas.

It's quite relaxing not having Dad around. No one bellowing, "Get off that bloody phone!" I'm beginning not to remember what he looks like.

So there's a silver lining to every cloud.

Jas's mum answered the phone and I asked to speak to Jas. She came down from her bedroom.

"Jas, I've got a good plan."

"Oh no."

"No, you'll like it."

"Why?"

"Because it's brilliant and also because it allows you to pay back your debt to me."

"Go on, then."

"Well, you know you said Robbie didn't know he was engaged, but Lindsay goes round with an engagement ring on . . . ?"

"Yes."

"Well, if she only wears it at school and then takes it off when she sees him, well, that means that she likes him more than he likes her."

"I suppose."

"Of course it does. He must be getting tired of her by now – what on earth does he see in her?"

"She's supposed to be quite clever. I think she is applying for Oxford."

"So, she's a swot, that's no reason to like her – anyway, learning stuff is not clever. Just because I can't remember the Plantagenet line doesn't make me not clever."

"Well, no, I suppose."

"Exactly."

"You have quite a lot of trouble with quadratic equations as well."

"Yes, all right, Jas . . ."

"And you can't do the pluperfect tense . . ."

"Yes, I know, but what I'm saying is . . ."

"You're hopeless at German – Herr Kamyer said he's never known anyone so bad at it in all his years of teaching."

"Look, Jas, can we just get back to the plan? What I think we should do is to stalk Lindsay."

"Stalk her?"

"Yes."

"What . . . follow her around and then phone her up and ask her what colour panties she has got on?"

"No, not that bit, just the bit where we keep her under observation."

"Why? What is the point?"

"The point is, I will then be able to tell whether Robbie likes her or not."

"Why do I have to be involved?"

"Because a) you are my friend and b) it looks less suspicious because we are always hanging around together and c) my mum is going away with Libby in a few weeks and you could come and stay the night and we could invite Tom."

"When do we start stalking?"

That's my girl.

friday april 16th

operation stalking lindsay begins
friday night

4.15 p.m. We had to hang around at the back of the Science block after final bell. Old Swotty Knickers (Lindsay) was chatting to Hawkeye. We could see them laughing together – how sad – fancy having to laugh with a teacher! Then, whilst Lindsay got her coat, we crept along the narrow alleyway that runs between the Science block and the main school building. It is disgusting down there, full of fag-ends from Jackie and co. But if you follow it right along you end up a bit beyond the main gate. The tricky part is getting

124

past Elvis's hut. I'd already made myself public enemy number one with him by putting a plastic skeleton with his hat on – and a pipe in its mouth – in his chair in his hut. I don't know how he knew it was me, but he did. Anyway, we got to Elvis's hut and he wasn't about so we shot across and into the last bit of the alleyway. We were wearing all black and had hats on – it was very like the French Resistance. We got to the end just as Lindsay (the stalkee) passed by. She looked at her watch and you could clearly see the flash of her ring.

5.15 p.m. Outside Lindsay's posh house, The Yews.
The house is all on one level, which means that Lindsay's bedroom would be on the ground floor, which means we might be able to see in through the window.
Teeheee.
First things first, though, time for a nourishing meal.

6.30 p.m. Double chips and Coke. Yum yum.

6.45 p.m. Stalkee spotted leaving the front room, did not reappear. We suspect she has gone to her room to start the long, desperate job of making herself look OK to go out with Robbie.

6.58 p.m. We decide to risk going round the back of the house. I whispered to Jas, "I hope they haven't got a cat," and she said, "Don't you mean a dog?" and I said, "Have you met Angus?"
There was a side path and we went really carefully down it. We had nearly reached the back garden when a head popped

125

up from behind next door's hedge. A really bald head, like Uncle Eddie's. Quick as a flash, Jas said, "Sshhh, we are giving Lindsay a big surprise . . ." She winked at the man and he disappeared. We crept on round the back of the house. Lindsay's bedroom faced on to the garden and she had her curtains half pulled back so you could see in.

Her bedroom was a nightmare of frilly white things, frilly pillows, frilly bedspread . . . Teletubby hot-water bottle cover!!!

Lindsay put on a tape and Jas and I looked at one another – it was Genesis. Jas mimed being sick. We had to keep bobbing our heads down if she turned directly to face the window. She disappeared off through another door and we could hear sort of gurgling noises. I said, "She's got an ensuite bathroom – that's very bad feng shui."

Jas said, "Why?" and I said, "I don't know but it's very bad, you'd have to have about fifty goldfish to make it OK again . . . Have you seen her alarm clock? It's got a sleepy face on it."

Lindsay emerged from the bathroom with her hair all scraped back from her face and wearing a bra and a thong. I don't understand thongs – what is the point of them? I tried one of Mum's that she uses for aerobics . . . well, she is supposed to use it for aerobics but she only went once. She said that she nearly knocked herself out during the running on the spot because her breasts got out of hand. Anyway, I tried her thong on and it felt ridiculous . . . they just go up your bum as far as I can tell. Then I saw something even more grotesque. Lindsay didn't have any hair on her womanly parts! What had she done with it? She couldn't have shaved it off, could she? I thought of the state of my legs the last time I had shaved them. I felt quite faint.

Lindsay was so skinny!! At least I filled my bra. Then, before our eyes, the stalkee did two things that were very significant and would have gone in our notebook had we had one:

1 She took off her ring and kissed it!!

2 She got some sort of pink rubber things and put them in her bra underneath her "breasts". The rubber things pushed up her "breasts" and made it look like she had a cleavage. What a swiz. I said to Jas, "I bet you Robbie doesn't know about that . . ."

But I noticed that I did not have Jas's full attention, she was looking over my shoulder at Mr Baldy-man, who had reappeared, peering at us over his fence. What is it with neighbours, don't they have lives of their own? He seemed a bit suspicious. So I said as naturally as I could, "She's certainly playing her music very loudly – she hasn't heard us tapping on her window. Do it again, Jas." Jas looked a bit stunned but fortunately had the presence of mind to do some mime. She mimed tapping on the window, then she mimed waving at Lindsay (who fortunately had gone back into the ensuite) and then she mimed hysterical laughter.

It's very tiring, this stalking business, but we seemed to satisfy Mr Baldy-man because he disappeared again and we crept round to the front of the house and along to the big hedge next door. We hid just inside next door's driveway to wait for Lindsay to come out.

7.40 p.m. Brrrr . . . bit chilly. At last the front door opened and Lindsay came out with her hair up (mistake) and in a black midi (mistake for long-streak-of-water type person). We huddled back into the shadows of the hedge as she passed and gave her a few minutes before we followed. When she got to the main street she stood under a

127

streetlamp and got out a compact to look at herself. Instead of running home screaming, she snapped the compact shut and walked on.

Suddenly I had the feeling that we were doing something wrong. Up until now I had been caught up in my French Resistance fantasy but what if I found out something I didn't want to know? What if she met Robbie and it was quite obvious that he really liked her? Could I stand it? Did I want to see him kissing her? I said to Jas, "Maybe we should go now," and Jas said, "What, after all this? No way. I want to see what happens next."

7.50 p.m. Outside the Odeon Robbie was waiting. My heart went all wobbly, he looked so cool. Why wasn't he mine? Lindsay went up to him. The moment of truth. I wanted to yell out, "She has bits of pink rubber down her bra . . . and she wears a thong!!!"

I held my breath and Jas's hand. She whispered, "Get off, you lezzer." Then . . . Lindsay put her face forward and Robbie kissed her.

8.00 p.m. Walking home, eating more chips, I said, "What sort of kiss do you think it was? Was there actual lip contact? Or was it lip to cheek, or lip to corner of mouth?"

"I think it was lip to corner of mouth, but maybe it was lip to cheek?"

"It wasn't full-frontal snogging though, was it?"

"No."

"I think she went for full-frontal and he converted it into lip to corner of mouth."

"Yes."

"He didn't seem keen though, did he?"

"No."

"Didn't you think so either?"

"No."

"No, neither did I."

outside jas's gate

8.40 p.m. I said, "The facts are a) – she doesn't wear her ring when she is out with him, so that makes it clear that she says they are engaged but they are not, and b) – he doesn't really rate her because he didn't do full-frontal with her."

Jas undid her gate. "Yes. Right, see you tomorrow. Don't forget to fix the sleep-over."

midnight So . . . the plot thickens. All I have to do is get rid of Lindsay, convince Robbie I am the woman of his dreams, stop Mum splitting up the home, grow bigger breasts and have plastic surgery on my nose and I have cracked it . . .

thursday april 29th

6.30 p.m. Phone rang and I answered it. A strange voice said, "G'day, is that Georgie?" I was a bit formal – it might be a dirty phone call. (I had had one of those from a phone box in Glasgow. This bloke with a Scottish accent kept saying, "What colour pa– . . . ?" and then the pips would go and I'd say, "I'm sorry, what did you say?" and then he'd start again, "What colour panties . . . ?" pip pip pip. Eventually he managed to say, "What colour panties have you got on?" and then the line went dead. So you can't be too careful.)

This strange, echoey voice said, "It's your dad, I'm calling from Whangamata."

I was a bit surprised and I said, "Oh-er-hello-Dad."

He was all enthusiastic and keen. "How's school?"

"Oh, you know . . . school."

"Is everyone all right?"

"Yes, Angus got next door's guinea pig."

"Did he give it back?"

"He did when I hit him with my tennis racquet."

"And Libby?"

"She can say 'tosser' now."

"Who the hell taught her that?"

"I don't know."

"Well, you should take better care of her."

"She's not my bloody daughter."

"Don't swear at me."

"I only said bloody."

"That's swear– . . . look, look, get your mum on the phone, this is costing me one pound a minute."

"She's not here."

"Where is she?"

"Oh, I don't know, she's always out."

"Well, tell her I called."

"OK."

There was a bit of silence then. His voice sounded even weirder when he spoke again. "I wish you were all here, I miss you."

I just went, "Hmmmpgh."

I wish parents wouldn't do that, you know, make you feel like crying and hitting them at the same time.

may

*i use it to keep
my balls still*

tuesday may 4th

8.10 a.m. Felt a bit sort of down in the dumps when I woke up. I'd had a dream that my dad had grown a Rolf Harris beard but it wasn't a beard really, it was Angus clinging to his chin.

Assembly, Maths, Physics . . . there is not one part of today that is worth being alive for.

4.30 p.m. Home, exhausted from laughing. My ribs hurt. Slim has made me be on cloakroom duty for the next term but I don't care, it was worth it.

Well . . . here is what happened. It was during double Physics and it was just one of those afternoons when you can't stop laughing and you feel a bit hysterical. For most of the lesson I had been yelling, "*Jawohl*, Herr Kommandant!" and clicking my heels together every time Herr Kamyer asked if we understood what he had been explaining. We were doing the molecular structure of atoms and how they vibrate.

Herr Kamyer was illustrating his point with the aid of some billiard balls on a tea towel on his desk. It was giving me the

132

giggles anyway, and then I put my hand up because I had thought of a good joke. I put my hand up with the finger pointing forward, like in 'Who ate all the pies?' and when Herr Kamyer said, "Yes?" I said, "Herr Kamyer, what part does the tea towel play in the molecular structure?"

That is when Herr Kamyer made his fateful mistake – he said, "Ach, no, I merely use the tea towel to keep my balls still." It was pandemonium. I could not stop laughing. You know when you really, really should stop laughing because you will get into dreadful trouble if you don't? But you still can't stop? Well, I had that. I had to be practically carried to Slim's office. Outside her office I did my best to get a grip and I thought I had just about stopped and was under control when I knocked on the door and she said, "Come."

In my head I was thinking, Please, please don't ask me anything about it. Just let it go. Please talk about something else, just don't ask me about it. Please please.

Slim was all trembly and jelloid. "Can you tell me, Georgia, what is quite so amusing about Herr Kamyer's experiment on the vibration of atoms?"

I tried. God knows, I tried. "Well, Miss Simpson, it's just that he used a tea towel . . . he used a tea towel . . ."

"Yes?"

"He used a tea towel to . . . keep his balls still." And then I was off again.

midnight   Bloody funny, though.

tennis tournament

2.30 p.m. Through to the semifinals. Beautiful sunny day. I think I will be a Wimbledon champion after all. White suits me. All the gang are cheering me on and this is very freaky deaky and karmic and weird but . . . if I win my semi against Kirsty Walsh (upper fifth) I will play Lindsay in the final. How weird is that? Pretty weird, that's what. Lindsay is such a boring player, I'm sure I could beat her. She plays by the book . . . baseline follow through to the net, but she hasn't met Mighty Lob (me) yet.

OK, if I beat her that must mean I am meant to have Robbie. Lindsay has white frilly knickers on under her tennis skirt. (Not the thong, thank goodness, otherwise Miss Stamp might have had an outburst of lesbian lust and put me off my game.) I think my shorts are much more stylish. They look like I've just remembered I'm playing in a tennis final and I've just grabbed something and thrown it on in an attractive way.

3.30 p.m. I won the first set and now I'm serving for the second and the match.

I feel pretty good. I'm a bit hot but I feel confident about my serve. Rosie and Ellen and Jools and Jas and all of my year are going mental. Chanting my name and "Easy, easy." Hawkeye keeps telling them to be quiet. (She is the umpire, worse luck.)

But even she can't make me lose. Hahahaha. I am ruler of the universe. Robbie is mine for the plucking.

First serve – an ACE!!! Yes! Yes! Yesssss!! Hawkeye says, "Fifteen–love."

Second serve – a brief rally and then a cunning, slicing cross-court forehand from me. Hawkeye says, "Thirty–love."

Third serve. *Whizzzz.* Oh yes, another ace!! Kirsty was nowhere. What a slack Alice. C'mon if you think you're hard enough!

Hawkeye says, "Forty–love."

The whole court is hushed as I serve for the match. I take my place behind the baseline. Jas is playing nervously with her fringe. I look at her. She stops.

I throw the ball up and bring my racquet down, putting a bit of top spin on it. Kirsty doesn't even try to get it. ACE!!!!

Hawkeye announces through tight lips, "Game, set and match to Georgia Nicolson." Yesss!!!!! Victory!!!!!!

I fall to my knees like McEnroe and the crowd is going mad. Full of euphoria I fling my racquet high up into the air.

It curves and falls down and hits Hawkeye right on the head. She is knocked off her umpire chair, unconscious.

in bed

8.00 p.m. I CAN'T BELIEVE IT. Hawkeye was only unconscious for about a minute but I was made to forfeit the match. Kirsty played Lindsay. I couldn't bear to watch – more to the point, I wasn't allowed to watch – I had to go and tidy all the gym mats.

Lindsay won the cup.

I don't know what this means karmically. I don't think I believe in God any more.

11.00 p.m. The only way I will believe in God is if something really bloody great happens to me soon.

june

pyjama party

friday june 4th

the pyjama party sleep-over

5.00 p.m. Mum will not get going. Why is she so slow? Libby still has not got any knickers on. I offer to put them on her and Mum says, "Oh, would you, love? Thanks. I cannot find my eyebrow tweezers anywhere. You haven't seen them, have you?"

(I remember they are in my pencil-case.) "Er . . . no, but I think I saw Libby with them."

"Damn, they could be anywhere."

Libby decided that "knickers on" was a game and I chased her around for ages before I could get hold of her. Then when I was putting her knick-knacks on she was stroking my hair, going, "Prrr prr. Nice pussycat. Do you want some milk, tosser?" I think she thinks "tosser" is like a name.

Once I got her dressed I raced upstairs and got the tweezers, then I put them in Angus's basket. (Fortunately he was out murdering birds or he would have eaten them.) Then I shouted to Mum, "Hey, Mum, guess where your tweezers are? Come and see!"

136

Mum came out of the bedroom and I pointed to the cat basket. She said, "Honestly!! Thanks, love. Right now, I think that's everything. We can get off now, Libby."

She grabbed Libby, who was struggling and licking her face. Libby said, "Bad, bad Mummy, stealing Libby."

As they went through the door Mum said, "You'll be OK, won't you? I'll be back late tomorrow – eat something sensible and don't stay up too late."

She went through the door and then came back a moment later. "Don't even think about doing anything to your hair."

6.00 p.m. Rosie was the first to arrive. She said, "Sven is going to come at about eleven thirty, after his restaurant shift finishes."

I said, "What have you got up to with him?"

She said, "Er . . . six and a bit of seven . . ."

We had this scoring system for kissing and so on, from one to ten:

1 holding hands;

2 arm around;

3 goodnight kiss;

4 kiss lasting over three minutes without a breath;

5 open-mouth kissing;

6 tongues;

7 upper-body fondling – outdoors;

8 upper-body fondling – indoors (in bed);

9 below-the-waist activity, and

10 the full monty.

I said, "What is he like at it?"

Rosie said, "He's good, I think Danish boys are better at it than English ones. They change rhythm more."

I said, "What do you mean?"

"You know English boys get really excited and just sort of kiss with the same pressure? Well, he varies the pressure: sometimes it's gentle and sometimes hard and then middley."

I said, "Oh, I like that."

Rosie said, "I know, I do too. Apparently all girls do. We like variety whereas boys like the same."

I said, "How do you know that?" and she looked a bit smug. "It's in *Men Are From Mars, Women Are From Venus*."

Jools, Ellen, Jas, Patty, Sarah and Mabs all turned up and we got out our jimjams. We watched *Grease* and kept stopping it and doing bits from it. I did "You're the One That I Want" on the sofa.

Then, at about eleven o'clock, the phone rang. I answered and it was Tom wanting to speak to Jas. So Jas went off into the hall and shut the door so we couldn't hear. When she came back her face was a bit pink. She sort of croaked, "He's coming round with his mate Leo . . . ohmyGodohmyGodohmyGod!"

11.30 p.m. Eating toast and Pop-Tarts when Leo and Tom arrived. They brought their pyjamas too and put them on. What a good laugh. Then Sven turned up – I'd forgotten how big he is . . . Rosie and he disappeared off and the rest of us watched *Grease* again. This time the boys joined in. Tom is quite a laugh. I desperately tried not to mention Robbie.

1.00 a.m. Still up and chatting about EVERY-THING!!!! Haven't seen Rosie and Sven for hours. Surely they must have got past seven by now???

1.30 a.m. Tom and Jas disappeared off and Leo and Ellen went off "to get some air". Why they think there is no air in the lounge, I don't know. The rest of us "Normans" (Norman-no-mates) decided to dare each other. It started off with taking your knickers off and putting them on your head, and so on, and then I dared Sarah to go and stand on the garden wall and drop her pyjama trousers and knickers.

She did.

2.00 a.m. Patty and Mabs dared me to streak down to the bottom of the street. They said they would buy me a new lipstick if I did. The "couples" were still away so I thought I'd do it. We went outside (us Normans), all in our jimjams. It was a nice summer night, and there were no houselights on in the streets except for ours. So I took my jimjams off and ran like mad in my nuddy-pants down to the bottom of the street and back. It made us die laughing – the others couldn't believe that I had done it!!!

We were all collapsed on the front doorstep when the "couples" came back. I hid behind the others whilst I scrambled into my pyjamas. Tom winked at me. "I should tell my brother what he's missing."

I went purple, "Don't you dare, Tom. Promise, promise me you won't!!"

Tom said, "Do you think that me and Jas should go out with each other again?"

139

I said, "Oh yes!! I think you are perfect for each other."

And he said, "I've always liked you because you are so sincere."

At about two thirty the lads went home and we cleared up the house. Please don't let Tom tell Robbie about the nuddy-pants incident.

All us girls snuggled up under duvets in the front room, chatting about everything – boys, make-up . . . lesbians.

Rosie said, "How do you get to become a lesbian?"

I said, "Why? Are you going to give it a go?"

Jas said, "You can't just give it a go. You can't just think, Oh, I'll give being a lesbian a go."

Ellen sat up. "A go at what?"

Jas went a bit red (which is a lot red in anyone else's language). "Well, have a go at, er, snogging a girl."

We all sat up then and went "Erlacck!"

Rosie said, "Is that what they do, then – snog each other?"

Jas (the lesbian spokesperson) said a bit smugly, "Of course they do. They have proper sexual whatsits."

Rosie said, "How can they have proper sexual whatsits when they haven't got . . . you know, any proper sexual whatsits."

I interrupted, "Jas, how come you know so much about it, anyway?"

She went ludicrously red. Rosie had got all interested now. "But, I mean, what do they do when they haven't got proper sexual whatsits?"

I said to Jas, "Go on, then, Miss Expert Knickers. What do they do in the privacy of their own lesbian love-nests?"

Jas sort of mumbled something under her duvet. I said, "You don't know, do you?" and she mumbled again, "Snnubbing."

140

I repeated, "Snubbing. They do snubbing? They snub each other?"

Jas sat up and said, "No, rubbing."

I said "Goodnight" really quickly and we all went to sleep.

wednesday june 16th

6.00 p.m. Got a note from Jackie today:

We are knocking off school this afternoon and going down town to "get a few things". We'll tell you all about the plan at lunch.

I knew that "getting a few things" meant shoplifting in Jackiespeak. I tried to hide from her at lunch-time but she found me in the loos. I was reading my mag in one of the cubicles – I had my feet off the ground so you couldn't see there was anyone there but she went into the next-door cubicle and looked over the top of the loo wall.

She said, "What are you doing?"

I didn't look up, I just said, "I'm practising origami."

She said, "Are you ready to go? We've got lists of what to get and where we will meet later."

Suddenly I snapped. I really was sick to death of her and Alison, they didn't make me laugh or anything, they just kept making me do things I didn't want to do. I was sick of it. I found myself saying, "I'm not coming and I don't think you should go either."

Jackie was amazed. "Have you become a Christian? I haven't seen your tambourine. Come on, get your coat and we'll go over the back fields."

I said, "No," and came out of the cubicle. She followed me and came up close – she is quite big.

141

She said, "I think you had better." Alison was just behind her.

Then this odd calm voice came out of me. I'd been watching *Xena, Warrior Princess* and for one stupid moment I thought I was her. I said, "Oh good, I didn't realise I'd be able to try out my new martial arts skills so soon. If I break anything I apologise in advance. I've only practised on bricks before."

Jackie looked a bit puzzled (who wouldn't?) but she kept coming nearer and suddenly with a yell I grabbed her arm and twisted it right up her back. I don't know how. But I was doing it for the little people everywhere (I don't mean dwarfs – I just mean, you know, vulnerable people).

8.00 p.m. Jas phoned. "Everyone is talking about you – it's brilliant!!"

8.30 p.m. I am cock of the walk. (I don't know what the girl equivalent of "cock" is . . . surely it can't be "vagina". I am vagina of the walk doesn't have the same ring to it, somehow . . .)

midnight Yesssss!!!!!

saturday june 19th

9.00 a.m. The Stiff Dylans are playing at The Market Place. Tom and Jas are going, and all the gang. Shall I?

11.30 a.m. Mum is being ridiculous – she refuses to

142

let me dye my hair blonde. I said, "Where would Marilyn Monroe have been if Mrs Monroe had said, 'No, Marilyn, you'll ruin your hair'?"

Mum said, "Don't be ridiculous."

But I went on, "And what about Caprice? . . . Do you suppose Mrs Caprice said . . ."

Mum threw her slipper at me. Oh great, now she has turned to violence. I may yet ring Esther Rantzen's childline.

2.00 p.m. Nngut naface-musk on, I cnt muv mi face.

2.30 p.m. Blocked the sink with my egg yolk mask.

4.00 p.m. I'm going to start my make-up now.

4.30 p.m. Double *merde*. I'll have to start all over again, I've stuck the mascara brush in my eye. It's all watery and red.

5.30 p.m. Lying down with cucumber slices on my eyes to take down the swelling.

5.50 p.m. Libby crept in and ate one of my cucumber slices. It gave me a terrible shock to see her face looming over me when I wasn't expecting it.

6.00 p.m. Ellen rang, we are meeting outside The Market Place at eight thirty.

midnight What an unbelievably BRILLIANT night. Double cool with knobs. Robbie KISSED me. The Sex God has landed. It was so mega.

The Stiff Dylans played some great music and Jas, Tom, Leo, Ellen and me worked out these funny dance routines. Lindsay was there, all po-faced. Robbie was great in the band. I felt a bit self-conscious about dancing at first but then I began to enjoy myself. I showed Tom and Jas a little routine I had made up in my bedroom – and then it was like in a film because everyone – loads of people – started copying it and joining in.

I was a bit out of breath at the end and hot, so when the band took a break I went outside the back door. There was this sort of patio area. As I was standing there Robbie came out . . . I felt really awkward and was going to go back in when he put his arm on mine and said, "Can I just speak to you for a minute, Georgia?"

I said, "Yes, fine . . ." He looked a bit embarrassed so I said, "Look, if it's about Jas and Tom I'm sorry that you were angry with me . . . I think he's really nice and Jas likes him a lot."

Robbie said, "Well, I'm glad, but it's not that. I've just been meaning to give you this." Then he kissed me!!! I went completely jelloid – it was like being part girl, part jellyfish. It was mega brilliant. Twenty out of ten type kissing. I got all that stuff you're supposed to have – fireworks wooshing in your head, bands playing, sea crashing in and out . . . I don't know how long it went on for, I was so faint.

Eventually he said, "I've wanted to do that for a long time, but I know it's wrong."

I could hardly speak, it came out all mad. "Ng ng – 's OK, not wrong, no wrong, ngng ng – I mean it's, I, what I, you and, always, even when I ng." He looked at me as if I was talking a foreign language. But I wasn't, I was just talking rubbish.

Then one of the lads in the band came out and Robbie sort of leaped away from me like a leaping thing. Then he went back in, saying to me, "OK, so Georgia, will you pass that on to Tom? See you later."

"See you later?" What does that mean? Here we go again!!! I told Jas and she said, "What's going to happen now? Are you his bit on the side? What does he mean, 'See you later'? Does he mean see you later or see you later?" I had to stick my hand over her mouth to shut her up. When Robbie took the stage again I had to stop myself gazing at him like an idiot. He was so gorgeous and he had kissed me!!

When the gig was over Robbie passed by me and said, "I'll call you." Then he went over to Lindsay. She put her arms round his neck and I couldn't watch any more.

When will he call me?

Angus was in my bed when I got home, and Libby, I had to sleep in a sort of S-shape with my feet hanging out of the bed. But I don't care!!!!

tuesday june 22nd

5.10 p.m. I don't know if it's me or the weather but I am so hot all the time.

No call for three days.

wednesday june 23rd

11.00 p.m. No call today.

6.00 p.m. Phoned Jas.

"He's not called yet."

Jas said, "Look, leave it with me, I'll try to find out something from Tom."

"Will you do it subtly though, Jas?"

She said, "What do you take me for? I know what's subtle."

And I said, "Well, I'm sorry, but I feel a bit sensitive and I don't want anyone to know about it until I know what is going on myself."

She said, "Look, relax, my middle name is 'cool'."

I said, "Is it? I thought it was Pollyanna."

She said, "Well, it is, my mum liked the film, but that's not what I mean – and anyway, you said you'd never mention that I told you that."

I said, "OK, but just remember to be subtle, all right?"

She said, "Of course. Hang on a minute." Then I heard her yelling up the stairs, "Mum, will you ask Tom to come down here!"

I heard a bit of faraway noise then Jas's mum yelling from upstairs, "Tom says what do you want? He has just set up the computer and can't come away at the moment."

Then I heard Jas yell back, "Well, will you say that Robbie kissed Georgia and said he would call her later and he hasn't called her yet. Does he know anything about it?"

I couldn't believe my ears and it got worse because Jas's mum joined in, "Robbie kissed Georgie – but he's going out with Lindsay, isn't he?"

Jas yelled back, "Yes, but he's confused."

Then I heard Tom yelling, "What kind of kiss was it?" and Jas said, "I think it was six."

I REALLY WANTED TO KILL HER.

"Jas, Jas, SHUT UP!!!"

friday june 25th

1.00 p.m. Lindsay came up to me at lunch-break. She's so wet close up, she's got really blinky blue watery eyes like a blue-eyed bat. Anyway, old blinky said, "I've heard what happened on Saturday."

I went a bit pale. "You've heard what?" I played for time.

"I heard that you have been going after my boyfriend."

How dare she suggest that I would do such a thing!! I went red and said, "What idiot has been saying that?"

Lindsay glared at me. "Robbie told me." I couldn't take it in. She went on, "He told me how you followed him at the break and then you just flung yourself on him. He said he was sorry for you but also very embarrassed."

I spluttered, I couldn't speak. She went on, "So I'm giving you a warning – don't be so sad. You're a silly little girl, don't let it happen again." I couldn't help thinking about the Ancient Egyptians – they used to put long-handled spoons up people's noses and scoop their brains out. Of course, the people were dead first but in Lindsay's case there was hardly any difference between alive and dead. I was going to get some spoons and poke them up her beastly, sticky-up nose.

6.00 p.m. Jas is going to gang up on Lindsay with me. I said to her, "Do you think Robbie really said I was sad and I flung myself on him?"

Jas was a real pal. "No, no, of course not . . . er . . . you didn't, did you?"

6.30 p.m. Oh why this? Why would he be such a pig as to say that? Oh I hate him, I hate him.

midnight I hate him, I hate him.

12.30 a.m. Oh I love him, I love him.

july

the sex god has landed

canteen

1.00 p.m. Lindsay put her coffee cup down while she went to get her bag and I spat in it (the coffee cup, not her bag – although I will spit in her bag if I get the chance). I hate her.

Jackie and Alison get on my nerves even more now they have decided to be my friends. Jackie bought me a bar of chocolate today. It will be an apple next. It's a pathetic world when twisting someone's arm up their back gets them buying you things.

4.00 p.m. I'm so angry with Robbie. I want to tell him what I think about him but I have too much pride.

4.30 p.m. Phoned Robbie at home (I got the number from Jas). He answered the phone but I just slammed down the receiver. (And I had done one-four-one as well, hahahahaha.)

4.45 p.m. Phoned Robbie. He answered and I said, "Robbie, it's Georgia."

He sort of breathed out and then he said, "Er . . . I can't really find that Science paper you asked me about, Mike, can I call you later? Thanks. Bye."

4.50 p.m. Phoned Jas. "What does he mean by calling me Mike?"

Jas said, "Well, I suppose Lindsay must have been there."

5.30 p.m. In bed with the curtains closed.

5.45 p.m. Mum came into my room.

She said, "Do you want to talk about anything?"

I said, "Yes, suicide."

She said, "It can't be as bad as that."

I said, "Well it is, it's worse. I don't want to be here any more, I hate school, I hate England."

She said, "Well, do you think that maybe a summer trip to New Zealand might cheer you up? We could go over to Disneyland on the way."

I said, "I don't care what I do."

6.30 p.m. So this is what men are like. Well, that is it, then, I am going to be a lesbian.

7.00 p.m. I got out some photos of Denise Van Outen and tried to imagine kissing her.

7.05 p.m. I can't do it. And I can't help thinking about Miss Stamp's moustache. And the rubbing.

7.10 p.m. I'll have to be a nun, then.

8.00 p.m. It's no use, if I pull all my hair back like a nun, it makes my nose look huge. Still, I don't suppose that matters when you are only saving poor people and making soup for them, like nuns do.

9.00 p.m. The phone rang for me. I said to Mum, "Who is it?" and she said, "I don't know, it's a boy."

9.30 p.m. Robbie is going to meet me tomorrow after school at my house. He was in a phone box and said that he couldn't really explain, he'd talk tomorrow. If he thinks he can "explain" this away he's very much mistaken. I have got some pride. I've got a lot to say to him about his "explanation"!!!

9.45 p.m. What shall I wear? Maybe I won't go to school tomorrow to give myself time to get made up in a natural way.

friday july 2nd

8.05 a.m. Said goodbye to Mum and Libbs and went as normal to Jas's. She was waiting

151

for me on the corner. I said, "I'm not coming to school today, I'm meeting Robbie. Will you say that I have got the painters in very badly? Thanks."

Then I went back home. I waited until Mum and Libbs left and then I slipped back into the house.

Day plan:

1 Steam face.
2 Apply face-pack.
3 Sort out clothes to wear.
4 Tidy bedroom (well, put everything on the floor and bed under the bed).
5 Put some interesting books near my bed (hide comics and boy mags).
6 Remove nuddy-pants poster of Reeves and Mortimer.
7 Make sure Libby has not peed or pooed in any secret corner.

11.02 a.m. In my room tidying when I heard the front door open. If it was a burglar I only had Mum's tweezers to defend myself with. Where was Angus when you needed him? I hadn't seen the mad furry thing for hours.

11.02 a.m. Not burglars, it's something much worse . . . it's Mum. And she's not alone! She has Jem the decorator with her. Oh fabulous, my mum is having an affair with a builder. Also she is older than him – also I already have a dad, who is bad enough, but better the dad you know than the builder you don't.

They went into the lounge so I crept downstairs to see if I could hear what was going on. I put my ear against the door but I couldn't quite hear. I pressed my ear quite hard up against the keyhole. I heard Jem say, "This is the door that sticks. I'm going to . . ." and that's when he opened the door and I crashed into the room.

noon In bed. I had to pretend that I had fainted. I lay still on the floor until Mum put something disgusting (smelling salts) under my nose. I thought my head was going to come off. I sort of pretended that I was all confused and that I had felt ill on the way to school.

Mum made me come to bed with an aspirin. Soon after, I heard the door slam. Mum came up. "Er – I just took an hour off to discuss the final details about the lounge with Jem."

I said, "He's taken about a hundred years to decorate one room. Libby thinks he is our new dad."

Mum laughed. "Don't be so silly, why would you think she thought that?"

I said, "Because she calls him 'my new dad'."

Mum ignored that and went on, "Well, I must get back to work, are you sure you will be all right?"

I said, "Oh yes, I'll be all right – will YOU be all right?" (I said it really meaningfully but she didn't know what I meant.)

Minutes later she came back in the room and said, "Georgia, I know that you like a bit of drama, but I'm afraid that Jem and I are not having a passionate affair."

I said, "Oh, what is it, then? A really lukewarm affair?"

She sat down on my bed. "It's not any kind of affair. Look, love, I really, really miss your dad." And it was horrible because her eyes were all leaky.

I said, "You can't miss his moustache."

She said, "No, I don't miss that. But I love him. Don't you?"

I said, "He's all right."

She kissed me. "I know you do love him, you're just moody and someone has to suffer, but never mind, we'll be seeing him soon."

Then she left. God, I can't stand this having to talk about grown-ups all the time! I do wish my dad was here, then I could forget all about him!

4.00 p.m. Robbie will be here in half an hour. I'd better just go to the loo again. I've only been ten times in the last ten minutes. I hope I'm not incontinent, I'll have to wear big nappies . . . Robbie will never stand for that – if he gets famous he won't want a girlfriend who wears nappies.

6.30 p.m. Robbie has just gone. I feel all hollow inside like a hollowed out coconut. He looked so gorgeous, all in black, and sort of sad. He gave me a brilliant smile when he saw me and then he just pulled me towards him (quite roughly, actually . . .). I remembered how cross I was though, so I only snogged him for half an hour before I said, "How could you tell Lindsay that I was sad and that I followed you outside and flung myself on you?"

He looked puzzled. "I didn't say that."

"Didn't you?"

"No, I didn't . . . I haven't said anything to anyone."

"Well, that's what Lindsay said to me."

He looked uncomfortable.

I went on, "And are you engaged to her or not?"

He looked really puzzled then. "Engaged to her? Why should you think that?"

"Well, because she wears an engagement ring at school that she tells people you gave her."

He sat down. "This is bad."

I tried to go on being cross but he looked so gorgy porgy that I couldn't keep it up. Then he looked right into my eyes. I tried not to blink because not blinking is supposed to be attractive. He said, "Look, Georgie, I'm having real trouble with this. The truth is, I've been trying to find a way to end it with Lindsay but I don't want to hurt her feelings."

I said, "Yes, it's tricky, isn't it? Because she obviously likes you a lot. Still, I've got an idea . . ."

He looked hopeful. "What is it?"

"I'll tell her, in a nice way of course, that she is a wet weed and that she is dumped. That should do it."

He did actually laugh! He said, "You're mad. Anyway, it's my problem and I'll sort it out, but there is something else I have to tell you."

Here it comes, I was thinking (but not blinking). He's going to say, "You are the girl of my dreams, will you be my girlfriend? You are the most gorgeous girl I have ever . . ."

I'd just got to that bit in my head when he interrupted me. "I have to tell you, it wouldn't be fair to you not to . . . but well, I am attracted to you [I tried not to smirk or smile too much in case he had second thoughts when he saw my nose spreading all over my face] but I can't go out with you."

I said, "Why not?" and he said, "Because you are too young. I'm nearly eighteen – it would not be right, it would be like cradle-snatching."

I argued with him. I even said, "I'm not really fourteen, I'm actually fifteen and a half, it's just that I'm not very bright and they've kept me back a year."

He laughed, but in a sad way. Then he gave me a last kiss sort of thing and went.

midnight Too young for him. Oh *merde merde merde, double merde*.

I wonder where Angus is? I could do with something to cuddle even if I did get a savage biting.

monday july 5th

11.30 a.m. Mucho excitemondo!!! Robbie has dumped Lindsay!!! Hurrah!!! She came into school with her eyes all swollen up like little boiled sweets. I passed her in the corridor and she said, "I hope you're satisfied now, you horrid little girl." Horrid little girl, that's nice.

I could have said, "At least I don't wear bits of rubber down my bra and a piece of string up my bottom." But unfortunately I began to feel a bit sorry for her – after all, she would never get another boyfriend, whereas even if I had to wait a whole year I would one day be older and then I could get Robbie.

5.30 p.m. I'm glum, though – a year seems a long, long time and what if he finds someone else before I get old enough?

6.30 p.m. Still no sign of Angus. This is a bit unusual. He always comes back for his dindins.

7.00 p.m. Looking round the street for Angus. I had a dead mouse and a chop to entice him.

7.15 p.m. Just stumbled into Mark, snogging in his driveway with some girl . . . he's always at it!! If it's true that stimulation makes things bigger (breasts, etc.), perhaps he had very tiny lips when he was born and he has just overstimulated them by snogging all the time.

9.30 p.m. No Angus. I hoped he might be at home lurking behind the curtain ready to attack my legs, but he's not.

11.00 p.m. No phone calls, no Angus. Libby came into bed with me. "Where big pussy tosser?" she asked me. I almost cried. I really cuddled her but it made her too cross and she bit me on the chin.

Had a dream about Robbie. I had blonde hair in the dream.

tuesday july 6th

7.30 p.m. Eureka!!! I've got it!!! I know what my dream was trying to tell me. There is a way I can convince Robbie that I am more mature than my fourteen years . . . I have to dye a blonde streak in my hair. A blonde streak will add years to my appearance!!!

Still no sign of Angus. Mum said, "I don't want to upset you, but you know that he stalks cars and attacks them – it may be that this time he's had a bit of an accident."

I can't bear to think of this.

midnight I think of all the animals in the world and all the sad things that happen to them. Little chickens whose parents go for a day's outing on the farmyard truck and never come back because they have gone to be on somebody's table. And all the little sheep who see their mummies and daddies loaded into vans . . . oh I cannot stand this. I'm never going to eat meat again.

1.00 a.m. They say vegetables feel pain. What about the little baby potatoes all snug underground with their brother and sister potatoes and then a big hand comes and uproots them and . . . slices them up. Oh God, now I can never eat chips again.

2.30 a.m. What can I eat, then?

4.00 a.m. If I starved myself to death would Robbie think I was grown-up enough?

wednesday july 7th

8.00 a.m. I'm shattered this morning, and upset. I miss Angus. Even Mum does. Mrs Next Door doesn't, though. When I asked her if she had seen him, she said, "No I haven't. And I know he hasn't been in my yard because nothing is dead or dug up and my dog is not a nervous wreck." I hate her – I hope her husband gets stuck in his greenhouse and then she will know what I feel like. She will know what true pain is.

And suffering.

2.30 p.m. Ink fight in RE, which generally cheers me up, but I couldn't even flick properly I was so upset.

The gossip at school is that Lindsay is not eating and has got what's it – anorexia. I don't know how you would know, she's so skinny anyway.

Nearly the summer hols, so it will be the last I see of this hell-hole for a bit.

friday july 9th

8.50 p.m. I really think Angus must have been run over or something. I miss him, we've been through a lot of stuff, me and him. Stupid furry freak. But I love him. It seems I am destined to lose everything I love.

sunday july 11th

2.00 p.m. Jas and I looked in all the streets around her house, just in case Angus had followed me one day and then lost his way. We were just by her place when Robbie pulled up in his mini. He looked a bit ruffled but I was too down in the dumps to think about it much. He said, "Have you found Angus?"

I said, "No, we've looked everywhere."

wednesday july 14th

3.30 p.m. Every cloud has a bit of a silver lining. I was sitting against the school wall in the shade, just thinking. The others were all sprawled out in their knickers sunbathing by the tennis courts. The bit of wall I was leaning against was just near Elvis's hut. I saw him put on his coat and get his shopping bag . . . what a wally he looked. He closed the hut door but he didn't lock it and then he went off. I'd nothing else to do so I thought I'd go and sit in his hut for a while, see what it would be like to be a school caretaker.

There was nothing much in the hut – a chair and a table and a little fridge and some magazines he'd been reading. I sat down and flicked through them . . . and my jaw nearly dropped off. Because they were naughty magazines, if you know what I mean. Called *Fiesta* and *Big Girls.* One of them was called *Down Your Way*, and was all full of candid photos of readers and their wives in the privacy of their own bedrooms. Some of them were so fat!! I flicked through the pages to the centrefold. And the centrefold was ELVIS and MRS ELVIS!!!! In the NUDDY-PANTS!!!! I couldn't believe it. Elvis in the nuddy-pants. Elvis was standing by the kettle in the nuddy-pants, pretending to make a cup of tea and Mrs Elvis was doing the washing-up in the nuddy-pants!!!

I took the mag with me and passed it around the whole class. We were laughing for the whole afternoon, someone only had to say, "Fancy a cup of tea, my dear?" and we'd be off again. Ooohhhhh, it made my stomach really hurt with laughing.

Elvis knows someone has got his mag but he can't say anything. If I see him I just let my eyes drift down to his trousers . . .

saturday july 17th

12.00 p.m. Joy joy, double bubble joy. Hadiha-hahaha. Robbie has just phoned me.

He has found Angus!! Robbie had been out searching for him and he heard all these dogs barking so he went to see what they were barking at. And it was Angus, tied up. Some people had found him, he had a bad paw so they had bandaged it up and tied him up until they found his owners. They had put up notices but I hadn't seen them.

Robbie said the people were bloody glad to get rid of him as he had already eaten two doormats and a clothes line. They were lucky they got off so lightly.

Anyway, Robbie is going to bring him round to me at five o'clock.

1.00 p.m. Mum's out and I am determined to make Robbie realise that I'm a great deal older than I was fifteen days ago. I haven't any money and Mum has selfishly taken her purse with her, but I HAVE A PLAN.

2.00 p.m. There is some peroxide that Gran uses to clean her dentures when she comes to stay. It's kept in the bathroom cupboard and I'm going to use it to bleach a really sophisticated streak of blonde in my hair at the front.

2.30 p.m. I've put it on, I wonder how long you have to leave it? It's stinging my scalp so that must be a good sign.

3.30 p.m. It's gone a sort of orange colour! Oh bloody hell, I'll have to put some more on.

161

4.15 p.m. Now it's gone sort of bright yellow. I look like a canary.

5.00 p.m. Thank goodness it's gone white. I think it looks quite good. It feels a bit stiff, though. Oh well, it'll soften up in time. I think it makes me look at least four years older.

5.30 p.m. Robbie here with Angus. I was so pleased to see him I tried to give him a cuddle but he lashed out at me and was hissing until I gave him a rabbit leg. Then he started purring. (Angus, not Robbie.)

Robbie noticed my hair when I stood up. He was obviously impressed because he said, "Er – you've got a white streak in your hair."

I said, "Oh yes, do you like it?"

There was a bit of a silence between us. I was thinking, Go on, kiss me, kiss me! but he said, "Look, this is not easy for me, I think I should go now."

I said, "Thank you for Angus."

He said, "Oh, that's OK, I knew you liked him and the scratches will heal in time and I should be able to replace the trousers."

As he was leaving I had one final go to make him see that I was mature and sophisticated beyond my years. I flicked my hair back like they do in movies and then I made the mistake of running my fingers through my hair. The white streak snapped off in my hand. I was just left holding it there, in my hand. Robbie looked amazed. He looked at the hunk of hair in my hand and then he looked at me and then he started laughing. He said, "God you're weird," and then he kissed me. (I

162

shoved the hunk of hair on the sofa and Angus pounced on it – he must have thought it was a hamster or something.)

After a bit of number six kissing Robbie said, "Well, look, let's take it easy and start seeing each other, shall we . . . see how it goes, maybe keep it a bit quiet from people at first?"

So all is well that ends well. I am now nearly Robbie's girl-friend, hahahaha. Summer love, summer love!!!

the end

9.00 p.m. Mum came in. "Right, we're all set – I've got them!!"

I said (in a sort of romantic daze), "What have you got, Mutti?"

"I've got the tickets for us!"

"Tickets for what?"

"Tickets for New Zealand. When you said you wanted to go I went and booked them. Dad paid for them and we're off to Whangamata next week."

Sacré bloody *bleu* and *merde*!!!

It's OK, I'm wearing really big knickers!

Further confessions of Georgia Nicolson

july

*the sex god has landed . . .
and, er, taken off again*

<u>*sunday july 18th*</u>

<u>*my room*</u>

6.00 p.m. Staring out of my bedroom window at other people having a nice life.

Who would have thought things could be so unbelievably pooey? I'm only fourteen and my life is over because of the selfishosity of so-called grown-ups. I said to Mum, "You are ruining my life. Just because yours is practically over there is no reason to take it out on me."

But as usual when I say something sensible and meaningful she just tutted and adjusted her bra like a Russian roulette player. (Or do I mean disco thrower? I don't know and, what's more, I don't care.) If I counted up the number of times I've been tutted at . . . I could open a tutting shop. It's just SO not fair . . . How can my parents take me away from my mates and make me go to New Zealand? Who goes to New Zealand?

In the end, when I pointed out how utterly useless as a mum she was, she lost her rag and SHOUTED at me.

"Go to your room right now!"

I said, "All right, I'll go to my ROOM!! I WILL go to my room!! And do you know what I'll be doing in my room? No you don't, so I'll tell you! I'll be just BEING in my room. That's all. Because there is nothing else to do!!!!!!"

Then I just slammed off. Left her there. To think about what she has done.

Unfortunately it means that I am in my bed and it is only six o'clock.

7.00 p.m. Oh Robbie, where are you now? Well, I know where you are now actually, but is this any time to go away on a footie trip?

On the bright side I am now the girlfriend of a Sex God.

7.15 p.m. On the dark side, the Sex God doesn't know his new girlfriend is going to be forced to go to the other (useless) side of the universe in a week's time.

7.18 p.m. I can't believe that after all the time it has taken to trap the SG, all the make-up I have had to buy, the trailing about, popping up unexpectedly when he was out anywhere . . . all the planning . . . all the dreaming – it's gone to waste. I finally get him to snog me (number six) and he says, "Let's see each other but keep it quiet for a bit." And at that moment, with classic poo timing, Mutti says, "We're off to New Zealand next week."

My eyes are all swollen up like mice eyes from crying. Even my nose is swollen. It's not small at the best of times, but now it looks like I've got three cheeks. Marvellous. Thank you, God.

9.00 p.m. I'll never get over this.

9.10 p.m. Time goes very slowly when you are suicidal.

9.15 p.m. I put sunglasses on to hide my tiny mincers. They are new ones that Mum bought me in a pathetic attempt to interest me in going to Kiwi-a-gogo land. They looked quite cool, actually. I looked a bit like one of those French actresses who smoke Gauloise and cry a lot in between snogging Gerard Depardieu. I tried a husky French accent in the mirror.

"And zen when I was – how you say? – *une teenager, mes parents, mes très, très horriblement parents*, take me to *Nouvelle Zélande.* Ahh *merde!*"

At which point I heard Mum coming up the stairs and had to leap into bed. She popped her head round the door and said, "Georgie . . . are you asleep?"

I didn't say anything. That would teach her.

As she left she said, "I wouldn't sleep in the sunglasses if I were you, they might get embedded in your head."

What kind of parenting was that? Mum's medical knowledge was about as good as Dad's DIY. And we had all seen his idea of a shed. Before it fell down on Uncle Eddie.

Eventually I was drifting off into a tragic snooze when I heard shouting coming from next door's garden. Mr and Mrs Next Door were out there, banging and shouting and throwing things about. Is this really the time for noisy gardening? They have no consideration for those who might want to sleep because they have tragedy in their life. I felt like

169

opening the window and shouting, "Garden more quietly, you loons!"

But then I couldn't be bothered getting out of my snuggly bed of pain.

mucho excitemondo police raid

12.10 a.m. When the doorbell rang I shot out of bed and looked down the stairs. Mum had opened the door wearing a nightdress that you could quite easily see through! Even if you didn't want to. Which I didn't. She has no pride. There were a couple of policemen standing at the door. The bigger one was holding a sack up in front of him at arm's length and his trousers were shredded round the ankles.

"Is this your bloody cat?" he enquired, not very politely for a public servant.

Mum said, "Well, I . . . er."

I ran down the stairs and went to the door.

"Good evening, constable. This cat, is it about the size of a small labrador?"

He said, "Yes."

I nodded encouragingly and went on, "And has it got tabby fur and a bit of its ear missing?"

PC Plod said, "Er . . . yes."

And I said, "No, it's not him then, sorry."

Which I thought was very funny indeed. The policeman didn't.

"This is a serious business, young lady."

Mum was doing her tutting thing again, and combining it with head shaking and basooma adjusting. Deeply unattractive. I thought the policeman might be distracted by her and say, "Go and put some clothes on, madam," but he didn't, he just kept going on at me.

"This thing has had your neighbours penned up in their greenhouse for an hour. They managed to dash into the house eventually but then it rounded up their poodles."

"Yes, he does that. He is half Scottish wildcat. He hears the call of the wilds sometimes and then he . . ."

"You should keep better control of it."

He went moaning on in a policemany way for hours and hours. I said, as patiently as I could, although I had enough things to think about as it was, "Look, I'm being made to go to Whangamata by my parents. It is at the other, more useless, side of the universe. It is in New Zealand. Have you seen *Neighbours*? Is there nothing you can do for me?"

My mum gave me her worst look and said, "Don't start, Georgia, I'm not in the mood."

The policeman didn't seem"in the mood" either. He said, "This is a serious warning. You keep this thing under control otherwise we will be forced to take sterner measures."

Mum was hopeless as per usual. She started smiling and fiddling with her hair.

"I'm really sorry to have troubled you, inspector. Would you like to come in and have a nightcap or something?"

It was so EMBARRASSING. He probably thought we ran a brothel in our spare time. The"inspector" was all smiling and he said, "That's very kind of you, madam, but we have to get on. Protecting the public from vicious criminals, dangerous moggies, and so on."

I didn't say anything as I took the wiggling sack, I just looked ironically at his chewed trousers.

Mum went BERSERK about Angus. She said, "He'll have to go."

I said, "Oh yes, perfect, just take everything that I love and destroy it. Just think of your own self and make me go halfway round the universe and lose the only boy I love. You can't just leave Sex Gods, you know, they have to be kept under constant surveillance and . . ."

She had gone into her bedroom.

Angus strolled out of the bag and strutted around the kitchen looking for a snack. He was purring like two tanks. Libby wandered in all sleepy with her "blankin". Her night-time nappy was bulging round her knees. The last thing I need-ed was a poo explosion at this time of night so I said, "Go tell Mummy about your pooey nap-naps, Libby."

But she just said, "Shhh, bad boy," and went over to Angus. She kissed him on the nose and then sucked it before she dragged him off to bed.

I don't know why he lets her do anything she likes with him. He almost had my hand off the other day when I tried to take his plate away and he hadn't quite finished.

monday july 19th

11.00 a.m. I am feeling sheer desperadoes. It's a day and a half now since I snogged the Sex God. I think I have snog withdrawal. My lips keep puckering up.

I HAVE to find a way of not going to Kiwi-a-gogo land. I went on hunger-strike this morning. Well, apart from a Jammy Dodger.

172

2.00 p.m. Phone rang.

Mum yelled up at me, "Gee, will you get that, love? I'm in the bath."

I yelled back, "You can wash the outside clean, but you can't wash the inside!"

She yelled again, "Georgia!!!"

Dragged myself up from my bed of pain and went all the way downstairs and picked up the phone.

I said, "Hello, Heartbreak Hotel here," and all I could hear was just crackle, crackle, surf, swish, swish. So I shouted really loudly, "HELLO, HELLO, HELLO!!!!" and this faraway voice said, "Bloody hell!"

It was my father, or Vati as I call him, phoning from New Zealand. He was, as usual, in a bad mood for no reason.

"Why did you shout down the phone? My ears are all ringing now."

I said, reasonably enough, "Because you didn't say anything."

"I did, I said hello."

"Well I didn't hear you."

"Well you can't have been listening properly."

"How can I not listen properly when I am answering the phone?"

"I don't know, but if anyone can manage it, you can."

Oh, play the old record again, it's always me that does things wrong. I said, "Mum's in the bath."

He said, "Just a minute, don't you want to know how I am?"

"Er, let me guess . . . funny moustache, bit bulky round the bottom department?"

"Don't be so bloody cheeky! Get your mum. I give up on

173

you. I don't know what you learn at that school besides how to put on lipstick and be cheeky."

I put the phone down because he can grumble on like that for centuries if you let him. I shouted, "Mutti, there is a man on the phone. He claims to be my dear vati but I don't think he is because he was quite surly with me."

Mum came out of the bathroom with her hair all wet and dripping, just a bra and pants. She really has got the most gigantic basoomas, I'm surprised she doesn't topple over. Good Lord.

I said, "I am at a very impressionable age, you know."

She just gave me her worst look and grabbed the phone. As I went through the door I could hear her saying, "Hello, darling. What? I know. Oh I know. You needn't tell me that . . . I have her all the time. It's a nightmare."

That's nice talk, isn't it?

As I point out to anyone who will listen (i.e. no one), I didn't ask to be born. I am only here because she and Vati . . . urgh . . . anyway, I won't go down that road.

my room

2.10 p.m. I could hear her rambling on to Dad, going. "Hmmm – well I know, Bob . . . I know . . . Uh huh . . . I KNOW . . . I know. Yes, I know . . ."

In the name of pantyhose, what are grown-ups like? I shouted down to her, "Break the news to him gently that I'm definitely not in a TRILLION years coming."

He must have heard me because even upstairs I could hear muffled shouting from down the other end of the phone. I wasn't amazed by the shouting as my vati is prone to violence. Once I poured aftershave into his lager and lime when he was out of the room. For a merry joke. But he didn't get the joke. When he stopped choking he went all ballisticisimus and shouted, "You complete IDIOT!!!" really loudly at me. It's the kind of thing that will cost me hundreds of pounds in therapy fees in later life. (Should I have a life, which I don't.)

2.30 p.m. Playing sad songs in my bedroom, still in my jimjams.

Mutti came into my room and said, "Can I come in?"

I said, "No."

But that didn't put her off.

She came and sat on the edge of my bed and put her hand on my foot. I said, "Owww!!!"

She said, "Look, love, I know this is all a bit complicated, especially at your age, but this is a really big opportunity for us. Your dad thinks he has a real chance to make something of himself over in Whangamata."

I said, "What's wrong with the way he is now? Quite a few people like fat blokes with ridiculous moustaches. You do."

She came on all parenty then. "Georgia, don't think that rudeness is funny because it isn't."

"It can be."

"No it isn't."

"Well you laughed when Libby called Mr Next Door 'nice tosser'."

"Well Libby is only three and she thinks that tosser is like Bill or Dad or something. Can't you see this trip as an exciting adventure?"

"What, like when you are on your way to school and then suddenly you get run over by a bus and have to go to hospital, or something?"

"Yes, like when . . . NO!! Come on, Georgie, try to be a pal, just for me."

I didn't say anything.

"You know that your dad can't get a job here. What else is he supposed to do? He's only trying to look after us all."

After a bit she sighed and went out.

Life is *très merde* and double bum. Why doesn't Mutti understand I can't leave now? She can be ludicrously dim. It's not her that I get my intelligence from. It is certainly no thanks to her that I came top in . . . er . . . well anyway, it's nothing to do with her what I do. I am just the unfortunate recipient of some of her genes. The orang-utan eyebrow gene, for instance. She has to do a lot of plucking to keep her eyebrows apart and she has selfishly passed it on to me. Since I shaved mine off by mistake last term they seem to have gone even more haywire and akimbo. The shaving has encouraged them to grow about a metre a week. If I left them alone I'd be blind by October. Jas has got ordinary eyebrows, why can't I?

Also, while I am on the subject, the worst news of all is that I think I have inherited her breast genes. My basoomas are definitely growing. I am very worried that I may end up with huge breasts like hers. Everyone notices hers.

Once, when we were on the ferry to France, Dad said to Mum, "Don't stand too near to the edge, Connie, otherwise your chest might be declared a danger to shipping."

5.00 p.m. I've just had a flash of whatsit!! It's so obvious, I am indeed a genius! Simple pimple. I'll just tell Mum that I'll stay behind and . . . LOOK AFTER THE HOUSE!! The house can't just be left empty for months because . . . er . . . squatters might come in and

176

take it over. Anarchists who will paint everything black, including, probably, Mr and Mrs Next Door's poodles. They'll be begging for Angus to come back.

Excellent, brilliant fabulosa idea!! Mum will definitely see the sense of it.

I'll promise to be really mature and grown-up and responsible. I mainly want to stay in England because of the terrifically good education system. That is how I will sell it to Mutti.

"Mutti," I will say, "this is a crucial time in my schooldays, I think I may be picked for the hockey team."

Thank goodness I didn't bother Mum with my school report from last term. I saved her the trouble of reading it by signing it myself.

5.05 p.m. You would think that Hawkeye could think of something more imaginative to write than *Hopelessly childish attitude in class*. Just because she caught me doing my (excellent) impression of a lockjaw germ.

5.10 p.m. I could have groovy parties that everyone would really want to come to. I'm going to make a list of all the people I will ask to the parties:

First – Sex Gods
Robbie . . . er, that's it.

Second – the Ace Crew
Rosie, Jools, Ellen and, I suppose, Jas if she pulls her pants up and makes a bit more effort with me. She has been a bit of a Slack Alice on the pal front since she got Tom.

Third – close casuals

Mabs, Sarah, Patty, Abbie, Phebes, Hattie, Bella . . . people I like for a laugh but wouldn't necessarily lend my mum's leather jacket to . . . then acquaintances and fanciable brothers.

5.20 p.m. I may even allow crap dancers like Sven to come if they have pleasing or amusing personalities (and gifts).

5.23 p.m. I tell you who I won't be asking – Nauseating P. Green, that's who. She is definitely banned. If I am made to sit next to her again next term I will definitely kill myself. Why is she so boring? She does it deliberately to annoy me. She breeds hamsters. What is the matter with her?

Who else will be on the exclusion list? Wet Lindsay, Robbie's ex. It would be cruel to invite her and let her see Robbie and me being so happy and snogging in front of her, etc. Also she would kill me and that would spoil the party atmosphere.

Who else? Oh, I know, Jackie and Alison, otherwise known as the Bummer Twins. They can't come because they are too common.

9.10 p.m. Looking out of my window. I can see Mark, the boy with the biggest gob in the universe, going off to town with his mates. People are out there having fun. I hate that. I haven't got any real friends – as soon as a boy comes along they just forget about me, it's pathetic.

I could never be that shallow.

I wonder if the Sex God is having second thoughts about me because of my nose?

9.15 p.m. Jas phoned. Tearing herself away from Tom for a second. She said, "Have you told her you are not going, yet?"

"No, I try but she takes no notice. I told her that it is a very important time for me as I am fourteen and poised on the brink of womanhood."

"On the what?"

Jas can be like half girl, half turnip. I said, "Do you remember what our revered headmistress, Slim, said at the end of summer term? She said, 'Girls, you are poised on the brink of womanhood, which is why I want to see no more false freckles painted on noses. It is silly and it isn't funny or dignified.'"

"False freckles are funny."

"I know."

"Well why would Slim say they weren't?"

"Jas."

"What?"

"Shut up now."

9.30 p.m. I've got Libby, her scuba-diving Barbie doll, which has arms like steel forks, and her Thomas the Tank Engine, all in my bed. It's like sleeping in a toy box only not so comfortable. Plus Libby has been making me play Eskimo kissing; it has made my nose really sore. I said, "Libby, that's enough Eskimo now," but she just said, "Kwigglkwoggleugug," which I suppose she thinks is Eskimo.

What is the matter with my life? Why is it so deeply unfab?

10.00 p.m. Looking at the sky outside my window and all the stars. I thought of all the people in history and so on who have been sad and have asked

God for help. I fell to my knees (which was a bit painful as I landed on a plate of jam sandwiches I had left by my bed). Through my tears I prayed, "Please, God, let the phone ring and let it be Robbie. I promise I will go to church all the time if he rings. Thank you."

midnight So much for Our Vati in Heaven. What on earth is the point of asking God for something if you don't get it?

Decided to buy a Buddha tomorrow.

1.00 a.m. As time is short it might be all right to ask Buddha for something before I actually invest in a statue of him.

I don't really know how to speak to Buddha, I hope he understands English. I expect, like most deities, it's more a sort of reading your thoughts job.

1.30 a.m. Because I haven't been a practising Buddhist for long (half an hour) I'll restrict my requests to the essentials.

Which are:

1 When I suggest to Mum that she leaves me behind to look after the house, she says, "Of course, my darling."
2 The SG rings.

1.35 a.m. I'll just leave it at that. I won't go into the nose business (less of it and more sticky up) or breast reduction requests, otherwise I will be here all night and Buddha may think I am a cheeky new Buddhist and that I'm only believing to get things.

tuesday july 20th

10.00 a.m. My room . . . soon to be a shrine to Buddha. Unless God gets his act together. Birds tweeting like birds at a bird party. Lovely sunny day. For some. I can see the sunshine glancing off Mr Next Door's bald head. He's playing with his stupid yappy little squirt dogs. Just a minute, I've spotted Angus hanging about in the potting shed area. Uh-oh, he looks a bit on the peckish side, like he fancies a poodle sandwich. I'd better go waggle a sausage at him and thereby avert a police incident.

How in the name of Mr Next Door's gigantic shorts am I supposed to be a Buddhist with these constant interruptions? I bet the Dalai Lama hasn't got a cat. Or a dad in New Zealand. (I wonder if the Dalai Lama's father is called the Daddy Lama? . . . I amaze myself sometimes because even though my life is a facsimile of a sham I can still laugh and joke!!)

10.36 a.m. What is the point? Mum just laughed when I told her about looking after the house and told me to go and pack.

midday Even though it is quite obvious I am really depressed and in bed Mum comes poking around being all efficient and acting as if life is not a tragedy of a sham (which it is). She made me get up and show her what I had packed for Whangamata. She went ballisticisimus. "*Men Are From Mars, Women Are From Venus*, eyelash curlers, two bikinis and a cardigan?!"

"Well I won't be going out anywhere as I don't like sheep and my heart is broken."

181

"But you might wear your bikini?"

"I've only packed that for health reasons."

"What health reasons?"

"Well, if I can't eat anything because of my heartache, the sun's rays may keep me from getting rickets. We did it in Biology."

"It's winter over there."

"Typical."

"You are being ridiculous."

That's when all the pain came raging out of me. "I'm being ridiculous!!??? *I'm* being ridiculous??? I'm not the one who is dragging someone off to the other side of the world for NO good reason!!"

She went all red. "No good reason?! It's to see your dad!"

"I rest my case."

"Georgia, you are being horrible!" And she stormed off.

I feel a bit like crying. It's not my fault if I am horrible. I am under pressure. Why can't Dad be here? Then I could be horrible to him without feeling so horrible. (And without having to go to the other side of the planet. Most teenagers only have to go into the sitting-room to be horrible to their dads.)

It's not easy having an absent dad, that's what people don't realise. I am effectively (apart from my mum and grandparents and my crap cousin James, etc.) an orphan.

1.00 p.m. Libby crept into my room carrying a saucer of milk really carefully. She was on her tippy toes and purring. I said, "You are nice, Libbs. Just put it down; Angus is out hunting."

She very slowly and on tippy toes brought the saucer over to me and put it on my desk. She put her little hands on my head and started stroking my hair. My eyes filled up with tears. I said, "If I can't be happy in my life I can try and see that you have a nice life, Libbs. I will give up all thoughts of happiness myself and be like your Buddhist nurse. For your sake I will wear flat shoes and those really horrible orange robes and . . ."

Then Libby started pushing my head quite roughly down towards the saucer of milk. "C'mon, Ginger, come on. Milky pops."

She'll make me sleep in a cat basket soon. Honestly, I think it's about time she started kindergarten and mixed with normal children.

It takes twenty-four hours to fly to New Zealand.

6.00 p.m. Uncle Eddie roared up on his pre-war motorbike. He's come round to collect Angus. How can I live without the huge furry fool? How can he live without me? No one else knows his special little ways. Who else will know that he likes you to trail his sausages around on a string so that he can pounce on them from behind the curtains? Who else will know about mouse racing? Not Uncle Eddie, that's for sure. He truly does come from Planet Bonkers. He came in wearing his motorbike leathers, took off his helmet and said, "How're you diddling?"

What is the matter with him? Why Mum thinks anyone as bald and barmy as him could look after an animal I don't know. Anyway, it's irrelevant what anyone thinks as he will never in a zillion years catch Angus and get him in a basket.

6.30 p.m. I don't think I could be more sad. We are going to be away for months: I will miss all my friends; I'll lose the SG. My hockey career will be in ruins. Everyone knows the Maoris don't play hockey. They play . . . er . . . anyway, we haven't done New Zealand in Geoggers yet, so I don't know what they do. Who cares?

6.35 p.m. Time ticking away. It's like waiting to be buried, I should think. Or being in RE.

Phoned Jas. I wanted to know if Tom had heard anything from his gorgeous older brother, the Sex God, but I didn't want to let Jas know that I wasn't interested in her life. So I asked her a few questions about her "boyfriend" first.

"Hi, Jas, how are you and Tom getting along?"

She went all girlish and giggly. "Well, do you know, we were just laughing so much because Tom said that he was in the shop the other day and . . ."

"Jas, did he mention anything, you know, interesting?"

"Oh yeah, loads."

There was a pause – she drives me INSANE!

I said, "Like what?"

"Well, he was thinking of suggesting that they start selling more dairy products in their shop, because . . ."

"No, no, Jas, I said interesting – not really, really boring. Has he, for instance, mentioned his gorgey older brother?"

Jas was a bit huffy but she said, "Hang on a minute." Then I heard her shouting, "Tom! Have you spoken to Robbie?"

In the distance I heard Tom shouting, "No, he's gone away on a footie trip."

I said to Jas, "I know that."

Jas shouted again, "She knows that."

Tom shouted, "Who knows that?"

"Georgia."

Then I heard Jas's mum shouting from somewhere, "Why

184

does Georgia want to know about Robbie? Isn't she off to New Zealand?"

Jas shouted, "Yes, she is. But she's desperate to see him before she goes."

I said to Jas urgently, "Jas. Jas, I wanted to find out when he's back. I didn't want to discuss it with your street."

Jas went all huffy. "I'm only trying to help."

"Well don't."

"Well I won't, then."

"Good."

There was a silence. "Jas?"

"What?"

"What are you doing?"

"I'm not helping."

I'm going to have to kill her.

"Ask Tom when Robbie is due back."

"Huh. I don't see why I should, but I will."

She shouted out again, "Tom, when is Robbie back?"

Jas's mum yelled, "I thought he was going out with Lindsay?"

Tom yelled back, "He was, but then Georgia and him got together instead."

Jas's mum said, "Well, Lindsay will be very upset."

This was UNBELIEVABLE.

Tom yelled back again, "Tell Georgia he's not back again until late Monday."

Next Monday! Next Monday. By that time I would be being bored half to death by Maoris. I tried to be brave so that I wouldn't upset Jas. "I know I can joke about it and everything, but I have fancied Robbie for so long. And it's not just because he is in The Stiff Dylans. You know that. It's a whole year since

185

I started stalking him. It was so groovy when he kissed me, I thought I would go completely jelloid and start dribbling. Luckily I didn't. And I think he will forget about that chunk of my hair snapping off, don't you?"

There was this clanking noise and then Jas said, with her mouth full, "Hello? Hello? What were you saying? I just went and got myself a sandwich while Tom was shouting at you."

Qu'est ce que le point?

7.30 p.m. I can't believe Jas. She is dead to me. Like in the Bible, when somebody goes off and becomes a prostitute or something. She is now the girl who has no name.

9.00 p.m. Phone rang. I leaped downstairs.

It was Rosie, Ellen, Jools and She Who Has No Name (Jas) calling me from the phone box at the end of our road. Rosie said in a fake Chinese accent, "Bringey self-ey to phone boxey."

I put on some mascara and lippy so that no one would know about my broken heart. Not that it made the slightest difference to Mutti and Uncle Eddie – they were too busy trying to trap Angus.

He's lurking on top of my wardrobe. I know he's got a few snacks with him because he dropped a piece of mackerel on my head when I passed. He'll be happy up there for hours. Serve them right if they can't find him. Cat-nappers!

I don't want to be rude to the afflicted but Uncle Eddie is bald in a way which is the baldest I have ever seen. He looks like a boiled egg in leather trousers. Once he came round and after he and Mum had had their usual vat of wine he fell asleep in the back garden face down. So I drew another face on the back of his head. Very, very funny indeed, especially as I did it in indelible pen. He got his own back, though, by turning up to a school dance on his pre-war motorbike and asking all my mates where I was because he was my new boyfriend.

Still, that is life for you . . . one minute you are snogging a Sex God and have got up to number six on the snogging scale without crashing teeth. The next minute you are made to go to the other side of the world and hang out with Kiwi-a-gogos. Whose idea of a great time is to sit in mud pools and eat toasted maggots. (This is very, very true as I have been reading a brochure about Kiwi-a-gogo land and it says it in there.) Oh pig's bum!! Or as our tiny French friends say, *Le grand bum de le porker!!!*

9.30 p.m. When I got to the phone box the gang were all in there. They squeezed open the door and Jools said, "Bonsoir, ma petite nincompoop."

Once I was in we were all squashed up like sardines at a fish party. Rosie managed to get a hand free and give me one of those photobooth photographs.

"We brought you a present to remember us by."

It was a picture of her, Jools, Ellen and Jas (She Who Has No Name), only they had their noses stuck back at the tip with Sellotape so that it made them look like pigs with hair.

On the back it said, *GRUNTINGS from your mates. STY in touch. This is a PIGTURE to remember us by.*

It made me feel a bit tearful, but I put on a brave face. "Cheers, thanks a lot. Goodnight."

We had to get out of the telephone box because Mark (the boy from up the road with the enormous gob who I went out with for a fortnight but dumped me because this other girl Ella let him "do things to her") came to use the phone. He just looked at us as we all struggled out. He really has got the biggest mouth I have ever seen. I was lucky to escape from snogging him with my face still in one piece.

BG (Big Gob) said, "All right?" in a way which meant, "All right, you lesbians?"

What do I care, though? My life is over anyway.

We all walked back to my house arm in arm. I wouldn't link up with Jas though because she has annoyed me. Uncle Eddie must have eventually got Angus into the cat basket because the gardening gloves he was wearing were lying in the driveway with the thumbs torn off.

We all hugged and cried. It was awful. I'd nearly got to the door when Jas sort of threw herself at me. She couldn't speak because she was crying so much and she said, "Georgia, nothing will be the same without you . . . I . . . I love you. I'm sorry I ate my sandwich."

wednesday july 21st

dawn — well, 10.00 a.m. Phoned my dearest friend Jas who loves me. Huh.

Now that she thinks she has got a "proper" boyfriend she acts like she is one hundred and eighty.

"Look, Gee-gee, I can't talk really because I am on the dash to meet Tom. Dig you later, though. *Ciao* for now."

. . . *Ciao* for now? I wonder if she has finally snapped? Nobody really cares about me. No one wants you when you are in trouble; no one is interested when you are not the life and soul of the party. I may have to try to make it up with God again at this rate.

2.30 p.m. I don't care what happens. I am not going to New Zealand. Not. Definitely. They will have to carry me on to the plane. Or give me knock-out drugs.

That is it. I am not going.

3.00 p.m. I am not speaking to Mum but as she has gone out shopping (again) she probably hasn't noticed.

3.19 p.m. Sitting by the phone and using telepathy to make it ring. I've read about it a lot – it's where you use your willpower to make something happen. In my head I was saying, "Ring, phone!" and "The phone will ring and it will be Robbie . . . by the time I count to ten."

3.21 p.m. "OK, the phone will ring and it will be Robbie by the time I count to a hundred . . ."

3.30 p.m. ". . . in French. By the time I count to one hundred in French the phone will ring and it will be SG." (God, or whoever it is that deals with willpower, will respect that I am making a bloody huge effort by counting in a foreign language.)

Everything really is sheer desperadoes and in tins. In two days' time I will be on the other side of the world and the Sex God will be on this side of the world. And, what is more, I will be a day ahead of him. And upside down.

3.39 p.m. I've got an appalling headache now.

While we are on the subject of French, why in the name of Louise the Fourteenth did Madame Slack (honestly – that is her name) make us learn a song called "*Mon merle a perdu une plume*"?

My blackbird has lost a feather. That will be a great boon and help if I ever get to go to Paris. I won't be able to get a sandwich for love nor money but I will be able to chat to *le* French about my blackbird's feathers. Not that I have got a blackbird and, if I did have one, believe me it wouldn't be just the one feather it would lose with Angus around. Not that he is around.

I really miss him already. He is the best cat anyone ever had. I can still imagine his furry head snuggled up in my bed. Bits of feather round his mouth. The way he used to bring me little presents. A vole, or a bit of poodle ear or something.

3.41 p.m. How do you say my blackbird has had its legs chewed off by my cat? *Mon merle a perdu les jambes . . .*

phone rang

3.45 p.m. Thank goodness, because I thought I was going to have to count up to a hundred in German and nobody wants that. (And besides, I can't.)

"It's me, Jas."

"Oh . . . What do YOU want?"

"I've just called to see how you are."

I said, "Dead actually, I died a few hours ago. Goodbye."

That will teach her. I'm not going to answer the phone if she rings back, either.

5.00 p.m. She didn't ring back. Typical.

my room
in bed

10.30 p.m. Mum and Libby came back in. When they popped their heads round my door I pretended to be asleep. Libby crept over quietly – well, her idea of creeping quietly, which is the loudest thing I have ever heard.

Mum whispered, "Give your big sister a kiss, Libbs, because she's upset."

Then I felt this wet thing sucking on the end of my nose. I shot up in bed. I said, "Does anyone else's sister kiss like that? Why is she so obsessed with my nose?"

11.15 p.m. After the nose sucking incident I am as awake as two awake things. Just gazing out of my bedroom window into the dark night. When you gaze at the stars it makes you feel really small. We have been discussing infinity in Physics: you know, how there is no end to the universe, and so on. Herr Kamyer said there might even be a parallel universe to the one we live on somewhere out there. There might be another Georgia Nicolson sitting in her bedroom, thinking, What on earth is the point?

11.17 p.m. Another Georgia Nicolson who is being forced to leave a Sex God and all her mates (and this does not include Jas). To go to the other side of the world. Double *merde*.

191

11.29 p.m. I've just had a horrible thought. If there is a parallel me, there will be a parallel Wet Lindsay. And a parallel Nauseating P. Green. And two pairs of Mr Next Door's shorts. Good grief.

thursday july 22nd

day before the last day of my life
hunger protest

2.00 p.m. Even though it is quite obvious even to the VERY dim that I am not eating, Mum hasn't noticed. She said, "Do you want some oven chips and beans?"

And I said, "I will never eat again."

She just said, "OK," and tucked in with Libbs.

I had to creep into the kitchen and finish off the chips she had left.

4.00 p.m. In my room. Practising feeling lonely and friendless in preparation for the months ahead.

4.05 p.m. I haven't heard from my so-called mates for days. Well, since this morning, anyway. I don't need to practise. I AM lonely and friendless.

4.10 p.m. I went into the front room to watch TV. Libby was snoozing but woke up when I sat down. She stood up on her little fat legs and put her arms up to me.

"I love my Georgie, I lobe my Georgie."

She made it into a little song:

"Haha, I lobe my Georgie,

I love my little Girgie,

Gingie, Gingie,

Hahahaha. Ginger, I love Ginger . . . my Ginger."

In her tiny mad brain I am half cat, half sister. I picked her up and we snuggled down on the sofa together. At least I have someone who loves me in this family, even if she is bonkers.

Mum came in and said, "You look really sweet together. It only seems a little while ago that you were that size, Georgie. Dad and I used to take you to the park and you used to have a little hat with earflaps that were like cats' paws. You were such a sweet little girl."

Oh good Lord, here we go. It will be, "How did my little girl get so big . . . ?"

Sure enough, Mum's eyes got all watery and she started stroking my hair (very annoying) and doing the "How did my little Georgie get so . . ." routine.

Fortunately (or unfortunately, depending on where you were sitting) Libby let off the smelliest, loudest fart known to humanity. It came out of her bum-oley with such force that she lifted off my knee – like a hovercraft. Even she looked surprised by what had come out of her.

I pushed her off my knee and leaped up. "Libby, that is disgusting!!!! I blame you, Mum, for the bean extravaganza. It's not natural, the amount of stuff that comes out of such a little girl."

Phwaaor . . .

Grandad farted once when we were out in the street. Really loudly. When he looked around behind him there was a woman walking her dachshund dog. You know, those little sausage dog things. The woman heard Grandad's fart (who didn't?) and she said, "Well, really!!"

And Grandad said, "I'm terribly sorry, madam, I seem to have shot the legs off your dog." Which was possibly the last semi-sane thing he said. I'd still rather stay here with him than go to Kiwi-a-gogo.

I said to Mum, "Well, can I go and live with Grandad, then?"

And she said, "He lives in an old people's home."

And I said, "So?"

But she is so mad and unreasonable she wouldn't even discuss it.

11.30 p.m. All my mates came and did a candlelit vigil underneath my bedroom window. Sven wore a paper hat. I don't know why. Does it matter? It was just his Swedish way of saying goodbye. They all sang *"Mon merle a perdu une plume"* as a tribute. Well, they sang the first verse before Mr and Mrs Next Door came and complained that they were frightening their dogs. Jas said, "I'm going to stay silently here all night."

But then Sven said, "Chips, now." And they all went off.

It was so sad.

friday july 23rd

the day the world ends

midday Decided to have to be dragged out of bed by the police so that the world will know how I have been treated. I have tied myself to the bedhead with my dressing-gown sleeves. I can imagine the newspaper headlines: *Promising hockey superstar teenager fights attempts to force her to Kiwi-a-gogo land*. I've put on a hint of make-up just in case, for the photos.

12.10 p.m. Mum surprised me by bursting into my room all flushed like a pancake.

"Guess what?!!!! We're not going to New Zealand because your dad is coming home!!!!!"

I said, "What?"

She was hugging me and didn't seem to notice I was like a rigid hamster in bed.

I was a bit dazed. "Vati, home, coming?"

1.00 p.m. Great news!!!!!!!!
My dad has had his shoes blown off by a rogue bore!!!!! All this hot steam shot out of something he was fixing and he leaped off and broke his foot. Mum has put her foot down with a firm hand and said she will not take her children to a place where steam shoots out of the ground.

She said to me, "It's hard enough getting you to get out of bed as it is, I'm not giving you more excuses." Which is incredibly unfair, but I didn't say anything, because inside I was saying "Yessssss!!!!!!"

The only fly in the manger is that Vati is going to be coming home when his contract is finished. Still, if it is a choice of going to live in Kiwi-a-gogo land or having to put up with Vati snooping around my bedroom and telling me what it was like in the seventies, I suppose I will choose having the grumpy moustachioed one.

Mum is hideously happy. She won't stop hugging me.

Which I think is on the hypocritical side but I didn't say anything. I just hugged her back and asked her quickly for a fiver. Which she gave me. Yesss!!!!

Beautiful English summer's day. Lovely, lovely drizzly rain!!! We don't have to go to Kiwi-a-gogo!!!

Thank you, God. I will always believe in you. I was only pretending to become a Buddhist.

3.00 p.m. I put on some really loud music in my room and started to unpack my bikini. Lalalalala . . . fabbity fab fab. Marvy and double cool with knobs.

Uncle Eddie turned up with a bottle of champagne and Angus in a basket. I noticed Uncle Eddie had put a muzzle on him. What a weed. Angus soon had it off and I could see him strolling around his domain. (The dustbins.) When I went downstairs Uncle Eddie had picked up Libby and was dancing around with her. She was singing, "Uncle Eggy, Uncle Eggy," which is quite funny when you think about it.

4.20 p.m. My little room. I love you, my little room!!! Lalalalalala. Fabbity fab fab. Ho-di-hum. Everything is so lovely: my little Reeves and Mortimer poster with them in the nuddy-pants, my little desk, my little bed . . . my little window overlooking next door's garden.

5.00 p.m. Phoned the Ace Crew and they went mental. Just put the phone down when there was a ring on the doorbell. It was Mr Next Door. His glasses were on all sideways. He did not say, "I am so glad you are not going, Georgia." In fact, he didn't say anything but just handed over a sweeping brush and stomped off.

Attached to the bottom part of the brush was Angus. He dragged the brush into the kitchen. There was the sound of pots and pans and chairs crashing over. I called out, "Libbs, Angus is back."

11.00 p.m. Before I went up to bed I looked into the kitchen. Libbs was feeding Angus cat food by hand. Aaahhh, this was more like it!! Back to normal.

saturday july 24th

11.00 a.m. Summer. Birds tweeting, voles voleing. Poodles poodling. I notice that we have new neighbours across the road. I hope they are a bit more considerate than Mr and Mrs Mad who used to live there.

Oh, they've got a cat! It looks like one of those pedigree Burmese ones, all leaping around. In a sort of fenced enclosure. They are very expensive, pedigree Burmese cats. They are the Naomi Campbells of the cat world. Not that they do a lot of modelling. Too furry. And not tall enough. Although they would be really good on the catwalk!!! Hahahahaha. Lalalalala. I think I am a comedy genius. Now if only the SG would phone and say, "I'm coming round now, oh gorgeous one. I didn't realise how close I came to losing you. I am mesmerised by your beautosity." Life would be beyond fab and entering the marvy zone.

midday Met Jas and we went to the park. I've got a spot on my chin but I've made it look like a beauty spot with an eyebrow pencil. With my shades on I look a bit like an Italian person. I think Jas was embarrassed about me not going to NZ after what she said. I am too considerate to mention it so I just said, "Do you really love me, Jas?"

She went all red.

As we strolled by the tennis courts we saw Melanie Andrews sunbathing. I may have mentioned this before but she has got the largest breasts known to humanity. Some lads went by and went "Phwooar!". One of them pretended to be juggling. Sometimes I feel that boys will always remain a mystery to me. I've felt that particularly since BG from up the road rested his hand on my basooma for no particular reason. Mel saw us looking so I said, "Oh, hi Mel!" sincerely.

She said, "Hi!" but I don't think she meant it.

I said to Jas, "Where does she get her bras from? They must be made by those blokes who built the Forth Bridge. Ted and Mick Forth." I just made that up; I don't know what they were called.

We lay down on the grass to sunbathe and Jas said, "Do you think I should get a bra?"

I was thinking what I should wear when I saw Robbie again. I said, "Robbie hasn't phoned yet, you know."

Jas was silent. I squinted round at her and she was sort of wobbling her shoulders around. I said, "What in the name of pantyhose are you doing?"

She said, "I'm seeing if my basoomas wobble."

Jas can be spectacularly dim. I think that if I dressed Angus in her school uniform probably no one would notice for days. Unless they tried to take a snack away.

I said, "Do the pencil test. You put a pencil under a breast and if it falls out you are OK. If it stays there, sort of trapped by your basooma, you're not and you should get help and support in the bra department."

She was full-on, attention-wise, then. "Really?"

"Yeah. Sadly my mum can get a whole pencil-case up there."

Jas was rummaging about. "I've got a pencil in my rucky, I'm going to try it."

"Jas, Tom hasn't said anything about Robbie, has he?"

As per usual Jas had gone off into the twilight world in her head. She was fiddling about with a pencil up her T-shirt. She said, "Hahahahaha, it fell out!!! I passed, I passed . . . you try it."

I wasn't interested. "Why would SG snog me and say 'see you later' if he didn't mean 'see you later'? Do you think he's worried about me being younger than him? Or do you think it's my nose?"

You might as well be talking to a duck. Jas was shoving the pencil at me. "Go on, go on . . . you're scared."

"No I'm not. I'm not frightened of a pencil."

"Try it, then."

"Oh for goodness' sake."

I grabbed the pencil from her and pulled up my top and put the pencil underneath my right basooma. Actually it stuck there, but I jiggled a bit. I said, "Yeah, it falls out."

Jas said, "You jiggled."

"I did not."

"You did. I saw you."

"I didn't. You're a mad biscuit."

"You did. Look, let me do it, I'll show you."

She grabbed the pencil and was trying to put it under my basooma when Jackie and Alison, the Bummer Twins, came round the corner of the tennis courts. Jackie removed the fag from her mouth long enough to say, "Well, well, well, our lezzo friends are out for an afternoon fondle."

Oh no, here we go again with the lesbian rumours. That will be something to look forward to next term.

monday july 26th

2.00 p.m. Phew, what a scorcher!!! Sun shining, birds tweeting. Mr and Mrs Next Door in their garden. They are wearing shorts – again. Mr Next Door's shorts really are gigantic in the bottom department. You'd think that out of courtesy to others he'd keep out of public view when he was wearing them. What if a very, very old person – even older than him – came along unexpectedly? And what if they weren't in peak medical condition? The sight of Mr Next Door in his shorts could bring on a dangerous spasm. Still, that is another example of the bottomless (oo-er!) selfishosity of so-called grown-ups for you.

tea-time

4.50 p.m. Fabulous day . . . not. Grandad came round. Even he was wearing shorts. As I said to Mum, "There is really no need for that."

He is so bow-legged that Angus can walk in between his legs with a stick and Grandad doesn't even notice. Mind you he doesn't notice much as he lives in the twilight world of the elderly mad. After fiddling in his prehistoric shorts he gave me twenty pence and said, "There you are, don't spend it all at once." Then he laughed so much his false teeth shot out. He was wheezing away for so long I thought he'd choke to death and then I'd have to do the Heimlich manoeuvre. Miss Stamp

(Sports Kommandant) made us learn it in First Aid. If someone swallows a boiled sweet or something and chokes, you grab them from behind and put your arms round below their breastbone. Then you squeeze them really hard until the sweet shoots out. Apparently some German bloke called Mr Heimlich made it up. Why Germans have to go round grabbing people innocently choking on sweets I don't know. But they do. That is the mystery of the German people.

8.00 p.m. Well, that is it. No call from the SG. He must be back. I can't call him because I have pride. Well actually, I did phone him but there was no reply. I didn't leave a message. I don't understand boys. How could you do number six type snogging and then not call someone?

8.10 p.m. Buddhism is the only way. I must meditate and be calm.

my room

8.20 p.m. I found one of Mum's kaftans that she got when she went to India on the hippie trail. She has some very sad photos of her and Dad with hilarious haircuts in Kathmandu. Dad looks like he has got a big nappy on. She gets the photos out when she is drunk, especially if you beg her not to.

I put on the kaftan and was listening to some dolphins on a meditation tape. It was called "Peaceful Universe". Squeak, squeak, squeak. On and on – it would go quiet for a bit and then squeak, squeak, squeak. If dolphins are so intelligent why don't they learn to speak properly? Instead of squeak-ing? It is fantastically irritating. I would turn it off but I am too depressed to get off the bed.

8.40 p.m. Phone rings. Of course, everyone else is far too busy to answer it. So I'll tramp all the way downstairs and get it.

I yelled out, "Don't worry, Mum, I'll come all the way down and answer the phone which is probably for you. You try and get some rest!"

Mum shouted from the living-room, "OK, thanks."

I picked up the receiver. "Yes?"

It was Robbie!!! Yes and treble fabuloso!! He's got such a lovely voice; quite deep – not quite as deep as Grandad's, but then he doesn't smoke forty cigarettes a minute. He said he'd been away.

I was thinking, I know you have, you great huge sexy hunk!!! My lips are stiff with puckering!!! But I didn't say that, I said, "Oh, have you?" which I thought was quite cool and alluring. Anyway, the short and short of it is that he's really, really glad that I didn't go to Kiwi-a-gogo and I'm going round to his place tomorrow!!! His parents have gone away.

Oooooooohhhhhh. I'm all shakey and nervous now. I'm like a cat on a hot tin roof. We did *Cat On a Hot Tin Roof* in English. There was no cat in it . . . or a tin roof . . . or . . . stop it, brain, stop it!!!!

8.45 p.m. Phoned Jas.
"He called me!!"
"Who?"

It's like talking to a sock. "Jas, HE called me. HE – the one and only HE in the universe."

202

Jas came round to discuss what I should wear. We went up to my room. Unfortunately I forgot to warn Jas about the hammock that Libby had made for her dolls. She'd made it out of one of Mum's commodious bras and tied it across the landing. Jas grazed her shins quite badly when she fell over. She was going, "Ow, ow!", but I can't be bothered with minor injuries just now.

She hobbled into my room and we looked through my wardrobe. I held things up and Jas went, "No. No. Maybe. No, too tarty. No, no . . . er . . . maybe."

I was trying on a suede mini and she said, "Erlack!! The front of your legs are quite hairy but the backs of your legs are all baldy."

I had a look. She was right!!! Time for operation smoothy legs. I grumbled to her as we went down to the bathroom. "What is the point of evolution? Why bother giving us hairy front legs and baldy back legs? When can that ever have been useful in our fight for survival?"

Jas said, "Perhaps it was to frighten things off."

I said, "Oh yeah, that will be it. Stone Age girl would have said, 'Here comes a big dinosaur chasing me from behind. It thinks I am a push-over because of my baldy legs, but wait till I turn round! I'll scare off the big lug with my terrifying hairy front legs.' That will be the explanation."

Jas wasn't interested in my scientosity because she was looking through the bathroom cabinet. "Your mum has got loads of anti-ageing creams, hasn't she?"

"I know. It's sad. Why doesn't she save all that money and put it towards some new spectacles or a hat? Or a decent bra that can contain her gigantic basoomas."

9.30 p.m. Mum's hair remover worked a treat; my legs were smoothy smooth. I was tempted to use a bit on my eyebrows but I remembered the last time I had shaved them and they had taken two weeks to grow back.

Clothes-wise we decided on a turtle-necked crop top (implies that I am mature for my years, on the brink of womanhood, etc . . . but doesn't go as far as saying "I am desperate for a snog"). In the leg department it was the tight Capri trousers.

Jas said, "Tom is going away on work experience this term. I will be on my own for weeks. I'll really miss him. Do you know, he said the other day that he . . ."

In a caring way I said, "Go home now, Jas, I have to get my beauty sleep."

11.00 p.m. In bed nice and early. I've barricaded my door so that Angus and Libby can't get in.

midnight I am SO nervous . . . What if I have forgotten how to snog? What if all my snogging lessons go out of my mind at the last minute and we bump teeth?

1.00 a.m. Or I lose my grip altogether and go to the same side with my head as he is going, and knock him out? Heeeeelp!!!!

What if I have one of those laughing fits that you can't stop? You know, when you remember something . . . like for instance when Herr Kamyer took us on a school trip and when we arrived at the railway station he said, "Ach yes, here ve are!" and then opened the door on the wrong side of the train and fell out of the carriage.

Hahahahahahahaha . . . hahahahaa. You see, I'm doing it now, I'm laughing by myself in the middle of the night in my room.

OhmyGodohmyGodohmyGod. Hahahahahahahahaha.

tuesday july 27th

sg day

7.00 p.m. Setting off to his house.

It's taken most of the day to achieve my natural make-up look. Just a subtle touch to enhance my natural beauty (!). I wanted the just-tumbled-out-of-bed look, so I only used undercover concealer, foundation, hint of bronzer, eye pencil, eight layers of mascara, lip liner, lippy and lip-gloss, and I left it at that.

7.20 p.m. Jas phoned to wish me luck. She said, "Tell me all about it when you get home. Remember what number you get up to on the snogging scale. Are you wearing a bra? I think it would be wise because you don't want to wobble all over the place."

I said, "Goodbye, Jas."

I'm not wearing a bra; I thought I would go free and akimbo. I just won't make any sudden movements.

walking down arundel street

7.30 p.m. Brrr, not quite as warm and bright as it was earlier. A bit overcast, actually, and . . . oh no . . . it's starting to rain! It's too far to go back home for an umby . . . it will probably stop in a minute.

7.40 p.m. Outside Robbie's gate. It really is raining quite hard now. I'm wet through and really cold. I think my trousers have shrunk; they are hugging my bottom in a vice-like grip. I wonder if I look all right?

I'll nip into the telephone box opposite his house and check my mirror.

in the telephone box

7.45 p.m. My trousers have shrunk so tight around my bottom that I can't bend my legs. This is hopeless. Brrr. Why is everything going wrong? I can't go to see the Sex God looking like this. I'll have to phone him up and say I'm ill.

7.50 p.m. SG answered the phone. "Hello." Swoon swoon.

I said, "Roggie, nit's ne, Neorgia."

"What's wrong with your voice?"

"Der nI'd gut a trrible cold nd Im nin bed."

"Do they have beds in telephone boxes?"

"Dnno."

"Georgia, I can see you through the window."

When I looked across at his house, he waved at me. Oh GODDDDDD!!!!!!

He said, "Come over."

What can I do, what can I do? My top is all wet. And there are two bumpy things in it. Great! It looks like I've got two peas down the front of my top. Typical, the only thing Mum has ever ironed for me and she has ironed it wrong.

As I walked up to the door I tried to flatten out the bumpy bits. But it wasn't my top sticking up . . . it was ME!!! My nipples!!!!! What were they doing?!!! Why were they sticking out? I hadn't told them to do that. How could I get them back in again? I'd have to cross my arms in a casual way and hope he didn't offer me a cup of coffee.

7.55 p.m. The back door opened and there he was!! The Sex God had landed. I went even more jelloid. He was so gorgey . . . so . . . oooooh and er and yum yum and scrumbos and yummy scrumbos. His hair was all floppy, he had on dark jeans and a white T-shirt and you could see his shoulders (one on each side). He's got really, really dark blue eyes and long dark eyelashes and a big mouth, sort of soft looking. He's not a girlie boy though, he's definitely a boyie boy, which I think is handy in a boy myself.

midnight I love him, I love him. I love you, Robbie, oh yes I do. When I'm not near to you I'm blue . . . What else rhymes with Robbie? Gobbie? Snoggie? Knobbie?

12.30 a.m. I can't sleep, life is too brilliant. I may never sleep again.

It was such a fab night. We talked for a bit – well, I said, "My dad had his shoes blown off by a rogue bore," and he said, "Does anything normal ever happen to you?" Which I took as a compliment.

He played me a song on his guitar. I didn't really know what to do when he did that. I just sat on the sofa next to him with an attractive half smile on my face (and my arms crossed). It was quite a long song and by the end of it my cheeks ached like billy-o. In fact, I think I might have cheek strain. I tried to keep my nose sucked in at the same time; I didn't want it wandering across my face.

He told me that he is going to go to university to do music properly. I said, "I'm going to be a vet." I don't know why as I'm not. I didn't seem to be able to make anything come out of my mouth that had anything to do with my brain. He looked into my eyes and went quiet, and I went quiet and looked back at him. I tried not to blink. That seemed to go on for about a million years. In the end I had a sort of nervy spasm and went and looked at a photograph of a dog that was on a table. He probably thinks I am obsessed with animals as I am a trainee vet (not).

He came over and put his arm round my shoulder. I had an overwhelming urge to start doing Cossack dancing as a very funny joke, but just in time I remembered that boys don't like girls for jokes. Then he kissed me. I think he may be the best snogger in the universe. Although I have only snogged two other boys so far, and one of those was part boy part whelk, so I can't be entirely sure. SG does that varying pressure thing that Rosie says foreign boys do. You know, soft and then hard and then medium and then hard again. I could have quite literally snogged until the cows came home. And when they came home I would have shouted, "WHAT HAVE YOU COWS COME HOME FOR? CAN'T YOU SEE I'M SNOGGING, YOU STUPID HERBIVORES???"

I think I may be a bit feverish.

1.30 a.m. I am going to be nice to everyone from now on. Even Wet Lindsay, Robbie's ex. I won't say to her, "Yesssssss!!!!" I will be grown-up and nice.

The only fly in the landscape is that when he walked me to my gate and said goodnight he tweaked my nose. And he said, "I'll see you later."

1.35 a.m. What does that mean? Not the "see you later" bit, because no one knows what that means. I mean the tweaking the nose business.

1.40 a.m. Does it mean, "Hey, you adorable cute thing," or does it mean, "Cor, what a size that conk is, I wonder if I can get all of it in one hand?"

wednesday july 28th

3.35 p.m. I am a Sex God's girlfriend. But I will not let it spoil my naturalness.

Phoned Jas: "Even when I have loads of interesting and glamorous friends I would still want to be friends with you. Because we are proper friends. We should never let boys come between us."

Jas said, "Tom is going to buy me one of those stick-on transfer tattoos. I'm going to put it on my bottom while he is away and not wash it off until he gets back."

"Jas, can you leave your bottom out of this? Please."

friday july 30th

5.00 p.m. Made my dear mutti and sister a meal today. Mashed potatoes and sausages. I thought Mum was going to cry.

10.00 p.m. Early to bed, early to rise, makes a girl . . . er . . . anyway, it gets a girl out of the way of her mutti who had a nervy b. when she saw the state of the kitchen.

10.15 p.m. Why do I always get the blame for every little thing? Is it really my fault that a couple of pans caught fire? I put them out.

Still, I refuse to be upset. I will remain calm beneath my egg and olive oil face mask.

saturday july 31st

7.55 p.m. Dreamy dreamy, smiley smiley.
However no phone calley.

Never mindey.

august

snogging withdrawal

sunday august 1st

8.00 a.m. I've persuaded Jas to come to church with me to thank God for making Dad have his shoes blown off and also for giving me a Sex God as a plaything.

10.00 a.m. When I got round to Jas's house she was sitting on her wall in the shortest skirt known to humanity. When I wear skirts like that my grandad says, "You can see what you had for your dinner." I don't know what on earth he is talking about but then neither does anyone else, except probably dogs.

Jas leaped off the wall. Her skirt was about four centimetres long.

I said, "Is it a long time since you went to church, Jas?" and she said, "It's OK, I'm wearing really big knickers."

church

10.40 a.m. Good grief. Now I know why I don't go to church much. It is not what is generally known as Fun City Arizona. I was forced to sing "All Things Bright and Beautiful" which is bad enough, but there was a further treat in store. The vicar, ("Call me Arnold") tries to be "modern". So to really get "with it" Call me Arnold had got some absolute saddos to play guitars as an accompaniment. One of the boys on guitar was called Norman and as if that is not cruel enough he had acne. And not just ordinary acne, he had acne of the entire head.

But as we left I remembered I was supposed to be being grateful so I said, "Sorry about Spotty Norman, God, I will be nice to him next time I see him," (inwardly) and put a pound in the collection box.

monday august 2nd

12.10 p.m. Still no news from the SG. I've been going to bed really early to make the hours pass more quickly.

I tried snogging the back of my hand to stave off snogging withdrawal but it's no good.

3.30 p.m. Cor, phew . . . boiling again. The sun was shining like a great big fried egg. Jas and Jools and Ellen and me went sunbathing in the park. I took off my shades and got the shock of my life: in the sunshine my legs looked like Herr Kamyer's legs. They were all pale-looking. Not as hairy or German as his legs, obviously.

I said, "Ellen, why are your legs so brown?"

She said, "Oh, I used some of that Kool Tan stuff."

Maybe the SG noticed my Herr Kamyer legs? I must get some Kool Tan.

tuesday august 3rd

10.30 p.m. When Jas came round for us to practise hairstyles I made her let me kiss the back of her calf to see if she could feel any teeth. She leaped about, going, "Erlack, erlack, get off, get off, it feels disgusting, like a sort of sucky Spotty Norman." Which is not very reassuring.

She said Tom touched her basooma the other night. In revenge I said, "How would he know it wasn't your shoulder?" She honestly does think she is like Kate Moss. It is very, very sad.

midnight SG didn't touch my basooma. I wonder if that is bad? Mind you, I had my arms folded for a lot of the time because of the nipple emergency.

wednesday august 4th

4.00 p.m. Phoned Jas.

"I'm really worried now. It's been over a week. I wonder if it is my nose? Perhaps SG only likes little sticky-up noses like Wet Lindsay's?"

Jas said, "Maybe a headband would help. You should make more of your forehead and that would take the emphasis away from your nose."

"At least I've got a forehead, not like Wet Lindsay who has got a tiny little forehead. In fact, she is really just hair and then eyebrows. How could the SG go out with someone with no forehead?"

"She's got quite nice legs."

213

"What do you mean? Nice – not like mine? Shut up, Jas."

"OK, keep your hair on."

"Nauseating P. Green, on the other hand, has got the HUGEST forehead known to humanity. In fact, she is a walking forehead in a frock. I must get away from this forehead business, it's making me feel a bit mad."

4.30 p.m. In the bathroom experimenting with a headband. Hmmm, headband seems to emphasise my nose. In fact, it's like wearing a big notice on my head that says, "Hey, everyone!!! Look at my incredibly big schnozzle!!"

4.40 p.m. While I had been doing headband work I hadn't been paying much attention to Libbs. She had come into the bathroom and got up on the lavatory seat. Her hair was all sticking up like a mad earwig but she won't let you comb it. I said, "Libby, things will start nesting in it," and she said, "Aaahh nice." Then she started going, "Bzzz, bzzz, bzzy bzz, bzz," like a mad bee.

I was experimenting with sucking in my nose to see if it made it look any smaller when Mum came barging in. (Not bothering to knock or anything.) Anyway, she went even more bananas than usual. Libby had put all of the loo paper down her knickers because she wanted to be a bumble bee. I'd heard her buzzing but I didn't pay any attention. Mum was all red-faced.

"Georgia, all you think about is how you bloody look. The house could burn down around you before you would stop looking in that mirror."

I raised my eyebrows ironically. Talk about the pot calling the other pot a black kettle, er . . . well whatever. She really has got a volatile temper; she should go to anger management classes. I will suggest it to her. But not just now as she has got a brush in her hand.

4.50 p.m. My violent, bad-tempered mother has gone out. Nothing in the fridge. Oh, I tell a lie, there is a half eaten sausage. Yum yum.

4.55 p.m. Grandad said that as you get older gravity pulls on your nose and makes it bigger and bigger.

5.00 p.m. Why couldn't I come from a decent gene bank? Nice, well-formed parents, like Jas's mum and dad. Nice and compact, nothing too sticky-outy. Instead I get massive "danger to shippings" from Mum and a massive conk from my dad. If Robbie doesn't like me it is Vati's fault. If it is true about the gravity business then Dad will need a wheelbarrow to carry his nose around in soon. Good, serve him right for ruining my life.

7.00 p.m. I'm so hot and restless. Oh Robbie, where are you? My nose feels tremendously heavy.

8.00 p.m. I put on a really loud record and danced about to get rid of my excess snogosity.

8.05 p.m. When I looked in the mirror I could see my basoomas bobbling about. Good grief and *sacré bleu*!! They look like they are doing their own dance!

In Mum's *Vanity Fair* it says that all the posh type ladies go to a special woman behind Harrod's to get their bras properly fitted.

8.15 p.m. The Queen must go there, then. Apparently this woman who does the bras is such an expert that she can just look at someone and say what size bra they should have. No suggestion of pencil-cases. I wish I could go to her.

8.30 p.m. When the Queen goes, this woman must just look at her and yell to her assistant, "Get the Queen a bra in size forty-eight D." Or whatever the Queen is.

9.00 p.m. The Queen is about five foot high, so if she was a size sixty D that would make her like a five-foot ball.

9.30 p.m. I wish I didn't have that in my head.

midnight Should I call him? Oh I don't know what to do, I don't know what to do.

thursday august 5th

still boiling

4.00 p.m. Jools, Ellen, Rosie, Jas and me went to town to try on make-up in Boots and

216

Miss Selfridge. I cheered up a bit, especially as we did this limping thing on the way home. You link up and all limp together. And you're not allowed to break arms no matter what happens. This tremendously old bloke got shirty with us because we accidentally stampeded his labrador. After that we went into the park and sat on the swings for a rest. Rosie said, "Oh I fancy a fag."

I was shocked. I said, "I didn't know you smoked."

And she said, "It's just to relax."

Rosie put a cigarette in her mouth and got out her lighter. We were all looking. Unfortunately she must have set the flame too high because when she flicked it a flame shot up about twelve centimetres and set fire to her fringe. We beat it out but the hair was all singed and short. She went home with her hand over her fringe. After she had gone the rest of us swang backwards and forwards for a few minutes.

I said, "Rosie smokes quite a lot, doesn't she?"

And then we all got the helpless laughing. You know, that laughing that makes your tummy hurt and makes you cry and gulp and choke? And you've laughed for long enough and you want to stop but you can't. Then you do stop and you think it's all right but then someone starts again. I just couldn't stop. And that's when I saw HIM. The Sex God. With his mates from The Stiff Dylans. He looked like he was coming across to say hello. And you know when you really, really should stop laughing because otherwise it will be really bad and everyone will hate you? But you can't? Well I had that.

10.00 p.m. Rang Robbie. His mum said he was at rehearsal. Still he likes a laugh himself, so it will be all right.

midnight On the other hand I wasn't by any means doing my attractive half smiling when he saw me. I had a look at myself in the mirror doing proper, unadulterated laughing, the kind of laughing where you just let your nose and mouth go free and wild.

12.15 a.m. That is it, my life is over; I must go to the ugly home immediately.

friday august 6th

11.00 a.m. A letter arrived for me. From Robbie. My hands were shaking when I opened it.

11.30 a.m. Back in bed. I CANNOT believe my life. It is beyond pooiness. It has gone well beyond the valley of the poo and entered the galaxy of merde.

11.45 a.m. I reread the letter from Robbie again. It still says the same thing though.

Dear Georgia,
I have been thinking and thinking about this. And although I think you are great, and I really do like you, well, I saw you with your mates yesterday having a laugh and you seemed so young. The facts are that I am seventeen, nearly eighteen, and if anyone knew I was even thinking about going out with a fourteen-year-old I would never hear the end of it. Where would we go for our dates? Youth club or something? You see what I

mean, don't you?

I think it is best we stay away from each other for a year or so. You need to see someone more your own age. My brother has a really nice mate called Dave. He's a good laugh. You'd like him.

I'm really sorry.

Love Robbie xxxxxxxxx

midday
On the phone to Jas. I was shaking with rage.

Jas said, "Well, erm . . . if he's a good laugh, maybe you should meet him."

"Jas, are you really saying that I should just stop liking one person and start liking another one, just like that? What if I said, 'Hey, Jas, forget about Tom, why not go out with Spotty Norman? He's got a really great shaped head underneath the acne?'"

saturday august 7th

6.20 p.m.
I hate him, I hate him.
On the phone to Jas.

"How dare he find another boyfriend for me? I hate him!!!"

sunday august 8th

3.50 p.m.
That is absolutely it for me now. He can't treat me like that. I have my pride. How dare he question my maturiosity?

On the phone to Jas. "Jas?"

"What?"

"You don't think I should just pop round to his house and sort of beg and plead, do you?"

monday august 9th

11.40 a.m. I will never get over this, never.

Mum says there are plenty more fish in the sea. Why is she so obsessed with fish? At a time like this! She doesn't care about my feelings anyway.

No one does.

wednesday august 11th

2.45 p.m. Took Angus for a long, moody walk. Part of me really hates the Sex God. Sadly it's only a little tiny part of me (near my knee), the rest of me really, really likes him!!!

3.00 p.m. Even my breasts like him. They want to break out of my T-shirt and yell, "I love you, I love you!!!"

3.32 p.m. I hope I am not being driven to the brink of madness by grief. They say that some people never get over things, like whatshername, Kathy Thing. The one who wandered over the moors at night yelling, "Heathcliff, Heathcliff, it's me a-Kathy come home again." Was that Kathy Brontë, one of the Brontë sisters? Or was that Kate Bush? Anyway, whoever it was wandered off into the rain and died from heartbreak. That will be me. I feel a bit tired now. If I just lie down here in the grass I might never be found.

3.35 p.m. Angus keeps tugging at his lead. It was murder getting it on him but at least it means he can't savage any small dogs that we see.

4.00 p.m. Famous last words. Angus saw a Pekinese and dragged me to my feet and halfway across a field before I managed to get him under control. He's senselessly brave. There is something about small dogs that really irritates him.

4.30 p.m. Angus can fetch sticks!!! I was just carrying a stick along, hitting things with it. Then my arm got tired so I flung it away. And Angus pounced on it and dragged it back!! Superdooper cat!!!

5.00 p.m. I wonder if I could get him to carry a little flask of tea round his neck in case I fancied a cuppa when we were having our walk?

friday august 13th

my bedroom

1.00 a.m. Hot and stuffy. Big full moon. Sitting on the windowsill. (Me, not the moon.)

1.05 a.m. I hate him.

1.06 a.m. Oh I love him, I love him.

1.10 a.m. I hate him, but he will not break me. I will make him regret the day he said, "I know a bloke called Dave. He's a good laugh."

She who laughs last laughs last.

2.00 a.m. I am going to be a heartless babe magnet as revenge.

2.05 a.m. Oh no, no, that's not what I mean. I don't want to be a babe magnet, that would mean I was a lesbian.

2.05 and 30 secs Still, what is wrong with that? Each to their own, I say. After all, Mum must have kissed Dad (erlack).

2.06 a.m. If anyone asked me to comment on sexuality, say in the *Mail on Sunday* or something, I would say that it is a matter of personal choice and nothing to do with nosey parkers. Or else I would say, "Don't ask me, I am on the rack of love."

sunday august 15th

in bed

9.40 p.m. In bed early, healing my broken heart in the "privacy" of my bedroom.

9.41 p.m. How can I stop Libby hiding her pooey knickers in my bed?

monday august 16th

9.00 a.m. Up. Up at nine a.m. in the holidays. Nine a.m.!! This just proves how upset I am.

Mum hasn't even noticed, of course.

"Mum, shouldn't even you be able to potty-train Libby by now? At this rate she'll be a pensioner and still pooing all over the place. She'll never get a boyfriend . . . Still, that will make two of us."

tuesday august 17th

8.30 a.m. I think I've lost a lot of weight from my bottom. No one has noticed. Mum just wanders around in a dream. She has got a calendar up in the kitchen with the days marked off until Vati gets back and a heart drawn round the date. How sad is that at her age? I said, "Don't worry yourself about my breakfast, Mutti. I'll get it myself, you get on with your own very important life."

She was humming and slathering herself with creams and ignoring me. So I said even louder, "Something quite interesting happened last night; I slit my throat and my head fell off. Have you seen it anywhere?"

Mum called from the bathroom, "Has Libby got her shoes on?"

"I think Mr Next Door might be another transvestite like Vati."

She came out of the bathroom then. "Georgia, is it possible for you to help at all? Where is your sister?"

"Mum, have you noticed anything unusual about me? I am

223

not happy . . . in fact, I am very unhappy."

"Why? Have you broken a nail?" And she laughed in a very unpleasant way. Then she called out, "Libbsy, where are you, pet? What are you doing?"

I could hear Libby's muffled voice from Mum's bedroom and a bit of miaowing. Libby called, "Nuffing."

Mum rushed in there, saying, "Oh God."

I heard bang bang, and Mum yelling, "Libby, that is Mummy's best lipstick!"

"It looks nice!!!!"

"No, it doesn't . . . Cats don't wear lipstick."

"Yes."

"No they don't."

"Yes."

"Owww, don't kick Mummy."

"Bad Mummy!!!"

Hahahaha. She who laughs last laughs . . . er . . . the last.

thursday august 19th

11.00 a.m. Raining. In August. Typical. Squelching along on my way to meet Mrs Big Knickers, I was thinking . . . I could either give in and be a miserable, useless person, like Elvis Attwood our barmy, sad old school caretaker. Or if I truly gave up I could be like Wet Lindsay. When Robbie dumped her she got all pale and even wetter than normal. She was like an anoraksick. (A person who is both very thin and wears tragic anoraks.) I just made that up as a joke. Even though I am very upset I can still think of a joke. I'll tell Jas when I see her. As I was saying, before I so rudely interrupted myself, I could be a sad old sadsack or I could gird my loins and be like in that song. The one where you have to search for the hero within yourself.

Jas was waiting for me at the bus stop. She said, "Why are you walking in that stiff way?"

"I'm girding my loins."

"Well, it looks painful, like you've got a stick up your bottom. You haven't, have you?"

"You really are sensationally mad, Jas. In olden days people would have thrown oranges at you."

As I said, I can sometimes surprise myself with my own wisdomosity. And humourosity. Even in adversosity.

monday august 23rd

2.10 a.m. In bed. Oh God, it's so boring being broken-hearted. I've spent so much time in bed I'll probably start growing a long white beard soon, like Rip van Thing.

2.15 a.m. Or perhaps I could just grow my eyebrows and train them into a beard.

2.48 a.m. I can't sleep. I've gone all feverish now. I'm going to creep downstairs and get Mum's *Men Are From Mars* book and do some more research.

3.35 a.m. God it's too weird. Apparently boys might seem like they like you to be all interested in them, but really they want you to be like a glacier iceberg sort of girl. So you have to play hard to get. That's where

I must have gone wrong. I have been too keen, I must do glacial.

thursday august 26th

10.33 p.m. Same bat time. Same bat place. Same scuba-diving Barbie digging me in the back.

According to the next bit in Mum's book, boys are like elastic bands. Good Lord!

It doesn't mean that boys are made of elastic, which is a plus because nobody wants a boyfriend made out of rubber. On the other hand, if they were made out of rubber you could save yourself a lot of time and effort and heartache by just rustling one up out of a car tyre. But that is not what the book means. Boys are different from girls. Girls like to be cosy all the time but boys don't. First of all they like to get all close to you like a coiled up rubber band, but after a while they get fed up with being too coiled and need to stretch away to their full stretchiness. Then, after a bit of on-their-own stretchy, they ping back to be close to you.

Hmmm. So in conclusion on the boy front, you have to play hard to get (the glacier bit), and also let them be elastic bands. *Sacré bleu!* They don't want much, do they?

friday august 27th

4.20 p.m. Round at Jas's house. Been to town. I bought myself some new lippy to cheer myself up and Jas got a new hot air brush thing that gives you bouncability. She was making her hair all turn under at the ends.

As she was tonging away at her hair she said, "I looked for a bra but I can't get one small enough. In fact, I don't need one, I'm more like Kate Moss. You have to wear one though, don't you? . . . Because of the pencil-case test thing."

"Just pencil . . . the case was my mum."

"Yeah, but the pencil stuck, didn't it? You said that if it did you had to have help and support."

"I know what I said."

When Jas really annoys me (i.e. all of the time) I notice that her fringe is more fringey than normal, if you know what I mean.

Fringey went on, "I'm only saying – there's no need to have a nervy b."

Jas was really, really beginning to annoy me. A lot. All her things are really neatly put away which is the sign of a very dull person in my opinion. When Jas and I stalked Wet Lindsay and looked through her bedroom window all her things were very tidy as well. Jas even puts all her knickers in the same drawer.

Besides it being VERY dull to do that it would also be useless at my house as Libby mostly uses my knickers as hats for her dolls. Or Angus eats them.

To change the subject I said, in a really caring way, "When does Tom go off to work experience?"

Jas stopped hot brushing her hair then and looked all mournful. Hahahahaha. She said, "Next Saturday – it's going to be really horrible. Do you think he'll meet someone else in Birmingham?"

I looked wise and oracle-like and like I was really thinking (which I wasn't). I said, "Well, he's a young bloke and we all know what young blokes are like."

227

"Do we?"

I laughed bitterly.

She said, "Just because Robbie went off doesn't mean all boys do."

"It does . . . in Mum's book *Men Are From Mars* it tells you all about it."

She was interested then and came and sat next to me. "What does it say in the book? Does it say Tom is going to go off with someone else?"

I said, "Yes it does, Jas. It says in the worldwide number one bestseller written by some bloke in America who has never met Tom, it says in Chapter Two, 'Tom Jennings definitely goes off with someone else when he goes to do work experience in Birmingham for a month.'"

She looked a bit miffed. "Well, what do you mean, then?"

I waited for a bit. Teach her to go on and on about my breasty problem and the fact that SG had left me.

"Can I try your new shiny lippy?"

She wasn't interested, it was all just me, me, me with her. She just went on about her problems.

"Anyway, Gee, what do you mean about this book? Isn't it American?"

"Yeah."

"Well it will be about American boys, then, won't it?"

"No, it's about boykind."

"Oh."

I paused. She looked all goggly and attentive, it was quite a nice feeling. Perhaps I might reconsider my career and think about becoming an Agony Aunt rather than a backing singer. Especially since I can't sing. But I know all about agony.

Jas was as agog as two gogs. She said, "Go on."

I explained, "Boys are like elastic bands."

"What?"

"Boys are like elastic bands."

"What?"

"Jas, if you keep saying 'what?' every time I say something we may be here for some centuries."

"Well, what do you mean 'like elastic bands'?"

"They like to be all close and then after a bit of being close they have to stretch and get far away . . . and you have to let them and then they spring back."

"What?"

"You're doing it again and it really annoys me. In fact, I will have to kill you now because I have a lot of untamed energy because of the Sex God. I'm going to have to give you a bit of a duffing up." And I shoved her.

She said, "Don't be silly and childish."

I said, "I'm not."

She got up and started making her hair have more boun- cability with the air brush thing again. I waited until she had got it just right (in her opinion), then I hit her over the head with a pillow. She started to say, "Look, this is not funn–" but before she could finish I hit her over the head again with the pillow. And every time she tried to talk I did it again. She got all red-faced, which in Jas's case is very red indeed. It made me feel much better. Violence may be the answer to the world's problems. I may write to the Dalai Lama and suggest he tries my new approach.

my room

midnight

I've got a plan. It involves the two "isities". They are "maturiosity" and "glaciosity". Firstly I have to prove to SG that I am very sophis and grown-up. Not a laughing hyena in a school uniform as he thought the last time he saw me. (This is the maturiosity bit.) Secondly I must be distant and alluring and play hard to get. (This is the glaciosity bit.)

The conclusion of these two parts is that SG comes springing back like an elastic band.

saturday august 28th

2.10 p.m.

Phoned Jas.

I said, "I've worked out a plan."

She said, "I can't talk, Tom and I are going to choose my tattoo."

Huh. Typico.

Well, old huge knickers always puts her boyfriend first. Just as well I am so popular.

10.00 p.m.

In bed listening to a tape. Sadly it is "The Teddy Bears' Picnic". Libby has made me listen to it five times. If I try to turn it off she has a nervy spaz and growls at me.

I phoned my "mates" earlier to go out, but they were all busy.

11.00 p.m.

I wonder if I had an emergency, like appendicitis or something, would my mates be too "busy" to come to the hospital?

11.30 p.m. I have got a pain in my side. It might be a grumbling appendix.

11.32 p.m. In Blodge we learned that rabbits have got some sort of shrub growing in their appendix. How normal is that?

sunday august 29th

6.30 p.m. Mutti and Libbs have gone to visit the elderly mad (Grandad). Mum asked me if I would like to go, but I just looked at her with pity. Sadly she didn't get it and asked me again. I explained politely that I would rather put my head in a pair of Elvis Attwood's old trousers. She said I was a "horrid, bad-tempered, spoiled brat". Fat chance I'm spoiled. I'm lucky if I get one square meal a week. I'm getting really, really thin. Apart from my nose. And basoomas.

8.00 p.m. Ellen, Rosie and Jools came round and we sat on the wall, looking at boys. There are, it has to be said, a lot of fit-looking boys, but they haven't got that certain Sex God factor for me.

Mark (BG) went by with his girlfriend Ella. She is practically a midget. I thought he was taking a toddler for a walk. Rosie said, "So what happened with you and Robbie?"

I said, "He sent me a note and said that I should go out with some loser called Dave the Laugh."

Rosie said, "That's sort of dumping by proxy, isn't it?"

I said, "Are you supposed to be cheering me up?"

"But I thought you got to number six and everything."

231

"Yeah, but he said his parents would go ballisticisimus because I am so young. They'd think I was jail thing."

The Ace Crew were all full-on, attention-wise. Ellen even took her chewing-gum out.

Jools said, "What is jail thing?"

I didn't really know actually but I improvised (lied). "Er . . . it's when you are underage and you go to . . . er . . . number eight with a boy."

Rosie said, "What, if you let a boy touch you above the waist you have to go to jail?"

I said patiently, "No, he has to go to jail."

Rosie said, "Well, that's it for Sven, then."

I said, "Fair enough." But I don't know what I am talking about really. I'm all upset and confused and still have Herr Kamyer legs, even though it's the end of August.

monday august 30th

1.43 p.m. Borrowed Ellen's Kool Tan. Soon my Herr Kamyer legs will turn into sun-kissed boy magnets. Hmmm, smooth it on smoothy smooth and leave for an hour.

2.00 p.m. If I move my bed and open the window I can sort of sunbathe on my bedroom floor. SG is going to find it damn difficult to resist the new tanned me.

4.05 p.m. Woke up to orange Herr Kamyer legs and a huge red nose!!

5.00 p.m. I've just scrubbed my legs off. They are not quite so orange but my nose looks like one of those red clown noses. Brilliant.

september

operation elastic band

wednesday september 1st

7.00 p.m. It's boiling having to wear stockings in this weather, but better than being blinded every time I look down at my still orangish legs.

Eight days till we go back to Stalag 14. I'm going to put my foot down with a firm hand this term and make sure I don't have to sit next to Nauseating P. Green.

Mum has gone out to Uncle Eddie's with Libbs. He is teaching Mum salsa dancing – can you imagine? How very sad. The tremendously old can be very embarrassing. Imagine my mum salsa dancing with Uncle Eddie the human boiled egg.

In public.

Or private.

7.05 p.m. Jas called. Tom has gone off to work experience and she wants to come round. I am a substitute boyfriend. Well she can think again if she thinks I am going to be constantly available when Tom goes off to work experience. I am not so cheap.

7.08 p.m. I may make her give me some expensive present that I choose from Boots. Oh no, hang on, I've got a better idea.

7.30 p.m. Jas moaning on about Tom.
I listened sympathetically and said,
"Shut up, now, Jas."

Then she looked at me. "Why have you got pink panstick on your nose?"

I said, "Shut up, now, Jas."

7.42 p.m. I made my famous French toast for Jas.
(Beat an egg and put bread in it and
then fry it. The French bit comes in when you are eating the toast and you have to speak with a French accent.) As we were munching through the toast I said, "Jas, *ma petite*."

"*Quoi?*"

"I've got *le plan* to *impressez* the Sex God *avec* my matur-iosity. It involves *vous*."

She almost choked on her toast. "*Non*."

"You will *aime* it."

"Oh *mon Dieu*."

The first part of my plan was that we got dressed up to look as old as we could and get on a bus and get full fares. As an experiment. She was grumbling as she got made up but at least she was on the move.

8.30 p.m. Ready. I must say I think we looked v.
sophis. We'd got loads more make-up
on than we normally wear, and darker lipstick. And we wore all black. Black is very ageing, as I continually tell Mum so I can get her black T-shirt and leather trousers. I said to Jas, "We'd better get back before she gets home

235

because I have borrowed her Gucci handbag. She specifically said she would kill me if I ever borrowed it. She is very, very mean with her things, which is why I have to borrow them in secret."

As we walked down the street I had another idea. "Let's keep pretending we are French as well."

"Why?"

"Don't you mean *pourquoi*?"

"No, I mean why?"

"Just *parce que, ma petite* pal."

midnight *Ouiii!!! Très, très bon!! Merveilleux!!!!* It was *très, très bon plus les grandes* knobs.

The bus driver was like a sort of mobile version of Elvis Attwood, our school caretaker – i.e. very old, mad and bad-tempered, but sitting in a bus rather than a hut. I said to Mobile Elvis, "*Bonsoir, mon très* old *garçon. Mon amie et moi désire deux billets pour Deansgate, s'il vous plaît.*"

He understood we wanted to go to Deansgate but unluckily, like all very old mad people thought he could be funny and witty. He gave us the tickets (full fare! Yesss!!! Result!!!!). I handed over the money and he said, "*Merci* buckets." Then he laughed himself senseless (easy enough as he was mad in the first place). I thought he would choke to death because he was laughing so much, but sadly he didn't.

What is the matter with people?

12.20 a.m. Snug in my bed. Maybe I should leave school as I look so old.

236

12.30 a.m. I could go off and have sophisticated adventures instead of hanging around with very young people.

12.35 a.m. I could go to India and visit the Dalai Lama, or is it Ghandi who lives there? I don't know. We haven't done India in Geoggers yet. All I know is what Mum tells me about it, and that is mostly, "Oh it was just so . . . you know . . . great." Anyway, even if we had done India in Geoggers Mrs Franks is so bad at explaining things that I wouldn't know any more than I do now. She called concentration camps "contraception camps" when we were doing world affairs.

1.00 a.m. Now on to part two of the plan. The glaciosity bit. I must look for an opportunity to show SG how stand-offish I can be.

saturday september 4th

5.50 p.m. Five days to Stalag 14 (school) and counting. I got my uniform out of the back of the wardrobe. Angus must have been using it as his lair by the look of it. I bunged it in the washing machine and hoped the bits of feather would come off.

I did cheer myself up a bit because I thought of something funny to do with my beret. Which we are forced to wear by the Oberführer (Miss "Hawkeye" Heaton).

6.00 p.m. Phoned Rosie.
"I've thought of something really

237

cool to do with the beret this term."

Rosie said, "I thought we were going to do the rolling it up into the sausage and pinning it under our hair at the back routine again?"

"Yeah I know, but what about this . . . what about if we use it as combination beret and lunchbox?"

Rosie said, "How do you mean?"

I had to explain, patiently. It is not easy being the leader of the gang. I sympathise with Richard Branson on this one, although I still see no reason for his ridiculous beard.

Anyway, I said, "Pop your sandwiches or crisps or whatever into the beret, then tie it on to your head with your scarf. *Voilà*, beret and lunchpack all in one."

"Hawkeye would go mad."

"*Exactamondo, ma petite amie.*"

Rosie said, "You are a genius." She is not wrong.

sunday september 5th

5.10 p.m. *Au secours* and *sacré bleu*!! Just walking to the park to meet the gang when I saw "Call me Arnold", the vicar. I ducked down behind a car to hide until he had gone by. But the car was his car. When he got in he saw me crouching down. I had to pretend I was looking at a really interesting pebble.

God will know that I was hiding from his maidservant. Still, I don't know how I could possibly be made to suffer more than I am already.

5.45 p.m. Now I know. Cousin James is coming round tomorrow.

238

midnight If he gets all weird like he has done in the past and attempts to kiss me or anything, I may go mad.

monday september 6th

10.00 p.m. Cousin James asked me if I wanted to play strip poker. I was so embarrassed, I just said, "I don't know how to play poker," and he said, "Well, let's play strip snap, then."

I pretended I could hear the phone ringing. When he left, five million years later, I noticed there was something lurking under his nose. I thought it was a bogey at first, but sadly I now think it was a sort of moustache. Erlack!

wednesday september 8th

10.00 p.m. Mum came in my bedroom and asked if I wanted a wake-up call for Stalag 14 tomorrow. I said, "Oh, hello Mum, what are you doing in?"

She patted me on the head and said, "Goodnight, my sweet-natured little elf."

Nothing seems to bother her now that Vati is coming home. She might have put his moustache out of her mind but I haven't. In fact, to remind her I have drawn a moustache on the heart she put in the calendar.

10.30 p.m. Washed my hair but couldn't be bothered drying it. I know if I sleep on it while it is damp I will wake up with the "stupid hedgehog" look. There will be bits sticking up all over the place, so I am sleeping with my pillow tucked under my neck and my head sort of drooping over the other side.

This is how Japanese Buddhist people sleep – it's probably whatsit . . . zen. They probably do it because it lets their *chi* flow free. *Chi* is energy that is in your body it says in my Buddhist book. Heaven knows I need as much energy as I can get for working out my plan for SG retrieval.

I think all the blood may have drained into my head from my shoulders.

11.00 p.m. What happens if you get too much extra blood in your head? If you were meant to have two shoulders and a neck's worth of extra blood in your head you would have a bigger head, surely?

Or inflatable ears that could accommodate the extra blood and so on. Do Japanese have big ears?

Perhaps that is why Wet Lindsay's ears are so huge – because she's got Japanese ancestors. I wouldn't be surprised.

That would explain her tiny legs.

But not her big goggly eyes.

thursday september 9th

8.00 a.m. Woke up all snuggled down under the covers. I must have dropped asleep and forgotten about my zen position. My awake mind said, "Ha-so, I am a Japanese zen person ha-sleep with head h-over end of bed." But my English subconscious took over when I was asleep and said, "Snuggle down, you know you want to . . ."

bathroom

8.10 a.m. OhmyGodohmyGod . . . my hair looks like I've been electrocuted. No time to wash it. I'll have to gel it down.

8.30 a.m. Pant pant, rush rush. Jas waiting for me. She said, "Why do you look like Elvis Presley?"

As we ran up the hill towards school, we could see Hawkeye standing like a ferret by the gates. Oh here we go again . . . the beret patrol!!! I hadn't got mine on. No time for the "sausage" or the "lunchpack". Only one thing for it. I fished the beret out of my bag and pulled it right down over my ears. You could only just see my eyes.

When we ran past Hawkeye she shook herself like something nasty had made a nest in her knickers.

"Two minutes to assembly; don't start the term with a detention."

Oh very caring. "Hello, Georgia, welcome back," would have been nice.

As we dashed to the cloakroom I said to Jas, "Imagine her having a boyfriend! Erlack, no no, I must pull my mind away from that otherwise I'll start imagining her snogging or something. Urgh!!!! Urgh! I've done it now; I've let it in my brain!!! Hawkeye getting up to number seven on the snogging scale. Putting her tongue in someone's mouth. Maybe Herr Kamyer in his *lederhosen*. Urghhhh. Erlack. Get out, get out!!!"

I ripped off my beret and coat and went into the main hall.

Rosie, Ellen, Jools and Mabs – otherwise known as the Ace Crew – were all there. I gave them our special Klingon salute.

They looked at me like they had never seen me before. Had they forgotten all we had shared after so little time? I felt a hand on my shoulder. It was Hawkeye. What fresh hell? She looked down her big beaky nose at me and hissed, "Take this, make yourself presentable and get back here as quickly as you can, you stupid girl."

I looked down and saw that she had given me a comb. When I went into the loos I saw my hair had gone the shape of my pulled down beret because of the superdooper hair gel.

Sacré bleu! I feel like *un nincompoop.*

9.00 a.m. Took my usual place next to Rosie and Jas. Our revered headmistress "Slim" Simpson (so called because she weighs about a ton) lumbered on to the stage. I whispered to Rosie, "Crikey, she has got chins on her chins."

Slim bored us half to death by telling us what fabulous treats were ahead of us this term. Exams (yippee!); the challenge of modern languages *and* Physics with Herr Kamyer (superdooper!!!); a school trip to the escarpments of the Lake District (oh marvy!!!) . . .

As she said each thing Rosie and I were clapping our hands together in delight until Hawkeye gave us the evil eye. Good grief.

break

11.00 a.m. Jools, Ellen, Mabs, Rosie, Jas and I met behind the tennis courts for a confab. Elvis Attwood, the grumpiest caretaker in the universe, shouted at us as we passed his hut, "I've got my eye on you lot. Don't come sneaking into my hut otherwise there will be trouble."

He's beyond bonkerdom. He came to a school dance and did some exhibition twisting on stage until his back went and he had to be taken to Casualty. That's when we started calling him Elvis.

I waved and shouted back, "Greetings, oh mad one."

We were grumbling and moaning as we sat down. As usual in this fascist hell-hole we have been split up in class and not allowed to sit together. I have my "pal" Nauseating P. Green next to me. She wears those glasses that look like they have been made out of jamjars, which is very unfortunate. She's got really bulgy eyes anyway. Rosie said, "I think there must be a touch of the goldfish in her family genes."

As we ate our snacks you could see right up Jas's skirt. I said, "Jas, do you always wear those huge knickers? A small dog could creep up a knicker leg and you wouldn't know."

"Well I like to be comfy."

"They're not very sexy, are they?"

"You said you thought little knickers were stupid. Remember Lindsay's thongs?"

"Shut up, don't upset me. You know how visual I am. Now not only have I got Hawkeye snogging Herr Kamyer in my brain, I've also got Wet Lindsay's thongs."

Ellen said, "Anything happening with you and Robbie?"

I explained about my glaciosity and maturiosity plan. They all nodded wisely. We are a very wise group. Full of wisdomosity. I am almost certainly wiser than God, who doesn't seem able to grant the simplest of requests. Which is why I have turned to Lord Buddha.

Rosie spoilt the moment of wisdomosity by saying through a mouthful of cheesy snacks, "What in the name of pantyhose are you talking about?"

4.45 p.m. At the end of my glorious day today Elvis made me pick up a sweet wrapper in the corridor. All because I did my VERY funny impression of him doing the twist and then his back going. If he doesn't want people to make jokes at his expense he should stay indoors. He's a barmy old fascist. I bet he goes round dropping sweet papers on purpose.

5.05 p.m. Jas phoned, all breathless and excited. "I've got two letters from Tom."
I said, "He's only gone to Birmingham."
"I know, but . . . well . . . you know."
No, I don't know.

5.15 p.m. Libby and Mum came home. Libby has had her first day at kindergarten which I think is a good thing as it will make her less mad.

5.16 p.m. Wrong. Libby has made me something to wear at kindergarten. She was ramming it on my head. I said, "Steady on, Libby, be gentle with my head. What is it you have made?"
"It's nice!!!!"
"Yes. I know. But what is it?"
She looked at me like I was a halfwit and put her face nose to nose with mine. She said really slowly, "For . . . egg!!!"
"For my head?"

She hit me. "No, no, no, bad boy . . . for your EGG!"

Mum came in.

"Look, Georgie, she's made you an egg cosy."

"Well why is she trying to put it on my head?"

"She must have got mixed up. Maybe she thinks the teacher said 'head cosy'." And Mum started laughing like a drain. Libby joined in while I just sat there.

7.00 p.m. What is there to laugh at? I am on the rack of love. Life is a sham and a facsimile and a farce.

7.15 p.m. But at least I have an egg cosy.

8.00 p.m. I am soothing myself by pampering my mind and body. I am pampering my mind by reading (an article about mascara) and I am pampering my body by eating a LOT of chocolate.

9.00 p.m. Now I feel worried, fat, but very well informed about mascara. Which is a plus.

wednesday september 15th

assembly

9.00 a.m. Does Slim go to a special evening class on how to be boring? She was going on about tiny people with small heads or the poor or something. I don't know, who cares? Well obviously someone cares, and maybe I will care again one day, but at the moment all my caringness is used up on myself.

re

10.00 a.m. Despite my tragedy I did cheer up a bit in RE. Honestly, Miss Wilson lives in the land of the very mad. Where does she get her stockings from? It can't be a normal shop. It must be a circus shop. They are all thick and wrinkly like an elephant has been wearing them. Perhaps they are Slim's cast-offs?

Rosie sent me a note: *Dear Gee, Ask Miss Wilson if God has a penis.*

Even in my tragedy it made me laugh and Miss Wilson said, "Georgia, what is funny? Perhaps you could share the joke with us all."

"Er . . . well. I was just wondering if God had . . ."

Rosie looked at me in amazement.

Miss Wilson was encouraging me in my religious curiosity. "You were wondering if God had . . . ?"

"Yes, if God had a . . . beardy thing?"

Miss Wilson unfortunately did not realise how very funny I was being. She went on and on about the fact that he wasn't really a bloke with a beard in the sky but more of a spiritual entity. She didn't need to tell me that there is no big bloke in the sky. I know that. I've tried often enough to speak to him and get stuff. Hopeless. That is why if she had bothered to ask me I would have told her that I have become a zen Buddhist.

1.15 p.m. What is it with Elvis? Jas and me were innocently moaning by the back of the

Science block and he comes along. Ears flapping in the wind. Raving on and on.

"What are you two up to?"

I said, "Nothing."

"Don't give me nothing. I know you two. You've probably been messing about in my hut."

What is the matter with him? And why does he always wear a flat hat? I wonder if his head is flat underneath it? Probably. As we walked away I said to Jas, "He's obsessed with us going in his hut. He's ALWAYS saying we go in his hut. He goes on and on about it, like a budgie. Why does he go on and on about it?"

Jas was just walking along. I said, "Why? On and on and on about us going in his poxy hut. Why us? Why keep accusing us of going in his hut? Why?"

Jas said, "Because we go in his hut."

"So?"

5.00 p.m. Jas's room at her house. Jas has just popped down to the kitchen to make me some nutritious snack (Pop-Tarts) to cheer me up. I'm just not interested in anything, though.

5.03 p.m. God her room is tidy. It's pathetically tidy. All her cuddly toys are neatly lined up in size order on her bed. I'm going to mix them up for an hilarious laugh. Ho hum, pig's bum. She's even got a box with "letters" written on it. I wonder if she's got a drawer that says "enormous pants" on it. There are some letters in the box. Probably private ones. It says PRIVATE on the top of them. Probably private, then. Probably letters that Tom has written to Jas. Very personal and private, I'd better put them away.

5.16 p.m. She calls him HUNKY!!!! That is hilariously crap!! *Absolutemento pathetico!!!* HUNKY!!! Tom!!! Hahahahahaha.

5.18 p.m. He calls her Po!!! Like in the *Teletubbies*. Good grief, that is sad.

5.19 p.m. Po, for heaven's sake.

5.20 p.m. My lips are sealed *vis-à-vis* Hunky and Po.

5.21 p.m. Even though it is very very funny I must never mention Hunky or Po.

5.23 p.m. Jas comes back in. I say, "How is Hunky?"

my bedroom

7.00 p.m. Jas is not speaking to me because I happened to find some personal letters of hers . . . She's so touchy.

10.30 p.m. And unreasonable.

248

8.20 a.m. On the way to school. When I got to our usual meeting place Jas had already set off, walking really fast ahead of me. I yelled, "Hang on a minute, Po!!" But she ignored me.

Honestly, people really take themselves seriously when they have got a so-called boyfriend.

In a sort of a way it was very funny walking behind Jas. She walked really fast for about five minutes but she is not in tiptop physical condition. In fact, the only exercise she gets is lifting Pop-Tarts and putting them in her mouth. Anyway, she got tired and had to slow down so then I could catch her up. I walked about half a metre behind her: it was annoying her quite a lot but she couldn't say anything as she is not speaking to me.

By the time I got to the school gates I was walking about ten centimetres behind her. Her beret was practically sticking up my nose.

She tried to escape me in assembly by standing next to Rosie but I squeezed in between them and looked at her with my face really near hers. She was all red and furious. Even her ears were red. Tee hee.

11.00 a.m. Followed Jas into the loos. I went into the next cubicle to her and talked to her through the walls.

"Jas, I love you."

"What are you doing? You're being stupid!"

"No. YOU'RE being stupid, Po."

"It was really mean of you to read my private letters."

"They were only from Hunky."

"You shouldn't read people's private things."

"How would I know anything if I didn't?"

There was a bit of a silence from the other side of the wall. Then she said, "What do you mean?"

I went on reasonably, "I wouldn't even know you were called Po if I hadn't read the letters."

She was on the edge of bamboozlement. "Yeah, but that's not the point . . . I . . ."

"You shouldn't have secrets from your very best pal."

"YOU have secrets."

"I don't – I even told you about my sticky-out nipples."

"Well, Tom says they stuck out because it was cold."

I couldn't believe it. The bell went for the end of break and I heard Jas flush the loo and go out. I rushed out of my loo and set off down the corridor, following her. "You told Tom . . . about my sticky-out nipples???"

I couldn't believe it. My nipples had been made a public mockery of a sham . . . I was so incensed I barely noticed Wet Lindsay talking to some unlucky Fourth Former. Although I did notice that she looked like an owl in a school uniform.

I was hissing at Jas, "You discussed my nipples with Hunky . . . I can't believe it!!!"

Then from behind me I heard Wet Lindsay's voice, "Georgia, your skirt is tucked up in your knickers . . . I don't think it sets a very good example to the younger girls."

Then she went off, sniggering in a pathetic sniggering owl sort of way.

5.00 p.m. In the bath. That is it. I am on the warpath. I am now a loner. I have no

250

friends. My so-called best friend only likes stupid Hunky and discusses my private body parts with him. And then he probably goes and discusses it with his older brother. And he and the SG have a good laugh.

5.15 p.m. Angus is sitting on the side of the bath. He is drinking the water even though it has got bubble bath in it. His whiskers are all soapy.

5.20 p.m. Now Libby has wandered in. Come in, everybody, why don't you? I'm only having a bath. Naked. I'm surprised Mr and Mrs Next Door don't pop in for a bit of a look.

I said to Libby, "Libby don't push Angus like that, he'll . . ."

5.21 p.m. Angus is soaking and furious. When I fished him out of the bath he savaged my hand. Libby couldn't stop laughing. What a life.

6.00 p.m. Jas phoned. I said, "What do you want, nipple discusser?"

She said, "Look, can't we call it quits? I won't mention the Hunky business again if you forget about the nip nips incident."

I didn't want to give in because I was in too bad a mood so I just went, "Huh."

But then I was all agog attention-wise because she said, "Tom phoned and told me The Stiff Dylans are doing a gig at the Crazy Coconut club a week Wednesday. AND WHAT'S MORE Dave the Laugh is going to be there. AND WHAT'S MORE my mum is staying at my aunt's in Manchester."

6.02 p.m. Thinking.

6.05 p.m. Thinking and eating cornflakes. Hmmm.

6.07 p.m. Obviously this is it!!! This is my chance to implement the elastic band theory. I have to go to The Stiff Dylans gig and get off with Dave the Laugh. In front of the SG. This will serve the twofold purpose of maturiosity (being at a nightclub) and glaciosity (getting off with another boy). SG will be very jealous. He will want to come pinging back (the elastic band theory).

11.00 p.m. I must start softening Mum up so that she will not be suspicious when I say I am staying at Jas's on Wednesday night.

saturday september 18th

weekend morning

10.00 a.m. Mum nearly dropped Libby when I said, "Do you want me to get anything for you while I am in town this afternoon?"

She said, "Sorry, love, I thought for a moment you offered to do something for me. What did you really say?"

Even though I was irritated by her I kept a lovely smile on my face. "Oh Mutti . . . as if I never do anything for you!"

She said suspiciously, "Why are you smiling like that? What

have you got on that is mine? If you have borrowed my gold necklace I'll go mad."

I snapped then. "Look, what is the matter with you? How can I ever be a nice person if you are so suspicious all the time? What are you, a mother or a police dog? Do you want to do a body search before I go out? Honestly!!!"

Then I remembered my Operation Elastic Band just in the knickers of time. I said nicely, "I just thought you might want me to bring something back for you. I know how busy you are, that's all."

In the end I think I convinced her, which is a bit of a drag as now I've got to lumber home with waterproof panties for Libbs. Hey ho. What sacrifices I make for the SG. I've almost forgotten what he looks like.

10.05 a.m. I've remembered what he looks like. Yum yum yum.

1.00 p.m. Miss Selfridge changing-room. I tried on a size twelve T-shirt and I couldn't get it on. Jas (very loudly) said, "I think your breasts are definitely getting bigger, you know."

This was in the packed communal changing-room and everyone looked round.

I said, "Er . . . Jas . . . I think there is someone in Australia who might not have heard you properly . . ."

Rosie and Ellen met us in Luigis coffee bar. I told them about The Stiff Dylans gig and my plan *vis-à-vis* Dave the Laugh. Rosie was eating the foam from her coffee with a spoon and slurping. So was Ellen. It was stereo foam slurping. After ten years had gone by Rosie said, with the spoon in her mouth which was very unattractive but I didn't say . . . anyway, she said, "So you're going to the gig so that you can get off with Dave the Laugh and that will make the SG into an elastic band?"

How difficult can life be? Very, very difficult, that's how. I said patiently (well, at least without hitting her), "Yes, yes, thrice yes!!!"

More slurping. She was obviously thinking about my master-plan (or mistressplan actually, as I had thought of it and I am a girlie). Then she said, "Can I borrow your brown leather boots?"

4.00 p.m. Lugged home Libby's waterproof nick-nacks. All quiet on the home front when I got in. Where was everyone?

9.30 p.m. Early to bed, early to rise, makes a . . . whatsit.

10.00 p.m. I may wear some false eyelashes for the gig. I must be careful though, last time I tried them the glue tube burst and I couldn't get my eyes apart for twenty minutes.

tuesday september 21st

4.15 p.m. Boring day apart from when Wet Lindsay got her bag caught on her foot and fell up the Science block stairs.

11.00 p.m. Libby in bed with me. I don't know why she can't sleep the right way up, her feet keep poking me in the eye.

11.10 p.m. I wonder what Dave the Laugh looks like.

friday september 24th

morning break

11.00 a.m. Ellen told me that her brother and his mates go out on "cat patrol".

I said, "Do they really like cats, then?"

She said, "No, him and his mates are the cat patrol and they go out looking for birds . . . you know, chicks . . . girls."

Good Lord.

lunch-time

12.30 p.m. Ellen says that her brother also calls breasts "nunga-nungas".

I know I shouldn't have asked but somehow I just had to.

Ellen said, "Well, he says that if you get hold of a breast and pull it out and then let it go . . . it goes nunga-nunga-nunga!"

I may be forced to become either a celibate or a lesbian.

afternoon break

2.30 p.m. Me and Ellen were sitting in the loos with our feet up against the back of the doors, so that the Hitler Youth (prefects) wouldn't know we were in there and send us into the torrential rain. The Hitler Youth call it a "slight shower". They'd still say that if the First Years were being swept to their deaths by tidal waves. Or if Elvis's hut was bobbing along with a sail up, or . . . anyway, who cares what they say?

I said to Ellen through the cubicle wall, "Is your brother a bit on the mad side?"

I could hear her crunching her crisps. She thought about it. "No, he's quite a laugh, really. He calls going to the loo 'going to the piddly diddly department'."

I could hear her through the wall, laughing and choking. I just sat there staring at the loo door. After a bit she controlled herself and said, "If he's going to the loo to do number twos he says, 'I'm just off to the poo parlour division.'" And she was off, wheezing and choking again. *Sacré bleu*. I am surrounded by *les idiots*.

3.30 p.m. If it's cold, Ellen's hilarious brother says it is "nippy noodles".

4.15 p.m. Walked home. Thinking about the difference between girls and boys. For instance, when girls walk home we put on lippy and make-up. We chat. Sometimes we pretend to be hunchbacks. But that is it. Perfectly normal behaviour. When the Foxwood boys come out they hit each other, trip one another up and stuff leaves or caps down each other's trousers. Ellen told me that sometimes her brother sets fire to his farts.

On the way to my house we passed through the park. There is a park Elvis. He is supposed to be the park-keeper but mainly he prods at things with a pointy stick. Oh and his second job is to yell, "I can see you!" at innocent snoggers in bushes.

We hung around on the swings for a bit just to annoy Park Elvis. Rosie (who by the way, since the flaming fringe incident is an ex-smoker) said she had made it up with Sven her Swedish boyfriend. She fell out with him because he said to her parents, "Thank you for your daughter, she is, how you say? *Jah* . . . a great SNOG."

I said, "How can you tell he's sorry? No one can usually understand a word he says."

And she said, "He knitted me a nose warmer."

It's really not worth asking.

Ellen said, "What about Dave the Laugh?"

I said, "What about him?"

"Well, do you really fancy him?"

"I don't know. I don't know what he looks like."

"Well, what is the point, then?"

"Well, he's like . . . erm . . . a red herring. In my elastic band strategy."

They all looked at me. It was no use them all looking at me like I know what I am talking about. I'll be the last one to know what I am talking about, believe me.

4.30 p.m. My so-called private bedroom.

Angus was in my bed. I suspect not alone. I daren't lift the cover in case it's like in that film where there was a chopped off horse's head in the bed.

6.07 p.m. Lying on the floor on cushions but at least Angus is nice and comfy. In Mum's *Cosmo* it says, "Buddhism is the new optimism."

Okey-dokey. That's what I'm going to do. Be a cheery Buddhist. Om hahaha om.

sports

2.50 p.m. It's windy and rainy. Naturally these two facts mean that Miss Stamp our games mistress (who is definitely Hitler reincarnated in a gym skirt . . . she even has the little black moustache) . . . Anyway, these two facts mean that Adolfa has decided that the best thing we can do is . . . play hockey outside!!! I'd write to the newspapers to complain but I'll probably drown out on the hockey pitch.

in bed

9.30 p.m. Brrr. If I have pneumonia and die and never get to number ten on the snogging table I'll blame Adolfa. Just because she doesn't have a life. Even now I'm only just getting feeling back in my bottom.

10.30 p.m. When Mum said goodnight I took my opportunity and said, casually, "Mum, can I go and stay round at Jas's on Wednesday night? Her mum says it's OK if it's OK with you. We're doing a Science project together . . . I mean me and Jas not me and Jas's mother – that would be stupid."

(Shut up, shut up now. Leave it! Don't babble on, she'll get suspicious and you will say something really stupid.)

Mum said, "You don't usually do your homework, Gee. This is a bit of a change of heart."

"Hahahaha – yeah right . . . I . . ." (Careful, careful, don't say anything stupid.) ". . . I . . . thought I might be a scientist."

(Too late, she's bound to rumble me now!)

"A scientist – not a backing singer, then?"

"No."

"Hmmm."

"So can I?"

"Oh yes, I suppose so. Night-night."

Result!!!!!! Yessss!!!!

wednesday september 29th

operation elastic band
kitchen

8.00 a.m. I grabbed a piece of toast and mumbled, "I'm off now, see you tomorrow night."

Mum didn't even look up from trying to fasten Libby into her dungarees. Libby had her porridge bowl on her head. Mum said, "OK, love, bye. Kiss your sister bye-bye."

I said, "Pass." I had kissed Libby before when she had been eating porridge and I didn't want the experience again. I blew her a kiss, "Byeeeeee!"

Phew. Now then, quickly out of the door. Victory!!!!! I've packed all my clubwear and make-up and so on in my rucky. Here we go with Operation Elastic Band.

Just at the end of the path when Mum came out of the house, shouting, "Georgia, what do you mean, 'See you tomorrow night'?"

OhmyGodohmyGodohmyGod.

I laughed casually (sounding a bit like a casual hyena). "Oh I knew you would forget, I'm staying at Jas's tonight – remember?"

She looked blank.

Inwardly I was shouting, "LET ME GO!! SHUT UP, SHUT UP!! I MUST HAVE THE SEX GOD. LET ME GO. LET ME GO. YOU HAVE HAD YOUR LIFE!!!!" Outwardly I said, "Mum, I have to go, I'll be late – see you tomorrow."

Yessss!!! I am cool as *le* cucumber. Or possibly *le* ice cube.

3.50 p.m. Last bell. Jas and I ran down the hill. Only five hours to get ready.

I said to Jas as we ran, "Mutti was really suspicious this morning when I reminded her I was staying at your house. It was like she didn't believe me. You know, like I am bound to be lying."

"You are lying."

"Oh picky, picky, Jas."

jas's house

5.00 p.m. A nourishing meal to set us up for the evening: oven chips, mayonnaise and two fruit Pop-Tarts (for essential vitamin C). In Jas's room we put on some groovy music and started getting ready. Jas had a bit of a moony attack when she looked at Tom's photo by her bed. She started sighing and saying, "I just can't seem to get in the mood to go out."

I pointed at her with my mascara brush. "Jas, snap out of it, you know that Hunky would want you to go out. He phoned you up to tell you about it. He wouldn't want you moping about; he wouldn't want you to let your mates down by stay-ing in. He wouldn't want to come home and find out that your mate had stabbed you with a mascara brush."

Jas was a bit huffy, but she got my nub. As she was putting her hair up she said, "What will you do with Dave the Laugh when you have got off with him?"

"How do you mean?"

I was stalling for time. I'd only really thought as far as getting my make-up on. The rest of it was a bit of a haze of a dream.

"Well, will you be . . . like his girlfriend then? Will you snog him?"

Luckily the phone rang. We both answered it. It was Rosie. She and Sven were calling from a phone box.

"We just rang to say we've made up this great new dance; it's called 'the phone box'."

She played a radio down the phone and in the background I could hear a lot of grunting and shuffling and Sven going, "Oh *jah* oh *jah*, hit it, lads!" or something in Swedish or whatever it is he speaks. Gibberish, normally. Not English, anyway. Then there was a bit of what sounded like tap-dancing. Rosie came back on the phone all breathless. "Brilliant, eh? See you in the next world . . . don't be late!!" And she slammed the phone down.

9.15 p.m. Left the house to catch the bus down town to the Crazy Coconut. I had so much make-up on I could hardly move my face, which is a plus really because it meant I wouldn't be tempted to go for full-on smiling. I was a vision in black leather. Prayed to God Mutti didn't go through her wardrobe before I could sneak things back in.

When the bus arrived and we got on I couldn't believe it. The driver was Mobile Elvis!! Sadly he remembered us and said "*Bonsoir*". And charged us full fare.

crazy coconut

Rosie and Sven turned up. Sven was wearing silver flares. Good Lord. When he saw us he started twisting his hips, saying, "Jah, groovy. Let's go, babies!!!"

The whole queue was looking.

I said to Rosie, "Does Sven always have to be so Svenish?"

Then the van with The Stiff Dylans in it arrived. Robbie got out. Oh bum, all my glaciosity turned to jelliosity.

He saw us and said, "Hi."

I went, "Nung." (I don't know what "nung" means, it just came out.)

The queue started to move and he sort of looked at me for what seemed ages, then he said, "Don't get into any trouble."

I was so mad. How dare he tell me not to get into any trouble? Now he had said that I was going to get into LOADS of trouble just to show him.

I'd show him how much maturiosity I had. At least I would if I managed to get in past the bouncers without them saying I was under-age. I said quietly to Rosie and Jas and Sven, "Be really cool."

That's when Sven lifted me up under one of his huge Swedish type arms and shouted at the bouncers, "Gut evening, I have the bird in the hand and one in the bushes, thank you!" and strode in.

I don't know whether they let us in because we looked mature or whether they were so amazed by Sven they didn't notice us.

Anyway, Operation Elastic Band was underway.

Us girls went to the loos and did some emergency make-up repair work. It was quite dark and sort of red lightish in the loos. I was just thinking we looked like groovy chicks around town when the Bummer Twins walked in. I say walked but they waddled. Jackie was wearing a dress that was SO tight. Not a wise choice for a girl who is not small in the bottom department. She is so common. They were both smoking fags (*quelle surprise*). Jackie said, "Oh look, they must be having a sort of crèche here while the grown-ups are clubbing."

She went off into the loo. I could hear her weeing. It sounded like a carthorse. Alison was looking down her nose at us. I'm surprised she could see anything past the huge spot that was on it. She looked like she'd got two noses.

The club was amazing. It had loads of flights of stairs all leading down to a big dance floor, and a stage at one end. You had to go down the stairs from the loos to get to the dance floor. I hoped that no one could see up my skirt because I couldn't remember what knickers I had on. Jas would be all right with her biggest knickers known to humanity.

There were flashing lights and mirror balls and laser beams. The music was really loud and rocking. Rosie and Sven did their phone box dance. Sven was yelling "Woop!" and "Hit it, lads!" They had loads of space to dance in because nobody wants to be flattened by a huge bloke in silver trousers.

Jas shouted in my earlug, "There's a gang of Tom's mates by the bar – can you see them? Over there. Dave the Laugh is probably one of them."

Jools said, "Yeah, but which one? There's ten of them to choose from."

I said, "Is anyone laughing?"

Jools looked at me. "Why?"

"Well, if he's called Dave the Laugh everyone will be laughing around him."

We looked across at the lads who were mostly looking around the room. Then I had another thought. "But what if he is called Dave the Laugh because HE laughs all the time?"

We looked again; now they were all laughing.

Jas for once in her life went all decisive and sensible (it was a bit scary, actually). She said, "I recognise one of them, he's called Rollo, he's been round to Tom's house. I could ask him who Dave the Laugh is."

I said, "Yeah, OK, but be really cool, Jas. Just find out which one is Dave the Laugh so we can look at him. But don't mention anything about anything."

Jas said, "I am not a fool, you know."

I didn't know that, actually.

Jas went over to the lads and I could see her going chat, chat, nod, nod, nod, wiggle, wiggle, wiggle, flickey fringe, flickey fringe . . . (Why does she do that? It is so annoying.)

I was acting really cool, doing a half smile and sort of nodding along to the music. Sipping my drink, waving at people, even ones I didn't know. Then Jas came back. She was all breathless. She POINTED really obviously at a dark-haired boy in black combats. "That's him!"

Naturally he saw her pointing at him and he shrugged his shoulders like he was asking a question. Jas then turned to me and POINTED again . . . AT ME, and nodded like one of those nodding dogs.

I couldn't believe it. It was unbelievable, that's why. My face was like a frozen fish-finger. All rigid and pale. (But obviously not with breadcrumbs on it.)

I said out of the corner of my mouth, "Jas, I'm going to kill you. What in the name of your huge knickers have you said?"

Jas said huffily, "I just said, 'Who is Dave the Laugh?' and Rollo said, 'This is Dave the Laugh,' and Dave the Laugh said, 'Why?' and I just said, 'Because my mate Georgia really rates you'."

I was going to kill her and then eat her.

Out of the corner of my mouth – because Dave the Laugh was still looking – I said, "Jas! You told him I FANCIED him? I cannot believe it."

Jas said, "Well I think he's quite cute. If I didn't have Hunky I would . . ."

Just then SG walked by carrying his guitar. On his way to the stage to do the first set. He smiled as he passed. Even though in my heart I wanted to leap into his arms like a seal I ignored him. I looked through him as if he was just a floating guitar in midair.

midnight The Stiff Dylans were playing and I was dancing with Rosie and Sven and Jas. Jools and Ellen had gone off with some of Tom's mates. They were all quite fit-looking boys, actually, but . . . there is only one Sex God on the planet. SG looked sooooo cool; it's not fair that he is so good-looking. All the girls were looking at him and dancing in front of him. They had no style. Every time he came off-stage there would be some girl talking to him. I tried not to look but I couldn't help it. What if he got off with someone in front of me? How could I bear it? There was a moment when our eyes met and he smiled. Ooohh, Blimey O'Reilly's trousers, he'd got everything . . . back, front, hair, teeth . . . I could feel my snogging muscles all puckering up but I thought NO! Think elastic band.

265

I made Jas go to the loos with me for a bit of a break from the tension. The Bummer Twins were still in there. I could hear them talking from one of the cubicles and a spiral of smoke coming under the loo door. Do they live in the lavatories? I said to Jas, "Perhaps the BUM-mer Twins have trouble in the poo parlour department!!" and we both got the hysterical heebie-jeebies. I had to hit Jas on the back to stop her choking to death. And we had to reapply mascara twice.

On our way back to the dance floor Dave the Laugh stopped me!! He said, "Hi."

I said, "Oh hi." (Brilliant.) And I half smiled, remembering to keep my nose sucked in.

He said, "Are you Georgia?"

1.00 a.m. Dave the Laugh is actually nice-looking in a sub SG way . . . and er . . . quite a good laugh.

2.00 a.m. Dave the Laugh has been dancing with me a lot. He's a cool dancer. He even did a bit of mad dancing with Sven. I don't think he expected Sven to pick him up and kiss him on both cheeks, but he took it well. We all left the club together. I saw SG looking over at us as he cleared up his gear. There was some drippy blonde hanging about wanting his autograph or something (oh yeah! Emphasis on the *something*). Time for a display of maturiosity and glaciosity. Dave the L. said, "Georgia, are you walking to the night bus stop?"

I made sure that SG was looking then I laughed like a loon on loon tablets. "Hahahahaha, the night bus! You make me die, Dave, you're such a laugh!!!!"

Dave looked a bit on the amazed side. He probably didn't think the night bus was his biggest joke. Me and Jas and Dave walked along. When we got to the bus stop there was a bit of an awkward pause. Jas was standing really close by like a goosegog. How was my plan *vis-à-vis* getting Dave the L. to go out with me going to happen if she just hung about like a goosegog? I kept raising my eyebrows at her but she said, "Have you got something in your eye? Let's have a look."

As Mrs Big But Stupid Knickers was prodding about at my eye Dave's bus came. He gave me a peck on the cheek and said, "Well, this is my bus. It was a great night; maybe see you later." He looked me in the eyes for a second, winked and then got on the bus.

As Mrs Loonyknickers Goosegoghead (Jas) and I walked home I was all confused.

"Does Dave the Laugh like me or not? He winked at me – what does that mean? SG definitely noticed us leaving, didn't he? And he saw me really laughing at what Dave the Laugh was saying."

Jas said, "That's when I thought Dave the Laugh might have gone off you, because he said, 'Are you catching the night bus?' and you nearly split your tights in half laughing. Your face went all weird and your nose sort of spread all over your . . ."

"Jas."

"What?"

"Shut up."

"Well, I was just saying."

"Well don't."

"Well I won't, then."

"Well don't."

"I won't."

"Well don't."

There was a bit of welcome silence for a bit then Jas said, "I won't."

She is so INCREDIBLY annoying.

3.00 a.m. And she takes up loads of room in bed. I had to make a sort of barrier out of her cuddly toys to put down the middle of the bed. To keep her on her own side.

What does Dave the Laugh mean, "See you later"?

3.30 a.m. Do I want to see him later even if he does mean "See you later"?

4.00 a.m. If the Sex God was really jealous he would ring me up tomorrow and try to get me back.

Or maybe he is not fully extended elastic band-wise.

thursday september 30th

3.00 p.m. I fell asleep in German. Herr Kamyer is a very soothing teacher. I drifted off when he started telling some story about Gretchen and a dove in a dovecote. (Don't even ask, as I have mentioned before, the Germans are a mystery to me since I learned about the Heimlich manoeuvre.)

4.30 p.m. On the way home we practised our new grasp of the German language.

I said to Jas, "What is 'a dove in a dovecote' in the German type language?"

Jas said, "Er . . . 'ein Duff in ein Duffcot,' I think."

"Ach gut . . . so . . . Jas . . . Du bist ein Duff in Duffcot nicht wahr?"

Jas said, "Nein, ich nicht ein Duff in Duffcot."

I said, "Jah."

Jas said, "You have just said I am a dove in a dovecote."

"You are."

"You're bonkers."

I think I might be hysterical.

4.45 p.m. So tired when I got in that I thought I would just have a little snooze.

5.00 p.m. "Ginger, ginger, me home!!!"

Oh Lord, it was my dearly beloved sister. I heard her clattering up the stairs. Then a bit of deep breathing, and bumping. "Here we are, Ginger."

Then she and Angus got in bed with me. And they weren't alone. There was scuba-diving Barbie and Charlie Horse. And something really cold and slimy.

I shot up in bed and looked down at her. "Libbs, what is that?"

She gave me her idea of a lovely smile, which in her case is terrifying. She scrunches up her nose and sticks her teeth out. I don't know why she thinks that is natural. She said, "It's nice."

I looked under the covers. "What is? Oh God."

Mum called up, "Libbs, where has your jelly rabbit gone?"

269

october

giganticus pantibus

monday october 4th

9.30 a.m. No news from either SG or Dave the so-called Laugh.

geoggers

10.00 a.m. Brrr. It's only October and it's like Greenland here. Well, apart from the ice floes and Eskimos and polar bears. It is, as Ellen's amusing brother would say, very "nippy noodles" today. I didn't mean ever to start saying things like that, but it is really catching. What's more, just because I said it all the gang is saying it. It's like brain measles. In Geoggers Rosie put up her hand and said to Mrs Franks (who is not what you would call "fun"), "Mrs Franks, could I just pop to the piddly diddly department, please?"

Mrs Franks said, really frostily, "What is the piddly diddly department, Rosemary?"

And Rosie said, "Well it's not the poo parlour division."

We all laughed like stuffed animals. Mrs Franks didn't. In fact she said, "Grow up, Rosemary Barnes."

She let Rosie go though, and started to explain some-

270

thing indescribably boring about the wheat belt. Behind her Rosie started lolloping out of the door like an orang-utan. She was trailing her arms on the floor. It made me laugh A LOT. But silently, as no one really wants to do two hours' detention.

break

11.00 a.m. They are a bunch of sadists here. We get forced to go out into sub-Antarctic conditions. Even Elvis Attwood won't come out of his hut and he is half human, half walrus. Meanwhile the so-called prefects and staff get to hang around in the warm. Wet Lindsay, the Owlie one, said to me, "If you wore skirts that were a bit longer you might not be so chilly."

I said to Jas, "Did you hear a sort of hooting noise, Jas?"

Me and Jas sheltered out of the icy winds behind a wall but we were still cold, so we had an idea. We thought we would button our two coats together to make a kind of big sleeping bag. We fastened the buttons of Jas's coat into the buttonholes of mine. Then we buttoned the buttons of my coat into Jas's buttonholes. With us in the middle. All nice and snug. It did make it very difficult to walk and unfortunately we had buttoned ourselves up a bit far away from our bags. Our bags with our nutritious snacks in them (Mars Bars and cheesy snacks). We tried synchronised shuffling to get to them but Jas tripped and we fell over. We were laughing, but not for long, because the Bummer Twins arrived.

Jackie looked down at us all tied together in our coats and said, "Look, Ali, the little girls are playing a little game. Let's join in."

271

And then they sat on us.

And they are not small girls.

Alison said, "Fancy a fag, Jackie?"

We heard them light up. We were just trapped there.

Then Jackie said, "Oooh look, someone has left some cheesy snacks for us. Fancy one, Ali?"

Me and Jas were the Bummer Twins' armchair.

my bedroom

5.30 p.m. No phonecalls.

Mutti came in.

I said, "Oh come in, Mum, the door is only closed for privacy." I said it in a meaningful way but she didn't know what I meant. She was all pink.

"Dad phoned again; he sends his love, he's really looking forward to seeing you. He's got you a present."

I said, "Oh goodie, what is it? Sheepskin shorts?"

She started that tutting thing.

I don't think she has asked me one thing about myself for about four centuries. What is the point of procrastinating . . . no I don't mean that, what do I mean? Oh yeah, procreating . . . What is the point of having children if you are not going to take any notice of them? You might as well get a hamster and ignore that.

5.35 p.m. Oh yippee.

This is my gorgeous life:

1 I haven't been kissed for a month; my snogging skills will be gone soon.

2 I have a HUGE nose that means I have to live for ever in the Ugly Home. Address:

  Georgia Nicolson

  Ugly Home

  Ugly Kingdom

  Ugly Universe

3 My Red Herring plan has failed.

4 I am the Bummer Twins' armchair.

6.00 p.m. Mum called up, "I'm just taking Libbs to the doctor's; she needs her ears cleaned out."

Oh please. Save me from that thought.

6.30 p.m. Phone rang. If it's Po moaning on about Hunky I'll go BERSERK!!

6.45 p.m. I'm seeing Dave in the swing park after school on Friday. He got my phone number from Tom through Jas! Good grief. The Red Herring has landed. I'm quite excited, I think.

Am I?

He said it would be "groovy" to see me again.

He also said he hoped it wouldn't be too nippy noodles in the park. He made me laugh.

I am still only using him as a red herring, though.

8.00 p.m. Mum came back with Libby. I was busily trying to save myself from starving to death by eating cornflakes.

I said, "The doctor didn't find my fishnet tights in Libby's lugholes, did he?"

Mum seemed to be in even more of a coma than normal. She said, "I borrowed them for salsa dancing with Uncle Eddie."

Charming. I'll have to boil them before I wear them again.

Mum said, "They've got a new doctor at the surgery."

Silence.

"He's very good."

Silence.

"He was so nice to Libby – even when she shouted down his stethoscope."

What is she going on about?

"He looked a bit like George Clooney."

9.40 p.m. When I went up to bed she kissed me and said, "You haven't had your tetanus injection renewed, have you?"

What is she talking about?

tuesday october 5th

10.30 a.m. Rosie said she might go across to Sweden land with Sven in the Chrimbo hols. I said, "Are you sure? You're only fourteen and you've got your whole life ahead of you. Are you sure you want to go to the other side of the world with Sven?"

She said, "What?"

I said, "Going to the other side of the world with Sven – is it a good idea?"

She said, "You don't know where Sweden is, do you?"

"Don't be stupid."

And she said, "Where is it, then?"

I looked at her. Honestly. As if I don't know where Sweden

274

is. I said, "It's up at the top."

"Top of what?"

"The map."

And she went, "Hahahahahahahaha."

I think she must be a bit hysterical.

I may forgive her. Because so am I.

maths

10.35 a.m. Oh good grief, welcome back to the land of the crap. The Bummer Twins sent round a note: *Meet in the Fourth Year classroom at 12.30 today. Everyone comes, and that means you, Georgia Nicolson and your lesbian mates.*

I wrote a note to Jas and the others.

> *Dear Fab Gang,*
> *This is it. Things have got sheer desperadoes. We have to put our feet down with firm hands. I for one am no longer prepared to be the Bummer Twins' armchair!!! Meet in the Science block at 12.15. Or be square.*
> *Gee-gee*
> *xxxxxxxx*

12.32 p.m. Hiding from the Bummer Twins in the Science block loos. Jas, Jules, Rosie, Ellen, Patty, Sarah, Mabs and me . . . all in one cubicle. We have to keep our feet off the floor so that no one will know we are in here. It's hard to keep your balance when there are eight of you standing on one loo seat.

Alert, alert!!! Two people came into the loos. I recognised their voices. It was Wet Lindsay and one of her mates, Dismal Sandra.

Wet Lindsay said, "Honestly, some of the younger girls are so dim. One of them came to see me and asked me if she could get pregnant from sitting on a boy's knee."

Jas mouthed at me, "Can you?" Which I thought was quite funny but I couldn't laugh otherwise we would end up quite literally down the pan.

I wanted to look over the top of the cubicle so that Owlie would know I had seen her in the loo. Seen her removing her thong from her bum-oley!!!

Then Owlie's weedy mate Dismal Sandra said, "What is happening with Robbie?"

I was full-on, attention-wise.

Wet Lindsay said, "Well he says he doesn't want to get serious because of college and the band and everything."

I nearly yelled out, "It's not that, Owlie, it is because he DOESN'T like you . . ."

Dismal Sandra said, "So what will you do, then?"

Lindsay said, "Oh, I've got my ways, I'll charm him back in the end. He's not seeing anyone else, he says. I expect he's still upset about us splitting up."

Oh yeah, in your dreams, Owlie.

physics

1.30 p.m. Herr Kamyer was twitching about in his sad suit. It's sort of tight round the neck and short round the ankles. Do normal people wear tartan socks? Anyway, he was adjusting his spectacles and saying, "So

276

zen, girls, ve haf the interesting question about ze physical world. Ver question is [twitch twitch], vich comes first . . . ze chicken or ze eggs?"

No one knows what he is talking about so we just carried on writing notes to each other or making shopping lists. Ellen was actually painting her toenails. You would think that Herr Kamyer would notice that she had her head underneath the desk, but he didn't seem to.

He really does jerk around. He sort of blinks his eyes and screws up his nose and flings his head round all at once. Someone said it was because he has had malaria. Once when he was walking across the playground and it was icy he had such a spasm that he slipped and crashed into the bike shed. Elvis had to restack sixty bikes. He grumbled for about forty years. You would think Elvis would have more sympathy for the afflicted. As he is so afflicted himself.

Suddenly about ten girls started sneezing really violently. *Really* violently, like their heads were going to blow off. Their eyes were streaming and they were stumbling for the door. Jackie Bummer managed to say, "Oh we must be . . . ATISHOO . . . ATISHOO . . . allergic to something in the Science lab, Herr Kamyer. ATISHOO!"

They all got sent home in the end.

I found out later what the Bummer Twins' meeting was about. They had made everyone at the meeting put bath crystals up their noses in the middle of Physics, and that had brought on the sneezing attacks. All because the Bummers wanted to go to some club in Manchester, and needed to be home early.

Good Lord. Three days to my date with the Herring.

5.00 p.m. Jas made me go home with her. She is planning a special celebration for when Tom gets home.

"It will be one year since we first met on the day he gets back!"

I just looked at her.

"And look!" Before I could stop her, she pulled up her skirt and pulled down her voluminous pants to show me her stupid heart tattoo. "I've been washing round it!"

She went on and on about what she was planning to do. Even though I found some matchsticks and put them over my eyelids so it looked like they were holding my eyes open. Eventually I said, "Look, why don't you do a nice vegetable display for him?"

midnight Honestly, Jas is so mad and touchy. And violent.

wednesday october 6th

4.30 p.m. After swimming today Miss Stamp came into the showers to make sure we all went in. She says we pretend to have a shower and that we are unhygienic. That is why she must supervise us. But really it is because she is a lesbian.

She watched a few of us go through (twirling her moustache). She shouted, "Come on, you silly ninnies, get in and get out!"

I dashed in in the nuddy-pants and was soaping myself like a maniac in order to get out quickly because Miss Stamp is a lesbian and might . . . well might . . . er . . . look at me. As if that wasn't bad enough I had to be on even more red alert because Nauseating P. Green lumbered into the shower next to me. What if she accidentally touched me? It's a sodding nightmare this place, like the Village of the Damned. If P. Green fell against me I would be smickled with Nauseatingness. She really is a most unfortunate shape. What on earth does she eat? All the pies, that is for sure. In fact, she has no shape, you can only tell which way up she is because of her glasses.

As I was getting dried I did feel a bit sorry for her because the Bummers had hidden her glasses while she was in the shower. She blundered around in the elephantine nuddy-pants, looking for them. The Bummers (who had managed to get out of games by "having the painters in" AGAIN! How many periods can you have in a month?) were singing, "Nellie the elephant packed her bags and said goodbye to the circus." Then the bell went and the Bummers slouched off.

After they'd gone I gave P. Green her silly specs. She would have been in the shower rooms for the rest of her life otherwise. I hope she doesn't think that makes me her mate.

my bedroom

6.00 p.m. No phonecall from SG. I wonder what Wet Lindsay means about using her charm on him? What kind of charm do owls have? Perhaps she will lay him an egg.

OhGodohGod. I'm getting the heebie-jeebies about my Red Herring extravaganza. How do I keep him as a herring without snogging him?

In the *Bliss* letters page there's a letter from a girl called Sandy. She didn't really like a boy and was just using him to

279

get off with someone else. Unfortunately the advice from Agony Jane was not "Carry on and good luck to you". The advice was "You are a really horrible girl, Sandy. You will never have a happy life, you cow." (Well, it didn't exactly say it in those words but that is what the gist and nub was.)

Decided to put the squeaking dolphins on and do some calming yoga. I used to be quite good at doing the sun salute last term until Miss Stamp surprised me in the gym with my bottom sticking up in the air.

Mmmmmm – much much better. All soothing and flowing. Lalalalala. Lift your arms up to worship the sun . . . breathe in . . . hhmmmmmm, then put your arms down to the floor like in "we are not worthy" in football . . . aahhh, breathe out. Much calmer. Then swing to the right and swing to the left.

That's funny . . . if I turned to the right, then the left, a funny noise came out of me. Like a sort of wheezy noise. Could it be the dolphins? I didn't know they did wheezing.

Turned the tape off.

Now then, to the right, to the left. Oh no. Wheeze wheeze. If I went really fast from the right to the left I could hear wheeze wheeze wheeze. Which is not what you want.

It was really quite loud. Wheeze wheeze.

I'd probably caught TB from being made to do swimming in freezing conditions.

Mum came in with a cup of tea for me (without knocking, naturally) and caught me doing my wheezing movements. She said, "Are you dancing?" and I said, "No I'm not, I'm wheezing. I think I may have caught TB. It's not as if I'm in tiptop physical condition, with the kind of diet that we live on."

She said, "Don't be so silly, what is the matter?"

I didn't want her to listen to my wheezing but I had really freaked myself out. I let her listen. Side to side, wheeze wheeze.

She looked worried. (Probably thinking she would be chastised by the local press for child abuse and neglect.) She said, "Look, I think maybe we should pop up to the surgery and see George Cloon– er . . . the doctor. Get your coat."

Before I could protest she grabbed Libby and we were out of the door. As she started the car I said, "Look, Mum, perhaps if I had a warm bath and you made me a nouris-hing stew . . ."

The next thing I knew I was in the doctor's waiting-room. It was full of the elderly mad, all coughing. If I wasn't sick now I was soon going to be.

Libby got up on a table to do a little dance for everyone. It must have been something she had learned at kindergarten. It seemed to be sung to "Pop Goes the Weasel".

Libby sang (loudly and with a lot of actions), "Ha ha pag of trifle atishoo atishoo all fall down." The finale was her throwing up her dress and pulling down her panties.

Mum hadn't expected that bit. Who could? There was a lot of muttering from the very old. One woman said, "Disgusting!" which was a bit rich coming from someone wearing a balaclava.

Eventually we got to see the doc. Mum practically threw herself through the surgery door and I was left dragging Libby because she wanted to do an encore.

Mum said, "Oh, hello, it's us again!" in a really odd girlie voice. When I had got Libby's knickers back on I looked at the doctor. He was quite fit-looking actually, not at all the surly red-faced madman that normally treated us. There was a bit of the young George Clooney about this one.

He smiled (yummm) and said, "Yes, hello again, Connie.

(Connie!) Hello, Libby." Libby gave him one of her very mad smiles.

Then he looked at me. I gave him my attractive half smile. (Curved lips but no teeth, nose snugly pulled in.)

He said, "And this must be Georgia. What can I do for you?"

Mum said, "Tell the doctor, Gee."

Reluctantly I said, "Well, when I do this . . ." (and I did the side to side thing) ". . . a wheezy noise comes out of me."

The doctor said, "Does it happen any other time?"

I said, "Er . . . no."

And he said, "Only when you go from side to side?"

And I said, "Yes."

And he said, "Well, I wouldn't go from side to side, then." And that was it.

Thanks a lot. All that money we (well, my parents) paid in taxes for his medical training not gone to waste, then!! He smiled at me. "When you move like that you force the air out of your lungs and it makes a sort of noise. That's all. They're just like bellows, really."

I felt like a fool. Two fools. It was Mum's fault for making me go. And she just hung around the doctor for AGES. Making conversation. Telling him she was learning salsa dancing. Did he like dancing? etc. She kept saying, "Oh, I mustn't keep you," and then going on and on. It was only when the nurse knocked on the door and said one of the pensioners had fallen off their chair that Mum pulled herself together.

It was so embarrassing. Mum was practically dribbling. She has zero pride. Now that my life was not in danger I noticed that even in the emergency of getting me to the doctor she had managed to squeeze herself into a tight top. You could see she was thrusting her "danger to shippings" at him. In a way, and

I never thought I would say this, it will be quite a relief when Vati comes home.

In the car going home she said, "He's nice, isn't he?"

I said, "Mum, honestly, have a bit of dignity. You have made your life choice and the large Portly One is on his way home in a fortnight. It is not a good idea to risk your marriage, and also incidentally make yourself a laughing stock this late on in life."

She said, "Georgia, I really don't know what you are talking about."

She does though.

Do I have to worry about every bloody single thing round this place? When do I get chance to be a selfish teenager? Jas's mum and dad have aprons and sheds, why do I have to have Mr and Mrs "We've Got Lives of Our Own" as parents?

thursday october 7th

11.30 a.m. The Bummer Twins have both got their knickers in a twist. They saw Nauseating P. Green coming out of a classroom, talking to Wet Lindsay. P. Green was probably telling her something about hamster feed. But the Bummers are saying she is a snitcher because they got done for knocking off school the other day. They call Nauseating P. Green "Snitcher the elephant" now. They stole her *Hamsters Weekly*. I thought she was going to cry which would have been horrific.

Rosie sent me a note in Maths; it said, *I am an equilateral triangle.*

I wrote back and said, *Does that mean all your angles are*

equal? and she wrote *I don't know. I'm a triangle*.

I looked over at her and pushed my nose back like a pig. She did the same thing back. We could wile away the hours much more amusingly if we could sit together.

I said that to Slim when she split us up last term. I said, "Miss Simpson, it is a well-known fact that if friends sit together they are encouraged to do more work." But she just shook in such a jelloid way I thought her chins would drop off.

She said, "The last time you two sat together, you set the locusts free in the Biology lab."

Oh honestly, not only has she got legs like an elephant, she has got a memory like one. How many times did we have to explain it was an accident? No one could have imagined they would eat Mr Attwood's spare overalls.

It is RE in a couple of hours so I will be able to have a decent chat to my mates instead of wasting time learning about stuff.

r e

1.30 p.m. Rosie bunked off, she said she was going to the pictures with Sven. It must be nice to have a boyfriend, even if it is Sven. Oh well, ho hum, pig's bum. While Miss Wilson raved on and hitched up her sad tights I chatted to Jas. She wasn't officially speaking to me because of the veggie business, but I put my arm round her every time I went near her. In the end, to stop me and also to avoid more lezzie rumours, she forgave me (ish).

I said, "My vati is back on the nineteenth."

"Are you glad?"

"No, Jas, I said my vati is back on the nineteenth."

"I like my dad."

"Yes, but your dad is normal, he's got a shed. He does DIY. He fixed your bike. When my vati tried to fix my bike his hand got stuck in the spokes. We had to walk to Casualty. I don't see why I had to go with him, everyone was calling out in the streets. And they weren't calling out 'What a brilliant dad you've got!'"

3.45 p.m. I've managed not to think about meeting Dave all day. I am a bit nervous, though.

7.30 p.m. In my bedroom. I've got my head under my pillow. This house is like a mental institution. In the front room Uncle Eddie and Mum are practising salsa. He turned up on his motorbike with a crate of wine. First of all he came snooping up to my room and opened my door (I don't know why we don't just take it off its hinges and leave it at that). I think he must have already had one crate of wine because he had a tennis racket he was pretending to play as a guitar and he said, "Georgia, this is a little song entitled, 'Get off the stove, Grandad, you're too old to ride the range'," then he laughed like King Loon and went off downstairs singing, "Agaddoo doo dooo."

Honestly, what planet do these people live on? And why isn't it further away? Libby is in the airing cupboard with Angus. She says they are playing doctors and nurses.

11.00 p.m. Does anyone care what happens to me? I've got to meet Dave the L. tomorrow and somehow cover up the fact that I have a broken heart. I must be glittering and glamorous and brave.

I could hear Mum and Uncle Eddie giggling. I called down, "Mum . . . Libby is still in the airing cupboard if you were wondering, which I don't suppose you were as you are busy drinking and carrying on, and so on."

I wondered if I should confide in Uncle Eddie about Mum and George Clooney. Maybe he could have a word with her? Then I heard him coming upstairs again. He popped his very bald head round my door, the light glancing off it almost blinded me, and he said, "We can go and meet your dad on my motorbike if you like!!"

Yeah, in your dreams, oh mad bald one.

friday october 8th

4.00 p.m. The Fab Gang came round and we hung around in my room, listening to the Top Twenty. We were discussing Operation Red Herring. Well me and Mabs, Rosie, Jools and Ellen were, Jas wasn't there. Too busy waiting for her "boyfriend" to come home to worry about her very best pal in the world, who would never dream of putting boys first.

Ellen said, "OK, this is the plan. Say to the herring you have to be home by nine thirty because you are grounded for staying out too late."

I said, "Yes, that's good because it makes me seem sort of like dangerous and groovy but it also means I can get away if I need to. Good thinking, Batwoman."

Ellen went on, "And me and the rest of the gang will sort of be around the park any time things might be getting heavy."

I said, "Yeah. Because that is like double cool . . . almost with knobs. It means I have loads of mates that I just

286

casually bump into at every whiff and woo AND it will stop any hanky panky in the snogging department."

Rosie said, "Exactamondo. Let's dance!"

And we did mad dancing to calm ourselves down.

7.00 p.m. Met Dave the L. in the park. I went for casual glamour: leopard-skin top (fake, because otherwise Angus would have followed me thinking he'd made a new big mate) and jeans and leather jacket. It was a bit awkward at first. You know, like a first date. He is quite a good-looking bloke if you like red herrings. He said, "Hi, gorgeous," which I think is nice. I admire honesty.

He told me he wanted to be a stand-up comedian when he leaves school and I said, "You should have my life, that would give you lots of material."

He laughed. It was funny but I didn't feel nervous, not like with SG. I didn't say I wanted to be a vet or anything. I very nearly made sense.

As we walked along chatting our arms sort of brushed against each other a couple of times. I didn't mind and he's got a nice crinkly smile. But then he grabbed hold of my hand. Uh-oh. Hanky panky. Also he is slightly smaller than me and I had to do the bendy knee business so I could be more his height. I don't know what it is about boys these days but they seem on the small side. Or perhaps I am growing. Oh no. That might be it. I might only be half the size I am going to be. I might turn out to be a female Sven and that might be God's punishment for me turning Buddhist. Anyway, I lolloped along as best I could, trying not to be like an orang-utan. But, oh *sacré bleu* and *merde*, then Dave pulled me round to face him and took hold of my other hand. I had to lift up my shoulders so that I didn't have excess arm. I felt like that woman in *The Sound of Music*, you know, Julie Thing. Surely he wasn't going to start dancing round with me? Nooooo, he wasn't. He was going to kiss me!! Oh no, this wasn't in the Herring plan . . . Where were all my so-called mates???

As he looked at me and started to bring his face closer I tried to say, really quickly, "Have you noticed how when you go from side to side there is this sort of wheezing noise?"

But I only got to "Ha . . ." when he put his mouth on mine. I could have bitten through my tongue. I kept my eyes open because I thought that wouldn't be like a real kiss. But it made me go cross-eyed so I closed them. It was, in fact, quite a nice kiss. (But what do I know? I've only ever been with SG, a whelk boy and BG (Mark) who had such a huge gob that no experience with him can be counted normal. You've just got to be glad to escape without being eaten).

my room
thinking

11.00 p.m. My so-called mates arrived at last. They gave us both a bit of a start, leaping out from behind a tree. Also if Rosie is thinking of taking up drama I would advise her against it. She said, "Oh hello, Georgia. It's YOU!!! What on EARTH are you doing here, I thought you were GROUNDED?" But she said it like somebody had hit her on the head with a mallet (which, incidentally, somebody should do).

11.30 p.m. Hmmm. I am in a state of confusosity. I'd rate him as seven and a half as a kisser.

Maybe even eight. He didn't do much varying pressure and his tongue work was a bit like a little snake. On the other hand he didn't do any sucking (like whelk boy) and there was no crashing of teeth. Or dribbling, which is never acceptable. He did nibble my lower lip a bit, which I must tell the gang about because it isn't on our list. It was quite nice. I might try doing it myself. When I retrap the SG.

midnight Also he didn't rest his hand on my basooma, which is a plus.

12.30 a.m. Maybe he didn't rest his hand there because he thought he might never find it again? I wonder if my basoomas are still growing?

12.32 a.m. Terrible news!! I can fit a pencil-case underneath my basooma and it actually stays there for a second!!

I feel all hot and weird. Still, what else is new?

saturday october 9th

11.50 a.m. Angus is in love!!! Honestly. With Mr and Mrs Across the Road's Burmese pedigree cat Naomi. (I call her that, they call her Little-Brook-Running-up-a-Tree-With-a-Sausage-up-its-Bottom Sun Li the Third, or something foreign.) I saw Angus on their wall, giving Naomi a vole he'd killed. He was parading up and down sticking his bottom up in the air and waggling his tail about. Disgusting, really. Especially as he had a clinker hanging out of his bum-oley. Cats think that is attractive. So does Libbs.

Mr and Mrs Across the Road didn't seem too thrilled by his attentions. In fact, they threw stones at him. They are going to have to try a lot harder than that, he was brought up having bricks thrown at him. They should try a bazooka.

my room

2.30 p.m. I must find some calm. I've got an instruction booklet on Buddhism from the library. Miss Wilson, who doubles as sad librarian, is beside herself with pleasure – she thinks I am taking religion seriously due to her excellent teaching. Sad really. She'll want me to go round for coffee at her house soon. I might go and ask her where she buys her tights. The book is called *Buddhism for the Stupid*. No, it's not really, but it should be.

Good grief. It's so boring. It's just all about world peace and so on, which is OK but you would think I could do that later. Once I was happy. And had got what I wanted.

4.00 p.m. Jas turned up. She was really mopey like a cod.

"I got all ready for Tom to come home and then he called up from Birmingham and said he was going to stay on for a few more days. He says that he likes Birmingham and has got some great new mates."

I was thinking, Oh, good grief! As if I haven't got enough to worry about without having Hunky and Po trouble. But I didn't say anything.

Jas moaned on: "He didn't use to like going out with mates, he used to like being with me."

I said wisely, "Remember he is a Jennings boy. He is the

290

same as Robbie. Remember the elastic band thing, Jas . . . let him have his space. In fact, why don't you say you think you should have a break from each other for a bit? You know, to sort of find yourselves."

Jas said, "I know where he is, he is in Birmingham."

It's easier chatting to Angus. I kept on, though. "Don't be silly, Po! Anyway, I want to talk to you about Buddha. Do you know what Buddha says?"

"Didn't he say quite a lot?"

"Yes, but he said, 'When a crow finds a dying snake, it behaves as if it were an eagle. When I see myself as a victim I am hurt by trifling failures.'"

There was a silence and Jas started fiddling around with her fringe.

"Do you see?"

"Er . . . what has that got to do with Tom? He's not an eagle."

Honestly she is so dim. I explained, as patiently as I could, "It means, if you think your life is poo it will be."

"Well why didn't he say that?"

"Because a) – he is Buddha and b) – they do not have poo in Buddhaland."

5.30 p.m. Phone rang. Mum yelled up, "Gee, it's for you . . . boyfriend."

Honestly, I could kill her. I went and answered the phone and sat down on a stool. It was Dave the Laugh. He said, "Hello, gorg. I had a great time last night. I've just about recovered from meeting your mates. What are you up to?"

As I was chatting to him Libby came humming into the hall. She wanted to get up on to my knee.

291

I said, "Libbs, I'm on the phone, go find Angus to play with."

She gave me her frowniest look. "NO . . . UP!!! NOW!!! BAD, BAD BOY." And she started spitting at me so I had to let her on my knee. Before I could stop her she was "talking" down the phone. "Hello, mister man. Grrrrrrr. Three bag pool, three bag pool."

Oh God. I struggled to get the phone off her and then she shouted, "Georgie has got a THERY big SPOT! Hahaha-hahaha."

I grabbed the phone back and put Libby on the floor. "Sorry about that, Dave, my little sister has . . . er . . . just learned to talk and, er, she must have . . . er . . ."

Libby was singing, "Georgie's got a THERY big spot, lalalalala, THERY, THERY big SPOT . . . on her bot . . . ON HER BOTTY."

6.00 p.m. She's right, actually. How can you get spots on your bottom? I must have more vitamin C.

6.05 p.m. Me and Jas chomping on bananas. Jas said, "Save the skins because they make really good face-masks."

6.30 p.m. As usual Jas is completely wrong. We washed off the banana on our faces, it felt disgusting.

I said, "I'm meeting Dave again tomorrow. He seems to really like me."

Jas was busy picking bits of banana out of her hair. "Does he? Why?"

"I don't know, he just does."

bed

11.00 p.m. Dave doesn't make my legs go jelloid and that is the point, isn't it? If a boy doesn't make you go jelloid you may as well be with your girlie mates . . . or boy mates that you are just mates with and no snogging involved.

11.30 p.m. Oh, I don't know.

midnight Angus still on the wall looking down at Naomi the Burmese sex kitten. She is rubbing herself against the wall, the little minx. I know what she feels like.

I wonder what the Sex God is doing now.

What shall I do about Dave?

1.00 a.m. I really would truly prefer to put my head into a bag of eels than kiss Wet Lindsay.

1.15 a.m. Sex God did take the bull by the nostrils and dump Wet Lindsay when he found true love (me). Even if he did then dump me.

1.30 a.m. He was true to his feelings. Even though it upset Owlie he dumped her because it was the right thing to do (and it is always the right thing to do to dump Owlie).

sunday october 10th

Dave the L. turned up at my door earlier, wearing a false moustache. He actually is quite a laugh. We went to the pictures and snogged again. He must be a bit surprised that my mates pop up every time we go anywhere. When Rosie put her head over the back of us in the pictures and said, "GEORGIA!!! How AMAZING!! What are you doing here?!!!" I thought he'd swallow his ice cream whole.

monday october 11th

school

8.30 a.m. I met Jas on the way to school. She was trailing her rucky along as we walked. I said, "Dave sent me a card today, it said, 'Merry one week anniversary, gorgeous. Lots of love, D, kiss, kiss, kiss'."

She didn't say anything. I said, "Jas, what are you doing?"

She was all pale, I noticed.

"I haven't heard from Tom and I tried to ring him and he was out."

"Ah yes, well."

"You said I should say, 'Have your own space, Tom'."

"Yes, well . . ."

"And now he's got loads of space."

"Ah yes."

"And so have I."

"Yes . . ."

"But I don't want it."

294

Oh good grief. I'm not going to be an Agony Aunt if all people do is moan on all the time.

last bell

3.50 p.m. Jas, Jools, Ellen, Rosie and me were lurking near the Science block, hiding from the Gestapo (Hawkeye) who wants to ask me about the lunchbox beret idea. Everyone has been doing it. Slim told us not to be so silly; she said in assembly, "You are making a mockery of the school's good name in the community."

Anyway, we have taken her advice to heart and we are going to have a "blind day" instead. After last bell we went to the alleyway in between the Science block and main school, waiting for an opportunity to dash out of the gates when Hawkeye was not looking. We all had our lunchpack berets on apart from old spoilsport knickers Jas.

Rosie said, "On the blind day next Wednesday the deal is we all shut our eyes for the whole morning and have to have minders that guide us around. From lesson to lesson."

I said, "Wait a minute, we have Sports on Wednesday, it's hockey. That will be a laugh."

Jas said gloomily – she had been an unlaugh all day – "Hawkeye will stop us, with detention and so on."

Rosie said, "No, because we will explain that we are being sponsored and are doing it so that we will have a better understanding of the poorly-sighted."

That's when we saw something awful. The SG drove up to the school gates in his car and Wet Lindsay ran out and got in!

7.00 p.m. In a way I feel free. If SG chooses Owlie over me then he is the loser. So be it. That is the Buddhist way. Omm. I will not be the crow finding the snake or whatever it found. Who cares? It's only a crow.

8.00 p.m. I need a break from being a Buddhist for a minute. POOO!!! DOUBLE *MERDE*!!! Life really is a pooburger.

9.00 p.m. Mum came in for a "chat".

"Dad's home in a week."

"Still time for a few serious medical complaints, then."

"What do you mean?"

"You and Doctor Clooney."

"Georgia, you're mad."

"Am I?"

"Look, all it is is that I think he's quite good-looking."

"Well that's because you are comparing him to Dad."

"Don't be rude."

"I'm not, I'm being factual."

"Anyway, you needn't worry, it's just innocent flirting."

"Yes it is for you, but what if Doctor Clooney really likes you? And what about if he will be really upset if he finds out you are just toying with him? Like a toying person?"

She went off looking all worried. Good. That's two of us all worried and guilty. And confused.

9.30 p.m. Dave phoned. He said, "I just called to say I really liked you. Night-night."

Good grief.

I wonder if all heartless babe magnets feel guilty?

tuesday october 12th

hockey pitch

2.30 p.m. Hockey match against boring old Hollingbury College. They really do think they are cool, but sadly they are about to find out that they are not.

I had a sneaky look in their changing-room when I pretended to be fastening up my boots. It was a nightmare of thongs. I noticed Miss Stamp busily popping in and out, saying things like, "Don't mind me, I was just wondering if you had enough towels."

She was all red and keen. Running on the spot, and so on. Very alarming if you're not used to it. I noticed quite a few of the Hollingbury girls were rushing off into the loos when she came in. They were getting a bit jittery. So I used sporting tactics. I said, "Miss Stamp, I wonder if the Hollingbury team would appreciate a bit of physio after the match. You know, if they had any little knocks or anything you could offer to . . . er . . . treat them yourself. Use those magic healing hands."

Adolfa was a bit suspicious. But she couldn't figure out my angle. I heard her go back into their changing-room and say something about treatment. All of the Hollingbury girls shot out of the door and on to the pitch. Ah good, a nervous team, desperate not to get injured!! Result!!!

It's very nippy noodles. I've got three pairs of knickers on. I probably look like Nauseating P. Green from the back . . . or Slim. Still, better a fat bum than a numb bum. There is a little crowd supporting us, most of my mates actually. Although not

297

Jas, she wasn't at school today. I hope she has not gone all weird because of Tom.

The slimiest wet weed who shall remain nameless (Lindsay) is captain of the team. Erlack . . . well I will not do anything that she says. In our pre-match talk she said, "So remember to watch me for instruction, and when you get into any kind of shooting position, watch for me to come and take on the shot."

Oh yeah, dream on, wet and weedy one. With a bit of luck someone will knock her stick insect legs from under her. I am not saying I want her to be badly injured, just badly enough that she has to go away to a convalescent hospital somewhere (Mars) for a year or two. Thank you, Buddha. (You can see how I am not taking poo lying down.)

2.50 p.m. Cracking match. I am playing a stormer, even if I say so myself. Zipping up and down the pitch, hitting the ball up to the forwards. Excellent passing!! I'm like David Beckham apart from the hockey stick and skirt and three pairs of huge knickers. Although who knows? Posh Spice may insist he wears sensible snug knickers in the winter time. She is a very caring person. But quite thin.

half-time
no score

3.15 p.m. Rosie, Ellen, Jools and Mabs are like cheerleaders. They have made up this song which goes, "One – two – three – four, go, Georgia, go!"

I said to them as I came off, "It doesn't rhyme," and Ellen said, "Well, it's too nippy noodles."

Brrr. She's right. I went into the loos to run my hands under the hot water tap. Oh no, the Bummer Twins had got Nauseating P. Green cornered in the changing-rooms. She was blubbing. They didn't even look round when I came in. Jackie said, "So, Snitcher, what did you tell Lindsay about us knocking off school?"

Nauseating P. Green was trembling like a huge jelly elephant. "I . . . I . . . didn't say . . . anything . . ."

I thought I should shout at her, to help, "Tell them about your hamsters, P. Green, that will bore them to death and you can run off." But I looked at Jackie's big arms and thought I wouldn't bother.

As I was going out again the Bummers started shoving P. Green against the loo doors. Oh bum, bum.

Alison said, "We don't like snitchers . . . do we, Georgia?"

I said, "Oh, they're all right, I . . ."

Jackie shoved P. Green so hard that her glasses flew off. That did it. I could no longer be the Bummer Twins' armchair. I said, "Leave her alone now."

Jackie looked at me. "Oh yeah, big nose, what are you going to do about it?"

I said, "I'm going to appeal to your niceness."

She laughed and said, "Dream on, Ringo."

I said, "Yes, I thought that might not work, so this is plan two."

Actually there wasn't a plan two, I didn't know what I was doing. I was like a thing possessed. I leaped over to them and grabbed Jackie's fag packet out of her hand. Then I ran into the loos with it and held it over the toilet. I yelled, "Let her go or the fags get it!"

Jackie was truly worried then and had a sort of reflex action to save her packet of fags. Alison came towards me as well, leaving Nauseating P. Green trembling by herself. I shouted, "Run like the wind, P. Green!!!"

She picked up her glasses and just stood there, blinking like a porky rabbit caught in a car's headlights. Good grief! I tried to give her confidence. "Well, not like the wind, then, but shuffle off as fast as you can."

Eventually she went off and I was left to face the Bummers. I charged past them shouting, "Uurgghhhhgghhh!", that well-known Buddhist warrior chant. I chucked the fags out of the packet on to the floor. When I looked back as I dashed out of the door they were scrabbling around picking them up. I raced out on to the pitch for the second half to a big cheer from the Ace Crew. I thought I may as well enjoy the game because the Bummers would be killing me immediately it was over.

I noticed there were a few boys gathered at the opposition end of the pitch. One of them cheered when I ran on. Probably Foxwood lads. They sort of appeared any time there was the least hint of knicker flashing. Or nunga-nunga wobbling. I don't know how they knew, or had found out we were playing today. Probably Elvis Attwood got on the tom-toms in his hut and drummed out a message to let them know there was a match on. He was lurking around pretending to be busy, wheeling his wheelbarrow. There was never anything in it. Old Pervy Trousers. Anyway, let the lads look at my nunga-nungas if they wanted! Let my nostrils flare free. Let my waddly bottom waddle, what did I care??? I was going to be dead anyway when the Bummers got hold of me.

4.10 p.m. Victory! Victory!!!!! We won one–nil.

It was a close match considering

we were playing such a bunch of wets. One of their team blubbed when I accidentally hit her on the shin with my stick. I wonder if all the times I have been savaged by Angus have made me immune to pain? Anyway, it was a nil draw until the last few minutes. I raced up the wing and found myself in the opposition's penalty area. The Ace Crew were going, "Georgia, Georgia!!" And then our so-called captain Wet Lindsay shouted from the left side, "Pass it to me, number eight!"

You know like in the movies when everything slows down and it's in slow motion? Well, I had that. I saw Owlie's face and her thin stupid legs and I thought, Haha-hahahahaha! (Only really, really slowly.)

I kept the ball myself and raced for goal with it. I dribbled past one opposition player, then another. Tripped. Picked myself up, nipped the ball through someone's legs. The crowd were cheering me on. They were going BERSERK!! Then there was the goalkeeper. Good grief, she was a giant!!! But I feinted to one side of her and got past. Then there was just the open goal. I whacked the ball and scored!!! . . . just as Lindsay tackled me savagely from behind.

4.30 p.m. Wet Lindsay tried to pretend that she had been "helping" me. Huh. Very likely . . . not.

Miss Stamp wanted Elvis to carry me to the sick bay but he said he had an old war wound and brought his wheelbarrow out on to the pitch. He said, "Get in. One of your mates will have to wheel it because I hurt my back serving this country."

Oh yeah. I said to Jools, "His back has probably seized up because he sits on his bottom all day."

Rosie wheeled me to the sick bay but I still couldn't walk even after the sadistic Adolfa Stamp had strapped up my ankle. While she was kneeling down in front of me bandaging it all my so-called mates were behind her doing pretend snogging. The Hollingbury girls didn't even bother to get changed, they just shook hands really quickly and got on their coach.

I hopped about a bit after I was strapped up but it was aggers. In the end Elvis said reluctantly that Rosie and Ellen and Jools could push me home in the wheelbarrow. Cheers, thanks a lot.

Elvis went grumbling back to his hut, saying, "Make sure you bring it back tomorrow . . . it's my own private equipment and shouldn't by rights be used for school business."

His own private wheelbarrow. How sad is that? Sensationally sad, that's how.

We set off, wheeling along. It wasn't very comfortable in the barrow and there was the suggestion of something brownish in one of the corners. But I was being all brave and heroic as I was the heroine of the hockey universe. And attractively modest. For a genius.

When we got to the school gates Dave the Laugh was there!!! He had been one of the lads at the match!!! He has seen my gigantic bottom bobbling around on the pitch. Closely following my gigantic schnozzle, bobbling around. OhmyGodohmyGodohmyGod.

He was laughing like a loon as we squeaked up to him in Elvis's wheelbarrow. Then he got down on his knees and was salaaming and chanting "We are not worthy" to me.

He said to Rosie and Ellen and Jools, "Let me push the genius home." And as he pushed me along he sang that really crap song by that band that Dad thinks he looks like the drummer from Queen. The song was "We are the Champions". The Fab Gang joined in really loudly. Everyone was looking at us as we went down the High Street. I don't suppose shoppers often saw anyone in a wheelbarrow. They probably had very narrow lives and travelled around by car. Or moped.

Dave the L. kissed me when he left me at my gate! In front of everyone! And he said, "Bye-bye, beautiful. See you soon. Let me know how the ankle is. I'll bring you pressies."

When he'd gone the girls went, "Aaaahhh."

Ellen said, "He really is quite cool-looking. Has he done that nibbling thing again? I quite fancy the sound of that."

But he is just a herring. We must not forget this.

6.15 p.m. Mum was quite literally ecstatic about my ankle. She just left me in the wheelbarrow outside the front door and got on the blower immediately. I could hear her talking to the doctor's receptionist.

"Yes, it really does seem quite bad. No, no, she really can't walk at all. Yes, well thank you."

Libby came trailing out with scuba-diving Barbie and got in the wheelbarrow with me. She gave me a big kiss. Don't get me wrong, I love my sister, but I wish she would wipe her nose occasionally. When she kisses me she leaves green snot all over my cheek.

Mum came outside and said, "The doctor will pop round after surgery, Gee. Will you just lend me your mascara? I've run out."

I said, "Huh, it's just one-way traffic in this house . . . if it was me, if the shoe was on the other boot, if I said, 'Mum, can I just borrow . . .'"

She wasn't listening. She called from indoors, "Hurry up, love, just get me it."

I yelled, "I can't walk, Mum! That is why the doctor is coming to see me. That's why I came home in a wheelbarrow."

"You don't have to walk, just hop out of the barrow and up the stairs and get the mascara."

Hop hop, agony agony, hop hop.

Why was I hopping around getting things for my mother who only wanted them so that she could make a fool of my father? (The answer to that question is I didn't want her poking around in my room. She might come across a few things that weren't strictly mine, things that in a word were – er – hers.)

I hopped into her bedroom and said, "It is pathetic and sad. You are trying to get off with a young doctor and my poor vati is coming home to a – a – facsimile of a sham!"

She just tutted and went on primping. She said, "The trouble with you is that trivial things are really serious to you, and stuff you should care about that is serious, you don't."

I said, hobbling off, "Oh very wise. Is that why you are stuffing yourself into things that are quite clearly made for people a) smaller than you and b) several centuries younger than you?"

She threw the hairbrush at me. That's nice behaviour, isn't it? – attacking a cripple.

7.00 p.m. Doctor home-wrecker arrived. He strapped up my ankle again and gave me painkillers. I said, "I suppose that is my hockey career over. Do you think that perhaps I have weak ankles because of my diet?"

He laughed. He had a good laugh, actually.

Mum said, "Can I get you a coffee, John?"

John? John? Where did that come from?

Mum went off into the kitchen and I heard her say, "Take Angus out of the fridge, Libbs."

"He likes it."

"He's eaten all the butter."

"Teehhheeeeeeheeee."

7.15 p.m. I hobbled off to my room and played moody music really loudly as a hint. It was ages before the door slammed. I looked out of my bedroom window. I could see John going off in his quite cool car.

7.45 p.m. Lying on my bed of pain. Well, it would be if I could feel my ankle.

Mum popped her head round the door. She was all flushed. "How is the ankle?"

I said, "Fine if you like red-hot pokers being stabbed in you."

"That's my little soldier." She was humming.

Brilliant, a week before my dad gets back my mum starts a torrid affair with a doctor.

8.00 p.m. Mind you, I would get tiptop medical priority.

8.30 p.m. He might be able to get me a good deal on my nose job.

9.00 p.m.	I must get revenge on Wet Lindsay.
10.00 p.m.	I wonder how the Bummers will kill me?
10.10 p.m.	Why is the Herring so nice to me? What is wrong with him?

wednesday october 13th

school

8.30 a.m. Mum made me hobble to school. Unbelievable. She said a bad ankle didn't stop me learning things. I tried to explain to Mum that it would be just a question of hobbling in to be killed by the Bummer Twins, but she wasn't interested.

I made Jas wheel the wheelbarrow as I hopped along with a crutch. The Foxwood lads had a field day with us, shouting, "Where's your parrot?" and so on.

Jas had perked up enough to say, "I wonder how the Bummers will kill you?"

She sounded quite interested. She's only cheered up because Tom is coming home.

I managed to keep out of the Bummers' way for the morning but eventually at lunch-time the fatal moment came. The Bummers cornered me in the loos. I tried to hobble off but they blocked the doorway. Here we go. Well at least death would solve the Dave the Laugh situation. Jackie just looked at me. She said, "Fancy a fag?"

306

What were they going to do, ritually set fire to me?

Jackie put a fag in my mouth and Alison lit it. Jackie said, "Cool," and Alison said, "Good call." And then they just went out.

What in the name of pantyhose did that mean? Why hadn't they duffed me up?

I hobbled over to the mirror to see what I looked like smoking. Quite cool, actually. I sucked my nose in. I definitely looked a bit Italian.

Out of the corner of my mouth I said, "*Ciao, bella.*"

But sadly smoke went up my nose and I had a coughing extravaganza.

I can't believe life. As I was having my coughing fit Lindsay walked in and booked me for smoking in the loos. I saw the Bummer Twins sniggering in the corridor.

Great. Stacking gym mats for the rest of the term. Elvis passed by and saw me hobbling and heaving mats around. He laughed.

4.00 p.m. Left school limping along next to Jas. I think it's quite attractive if you like Long John Silver. I said to Jas, "You know, I think I am going to give up on boys altogether – tell Dave the Laugh it's over, forget the Sex God and just concentrate on lessons and so on. I might ask Herr Kamyer to give me extra tuition."

"He'd have a spasm to end all spasms if you did."

I said, "I think I might be over the Sex God anyway. When I saw him pick up Owlie in his car, that did it for me. Anyone who can go out with Wet Lindsay, with her stupid no forehead and sticky insect legs, and . . . er . . ."

"Goggly eyes?"

"Yeah, goggly eyes. Anyone who can do that has got something very wrong with them. You know, if he asked me out now I would say n–ung."

I meant to say "no" but that was when I saw him leaning against his car. The Sex God. Oh don't tell me he was waiting for gorgeous (not) Wet Lindsay. Pathetic! Très pathetic and très, très sad.

I hobbled past him. He wasn't so very gorgey. Well actually, yes, he was. He was a Sex God. Really. He looked me straight in the eyes and I went completely jelloid. In fact, my other leg nearly gave way. He half smiled and I remembered what it was like to be attached to his mouth. Somehow I kept hobbling. We'd got past him and I was feeling all shaky when he called after us, "Georgia, can I talk to you for a minute?"

OhmyGodohmyGod. Was this an elastic band moment? Jas was just goosegogging at my side. I said, "You walk on, Jas. I'll catch you up."

She said, "Oh it's OK, I'm not in any hurry. Anyway, you might fall over and lie for ages with no one to help you. Like a tortoise on its back or . . ."

I opened my eyes really wide at Jas and raised my eyebrows. After about forty years she got it and walked on.

Robbie said, "Look, I know I'm probably the last person you want to talk to, but . . . well . . . I'd just like to tell you something . . . I'm really, really sorry about what happened between us . . . I handled it really badly, I know. She, you know, Lindsay, just was like, so upset, and you were so young and I couldn't . . . I didn't know what else to do. I thought I'd be going away soon and that would just sort things out . . . but then I was at the match . . ."

God, was there anyone in the universe who hadn't seen my

huge wobbly bottom and enormous conk bobbling around the hockey pitch?

SG was going on in his really sexy voice, ". . . and I saw how Lindsay deliberately hurt you . . . and I . . . I'm sorry. I've caused a lot of trouble and you're a really nice kid . . . Look, I'll . . ."

Then I heard, "Robbie!!"

Wet Lindsay was walking over towards where we were and I just couldn't handle any more. I hobbled off.

5.00 p.m. OhGodohGodohGod. I love him, I love him.

He thinks I am a kid.

It's all a facsimile of a sham.

And in tins.

And pants.

And pingy pongos.

And *merde*.

He was at the match. He saw my giganticus pantibus.

But he still spoke to me.

Perhaps Jas is not as mad as she seems. Perhaps big knickers are boy magnets?

Oh I don't know.

Why does he still make me go jelloid?

6.00 p.m. Dave the Laugh had left me a card at home which said, *One-legged girls are a push-over. Love Dave XXXXXX.* And some chocolates. Oh GODDDDDDDD!!!!

309

11.00 a.m. I am a horrible person. I have dumped Dave. I had to. It was really double poo. I thought he was going to cry. He turned up at my house with some flowers because of my injury. He is so sweet and it didn't seem fair to lead him on. I explained that he had only really been a red herring.

2.30 p.m. Phoned Jas.

"He said I was a user and, er . . . something else . . ."

"Was it 'selfish'?"

"No."

"The crappest person in humanity?"

"No."

"Really horrible and like a wormey . . ."

"Jas, shut up."

in bed

8.00 p.m. Am I really horrible? Perhaps I am one of those people who don't really feel things properly, like Madonna.

10.00 p.m. Personally I think I have shown great maturiosity and wisdomosity.

11.00 p.m. Dave will some day thank me for this.

Angus still on top of the wall across the road. Looking down at his beloved Naomi in her enclosure. He too is disappointed in love.

3.00 a.m. Libby came in all sleepy. She said, "Move." And climbed in with the usual accoutrements – Barbie, Charlie Horse, etc. I've got about half a centimetre of bed. Marvellous. Bloody marvellous.

monday october 18th

school
break

2.15 p.m. Well, at least life can't get any worse. Oh, I beg your pardon, yes it can. Raining again and cold and we have been forced outside by the Hitler Youth. I said to Wet Lindsay who was the prefect on duty, "It is against the Geneva Convention that we are forced outside in Arctic–" But she had locked the door and was sort of grinning through the window. She took off her cardigan as I was looking and wiped her forehead as if she was boiling. Oh *très amusant*, Owlie.

Jas and I wandered round to Elvis's hut to see if the old lunatic was in. If he wasn't we could sit in his hut for a bit and warm up. But oh no, there he was, reading his newspaper. Elvis had ear muffs on underneath his flat cap! Mrs Elvis must be very proud. I tapped on his little window so that I could say a friendly hello to him. But he couldn't hear because of the muffs.

I said to Jas, "As an hilarious joke I'll pretend to say something very urgent to him but I won't really be saying anything. I'll mime saying, 'Mr Attwood, my friend Jas is on fire!!!'"

So I went up to the hut door and I was mouthing, "Mr Attwood, my friend Jas is on fire!!!" and waving my arms wildly. In the end he took off his ear muffs, thinking that he couldn't hear me because of them. When he realised the joke he went ballisticisimus. He leaped up in a quite scary way for a one-hundred-and-eighty-year-old man and came charging at us out of his hut. I hobbled off quite quickly. Unfortunately he didn't remember he had parked his personal wheelbarrow round the corner of his hut and did a spectacular comedy fall over it. I thought I would die laughing. Me and Jas went and bent over a wall at the back of the tennis courts.

I said to Jas, in between laughing and gasping for air, "Jas . . . Jas . . . he . . . he has got a flat head."

God it was funny. I had a real ache in my stomach from laughing too much.

french

3.00 p.m. For a "treat" as it is Monday, Madame Slack taught us another French song. It was called *"Sur le Pont d'Avignon"*. About some absolute saddos dancing about on a bridge. All I can say is that the French and me have a different idea of having a cracking good time. Also, if I do go to French land, although I will be able to tell my new French mates that my blackbird has lost a feather, and be able to dance on bridges, I will not be able to get a filled baguette for love nor money.

At the end of the lesson Wet Lindsay came into the classroom in her role as Oberführer assistant. She smiled in a not attractive or friendly way and said, "Georgia Nicolson, report to Miss Simpson's office . . . NOW."

3.30 p.m. Outside Slim's office. Oh dear. *Quelle dommage. Zut alors* and *sacré bleu* even. Now what? Unfortunately Wet Lindsay was my guard and as I looked at her I was reminded of her thongs lurking under her skirt. Going up her bum-oley. And it started me off again.

The jelloid one called me in. I was like a red-faced loon trying not to laugh. She said, "Georgia Nicolson, this is an unforgivable offence. This time you have gone too far. Berets worn like lunchpacks, noses stuck up with Sellotape, false freckles painted on noses, all these childish pranks I have put up with . . . Last term there was the skeleton in Mr Attwood's uniform, the locusts . . ."

Slim raved on and on, shaking like a gigantic jelly. ". . . I was hoping that you had grown up a bit. But to lure an elderly man, not in peak condition . . ." Blah blah blah.

It was useless my trying to explain. Mr Attwood has dislocated his shoulder and I am being held responsible. Fab. Anyway, the short and short of it is that I'm suspended for a week and Jas is on cloakroom duty. Slim said she was going to write a stiff note home to my parents telling them the circumstances. I helpfully offered to take the stiff note home myself but Slim insisted on posting it.

Hobbling home with Jas and the gang. I was a bit depressed. Again. I couldn't even be bothered putting my lunchpack beret on.

I said to Jas, "Slim is so ludicrously suspicious! What she implied was that I would not take the note home and would pretend that I am not suspended!!"

Jas said, "Hmmm . . . What were you going to tell your mum after you had destroyed the note?"

"You're as bad as everyone else, Jas."

"I know, but just for interest's sake, what were you going to say?"

"I thought I might try the mysterious stomach bug. I haven't used it since last year's Maths test."

4.00 p.m. Home. Great. Life is great. Just *perfectamondo*. Suspended. Suspended just in time for Vati to come home and kill me. In love with a Sex God who calls me a kid. Called a heartless whatsit by Dave the Laugh. And the spot on my bum is like a boil. I wonder what Buddha would do now?

4.30 p.m. Waiting for Mum to come home so I can break the brilliant news.

5.00 p.m. Phoned Jas. Her mum answered.
I said, "Hello, can I speak to Jas?"

I heard her shouting to Jas, "Jas, it's Georgia on the phone."

And I heard Jas shout back, "Can you tell her I'll talk to her later. Tom is showing me a new computer game."

A new computer game? Are they all mad?

If I had called down and said that a boy was showing me a computer game my bedroom would have been full of parents within seconds!!

Unless that boy was my cousin James, in which case I would have been left up there for years, because my family doesn't seem to mind incest.

314

Mutti went ballisticisimus about the suspension. Even though I explained how it was not my fault and how provoked I was by Elvis.

When she calmed down she said, "Don't you think you might have a bit of a stomach bug?"

I said, "Here we go. Look, Mum, this is no time to be visiting Doctor Gorgeous. We should be thinking about Vati."

She said, "I AM thinking of Vati. And do you know what I'm thinking? I'm thinking that he'll go mad if he comes back and the first thing he hears is that his first born has been suspended. Now, are you feeling a bit poorly?"

my room

8.30 p.m. Mum "suggested" I went to bed early and thought about the important things in life for once. She's right. I will think about the important things in life. Here goes:

My hair . . . quite nice in a mousey sort of way. I still think that a blonde streak is a good idea, even after the slight accident I had last time I tried it. The bit that snapped off has grown back now, but I notice Mum has hidden all the toilet cleaners and Grandad's stuff that he puts his false teeth in when he stays. She really is like a police dog.

Anyway, where was I? Oh yes, eyes . . . Nice, I think, sort of a yellow colour. Jas said I've got cats' eyes.

Nose . . . Yes well, it doesn't get any smaller. It's the squashiness I don't like. It doesn't seem to have any bone in it. I still can't forget what Grandad said about noses, that as you get older they get bigger and bigger as gravity pulls on them.

8.35 p.m. You can make a sort of nose sling out of a pair of knickers! Like a sort of anti-gravity device. You put a leg hole over each ear and the middley bit supports your nose. It's quite comfy. I'm not saying that it looks very glamorous. I'm just saying it's comfy.

8.40 p.m. It's not something I would wear outside of the privacy of my own bedroom.

8.45 p.m. It's a good view from my windowsill. I can see Mr Next Door with his stupid poodles. He's all happy now that Angus has gone off poodle baiting in favour of the Burmese sex kitten.

8.46 p.m. Oh hello, here comes BG, my ex, the breast fondler. At this rate he will be the one and only fondler. I will die unfondled. He must be coming home from footie practice. I don't know how I could ever have thought about snogging him, he wears extremely tragic trousers. He is looking up at my window. He has seen me. He's stopped walking and is looking up at my window. Staring at me. Well, you know what they say – once a boy magnet always a boy magnet. I'm just going to stare back in a really cool way. All right, Mr Big Gob, Mr Dumper. I might be the dumpee but you still can't take your eyes away from me though, can you??? I still fascinate him. He's just looking up at me. Just staring and staring.

Mesmerised by me.

8.50 p.m. Oh my God! I am still wearing my nose hammock made out of knickers.

8.56 p.m.   Mark will tell all his mates.

8.57 p.m.   He will now call me a knicker-sniffer as well as a lesbian.

midnight   Oh for heaven's sake! What now? Woken by loud shouting and swearing. Surely Dad is not home already? Looked through the window. It was Mr and Mrs Across the Road. They were hitting things in their garden, shouting and shining torches. What on earth is the matter with them? This is no time for a disco inferno.

2.00 a.m.   Woke up fighting for breath from a dream about my nose getting bigger and bigger and my breasts getting bigger and bigger. And someone laughing and laughing at me. I couldn't seem to move anything except my head. Paralysis for being so horrid to Dave the Laugh. Libby was laughing like a loony. (Which of course she is.) She pulled my hair, "Look, bad boy!!! Aaahhh."

The weight was Angus curled up on my chest. Purring. I couldn't move, he weighs a ton. Big fat furry thing. I'm going to cut down on his rations. He's like a small horse.

Hang on a minute. He's not alone. He's got Naomi with him, curled up on top of him!!! Oh Blimey O'Reilly's trousers!

I managed to get them off me and they slunk off into the night – not before Angus had bitten my hand for my trouble. Naomi is a bit forward for a pedigree cat, she had her head practically up Angus's bottom as they went off.

I'll think about it in the morning. I mustn't do anything hasty. Like tell Mr and Mrs Across the Road.

8.45 a.m. All hell broke loose. Mr and Mrs Across the Road came round "asking" about the Burmese sex kitten. Mr Across the Road had a spade, and the words "Skinned and made into slippers" were mentioned. As she shut the door Mum said, "Honestly, Angus gets the blame for any bloody thing that goes on round here."

I said, "Yes . . . he's a scapewhatsit like me."

She said, "Shut up and get the balloons out."

4.00 p.m. Balloon city.

The house is covered in balloons. I even made a banner for the gate, it says VELCOME HOME, VATI.

Libby has made something disgusting out of Playdough and bits of hair. She is wearing ALL of her dressing up things; her Little Red Riding Hood outfit, fairy wings, deely boppers and, on top, her Pocahontas costume. She can hardly walk about.

No sign of Angus and Naomi. They will have made a love nest somewhere. Pray God my knickers are not involved in any way.

5.00 p.m. First of the loons arrive.

Grandad almost broke my ribs; he's surprisingly strong for someone who is two hundred and eight. He gave me a sweet (!) and said, "Don't send your granny down the mines, there's enough slack in her knickers!!"

What is he talking about? Mum gave him a sherry. Oh good grief. That means he will take his false teeth out soon and make them do an "hilarious" dance.

6.00 p.m. Excitement mounts (not). Uncle Eddie and Vati turned up on Uncle Eddie's pre-war motorbike. Vati leaped off the bike in a way that might have caused serious injury to a man of his years.

Mum and Dad practically ATE each other. Erlack!! How can they do that? In public.

I think Dad was crying. It's hard to tell when someone is as covered in facial hair as he is. He hugged me and went, "Oh, Gee . . . I . . . oh, I've missed you! Have you missed me?"

I went, "Nnnyeah."

Then Mum gave me a look and I pretended my stomach bug was quite bad. We'd "agreed" that we would do the stomach bug scenario early on, so as not to arouse suspicion tomorrow morning. I was beginning to feel quite ill, actually. It's weird having him back. At least Mum more or less ignores me. Vati tends to take an interest in, well, exam results and so on.

7.00 p.m. More and more people arrived. The drive was full of cars and old drunks. Mum and Dad were holding hands. It is so sad to see that sort of thing in people who should know better. I wondered if I should tell Vati he was in a love triangle with George Clooney. But then I thought no, can't be bothered.

12.30 a.m. What a nightmare! All the so-called grown-ups got drunk and started "letting their hair down". Well, those of them that had any.

Uncle Eddie was spectacularly drunk. He put one of Libby's rattles with a sucker bottom on his head, to look like a dalek. Libby laughed a lot. Uncle Eddie was going, "Exterminate, exterminate," for about a million years. But then Libby wanted it back and Uncle Eddie couldn't get the sucker off his head. All the drunkards had to pull on it together, and when it eventually came off Uncle Eddie had a round purple mark about a metre wide on his forehead. Which actually was quite funny.

1.00 a.m. I went down to tell them that some of us were trying to sleep, so could they turn down Abba's "Golden Hits", please. I saw them "dancing". God it was so sad. Dad was swivelling his hips around and clapping his hands together like a seal. Also he kept yelling, "Hey you! Get off of my cloud!!" like a geriatric Mick Jagger, and as Mick Jagger is about a million years old you can imagine how old and ludicrous Dad looked. Very old and ludicrous, that's how.

Mum was all red and flushed – she was TWISTING with Mr Next Door and they both fell over into a heap.

wednesday october 20th

12.30 p.m. Up at the crack of midday.

Mum in the kitchen in her apron making breakfast for us all. Oh no, sorry, I was just imagining being part of a proper family where that sort of thing happens. In Nicolson land the M and D are still in bed, even Libby was in there with them. I tried to get her to come into bed with me last night but she hit me and said, "No, bad boy, I go with Big Uggy!" (That's what she calls Dad – Big Uggy.) Angus was somewhere with the sex kitten and I was just . . . alone. In my room. In my bed of pain. Because my ankle still hurt, not that anyone cared. Very, very alone as usual.

As alone as a . . . er. . . an elk.

You never see elks larging it up with other elks, do you?

They are always on their own, just on a mountain. Alone.

Ah well, I decided to take a Buddhist viewpoint and just be happy that everyone else is happy . . .

12.45 p.m. Doorbell rang.

I called down, "The doorbell to your home is ringing."

No reply from the drunks.

The doorbell rang again. It would be Mr and Mrs Across the Road wanting to search the house for Angus and the Burmese sex kitten.

Ring ring.

I yelled as I hobbled down to answer it, "Don't worry about the fact that I have a limp and a very serious stomach complaint that makes me too sick to go to school . . . I will get up and answer the door. You recover your strength from lifting glasses up to your mouths!"

Silence. Well, just a bit of snoring from Libby.

I opened the door.

It was the Sex God.

At my door.

Looking like a Sex God.

At my door.

The Sex God had landed at my door.

I was wearing my *Teletubbies* pyjamas.

He said, "Hi."

I said, "Hhhnnnnngggghhh."

1.00 p.m. I got dressed as quickly as I could. The Sex God said he would meet me by the telephone box so we could go for a walk round Stanmer Park.

I dithered for about five minutes about lippy. I mean, if there is going to be snogging, is it worth putting it on? But then, if you don't put it on, does it look like you are expecting to snog, and is that too much pressure for boys who might go springing off in an elastic band way again?

Ooohhhh, I could feel my brain turning to soup. I knew I'd say something so stupid to the SG that even I would know it was stupid. That's how stupid it would be.

I didn't take any chances with the nipple department; I wore a bra and a vest. Let them get out of that if they could.

I must be calm. Om. Om. OhmyGodohmyGodohmyGod. My tongue seemed too big for my mouth. Do tongues grow? That would be the final straw if I had a tongue that just lolled out of my mouth. Shut up, brain!

1.25 p.m. There he was, leaning against the wall! He was just so cool. His hair was flopping down over one eye.

When he looked up I went completely jelloid. He said, "Hi, Georgia. Come here."

And I said, "My dad has grown a little beard and I thought I was going to be lonely as an elk."

What in the name of pantyhose was I talking about? I'd be the last to know as usual.

The SG HELD OUT HIS HAND . . . to me!!!! Something I had dreamed of. Do you know what I did? I shook it!!!

He really laughed then, and grabbed hold of my hand. We walked to the park. Holding hands. In public. Me and a Sex God. I honestly couldn't think of anything to say. Well I could, but it would only have made sense to dogs. Or my grandad.

In the park we sat down on the grass, even though it was a

bit on the nippy noodles side. Unfortunately I did feel like going to the piddly diddly department, but I didn't say.

He looked at me for what seemed like ages and ages, and then he kissed me. It was all surf crashing and my insides felt like they were being sucked out. Which you wouldn't think was very pleasant. But it was. He put his hand on my face and kissed me quite hard. I felt all breathless and hot. It was brilliant. We whizzed through the scoring system for snogging in record time. We got to number four (kiss lasting over three minutes without a break), had a quick breather and then went into five (open mouth kissing) and a hint of six (tongues). Yesss!!!! I had got to number six with the Sex God!!! Again!!!

Eventually we had a bit of a chat. Well, he chatted. I just couldn't seem to say anything normal. Every time I thought of something to say, it was something like, "Do you want to see my impression of a lockjaw germ?" or "Can I eat your shirt?"

He had his arm round my shoulder, which was good because then he got profile rather than full-frontal nose. He said, "I haven't been able to forget you. I've tried. I tried to be glad when you started seeing Dave. But it didn't work. I even wrote a song for you. Do you want to hear it?"

I managed to say "Yes" without putting on a stupid French accent or something. Then he sort of pulled me backwards on to him so that my head was resting on his lap. It was quite nice, but I could see up his nose a bit. Which I didn't mind, because he is a Sex God and I love him. It's not like looking up Cousin James's nose, which would make anyone immediately sick. But then I thought, if he looked down and saw me looking up his nostrils, he might think it was a bit rude. So I settled on closing my eyes and letting a half smile play around my lips.

Then he started singing me the song he had written for me.

There weren't many words – it was mostly, "And I really had to see her again." And then melodic humming and yeahing. Unfortunately he was sort of jiggling his knees for the rhythm so my head was bobbling about. I don't know how attractive that looked.

4.00 p.m. The Sex God has left the arena. He wants us to be, like, official snogging partners after my fifteenth next month. He's going to tell his parents.

I am irresistible.

I am truly a BABE magnet.

Even in my *Teletubbies* jimjams.

Even without mascara on.

Life is fabbity fab fab!!!!

Yesssssss!!!!!! And triple hahahahahaha-di-haha!!!!

5.00 p.m. M and D eventually got up. I didn't care because I am in the land of the very fab, in fact beyond the valley of the fab and into the universe of marvy.

Vati is in a hideously good mood. He keeps looking at things and going, "Aahh-h" and hugging me. I wish he would get back to normal. I wonder how long it will be before he drops this "happy family" nonsense and gets all parenty.

6.00 p.m. An hour, that's how long.

I was on the phone when it started. Telling Jas about SG. I said to her, "Yeah, come round and I'll tell you all about it. It is so FAB. How long will you be? OK. Good. Yeah anyway, he just turned up in his car. He looked BRILLIANT – you know those black jeans he has got, the really cool ones with the raised seam that . . ."

324

Vati had gone into the kitchen to get a cup of tea. He came out, stirring it. Jas had just asked me what sort of jacket SG was wearing and I was beginning to tell her when Dad interrupted and said, "Georgia, if Jas is coming round why are you talking to her on the phone? Phones cost money, you know."

Oh, I wondered how long it would be before the fascist landed. I said to Jas, "Have to go, Jas, I may already have wasted two pence. See you soon."

7.20 p.m. In my room, daydreaming about my wedding. Can you wear black as a bride? Dad came up and suggested we have a family "chat". I know what that means, it means they tell me what they are going to do and expect me to go along with it, and if I don't they call me a spoiled teenager and send me to my room.

But I don't care any more. I said to Dad politely, "Look, why don't we just skip the boring middle bit where I have to come all the way downstairs and you tell me what to do and I say no I don't want to and then you send me straight to my room. Why don't I just stay in my room?"

He said, "I don't know what you are talking about. Come into the front room. And what's wrong with your eyes? They look all bunged up, have you got a cold?"

"It's Vaseline, it makes your eyelashes longer."

He said, "Can't you stop messing about with yourself?"

As I went downstairs I was thinking he should try messing about with himself a bit more. He never had what you might call good dress sense but it's so much worse since he's been in Kiwi-a-gogo land. Today he's wearing tartan slacks which is a crime against humanity in anyone's language. Also he has

325

clipped his beard so that it is just on the end of his chin. No side bits and no moustache, just a beard thing . . . on the end of his chin. When we went in the room Mum kissed him on the cheek and stroked his beard . . . How disgusting.

Anyway, I don't care because I am going out with a Sex God and life is fab. I said, "OK, I am sitting comfortably. Rave on, El Beardo."

El Beardo said, "Great news!!! I've been offered a cottage in Scotland, I thought we would all go there for a week together as a family. Spend some quality time there together. Mum and Libbs, Grandad, Uncle Eddie, we could even ask Cousin James if you'd like a bit of company your own age. What do you think?"

Sacré bloody *bleu. Merde* and poo!!! is what I think.

Fortunately the doorbell rang and Mrs Huge Knickers and me scampered up to my room. My room, which as usual, was full. Libby was in my bed with scuba-diving Barbie, Charlie Horse, Angus and Naomi.

I said, "Go play downstairs with Daddy, Libbs."

But she just stood up on my bed and started dancing, singing, "Winnie Bag Pool, Winnie Bag Pool." She got to the bit where she takes off her panties, but I noticed they were suspiciously bulky, so I said, "Stop it, Libbs," and she said, "Me let my legs grow."

"No, leave them on."

Too late. I thought Jas was going to faint. She doesn't have a clue what it's like to have a little sister. Me and Jas went off to the utility room for a bit of privacy. I was dying to tell her all about my snogging extravaganza, but she went raving on about Tom: "We went to the country."

Oh good Lord. Still I thought I'd better pretend to be

interested otherwise I would never get to talk about myself. I said, "What for?"

"You know, to be on our own in nature."

"Why didn't you just go and sit in your room with some houseplants instead of tramping all the way to the country? You only snog there, anyway."

"No we don't."

"Oh yeah? What else do you do?"

"We looked at things."

"What things?"

"Flora and fauna and so on. Stuff we do in Blodge. It was really interesting. Tom knows a lot of things. We found cuckoo spit and followed a badger trail."

I clapped my hands together and started skipping round the room. "Cuckoo spit!!! No!!! If only I could have come with you! Sadly there was a Sex God I had to snog."

Jas got all huffy and pink. It's hilarious when Jas gets miffed, and a reason in itself to make her irritated. She goes all red and pink apart from the tip of her nose which is white. Very funny, like a sort of pink panda in a short skirt and huge knickers.

She was all sulky, but then I put my arm round her. She said, "You can stop that."

I said, "I feel a bit sad though, because I'm so lucky and I can't help thinking about Dave the Laugh. He was a really nice bloke, and you know . . . er . . . a good laugh. It's sad that I have broken his heart."

Jas was poking around in Dad's fishing bag, which is not a good idea as he sometimes leaves maggots in there which turn into bluebottles. She said, "Oh, I meant to tell you. He's going out with Ellen. Tom and I are meeting them later at the pictures."

midnight Bloody *sacré bleu*. Dave the Laugh was supposed to really like me. How come he is going out with Ellen? How dare she go out with him? He is only just my ex.

1.00 a.m. Still, I am going out with a Sex God. So I should be nice to everyone.

1.05 a.m. Dave was a laugh, though. Even if he didn't make me go jelloid.

1.10 a.m. I definitely go jelloid with the SG. Mmmmm, dreamy. But he doesn't make me laugh, he makes me stupid.

1.15 a.m. I wonder if Dave the Laugh did that nibbling thing with Ellen?

1.20 a.m. Looking through the window. Angus and Naomi are lurking about on Mr and Mrs Next Door's garden wall. Angus is just dangling his paw down at the poodles. I hope there is not going to be group sex. (Whatever that is.)

1.25 a.m. Perhaps I could have a jelloid boyfriend and an ordinary one for laughing with.

1.30 a.m. Good grief! What in the name of panty-hose is going to happen next?!?

Further further
confessions
of Georgia Nicolson

return of the loonleader

thursday october 21st

1.00 p.m. Looking out of my bedroom window, counting my unblessings. Raining. A lot. It's like living fully dressed in a pond.

And I am the prisoner of whatsit.

I have to stay in my room, pretending to have tummy lurgy, so that Dad will not know I am an ostracised leper banned from Stalag 14 (i.e. suspended from school). I'm not alone in my room, though, because my cat Angus is also under house arrest for his love romps with Naomi the Burmese sex kitten.

2.00 p.m. They'll be doing PE now.

I never thought the day would come when I would long to hear Miss Stamp (Sports *Oberführer* and part-time lesbian) say, "Right, girls, into your PE knickers!"

But it has.

3.30 p.m. All the Ace Gang will be thinking about the walk home from school.

Applying a touch of lippy. A hint of nail polish. Maybe even mascara because it is RE and Miss Wilson can't even control

333

her tragic 70s hairdo let alone a class. Rosie said she was going to test Miss Wilson's sanity by giving herself a face-mask in class and see if Miss Wilson had a nervy spas.

Jas will be practising her pouting in case she bumps into Tom.

3.50 p.m. How come Jas got off with cloakroom duty and I got banned? I am a whatsit . . . a scapethingy.

4.10 p.m. Robbie the Sex God (MY NEW BOYFRIEND!!! Yesss and three times yesss!!!!!) will be going home from college now. Walking along in a Sex Goddy sort of way. A walking snogging machine.

4.30 p.m. Mutti came in.
"Right, you can start making your startling recovery now, Georgia."

Oh cheers. Thanks a lot. Goodnight.

Just because Elvis Attwood, school caretaker from Planet of the Loons, tripped over his own wheelbarrow (when I told him Jas was on fire) I am banned from school.

Mutti rambled on, although she makes very little sense since Vati got home.

"It's your own fault, you antagonise him and now you are paying the price."

Yeah yeah, rave on.

4.45 p.m. Phoned Jas.
"Jas."

334

"Oh, hi Gee."

"Why didn't you phone me?"

"You're phoning me. I would have got the engaged tone."

"Jas, please don't annoy me, I've only been speaking to you for two seconds."

"I'm not annoying you."

"Wrong."

"Well, I've only said about two words to you."

"That's enough."

Silence.

"Jas?"

Silence.

"Jas . . . what are you doing?"

"I'm not annoying you."

She drives me to the brink of madnosity. Still, I really needed to speak to her, so I went on, "It's really crap at home. I almost wish I hadn't been banned from school. How was Stalag 14? Any goss?"

"No, just the usual. Nauseating P. Green smashed a chair to smithereens and back."

"Really?! Was she fighting with it?"

"No, she was sitting on it having her lunch. It was the jumbo-sized Mars bar that did it. The Bummer Twins started singing 'Who ate all the pies?' to her but Slim, our beloved headmistress, heard them and gave us a lecture about mocking the unfortunate."

"Were her chins going all jelloid?"

"Yeah. In fact it was Chin City."

"Fantastic. Are you all missing me? Did anyone talk about me or anything?"

"No, not really."

Charming. Jas has a lot of good qualities though, qualities you need in a bestest pal. Qualities like, for instance, going out with the brother of a Sex God. I said, "Has Hunky – I mean, Tom – mentioned anything that Robbie has said about me?"

"Erm . . . let me think."

Then there was this slurp slurp noise.

She was making slurping noises.

"Jas, what are you eating?"

"I'm sucking my pen top so I can think better."

Bloody *sacré bleu*, I have got *le idiot* for a pal. Forty-nine centuries of pen-sucking later she said, "No, he hasn't said anything."

7.00 p.m. Why hasn't Robbie mentioned me? Hasn't he got snogging withdrawal?

8.00 p.m. I can hear Vati singing "If I Ruled the World". Good Lord. I have only just recovered from a very bad bout of pretend lurgy. He has no consideration for others.

8.05 p.m. The worsterosity of it is that the Loonleader (my vati) has returned from Kiwi-a-gogo land and I thought he would be there for ages. But sadly life was against me and he has returned. Not content with that he has insisted we all go to Och-aye land to "bond" on a family holiday.

But . . . na-na-na-na-na and who-gives-two-short-flying-pigs'-botties? because I live in Love Heaven.

Lalalalalalala.

I am the girlfriend of a Sex God!!
Yesss!!! Result!!!!

8.15 p.m. The Sex God said I should phone him from Scotland when I go up there. But there is a fly in his ointment . . . I am not going to Scotland!!!

My plan is this: everyone else goes to Scotland and . . . I don't!

Simple enough, I think, for anyone to understand.

operation explain-brilliant-not-going-to-Scotland-plan-to-mutti-and-vati

8.30 p.m. The Olds were slumped in front of the TV canoodling and drinking wine. They are so childish. I had to leave the room in the end because Dad did this really disgusting thing. It makes me feel sick even thinking about it. He got hold of Mum's nip-nips (!) through her sweater and then sort of twiddled them around. He was going, "Calling all cars, calling all cars, are you receiving me?"

Like he was tuning a radio or something. With her basoomas.

Mum said, "Stop it, Bob, what are you like!"

But then they both were laughing and grappling about on the sofa. Libby was there as well. Laughing along. It can't be healthy for a toddler to be exposed to porn. I'm sure other people's parents don't do this sort of thing. In fact, some of my mates are lucky enough to have parents that are split up.

I've never really seen Jas's dad. He is usually upstairs or in his shed doing some DIY. He just appears now and again to give Jas her pocket money.

That is a proper dad.

11.00 p.m. Before I went to bed I explained to the elderly snoggers (from outside the door, just in case they were touching each other) that I will not in a zillion years be going on the family excursion to Scotland tomorrow and said goodnight.

friday october 22nd

scotland
raining
in a crap cottage in nowhere

10.30 p.m. I have come on holiday by mistake.

This is the gorgeous diary of my fantastic family holiday in Och-aye land.

Five hundred years driving with a madman at the wheel (Dad) and another two mad things in a basket (Angus and Libby). After two hours of trying to find the cottage and listening to Vati ramble on about the "wonderful countryside" I was ready to pull Dad's head off, steal the car and drive, drive like the wind back home. The fact that I can't drive stopped me, but actually I'm sure that, once behind the wheel, I could pick it up. How difficult can it be, anyway? All Dad does is swear at other cars and put his foot down on some pedal thing.

Finally arrived at some crap cottage in the middle of nowhere. The nearest shop is twelve hundred miles away (well, a fifteen-minute walk).

The only person younger than one hundred and eighty is a half-witted boy (Jock McThick) who hangs around the village on his pushbike (!).

In the end, out of sheer desperadoes, I went outside after supper and asked Jock McThick what him and his mates did at nights. (Even though I couldn't give two short flying sporrans.)

He said, "Och." (Honestly, he said that.) "We go awa" doon to Alldays, you ken." (I don't know why he called me Ken but that is the mystery of the Scottish folk.)

It was like being in that film *Braveheart*. In fact, in order to inject a bit of hilariosity into an otherwise tragic situation, I said, when we first saw the cottage, "You can tak' our lives, but you cannae tak' our freedom!!"

1.15 a.m. It's a nightmare of noise in this place: hooting, yowling, snuffling . . . and that's just Vati! No, it's the great Scottish wildlife. Bats and badgers and so on . . . Haven't they got homes to go to? Why do creatures wake up at night? Do they do it deliberately to annoy me? At least Angus is happy here though, now he is not under house arrest. It was about one a.m. before he came in and curled up in his luxurious cat headquarters (my bed).

saturday october 23rd

10.30 a.m. Vati back as Loonleader with a vengeance. He came barging into "my" (hahahahaha-ha) room at pre-dawn, waggling his new beard about. I was sleeping with cucumber slices on my eyes for beautosity purposes so at first I thought I had gone blind in the night. I nearly did go blind when he ripped open my curtains and

339

said, "Gidday gidday, me little darlin'," in a ludicrous Kiwi-a-gogo twang.

I wonder if he has finally snapped? He was very nearly bonkers before he went to Kiwi-a-gogo land and having his shoes blown off by a rogue bore can't have helped.

But hey, El Beardo is, after all, my vati and that also makes him Vati of the girlfriend of a Sex God. So I said quite kindly, "*Guten morgen*, Vati, could you please go away now? Thank you."

I think his beard may have grown into his ears however, because he ignored me and opened the window. He was leaning out, breathing in and out and flapping his arms around like a loon. His bottom is not tiny. If a very small pensioner was accidentally walking along behind him they may think there had been an eclipse of the sun.

"Aahh, smell that air, Georgie. Makes you feel good to be alive, doesn't it?"

I pulled my duvet round me. "I won't be alive for much longer if that freezing air gets into my lungs."

He came and sat on the bed. Oh God, he wasn't going to hug me, was he?

Fortunately Mutti yelled up the stairs, "Bob, breakfast is ready!" and he lumbered off.

Breakfast is ready? Has everyone gone mad? When was the last time Mum made breakfast?

Anyway, ho hum pig's bum, I could snuggle down in my comfy holiday bed and do dreamy-dreamy about snogging the Sex God in peace now.

Wrong.

Clank, clank. "Gergy! Gingey!! It's me!!"

Oh Blimey O'Reilly's trousers, it was Libby, mad toddler from

340

Planet of the Loons. When my adorable little sister came in I couldn't help noticing that although she was wearing her holiday sunglasses, she wasn't wearing anything else. She was also carrying a pan. I said, "Libby, don't bring the pan into . . ."

But she ignored me and clambered up into my bed, shoving me aside to make room. She has got hefty little arms for a child of four. She said, "Move up, bad boy, Mr Pan tired."

Then she and Mr Pan snuggled up against me. I almost shot out of bed, her bottom was so cold . . . and sticky . . . urghh.

What is it with my room? You would think that at least on holiday I might be able to close my door and have a bit of privacy to do my holiday project (fantasy snogging), but oh no. There will probably be a coachload of German tourists in *lederhosen* looking round my room in a minute.

I'm going to go and find the local locksmith (Hamish McLocksmith) and get two huge bolts for my door and you can only get in by appointment.

Which I will never make.

11.00 a.m. Libby has clanked off with Mr Pan, thank the Lord. I don't like to be near her naked botty for long as something always lurks out of it.

I think Mum and Dad are playing "Catch" downstairs. I can hear them running around and giggling "Gotcha" and so on.

Sacré bloody *bleu. Très pathetico.* Vati's only been back for eighty-nine hours and I feel more than a touch of the sheer desperadoes coming on.

11.10 a.m. Still, who cares about his parentosity and beardiness? Who cares about being dragged to the crappest, most freezing place known to humanity? I, Georgia Nicolson, offspring of loons am, in fact, the GIRLFRIEND OF A SEX GOD. Yesssssss!!!! Fab and treble marvelloso. I have finally trapped a Sex God. He is mine miney mine mine. There is a song in my heart and do you know what it is? It is that well-known chart topper, "Robbie, oh Robbie, I . . . er . . . lobbie you!!! I do I do!!!"

1.00 p.m. Hung around, sitting on the gate watching the world go by. Unfortunately it didn't. All that went by were some loons talking gibberish (Scottish) and a ferret.

Then Jock McThick or whatever his name is loomed up on his bike. He has an unfortunate similarity to spotty Norman, i.e. acne of the head. This is not enhanced by him being a ginger nob.

Jock said, "Me and the other lads meet oop at aboot nine just ootside Alldays. Mebbe see you later."

Yeah right, see you in the next life, don't be late. Nothing is going to make me sadly go and hang out with Jock and his mates.

8.59 p.m. Vati suggested we had a singsong round the piano tonight and started off with "New York, New York".

9.00 p.m. I took Angus for a walk to check out the nightlife that Jock McThick told me about. Angus is the only good thing about this trip. He's really perked up. I know he longs for Naomi the sex kitten inside his furry brain but he is putting a brave face on it. In fact, he is strutting around like he owns Scotland. This is, after all, his

342

birthplace. He can probably hear the call of the Scottish Highlands quite clearly here. The call that says, "Kill everything that moves." There were four voles all lined up on the doorstep this morning. Mum said she found a dead mouse in her tights. I didn't ask where she had left them. If I ask her anything she just giggles and goes stupid. Since Dad came home her brain has fallen out.

Angus has made a new furry chum. None of the other local cats will come near our cottage. I think there was a "duffing up" challenge last night. The black and white cat I saw in the lane yesterday has quite a bit of its ears missing now. Angus's new mate is a retired sheepdog called Arrow. I say he is retired but sadly he is too barmy and old to know that he is retired, so he keeps rounding things up anyway. Not usually sheep though . . . things like chickens, passing cars . . . old Scottish people doing their haggis shopping. Angus hangs out with Arrow and they generally terrorise the neighbourhood and lay waste to the wildlife.

9.30 p.m. It's quite sweet and groovy walking along with Angus and Arrow. They pad along behind me. At least I have got some intelligent company in this lonely Sex Godless hell-hole.

9.35 p.m. When the three of us got to Alldays, Scotland's premier nightspot, I couldn't believe it.

Alldays turns out to be a tiny twenty-four-hour supermarket.

Not a club or anything.

A bloody shop.

And all the "youth" (four Jock McThicks on bikes) just go

343

WILD there. They hang around in the aisles in the shop, listening to the piped music! Or hang about outside on their pushbikes and go in the shop now and again to buy Coca-Cola or Irn-Bru!

Sacré bloody *bleu* and *quel dommage*.

midnight That was it. The premier nightspot of Scotland.

I said to Mutti, "Have you noticed how exceptionally crap it is here?" and she said, "You have to make your own fun in places like this. You have to make things happen. Anyway, you do exaggerate."

Vati said, "Your cousin will be here tomorrow."

Double *merde*. Vati reaches alarming levels of bonkerosity sometimes. Why does he think I will be pleased to see my cousin James, also known as Pervy Jimjams, pervert *extraordinaire*?

12.30 a.m. Hoot hoot. Scuffle scuffle. Root root. Good grief, it's like a badger party out there . . . Oh no, no, hang on, I forgot – I am enjoying my lovely holiday. Mum was right. I am exaggerating. Something did happen at Scotland's premier hotspot. One Jock McThick lit up a fag and had such a coughing fit that he spilt his Coke on his trousers and had to go home.

1.00 a.m. Honestly.
I am not kidding.

1.30 a.m. I wonder if it would be uncool to walk the forty-eight miles into town and phone the SG?

1.35 a.m. Or walk home to England?

sunday october 24th

10.20 a.m. Still in Och-aye land. Tartan trousers for as far as the eye can see.

10.31 a.m. How many hours has it been since I saw Robbie now? Hmmm, ninety hours and thirty-six minutes.

10.46 a.m. How many minutes is that?

11.04 a.m. Oh God, I don't know. I can't do multiplication very well; it's too jangly for my brain. I've tried to explain this to Miss Stamp our Maths *Oberführer* (and part-time lesbian). It is not, as she stupidly suggests, that I am too busy writing notes to my mates or polishing my nails to concentrate, it is just that some numbers give me the mental droop.

Eight for instance.

It's the same in German. As I pointed out to Herr Kamyer, there are too many letters in German words.

The German types say *Goosegot* in the morning; how normal is that? In fact, how can you take a language like that seriously? Well you can't, which is why I only got sixty per cent in my last German exam.

11.50 a.m. I'm just going to lie in bed conserving my

345

strength for a snogging extravaganza when I get home.

midday Mutti came into my room with a tray of sandwiches. I said, "*Goosegot in Himmel, Mutti,* have you gone mad? Food? For me? No, no, I'll just have my usual bit of old sausage."

She still kept smiling. It was a bit eerie actually. She was all dreamy. Wafting around in a see-through nightie. Good Lord.

"Are you having a nice time, Gee? It's gorgeous here, isn't it?"

I looked at her ironically.

She raved on, "It's fun, though, isn't it?"

"Mum, it's the best fun I've had since . . . er . . . since Libby dropped my make-up into the loo."

She tutted, but not even in her usual violent tutting way. Just like, nice tutting.

Even though I started reading my *Don't Sweat the Small Stuff for Teens* book she still kept raving on. About how great it was to be a "family" again. I wish she would cover herself up a bit more. Other people's mothers wear nice elegant old people's-wear and she just lets her basoomas and so on poke out willy-nilly. And they certainly *do* poke out willy-nilly; they are GIGANTIC.

She said, "We thought we might go to the pencil-making factory this afternoon."

I didn't even bother saying anything to that.

"It will be a laugh."

"No it won't. When did we last have a laugh as a family? Apart from when Grandad's false teeth went down that woman's bra?"

1.00 p.m. The "lovebirds" went off to the pencil factory. They only got Libby to go with them because she thinks they are going to go and see the pencil people.

And I do mean pencil people. Not people who make pencils. Pencil people. People who *are* pencils. She'll go ballistic when she finds out it's just some boring Scottish blokes making pencils.

Oh I am SO bored. Hours and hours of wasted snogging opportunities.

1.20 p.m. I'd go out but there is nothing to look at. It just goes trees, trees, water, hill, trees, trees, Jock McTavish, Jock McTavish. What is the point of that?

On the plus side, I am going out with a SEX GOD!

1.36 p.m. Oh *Gott in Himmel*! What is the point of going out with a Sex God if no one knows? Not even me at this rate.

4.00 p.m. I wonder if I should phone him?

4.30 p.m. I was even nearly pleased to see James and Grandad arrive with Uncle Eddie. For about a second. Uncle Eddie had hired a van specially. He probably had to get a special kind that accommodates the very bald.

James's voice has gone all weird. It's sort of deep and then all squeaky. How normal is that? He is by no means a lurker-free zone either, I notice. *Tout au contraire.*

Dad said, "Cum awa' in!" in a really crap Scottish accent and Grandad started to jig around "dancing", and had to be helped into the cottage.

Uncle Eddie said, "Don't panic, don't panic! I've brought supplies of large Union Jack underpants!" What in the name of Louis the Fourteenth is he on about?

7.00 p.m. Forced to go and sit in the pub with the elderly loons (and James) to "celebrate". Yippeee! This is the life . . . (not). I asked Vati for a Tia Maria on the rocks with just a hint of Crème de Menthe but he pretended not to hear me. Typico. On the way home M and D and Uncle Eddie and Grandad were all linked up, singing "Donald, Where's Your Trousers?" whilst James and I skulked along behind them. It was incredibly dark, no street lamps or anything. As we tramped along the grown-ups were laughing and crashing about (and in Grandad's case farting) when this awful thing happened.

I felt something touch my basooma. I thought it was the Old Man of the Loch and I leaped back like a leaping banana. James spoke from out of the darkness, "Oh . . . er . . . sorry, was that you, Gee? I was just like . . . you know . . . feeling my way."

Dream on, saddo. Feeling your way? Feeling your way to where? My other basooma?

This was disgusting. He was my crap cousin. Molesting my nunga-nungas. Nunga-nunga molester.

11.00 p.m. Despite the incredible crapness of my life my nunga-nungas have made me laugh.

Nunga-nungas is what Ellen's brother and his mates call girls' basoomas. He says it is because if you pull out a girl's breast and let it go . . . it goes nunga-nunga-nunga. He is obviously a touch on the mental side.

11.10 p.m. But quite funny though.

11 20 p.m. I wonder what size nunga-nunga holder Mum wears?

11.30 p.m. Perhaps I could make some nunga-nunga protectors by electrifying my sports bra with a battery type thing. That would give Cousin James the perv a shock if he attempted to "accidentally" molest my nungas.

11.35 p.m. But it would also give me a shock, which is *la mouche* in the ointment.

midnight Angus has rediscovered his Scottish roots. Apparently they are in the middle of some bog because he had bits of horrible slimy stuff in his whiskers. He came into my bed purring and all damp and muddy. Still, he soon got nice and dry by wiping himself on my T-shirt.

God he smells disgusting. I think he's been rolling in fox poo again. He thinks it's like a sort of really attractive aftershave.

12.10 a.m. It isn't.

10.10 a.m. Why oh why oh why has the SG not called me? Oh hang on, I know why he hasn't, it's because we haven't got a phone in our fantastic cottage. I couldn't believe it when we first arrived. I said to Mutti, "There has been some mistake. I'm afraid we must go back to civilization immediately. I'll drive."

Dad raved on about "tranquillity" and the simple life.

I said, "Vati, you can be as simple as you like, but I want to talk to my mates."

He grumbled on about my constant demands. As I pointed out to him, if he would buy me a mobile phone like everyone else on the planet I wouldn't have to bother speaking to him at all.

2.00 p.m. I can't stand much more of this. The whole "family" has gone on a forced march. Well, Vati called it "a little walk in the woods". But I know about his little walks. I know exactly what will happen: the Loonleader will be all bossy and "interested" in stuff like cuckoo spit. Then he'll lose the way and argue with Grandad about the right way home. Grandad will fall over something and Uncle Eddie will be attacked by sheep. And those will only be the high spots.

I pretended I had a headache.

Vati said to me as I lay in my pretend bed of pain, "You've probably given yourself eyestrain looking in that bloody mirror all the time."

I said, "If I develop a brain tumour you will be the first person I will come to because of your great kindness and sympathosity."

350

4.20 p.m. On the edge of sheer desperadoes. Decided to go for a walk.

Arrow tried to round me up as I came out of the gate. So to make him happy I let him herd me into a hedge for a bit. Then I set off down the lane. Ho hum. Birds singing, ferrets ferretting, probably. Jock McThicks McThicking around. Good grief. Then I came across a phone box.

Uh-oh. Temptation.

The phone box was saying to me, "Come in and use me, you know you want to."

I have been practising maturiosity by not phoning the Sex God. It seems like a lifetime since he last snogged me. My lips have definitely got snog withdrawal. I found myself trying out kissing techniques on scuba-diving Barbie last night. Which is truly sad. I wonder if Rosie is right? Her theory is that if you snog a lot your lips sort of swell up and get bigger. It makes you wonder what in the name of Slim's pantaloons Mark the Big Gob has been doing.

I must pass by the phone box with complete determinosity.

4.30 p.m. Brring brring.
Please don't let it be Robbie's mum or dad. Please don't let me have to be normal.

Oh thank goodness, SG answered the phone. Jellyknickers all round.

He said, "Hello," in a Sex Goddy sort of a way.

Wow!!

Then he said, "Hello," again.

Wow.

Then I realised that normally when you phone someone you are supposed to say something. And that something is NOT "I

351

love you, I love you!" or "Ngyunghf". So I took the bullet by the horns and said, "Hi, Robbie . . . it's me. Georgia."

(Very good, I had even said the right name!!!)

He sounded like he was really pleased to hear from me. "Gee! How are you, gorgeous?"

Gorgeous, he, me called, gorgeous. Me, I.

Georgia to brain, Georgia to brain! Shut up shut up shut up!!!!!

He said again, "Gee, are you there? Are you having a good time?"

"Fantastic, if you like being bored beyond the Valley of Boredom and into the Universe of the Very Dull."

He laughed. (Hurrah!!!)

Oh, it was so dreamy to talk to him. I told him about everything. Well, apart from being molested by my cousin. He says some talent scouts are coming to see the next Stiff Dylans gig!!

Then he said, "Look, Gee, I'm really sorry but I have to go. I could talk to you all day but I have to go off to a rehearsal and I'm late now."

Ho hum. Well I suppose this is the price I must pay for being the GIRLFRIEND OF A SEX GOD POPSTAR!!! YESSS!!

He said, in his groovy voice full of gorgeosity, "See you later. I'd like to snog you to within an inch of your life. I'll phone you when you get back."

OOOhhhhhh.

After he had put the phone down I stroked my T-shirt with the receiver, pretending it was him. But then I saw that one of the Jock McTavishes was waiting outside the telephone box, looking at me, so I had to pretend I was cleaning the receiver.

352

Phew. To make Jock go away I have said I will go to Alldays later. Jock seemed to believe me because he said, "Awa' the noo hoots akimbo," or something. After he had done wheelies (!) and gone off on his bike I popped back into the telephone box to phone Jas.

"Jas, it's me!!!! God it's good to speak to you! What's been happening???"

"Er . . . well . . . I got this fab new foundation; it's got gold bits in it that make you . . ."

"Jas, no, no, no, be quiet, I have to tell you something."

I told her about talking to the Sex God. "It was SO dreamy. He is going to be a HUGE popstar and then I will be richey rich rich. But still your best pal, Jas."

She said, "Tom is thinking about doing Environmental Studies."

I nearly said "Who cares?" but you have to be careful with Jas because she can turn nasty if she thinks you are not interested in her. I tried to think of something to say.

"Oh . . . er . . . yeah . . . the environment . . . er, that's great, erm, there's a lot of . . . er . . . environment here – in fact, that is all there is."

Then I told her about the James fandango.

She said, "Erlack-a-pongoes. Did you encourage him? Maybe you gave out the wrong signals."

"Jas, I was not in the nuddy-pants."

"Well I'm just saying, he must have thought he could rest his hand on your basooma. Why is that? He has never rested his hand on my basoomas, for instance."

"What are you rambling on about?"

"I'm just saying, this is not the first time this has happened to you, is it? There was Mark the Big Gob . . ."

"Yeah but . . ."

"You say it just happened. That just out of the blue he put his hand on your basooma. No one else was there so we will never really know for sure."

"I didn't . . . it was . . ."

"Perhaps James has heard about your reputation. Perhaps he thinks it's all right to fondle your basoomas."

I hate Jas. I slammed the phone down. I will never be talking to her again. I don't forget things. Once my mind is made up that is it. The friendship is *finito*. She has made a mockery of a sham of my nunga-nungas. I would rather eat one of Libby's night-time nappies than talk to Jas again.

She is an ex-best mate. Dead to me. Deaddy dead dead. For ever.

phone box
5 mins later

4.55 p.m. Phoned Jas. "Jas, are you suggesting I am an easy fondleree?"

"I don't know. I might be."

"What do you mean, you might be?"

"Well, I might be . . . but I don't know what a fondleree is."

It is like talking to the very very backward.

I explained to her as patiently as I could, "Well, it's like dumping. If you dump someone you are the dumper. And they are the dumpee."

"What has that got to do with fondling?"

"Jas, concentrate. The verb is 'to fondle': I fondle, you fondle, he, she, it fondles, etc. But I am the recipient of the fondle so that makes me the fondleree."

She wasn't really concentrating, though, she was in a dream-world of her own. She was probably looking at herself in the mirror in their hall . . . imagining she is Claudia Schiffer. Just because some absolute prat told her she looked a bit like Claudia. Yeah . . . Claudia with a stupid fringe.

Walked back to Cottage Crap.

my room

6.00 p.m. Brilliant. Miles away from civilization and my so-called mate says I am an easy fondleree . . . Still, she is mad as a badger, everyone knows that. I went into the kitchen for a glass of soda and James came in behind me. He said, "I'll get a glass for you, Georgia." Then he sort of pressed himself into me and pretended he was reaching up for a cup from the cupboard.

Good grief. He's Stalker Cousin.

You would think that Mutti and Vati would notice but all they do is enjoy themselves and giggle.

9.00 p.m. Sitting around in the tartan lounge in Cottage Crap. Sitting as far away as possible from James just in case he looms around me. Mutti and Vati and Grandad and Uncle Eddie are actually playing Snap. James is pretending to be reading his stupid boy comic but I bet he is secretly looking at my nunga-nungas. My breasts are making me a mockery of a sham. They are like two sticky-out beacons attracting all the sadsacks in the universe.

11.00 p.m. Mutti came into my bedroom to get Libby out of my wardrobe. She's made a

sort of nest in there which she says is a "wee-wee house" –
I think she means treehouse.

Over the shouting and biting I said to Mutti, "Do you think
you could ask Dad if you and he could club together to let me
have some money for breast reduction surgery?"

It took her about a year to stop laughing.

It's pointless asking for money. I can't get a fiver out of Dad
for some decent lip-gloss. He would never give me the money.
Even if my breasts were so big that I had to have two servants
called Carlos and Juan to carry them around for me.

tuesday october 26th

10.00 a.m. The postman came this morning. He
didn't have any post; he just said "Good
morning to you. Welcome to Scotland." He was quite
groovy-looking.

10.15 a.m. Oh, Blimey O'Reilly's pantaloons, I think I
have got general snoggosity syndrome.

8.00 p.m. James followed me around all day, waiting for an opportunity to "accidentally"
touch me. I have tried hanging around with Mutti and Vati but
it is too sad.

Oh, Robbie, where are you now? Rescue me from the Valley
of the Loons.

9.00 p.m. How soon can I get them to set off for
home tomorrow? If we set off at dawn we
could be back in Normal Land by about four p.m.

9.30 p.m. I wonder if the Ace Gang might arrange a surprise welcome home party for me? It's half term now so I am no longer an ostracised leper on my own. So ha-di-ha-ha. She who laughs the last laughs, erm, a lot. Slim thought she was banning me for a week but she was banning me for two weeks!!!

10.00 p.m. In "my" bed, with the usual crowd. Libby and the entire contents of her travelling toybox: scuba-diving Barbie, one-eyed Teddy, Pantalitzer, Panda the Punk (Libby shaved his head). The only difference is that to celebrate our holiday in Tartan-a-gogo Libby has replaced Charlie Horse with Jimmy. Jimmy is a haggis with a scarf on. Don't even ask. Libby made him this afternoon and she "lobes" him.

I am sleeping in a bed with a stuffed sheep's stomach. With a scarf on.

wednesday october 27th

6.00 a.m. Up and packed. I tried to get Mutti and Vati to get up and make an early start but when I went into their bedroom Vati threw his slipper at me.

9.00 a.m. At last! Escape!!!! Soon I will be back in the arms of my Sex God. At last, at last. Thank the Lord!!! I love you, Jesus, really really I do. Uncle Eddie, James and Grandad drove off in the Loonmobile. Uncle Eddie was wearing his souvenir bagpipe hat but I didn't care. They were goney gone gone. Hurrah hurrah!!! With a bit of luck I can avoid them for the rest of my life. Arrow looked all mournfully at Angus when we left. He will miss his furry partner in crime. Angus and Arrow, *Los Dos Amigos Bonkeros*. Angus didn't even look back; he just shot into the car and started wrestling with the car rug.

11.00 a.m. Meanwhile in my fabulous life, another eighty-five years of my parents' company in the car home.

Libby has insisted on bringing Jimmy the haggis home with us.

1.00 p.m. Oh good grief. Angus ate half of Jimmy when Libby had to be taken to the piddly diddly department at the service station.

She went ballisticisimus when she found out. She hit Angus over the head with scuba-diving Barbie. I don't think he even noticed – well, he didn't stop purring. I nodded off for the whole of the Midlands because Dad started telling us about his hopes for the future. When I woke up I noticed that both Libby and Angus were nibbling away at Jimmy.

They are disgusting.

I sooooo hope that Robbie rings when I get home.

6.00 p.m. Home!!!! Oh thank you, thank you, Baby Jesus. I am SOOOO happy. I will never complain about my dear little home again.

6.15 p.m. God it's so boring here. Nothing is happening.

6.30 p.m. No phone calls.

All my so-called mates forgot to remember that I am not dead. Don't they even wonder where I have been for the last five days?

7.55 p.m. Jas, Jools, Ellen, Rosie, Mabs and Soph are ALL out. They've all gone to the cinema together. The Fab Gang but without one of the fab.

People can be so self-obsessed. Right, well I am going to eat the souvenirs that I brought back from Och-aye land for them.

8.25 p.m. Lying down.

Urgh, I feel sick. I may never eat Ye Olde Shortbreaddy again as long as I live.

9.00 p.m. Tucked up in bed. I have made a barrier with my bedside table so that no one can get in my room.

Now I really have got snogging withdrawal BADLY!!

9.05 p.m. I must see him. I must.

10.00 p.m. Undid my barricade and went downstairs. I am so restless.

Angus is driving everyone insane!! He is not allowed out at night until he learns his lesson *vis-à-vis* Naomi the sex kitten. He has to be kept away from her otherwise he is for the big chop. Although I would like to see the vet that could do the job and still have both arms.

He keeps yowling and scratching at the door. He is supposed to go to the piddly diddly department and poo parlour division in the laundry room. But he won't go in, he just hangs round the front door trying to get out, whining and scratching and occasionally licking his bottom.

Libby said, "C'mon, big pussy, I'll show you," and went and had a piddly diddly on his tray. Erlack.

She said, "It's NICE!!!"

Oh marvellous. Now we'll never get her to go to the ordinary piddly diddly department. She'll want her own tray.

Then Vati, Loonleader of the Universe, took over. "I'll deal with the bloody thing!"

He dragged Angus into the laundry to put him on the cat tray. It took him about half an hour, even using the spade. Anyway, he got him in there at last. There was a lot of yowling and swearing and Vati came out two minutes later covered in kitty litter. Like the Abominable Ashtray! Even his beard was grey.

10.30 p.m. In the end, after Angus had laid waste to four loo rolls, I was made to take him out on his lead to see if it would calm him down. God he's strong! I mean, normally I have very little control over him but his love has given him the strength of ten mad cats. When we got out of the door he just took off with me on the end of the lead. Straight to Naomi's love parlour. At Mr and Mrs Across the Road's place there was a reinforced fence round the garden but you could see the house and there was Naomi! The sex kitten. Languishing in the kitchen window. On the windowsill. Looking all longing. She was like me. All puckered up and nowhere to go. Poor furry thing. Angus yowled and started doing this weird shivering thing. When Naomi saw Angus she immediately lay on her back with her girlie parts flowing free.

360

She's a dreadful minx. No wonder Angus is a wreck, driven mad by her Burmese sex kitteny charms. Still, that is male and female for you. Sex God was probably at home even now thinking about me and shivering with excitement like Angus.

10.40 p.m. But hopefully not rubbing his bottom against a dustbin.

10.50 p.m. We would have been there all night but fortunately Mr Across the Road drew the curtains and I found a bit of old sausage and managed to get Angus to trail after it. He was so miserable that I didn't lock him in the kitchen, I let him sleep on my bed even though it is strictly *verboten*.

I said to him very seriously, "Angus, you are on best behaviour, just lie down and go to sleep."

He was all purry and friendly and licky. You see, that's all he needs – a bit of understanding.

Aahhh. It's nice having a loyal furry pal. He's a lot more loyal than some I could name but won't.

Jas.

10.55 p.m. Rosie, Jools, Ellen.

11.00 p.m. Night-night, Sex God, wherever you are.

midnight Vati went ballisticisimus in the middle of the night. Raving on and shouting, "That is IT, that is IT!!!"

Mutti was saying, "Bob, Bob . . . put the knife down."

Has he finally snapped and will have to go to a Vatihome?

12.15 a.m. Angus has pooed in Vati's tie drawer! Hilarious really. El Beardo, as usual, did not see the joke. He dragged Angus, who was spitting at him, into the kitchen and locked him in there. Then he shouted at me, "Right, that's IT! I'm going to the vet."

I said, "Why? Are you feeling a bit peaky?" But he didn't get it.

snog fest!

thursday october 28th

10.00 a.m. Vati said to me over our marvellous breakfast of . . . er . . . nothing, "He's going to the vet and having his chimney swept as soon as I can make an appointment."

What in the name of Sir Julie Andrews is he talking about now?

11.00 a.m. I've got much too much on my mind to worry about chimneys. I think I may have a lurker coming on. Emergency emergency.

11.15 a.m. Also the orang-utan gene is rearing its ugly head again. My eyebrows are so hairy they are now approaching the "It's a moustache! It's a hedgehog!!! No, no, it's GEORGIA'S EYEBROWS!!" stage.

It doesn't even stop at the head, this rogue hair business. I've just inspected my legs. I look like I have got hairy trousers on.

Dad's razor is lying there, calling to me, "Come on, use me. You know you want to." But no, no, I must resist after what

363

happened last time. My eyebrows took a thousand years to grow back after I accidentally shaved them off.

Hmm, but maybe Mum's hair removing cream? Just a little dab here and there.

midday   Mutti asked me if I wanted to go ten-pin bowling with them! Honestly! She and Vati went off with Libby skipping along. I think M and D were holding hands. Sweet really, I suppose. I just wish it didn't make me feel so sick.

12.30 p.m.   Jas came round AT LAST. I was a bit miffed with her about last night and not bothering to come round earlier. She was lying on my bed and I could see her vast pantibus underneath her skirt. I said, "Jas, do you mind? I'm not feeling very well. I think I might have jet-lag from coming home from Och-aye land."

"You haven't got a tan."

What is the point? I gave her my worst look. She didn't notice, of course, just went on putting on my mascara. She CANNOT stop pouting every time she sees herself in a mirror. She said, "We had a great time at the cinema. Dave the Laugh is really . . . you know . . ." (Pouty pout.)

"What?"

"Well, you know . . ." (Pouty pout.) ". . . a laugh."

I tried not to be sarcastic or raise my eyebrows ironically, because I didn't want to draw any attention to them. I had not quite achieved the sophisticated look that I wanted with Mum's hair remover. In fact, I had achieved the "someone has just stuck a firework up my bottom" look. But you couldn't really tell unless you pulled my fringe back.

364

Anyway, you'd have to be on fire for Jas to notice anything. She was rambling on, "Do you think I should get my hair cut really short at the back and kind of longer at the front?"

I hadn't the remotest interest in Jas's head but I know you have to let her rave on about herself a bit otherwise you never get to talk about yourself. Then she said, "Ellen really likes Dave the Laugh."

"Huh?"

"She stayed round at my place for the night and we talked until about four a.m. That's why I am so tired."

"It's nice that you have got a new lezzie mate, Jas, but what has that got to do with me?"

"She didn't sleep in my bed."

"So you say."

"Well she didn't."

"It's nothing to be ashamed of, Jas. If you swing both ways that is your personal choice. I'm sure Tom will understand if you tell him you are a bisexual."

"Oh shut up – you're being all moody and stressy because Robbie hasn't phoned you."

She's right, actually, which is annoying. I feel all pent up, like in *Cell Block H*. I said, "Let's put on some really loud CDs and go apeshit crazy."

We did this fab dance routine. It was duo head shaking, kick turn, jump on bed, snog teddy then back to the head shaking. I was feeling quite perked up. Then, of course, someone had to spoil it. I had forgotten about the Return of the Mad Bearded One. He came in the front door and it was stomp, stomp, "Bloody hell!", then crash, stomp stomp, yell: "Georgia!!! Are you deaf?!!! Turn that racket down, I could hear it at the end of the bloody street!!"

I shouted back, "Pardon? Can you speak up, Dad, there's really loud music playing!!!" Which made Jas and me laugh a lot. But not El Beardo.

4.00 p.m. Jas, my so-called best mate, had to go because she was doing her "homework". How sad is that? Very very sad. Also she was doing it with her "boyfriend" Hunky. Hell will freeze over and become a skating rink for the mad before I will do my homework with Robbie. Sex Gods and their girlfriends do not "do homework". Life is too short.

I tried to explain the tragedy of what she was doing but Jas just said, "I want to do well in my German exam."

I laughed. But she was serious.

I said, "It is so naff to do well in German, Jas."

Jas went all huffy. "You only say that because you can't do it."

"Oh that is so *nicht* true, Jas. *Ich bin ein guten* German speaker."

But old swotty knickers went off anyway. Hmmm.

5.00 p.m. Swiss Family Robinson have gone to the cinema together now. It's just fun fun fun, all the way for them.

All aloney. On my owney. It's bloody nippy noodles as well. What a life.

I have been back a whole day and a night and he has not called me. Why oh why oh why?

I am so fed up.

5.10 p.m. I might as well go to bed and grow my lurker.

5.20 p.m. Phone rang. Probably Jas asking me something about her homework.

I said, "Jahwohl!"

5.22 p.m. The Sex God wants me to go round to his house!!! His parents are out. I am so HAPPY!!!

5.30 p.m. I changed into my jeans and quickly got made up. I went for the "natural" look (lip-gloss, eyeliner, mascara and blusher) with a touch of pan-stick on the lurker. You could only see the lurking lurker if you looked up my nostril and what fool was going to do that? Then I dashed off.

outside robbie's house

6.00 p.m. I walked through the gate, breathing the atmosphere of Sex Goddiness, and knocked on the door.

My heart was beating really loudly. The door opened.

The Sex God.

Himself.

In person.

In his gorgeous black jeans and thingy top. And his dreamy armey things and gorgey leggy whatsits and mouthy thing and so on. He is SO dreamy. Every time I see him it's a shock. He smiled at me.

"Georgia . . . how are you?"

Excellent question. Excellent. Good. I knew the answer as well. That was the marvellous thing. I knew the answer was

"Great, how are you?" Unfortunately all the blood in my brain had gone for a bit of a holiday into my cheeks. I had a very very red face and a completely empty brain. I couldn't speak, all I could do was be very very red. I bet that was attractive.

He just looked at me and he smiled this really beautiful smile, all curly round the teeth. Like he really liked me. Yuuummy scrumbos.

Then he pulled me into the house and shut the door behind me. I just stood there trying not to be red. He put his arms round me and gave me a little soft kiss on the mouth, no tongues (Number Three on the snogging scale). But my mouth had gone into pucker mode so when he stopped my mouth was a bit behind and still a bit open. I hoped I didn't look like a startled goldfish.

He kissed me again, this time harder and longer. His mouth was all warm and wet (not wet like Mollusc Boy though). He put one of his hands on the back of my head, which was just as well as I thought my head might fall off. And then he started kissing my neck. Little sucky kisses right up to my ear. Fanbloodytastic. After a bit of that, and believe me I could have gone on doing that for years, he put his tongue ever so softly into my ear!! Really! Ear snogging!!! Fantastic.

I think I might have lost the use of my legs then because I fell over on to the sofa.

my bedroom

10.00 p.m. I am in Love Heaven. What a beyond fab day. He is Sex God of the Universe and beyond.

I crept downstairs and phoned Jas.

"Jas," I whispered.

"Why are you whispering?"

"Because M and D are in the front room and I don't want them to know I am calling you."

"Oh."

"I have had the most amazing time, I . . ."

"Well I haven't; I just can't decide whether to have my hair cut for the gig . . . Do you think yes or no? I mean, it's nice to have it long but then it's nice to have it short, but then . . ."

"Jas, Jas . . . it is my turn to talk."

"How do you know?"

"I just do."

"Oh."

"Ask me what I have just done."

"Why? Don't you know?" And she started laughing.

I forgot I was supposed to be whispering and yelled down the phone, "Jas!!!"

Then I told her. "I went round to Robbie's house to see him."

Jas said, "No!"

"*Mais oui!*"

"*Sacré bleu!*"

"*Aujourd'hui.*"

"Well, what happened?"

And I said, "Well, it was beyond marvy. We talked and snogged and then he made me a sandwich and we snogged and then he played me a record and then we snogged."

"So it was like . . ."

"Yeah . . . a snogging fest."

"*Sacré bleu!*"

Jas sounded like she was thinking which is a) unusual and b) scary.

369

I said, "But then this weird thing happened. He was playing me his demo CD and standing behind me with his hands on my waist."

"Oo-er . . ."

"*D'accord*. Anyway, I turned round and he sort of leaped out of the way like two short leaping things."

"Was he dancing?"

"No . . . I think he was frightened of being knocked out by my nunga-nungas . . ."

Then we both laughed like loons on loon tablets (i.e. a LOT).

my bedroom

10.20 p.m. Vati made me get off the phone and gave his famous "We are not made of money" speech first given in 1846.

11.00 p.m. Emergency snogging scale update:

1 holding hands;
2 arm around;
3 goodnight kiss;
4 kiss lasting over three minutes without a breath;
5 open-mouth kissing;
6 tongues;
6½ ear snogging;
7 upper-body fondling – outdoors;
8 upper-body fondling – indoors (in bed);
9 below waist activity (b.w.a.), and
10 the full monty.

11.10 a.m. Dreamed of Robbie feeding me chocolate sandwiches. Which was really cool. But then he started nibbling my ears in a sort of peckish way and he nibbled them both off. Then for some reason we were in the South of France at some big gig and it was really sunny and I got my shades out to put on and they just fell off because I had no ears to balance them on.

I don't know what this means. It means I am feverish with love.

Very nippy noodles again. Brrrr. Oh, it's snowed during the night, that's why.

When I got out of bed and stood in the cold air my nipples did that sticking out thing again. On the whole I seem to have very little control over my body.

Still, so what!!!

6.00 p.m. Spent the day in a love haze punctuated by rescuing bits of my underwear from Angus's basket. He is in an awful mood. He climbed up the curtains like a Tyrolean mountaineer in a furry suit. I don't know why.

watching tv

9.00 p.m. It's a programme called *Changing Rooms* where some sadists go into some other people's home and change their living-room into a water feature. With the aid of bubble-wrap. What amazes me is that there is no violence.

Phone rang. OhmyGod. I almost ripped it off the wall.

It was Rosie checking arrangements for tomorrow.

I could hardly hear her because there was such loud music in the background. She said, "Greetings, earth creature . . . SVEN!!!!! you adorable Norwegian fool, turn the music down!!"

I heard laughing and stamping and then the music went quieter. Rosie said, "Jas said you did ear snogging yesterday."

Oh thank you, Radio Jas.

saturday october 30th

10.30 a.m. Phoned Jas for gang discussion. Where we should all meet today and so on.

When she answered I came over a bit French. (Because I am in *Le Luurve* Heaven.)

"*Bonjour, Jas, it is moi, ta grande amie.*"

"Ah, *bonjour.*"

"Ah *d'accord,* I have just *manged* my breakfast. I *manged* the *délicieusement* toast and *le coffee de Monsieur Nescafé.*"

"*Magnifique.*"

"*De rigueur.*"

We are meeting at gang headquarters (Luigi's café) at one o'clock and then going on for a bit of heavy make-up trying-on in Boots, etc. I have only got a measly five pounds to spend. I hope Dad manages to persuade some poor fool to give him a job soon because I am running out of lip-gloss.

11.00 a.m. Bloody hell. You take your life in your hands going into the kitchen for a snack.

372

Angus is in there and he is not pleased. I had to fend him off with a frying pan to get into the fridge.

Still, lalalalala.

midday Still in a European mood I dressed French casual (same as sports casual – black Capri trousers, black roll-neck top, ankle boots – but with a lot more eyeliner).

In fact, the combination of Frenchosity and my snogging extravaganza made me come over all forgiving and relaxed. I even waved to Mr Next Door as I went down the road. Typically he just tutted. But hey ho, tut on, Fatty, nothing can spoil my mood. Mr Next Door was wearing an extraordinary pair of trousers; they seemed to start under his armpits and be made out of elephant. He was "armed" with a hoe.

He said, "I hope you are keeping that wild animal under lock and key. It's about time something was done with it."

Nobody can take a joke around here. All right, Mr Across the Road does have a point in that Angus did abscond with Naomi, but what does old elephant trousers have to complain about?

What they both fail to see are Angus's very good qualities. He has many attractive cat qualities. For instance he has EXCELLENT balance. Only last month he herded Snowy and Whitey, Mr Next Door's prat poodles, into the manure heap and then leaped down from the wall and had a ride around on Snowy's back. Like Snowy was a little horsey.

How many cats can do that?

12.30 p.m. When I was waiting at the bus stop for a bus to town two blokes in cars hooted their horns at me (oo-er). I really have become a babe magnet.

Then along came Mark Big Gob who I unfortunately made the mistake of going out with in my youth. Well, ten months ago, anyway. He was messing about with his rough mates, waiting for the bus. No sign of his midget girlfriend: perhaps he had mislaid her?

His mouth is sooo big; how could I have snogged him? And he rested his hand on my basooma. Still, let bygones be bygones. My basoomas were out of his hands now. I was after all the girlfriend of a Sex God and Mark was the boyfriend of some toddler. I smiled kindly at him and that is when he said to his mates, "You don't get many of those to the pound." And he meant my nunga-nungas! And all his mates laughed.

I stood there in a dignity-at-all-times sort of way, until the bus came. I sat as far away from the BG and his rough mates as I could.

12.45 p.m. It was a relief to get off the bus. As I got off I had to go past Mark and his mates. I made sure my nungas were not making a guest appearance by hunching my shoulders over.

12.50 p.m. I've just seen a reflection of myself in a shop window looking like the hunchback of Notre Dame in a mini skirt.

1.00 p.m. In the café I met up with Rosie, Ellen, Mabs, Jools and Jas. Yesssssssssss! The Ace Gang together again!! The girls are back in town, the girls are back in town!!! We had loads of really important things to talk about: make-up, snogging and, of course, berets. This term is not going so well on the beret front. Even the lunchpack beret has lost its charm.

Rosie said, "I walked past Miss Stamp with two oranges and a banana stuck under my beret and she just raised her eyes. Something must be done."

I had a flash of total whatsit . . . wisdomosity. "Mes huge amis I have given this seconds of thought, and I know what the answer is."

They were all as agog as two gogs. Jools said, "What?"

I brought out my gloves and beret from my rucky. "Voilà."

They looked at me. Honestly, it was like talking to the terminally deaf.

I said again, "Voilà . . . glove animal!!"

Rosie said, "What in the name of Slim's gigantic knickers are you talking about?"

Good grief. It is very tiring being the girlfriend of a Sex God and a genius at the same time.

"Glove animal!!! A way of dressing sensibly and snugly using both beret and gloves. You pin a glove over each ear so that it hangs down like big dog ears and then you pop the beret over the top."

I clipped my gloves over my ears and popped the beret over the top (risking my hair's bounceability factor).

"Voilà glove animal!!!"

Magnifique, I think everyone will agree.

8.00 p.m. Home again. To my lovely delicious supper of . . . er . . .

Mutti and Vati and Loonsister out AGAIN. Still. In Love Heaven you are never really alone.

Angus is tied up to the kitchen table leg. I gave him a hug

to cheer him up and he lashed out at me. Also I notice that he has a pair of Vati's Y-fronts in his basket. Good grief. He has gone beyond sheer desperadoes. He is really sad without Naomi. I know how he feels, every minute without the Sex God seems about sixty seconds long.

9.10 p.m. OOOhhhhh. If the SG was here now we could practise our ear snogging skills.

11.30 p.m. Hallowe'en tomorrow.
It's impossible to sleep in my bed with Libby's turnip lantern in here.

I suppose I should be pleased she hasn't insisted on having her witch's broom and . . .

"Libby, no not the broom and . . ."

"Move over, bad boy."

sunday october 31st

hallowe'en

10.30 a.m. I immediately annoyed Dad this morning by pretending that he was wearing a scary Hallowe'en costume. In fact his leisure slacks and Marks & Spencer's cardigan ARE very scary but he didn't get it.

Libby is in toddler heaven because some of her little mates from kindy are coming across this afty for apple bobbing and lanterns and stuff.

11.00 a.m. In a rare moment of sanity Vati has been over to see Mr and Mrs Across the Road and pleaded for Angus's manhood. He was all pleased with himself when he came back.

"I thought I'd take a look at that garden fence, Connie, see if we can keep Angus in a bit more. Then he might not have to have his biscuits nibbled."

Biscuits nibbled? What planet does he live on?

He started rooting around in the toolbox. I wish he would get a job and then he wouldn't be interested in DIY any more.

Mum said, "Bob, I beg you, please get someone competent to do the fence. You're only just back on your feet again."

Vati got all Daddish.

"Connie, I can fix a fence, you know."

We laughed. I helped Mum out: "Dad, there was the unfortunate leg through the ceiling incident when you last went into the loft."

"There was a weakness in the roof."

"Yeah, Dad, that was you."

"Don't be so bloody cheeky."

I am not wrong though. The electrician who came to look at the fridge that blew up after Dad had "fixed it" accused Dad of being a madman.

And the shed fell down on Uncle Eddie.

But grown-ups will never be told anything until it is too late. That is the sadnosity of grown-ups.

As Vati went into the cupboard under the stairs Mum looked at me, but what was I supposed to do? It's her husband, she should stop him. He came out of the cupboard with a hammer and a saw. I said, "Well, probably catch up with you later in Casualty then, Dad."

He swore in a very unpleasant way.

Actually, Mum is probably hoping he will injure himself.

377

She hasn't had any excuse to go see gorgeous Dr Clooney for a week or so. Libby can't have any more vaccinations – she's practically a pin-cushion as it is – and I am not going to sustain any more sports injuries to help her out.

As I was just going to escape through the door Vati put his foot down with a firm hand.

"Georgia, make yourself useful. Take Angus out on his lead. Get him out from under my feet."

I put Angus's lead on him while he playfully bit my shins. He's mad for fun. We reached the bottom of the hill in about two seconds flat because he caught wind of a tiny little Pekinese. The owner had to take refuge in a shop.

2.00 p.m. Dad has built an hilarious fence. It's sort of leany and falling-downy at the same time. It is supposed to keep Angus away from Naomi but when Dad was hammering in the final nail he said, "Yes, well, that should keep him safely in!" and the whole fence fell over . . . And Angus just walked straight over the fence into Next Door's garden.

3.00 p.m. Vati is having to pretend to be normal because Libby's kindy mates have arrived. Libby's an awfully rough hostess. When Millie and Oscar were bobbing for apples she "helped" them by banging them on the heads with her pumpkin lantern. Oscar couldn't walk straight for ages and Millie wanted to go home. Well, actually, all of the children wanted to go home.

I said to Mutti, "Why does she think that smiling like that at people is normal?"

Angus is having a huge laugh. He keeps appearing on the top of fences and so on. He ate Snowy's play Bonio. Mr Next Door said he will have to get a dog psychiatrist in.

Vati's been raving on and on. Outside I could see Mr and Mrs Next Door and Mr and Mrs Across the Road all muttering together and poking about with sticks. They are probably forming a lynch mob. For heaven's sake.

Vati said, "As soon as we find him that is it, he has his trombone polished once and for all."

As Dad was grumping around moaning on and on and banging things about in the kitchen I said to Mum, "Will you tell Vati that I don't want to discuss things of a personal nature with him but if he takes Angus to the vet and has his, you know, trouser snake addendums tampered with, he is no longer my vati. I will be vatiless."

Mutti just went tutting off into a world of her own.

Angus is a king amongst cats. He walks tall with his trouser snake addendas proudly dangling. Naomi is yowling all the time. Why don't they just let them be together?

away laughing
on a fast camel

back to school
sacré bleu merde and double poo
at "breakfast"

7.50 a.m. Angus is on his lead, yowling, tied to the kitchen table. It's like having a police car in the kitchen. He was brought back under armed guard this morning. The lynch mob only managed to get him because he tried to get in through Mr Across the Road's catflap. To see his beloved sex kitten. No one seems to appreciate the romance of the situation. Angus had even taken Naomi a midnight snack of half chewed haddock fillet. How romantic is that?

Vati has got a job interview this morning. With my luck he'll turn up serving hot dogs in a van outside school. With, as a *coup d'état*, Uncle Eddie as his assistant. Anyway, it means that Angus lives to polish his trombone another day.

Vati gave me a kiss on the head as he left!! Erlack!! I've asked him to respect my personal space. Well I said, "Please don't touch me as I don't want to be sick down my school uniform."

I made for the door before anyone else could kiss me – I had seen the state of Libby's mouth after her cornflakes and Jammy Dodger. As I went through the door Angus made a desperate bid for freedom. He was fastened to the kitchen table leg but that didn't stop him. He dragged the table with him. It really made me laugh because one minute Mum was eating her cornies on the table and the next minute the table and cornies were gone.

8.15 a.m.

Slouch slouch.

I saw Jas outside her gate. She was turning her skirt over at the top to make it short for the walk to school. We unroll as we approach Stalag 14 because of the ferret on guard there (Hawkeye). She lurks around the school gates like a lurking lurker. Hawkeye's life ambition is to give us bad conduct marks for breaking useless school rules. That's how fabulous her life is.

Anyway I crept up behind Jas and yelled, "*Bonjour, sexe bombe!!!*" and she nearly had a nervy spaz. Which was very funny.

I wasn't looking forward to facing *le* music. This was my first day back since I had been unjustly banned from school because Elvis Attwood had carelessly tripped over his wheelbarrow and injured himself. OK, he was chasing me at the time, but . . .

When we reached the school gates I didn't even do anything annoying with my beret. Even Jas noticed. She said, "Gee, you've got your beret on properly."

"That is because for the time being the party is over, Jas. You may also notice that I am not wearing lip-gloss."

"Crikey."

As I slinked through the gate to Nazi headquarters Hawkeye was there like an eagle on heat. She hates me. I don't know

381

why. I am victimised by her. That is the sadness of life. As I went by her, she said, "Walk properly."

What does that mean? Walk properly? As an amusing example of my hilariosity, I did a bit of a limp. Hawkeye shouted after me, "Georgia, don't earn yourself a reprimand before you even get your coat off! As soon as assembly is over report to Miss Simpson's office."

She is such a stiff! I said to Jas, "I bet she irons her knickers."

Jas started to say, "What is so wrong with that . . . ?" but I had gone into the lavatory.

I sat down on the loos. Same old bat time, same old bat place. Good grief. In my despairosity I said out loud to myself, "What in the name of pantyhose is the point?"

A voice from the next loo said, "Gee, is that you?"

It was Ellen. I grunted. But she was all chatty. Just because she's been to the cinema with Dave the Laugh. A dumpee of mine.

She said through the wall, "Do you know what Dave says when he is leaving? Instead of saying goodbye?"

I wasn't remotely interested. I thought if I flushed the loo she might get the hint but she didn't.

"He says, 'Well, I'm off then. I'm away laughing on a fast camel.'"

And she absolutely pissed herself laughing.

What is the matter with her? Away laughing on a fast camel?

assembly

9.00 a.m. Fab news! Slim told us that some nutcase from Tampax the tampon company is coming to talk to us in a few weeks' time. About "reproduction".

382

Lord save us.

Slim also said Mrs Tampax would be answering any questions we might have about "growing up and so on". Hahahahahahaha. Hell could freeze over before I would ask Mrs Tampax about my girlie parts.

After Slim had bored us to death for half an hour everyone else went off to English and I lolloped off slowly to her office for a spot of mental torture. I wasn't the only one waiting for a duffing: Jackie and Alison, the Bummer Twins, were sitting around in her anteroom. They looked at me when I sat down.

Jackie said, "Oohhhh! What have you been up to, Big-nose?"

She must die, she must die.

Then we heard the sound of a distant elephant (Slim) and Jackie stubbed out her fag and popped in a mint.

Slim said, "Come through, Georgia." Then she sat down at her desk and started writing. I just stood there. How many times had I been in this room for no good reason? Millions.

To pass the time I pretended in my head that I was Parker, Lady Penelope's chauffeur in that crap puppet show *Thunderbirds*. Parker is supposed to be driving a car but the puppeteering is so bad that his hands are about two metres above the wheel. Very, very funny in anybody's language. I was still pretending and slightly waggling my head like a puppet when Slim looked up and said, "Well," and I said, "Yes, milady?"

She glared at me. "What did you say?"

"Oh, sorry, I was just thinking about my English homework assignment, Miss Simpson."

She trembled in her jelloid way. It was amazing the way each chin could shake at a different rhythm. She said, "Well, it

383

makes a change for you to think of anything serious or useful, Georgia."

Oh, that is so UNFAIR. What about all the hours I had spent thinking up glove animal?

Slim was raving on: "I hope for a great improvement in your attitude to school and work after your suspension. I hope it has given you pause for thought. But first of all you will go to Mr Attwood and apologise to him for causing his injuries."

Oh great. Now I had to go and speak to the most bonkers man in the history of bonkerdom.

When I left Slim's torture chamber Jackie Bummer said, "Did the nasty teacher tell you off and make you scared?" but when Slim shouted, "You two articles in here now!!!" they leaped up like two salmon.

Jas said that the Bummer Twins had arrived this morning, had a fag and then stuck a first year to a bench with super-glue.

9.35 a.m. I walked really really slowly along to Elvis's hut. At least if I took ages to find Elvis I might miss most of English. Sadly that is when I saw his stupid flat hat bobbing around. Not on its own, unfortunately, he was underneath it. Pushing his wheelbarrow along. I walked up quietly behind him and said really enthusiastically, "MR ATTWOOD. HELLO!!!"

He leaped up like a perv in overalls (which he is). When he saw it was me he had a nervy spaz.

"What do YOU want?"

"Mr Attwood, it's me!!!"

"I know who you are all right. Why are you shouting?"

"I thought you might have gone deaf."

"Well I haven't."

"Well you might have. You see, I know what it's like at your stage of life – my grandad is deaf. And he's got bandy legs."

"Well I'm not deaf. What do you want? I'm still not right, you know. My knee gives me awful gyp."

"Slim . . . er . . . Miss Simpson said I had to come and apologise."

"Yes, well, quite right too."

He was SO annoying. And a bit pingy-pongoes when you got downwind of him.

I said, "So, then. See you around."

He said, "Just a minute – you haven't said you are sorry yet."

"I have. I just told you I had to come and apologise."

"I know, but you haven't."

I said patiently, "Well, why am I here, then? Am I a mirage?"

"No you're not a mirage, you're a bloody nuisance."

"Thank you."

"Clear off. And you should behave a bit more like a young lady. In my day you would have . . ."

I interrupted him politely, "Mr Attwood, interesting though the Stone Age is, I really haven't got time to discuss your childhood. I'll just say *au revoir* and if I don't see you again in this life, best of luck in that great caretakers' home in the sky."

He was muttering and adjusting his trousers (erlack!), but he shambled off. He daren't say too much to me because he suspects I have seen his nuddy mags, which I have.

lunch-time

12.30 p.m. Hours and hours of boredom followed by a cheese sandwich, that is what my morning has been like. And I wish Nauseating P. Green would stop ogling me. Blinking at me through her thick glasses like a goldfish in a uniform. Since I saved her from being duffed up by the Bummers last term she follows me around like a Nauseating P. Green on a string.

Rosie said to me, "She loves you."

Good Lord.

1.30 p.m. Madame Slack was so overjoyed to see me that she made me sit right at the front next to Nauseating P. Green and Slack Alice, both of whom can only see the board if it's an inch away from their glasses. Jas and Ellen (Jas's bestest new lezzie mate) and the rest of the gang sat together at the back.

On the plus side Madame Slack told us we are going to have a student teacher next week. That is usually *très amusant*. A bit of a light in a dark world.

3.50 p.m. Bell rang. At last, escape from this hell-hole. Jas and me were walking out of the gates. I said, "Do you like me the best, Jas?"

"Er . . . is this a trick question?"

"Do you like me better than Tom?"

She sort of looked like a startled earwig in a beret and went all red. "Well . . . well . . . he's, well . . . a boy and you're . . . a girl."

I said, "No really? You noticed? Was it the basoomas that blew my cover?"

She got all miffed. "You know what I mean, Gee . . . I like you best girl-wise and I like him best boy-wise. Just like you like me best girl-wise and you like Robbie best boy-wise."

I said, "Hmm, well actually, do I like you best girl-wise? That is the question. I mean, sometimes you go off people, don't you, if they, you know, for instance . . . are always too busy to see you because of their boyfriends and so on."

That worried her. Ha ha and ha-di-hahaha.

She takes me for granted. She goes to the cinema with other mates.

But I mean it.

7.15 p.m. Jas phoned.
"Gee."

"Yes, who is that?" (Even though I knew who it was.)

"It's me, Jas."

"Oh."

"Look, you could have come to the cinema with us but you were in Och-aye land."

"Huh."

"And, well, it was just, you know, couples, and well, I don't think Robbie would have wanted to come. He doesn't really hang out with Tom much, you know, Robbie's got his mates from The Stiff Dylans and because he's got the band and . . ."

She dribbled on for ages.

midnight The nub and gist of Jas's pathetic apology is that I am going out with an older Sex God. We came to an understanding. The understanding is that she has to show her remorse: she has to be my slavey girl for three days. And do everything I say.

387

lunch-time

12.30 p.m. I made slavey girl give me a piggyback to the loo. Hawkeye said we were "being ridiculous".

8.00 p.m. The Sex God was waiting for me outside school!!! How cool is that? And he was in his cool car. Fortunately I had abstained from doing anything ridiculous with my beret. So I was able to get into his car only having to concentrate on not letting my nostrils flare too much . . . or knocking him out with my nunga-nungas. SHUT UP, BRAIN!!!

10.00 p.m. I must stop being jelloid woman every time I see the Sex God.

Why oh why did I say "I'm away laughing on a fast camel" instead of goodbye? What is the matter with me?

However on the whole, taking things by and large . . . Yessss!!!!

I live at Snogging Headquarters. My address is:

> Georgia Nicolson
> Snogging Headquarters
> Snog Lane
> Snoggington

10.15 p.m. Phoned Jas.

"Jas, I've done car snogging, have you done that?"

388

"No . . . I've done bike snogging."

"That's not the same."

"Oh. Why not?"

"It's just not the same."

"It is."

"No it isn't."

"Well there are still four wheels involved."

Good grief.

11.00 p.m. In the car this afternoon Robbie put his head on my knee and sang me one of his songs. It was called, "I'm Not There". I didn't tell Radio Jas that bit.

I never really know what to do with myself when he does his song singing. Maybe nod my head in time to the rhythm?

How attractive is that from upside-down?

And also if you were passing the car as an innocent passer-by you would just see my head bobbling around.

1.00 a.m. Libby woke me up when she pattered and clanked into my room. When she had got everybody into my bed she said, in between little sobs, "Ohh, there was a big bad man, big uggy man."

She cuddled up really tightly and wrapped her legs round me. I gave her a big cuddle and said, "It's OK, Libbs, it was just a dream, let's think about something nice. What shall we dream about?"

She said, "Porridge."

She can be so sweet. I gave her a little kiss on her cheek and she smiled at me (scary). Then she ripped the pillow from underneath my head so that Pantalitzer and scuba-diving Barbie could be comfy.

wednesday november 3rd

7.00 a.m. Woke up with a crick in my neck and a sort of airtank shape in my cheek where scuba-diving Barbie had been.

Dad came into the kitchen in a suit. Blimey.

No one said anything. Apart from Libby, who growled at him. It turns out that it wasn't a nightmare she had last night, she just woke up and caught sight of Dad in his jimjams.

Mum was in her usual morning dreamworld. As she came out of her bedroom getting ready for work she was wearing her bra and skirt and nothing else. I said, "Mum, please, I'm trying to eat."

But then Vati did this GROTESQUE thing. He got hold of one of Mum's nunga-nungas (honestly!) and sort of squeezed it and went, "Honk honk!!"

In the bathroom I was checking the back of my head and profile. (There's a cabinet which has two mirrors on it. You can look through one and angle the other one so that you can look at the reflection of yourself sideways.) Then I put Mum's magnifying mirror underneath and looked down at myself, because say the Sex God had been lying on my knees sort of looking up at me adoringly and singing (which he had), well I wanted to know what that looked like.

I wish I hadn't bothered for two reasons.

Firstly when I looked down at the mirror I realised that my nose is GIGANTIC. It must have grown overnight. I looked like Gerard Depardieu. Which is not a plus if you are not a forty-eight-year-old French bloke.

Secondly you can definitely see my lurker from underneath.

Jas was waiting for me at her gate. I was a bit aloof and full of maturiosity. Slavey girl said, "I've brought you a Jammy Dodger all to yourself."

"You can't treat me badly and then bribe me with a Jammy Dodger, Jas."

She can though, because I was soon munching away.

On the way up the road I said to Jas, "Do you think my nose is larger than it was yesterday?"

She said, "Don't be silly, noses don't grow."

"Well everything else does – hair, legs, arms . . . nunga-nungas. Why should your nose be left out?"

She wasn't a bit interested. I went on, "And also can you see I have a lurker up my left nostril?"

She said, "No."

"But say you were sort of looking up my nose, from under-neath."

She hadn't a clue what I was talking about. She has the imagination of a pea. Half a pea. We were just passing through the park and I tried to explain.

"Well, say I was singing. And you were the Sex God and you were lying with your head in my lap. Looking up adoringly. Marvelling at my enormous talent. Waiting for the appropriate moment to leap on me and snog me to within an inch of my life."

She still didn't get it, so I dragged her over to a bench to illustrate my point. I made her put her head on my lap. I said, "So . . . what do you think?"

She looked up and said, "I can't hear you singing."

391

"That's because I'm not."

"But you said what if you were singing?"

Oh for Goodness O'Reilly's trousers' sake!!! To placate her I sang a bit – the only thing that came into my head was "Goldfinger". Singing it brought back horrible memories because Dad and Uncle Eddie had sung it the night Dad came home from Kiwi-a-gogo. They were both drunk and both wearing leather trousers. Uncle Eddie said, "To impress the ladies." How sad and tragic is that?

Anyway, I was singing "Goldfinger" and Jas had her head on my lap, looking up at my ever-expanding nostrils. Sort of on nostril watch!

I said, "Can you see my lurker up there?"

Then we heard someone behind us having a fit. We leaped up. Well, I did. Jas crashed to the floor. It was Dave the Laugh, absolutely beside himself with laughing. I said, "Er . . . I was just . . ."

Jas was going, "I was just looking up . . . Georgia's nose for . . . a . . . bit . . ."

Dave the L. said, "Of course you were. Please don't explain, it will only spoil it for me."

He walked along with us. I couldn't help remembering snogging him. And using him as a Red Herring. But he was funny. And he wasn't snidey. Just laughing a lot. In a Dave the Laugh way.

After he went off I said to Jas, "He seems to have forgiven me for being a callous minx, doesn't he? He is quite groovy-looking, isn't he?"

Uh-oh I hope I am not becoming a nymphowhatsit. It is true though, I did think he looked quite cool. And a laugh. He's going to The Stiff Dylans gig this weekend. I said to Jas, "Do you think that he is going with Ellen?"

Why do I care? I am the girlfriend of a Sex God.

Still, I wonder if he is going with Ellen??

german

11.15 a.m. Whilst Herr Kamyer was writing something pointless on the blackboard about Helga and Helmut I did an excellent improvised impression of a boy's trouser snake.

Everyone said it was very lifelike.

hockey

3.00 p.m. Adolfa (Sports*führer* and part-time lesbian) has been relatively quiet this term. She had extravagantly big shorts on today. As we got changed I said to Jas, "It's you she wants, Jas. I know because imitation is the sincerest form of flattery. Look at the size of her shorts, they are JUST like your knickers."

Jas hit me.

jas's place

6.00 p.m. Doing homework (peanut butter sandwich-making and hairstyling) with Ellen, Jas and Rosie. We were discussing the arrangements for The Stiff Dylans gig. Because of some trivial French test coming up all of our parents have turned into elderly Nazis. We can't go out late during the week and we have to be picked up by our Loonleaders (dads).

I casually found out that Ellen is meeting Dave the Laugh at the gig. I said, "Oh, are you a sort of item, then?"

She went a bit girlish. "Well, you know, he said, 'Are you going to the gig?' and I said, 'Yeah,' and he said, 'See you there, then.'"

Rosie said, "Yes, but does he mean 'If you are going I'll see you there because you will be, like, THERE to see'? Or does he mean 'See you there, like in see YOU there'?"

Ellen didn't know, she was in a state of confusosity. Join the club, I say.

As I wandered home I was thinking. One thing is true. He is not making the effort to meet her before the gig. Hahahahaha.

home

7.00 p.m. Hang on a minute, though, Robbie has not arranged to meet me before the gig either. Is he expecting me to just turn up because I am, like, his official girlfriend?

Oh well, it's only Wednesday, he'll call me and sort it out. Probably.

10.00 p.m. No call from Robbie.

I started softening up Dad for Saturday.

"Vati, you know how hard I have been working at school . . . well . . ."

He interrupted me. "Georgia, if this is leading up to any suggestion of quids leaping out of my pocket into your purse . . . forget it."

What an old miser.

"Vati, it's not to do with money. It's just that my friends and I are going to a gig on Saturday night and . . ."

"What time do you want me to pick you up?"

"It's all right, Dad, I'll just, you know, come home with the rest of the gang and . . ."

He's going to pick me up at midnight. It's hardly worth going out. I made him promise me that he'd crouch down behind the wheel and not get out of the car.

midnight SG hasn't called me. How often should he call me? How often would I call him? About every five minutes seems right.

Maybe that's too keen. It implies I haven't got any sort of life. I haven't.

1.00 a.m. OK, every quarter of an hour.

1.15 a.m. It says in my *Men Are From Mars* book that boys don't need to talk as much as girls. The bloke that wrote it has obviously never met my Uncle Eddie. When he came round the other day he didn't shut up for about five million years.

He ruffles my hair. I am fifteen years old. Full of maturiosity. And snoggosity. I would ruffle HIS hair to show him how crap it is. But he hasn't got any.

operation glove animal

8.30 a.m. This is GA day. (Glove Animal day.)
Everyone is going to turn up with ears in
place today. Jas was grumbling and groaning about getting a
reprimand. I said, "Jas, please put your ears on as a smack in
the gob often offends."

Even she got into the swing of it once her ears were in place.
It was, it has to be said, quite funny. Jas looked hilarious bobbing
along with her glove ears. She even did a bit of improvising
with her teeth, making them stick out and doing nibbly movements with them like a squirrel. We did a detour through the
back alleyway near the Science block. Elvis was in his hut
reading his newspaper. We just stood there in our glove animal way, looking in at him through the window. He sensed we
were there and looked up. We stared back at him. His glasses
were a bit steamed up so maybe he really thought we were
some woodland creatures. Woodland creatures who had
decided to go to school and get ourselves out of our woodland
poverty trap . . . But then he started shouting and raving on,
"Clear off and learn something instead of messing about. And
make yourselves look normal!!!"

Oh wise advice from the looniest-looking person in the
universe.

Unfortunately Hawkeye spotted us before we could scuttle
into the cloakroom. She went ballistic, unusually enough. I
tried to explain that it was a useful way not to lose your gloves
but I only got as far as "It's a really sensible way of . . ." before

she had snatched them off my head. She has very little sense of humour.

However the last laugh was on her because she was so busy telling me and Jas that we were ridiculously childish and ripping our ears off that she didn't see the rest of the Ace Gang bob into school. It was very very funny indeed seeing them bob through the gates and across the playground as if they were perfectly normal glove animals.

7.00 p.m. No call from the SG.

Mrs Across the Road came over. Mutti had gone to her aerobics class. Surely it can't be healthy for a woman of her size to hurl herself around a crowded room?

Mrs Across the Road or "Call me Helen" is OK but a bit on the nimby girlie side. If you hit her with a hockey stick she would probably fall over. She's fluffy and blonde (not natural, I think).

Vati was acting very peculiarly. He was being almost nice. And laughing a lot. And he got out of his chair. Hmmm.

After she'd gone he must have said at least two hundred and fifty times, "She seems very nice, doesn't she? Helen? Very . . . you know . . . feminine."

Oh no.

Also he said that they are going to get a pedigree sort of boyfriend for Naomi. I said, "She won't go out with anyone else. She loves Angus."

Dad laughed. "You wait, there will be little Naomis running about the place before you can blink. Women are very fickle."

Hmmmm.

9.10 p.m. Pre-gig nervosity. Not helped by the fact that when I went down on to the field to take Angus for his "constitutional" Mark Big Gob threw a jumping-jack at me. I wonder if he is quite normal in the brain department?

Oh God, it's Bonfire Night tomorrow, an excuse for all the sad boys in the world to set fire to themselves with fireworks whilst showing off to their mates.

9.30 p.m. Mum came in, flushed as a loon. I said, "You are looking particularly feminine, Mum." But Vati didn't get it.

in my room

9.50 p.m. Vati knocked on my door!!! I said, "I'm sorry, but sadly I'm not in."

He ignored that, came in and sat on the edge of my bed.

Oh God, he wasn't going to ask me if I was happy, was he? Or tell me about his "feelings"?

He was all embarrassed. "Look, Georgia, I know how you feel about Angus . . ."

"Yes . . . and?"

"It's just not fair on him being all cooped up in the house."

"Well that is not my idea."

"I know, but he won't leave that bloody Burmese alone."

"He loves her and wants to share his life and dreams with her, maybe buy a little holiday home in Spain for those cold . . ."

"He's a bloody cat!!!"

10.00 p.m. Dad is going to take Angus to the vet tomorrow to have his trouser snake addendums taken away. He said, "I know you will think about this and be grown up about it."

I said, "Dad, as I have mentioned before, if you do this to Angus you are no longer my vati. You are an ex-vati."

I mean it.

10.10 p.m. Phone rang. Vati answered it, still all grumpy.

I was in my room, shaping the cuticles in my nails for Saturday.

If I don't start my beauty routine now I'll never be ready in time.

I heard Dad say, "I'll see if she's still up, it's a bit late to call . . . Who shall I say it is?"

By that time I had thrown myself down the stairs and ripped the phone out of his hand. How could he be so deeply uncool?

I calmed my voice and said "Hello" in a sort of husky way. I don't know why, but at least I wasn't assuming a French accent.

It was the Sex God!!! Yeahhh!!! I got jelloid knickers as soon as I heard his voice. It's so yummy scrumboes . . .

He said, "Is that your dad?"

I said, "No, it's just some madman who hangs around our house."

Anyway the short and long of it is that he'll see me Saturday at the gig. He's rehearsing so can't see me before. *C'est la vie*, I think you will find, when you go out with *le* gorgeous popstar.

bonfire night

4.00 p.m. Some of the Foxwood lads sneaked into school today and put a banger down a loo and the loo exploded! You could hear the explosion even in the Science block. Slim was so furious that her chins practically waggled off.

6.30 p.m. Vati has actually taken Angus to the vet. I cannot believe it. I am not speaking to him.

He said, "The vet said he would be fit as a flea on Monday and we can pick him up then."

Libby and me might go on dirty protest, like they do in prison. Not bother going to the loo, as a protest, just poo on the floor. Mind you, Libby is almost permanently on dirty protest, so they might not notice.

8.00 p.m. Mutti and the bloke that she sadly lives with have gone to the street bonfire. Mr and Mrs Next Door and Mr and Mrs Across the Road and the saddos from number twenty-four are all going to be there and then they are off to a party at number twenty-six. Can you imagine the fun that will be? Vati was wearing a leather cowboy hat. How tragic is that? Very very tragic. Mutti asked me if I was coming. I just looked at Dad's hat. Anyway as I am not speaking to any of them I can't reply. Dad leaped over the garden wall instead of going through the gate. Sadly he didn't do himself a severe injury and so he

400

lives to embarrass me to death another day.

Angus normally loves Bonfire Night. I wonder where he is now? Does he know his bottom sniffing days are over?

8.30 p.m. Jools, Rosie and Jas came round. They're all off to a bonfire party at Kate Matthew's place. SG is rehearsing again, but we're going to meet up later.

The girls managed to find something to eat in the kitchen which is a bloody miracle.

We sat munching and crunching our cornflake sarnies. Jools said, "I must get a boyfriend. I quite fancy that mate of Dave the Laugh's. What is he called? Is it Rollo? You know, the one that's got a nice smile."

He was quite cool-looking now she mentioned it. I said, "I wonder why he hasn't got a girlfriend? Maybe there is something wrong with him."

Jools was all alert. "Like what?"

"Well, you know spotty Norman has acne of the head?"

"Rollo hasn't got any spots."

"He might have secret acne."

"Secret acne?"

"Yeah, it only starts at the top of his arms."

"Who gets acne like that?"

"Loads of people."

"Like who?"

"Loads of people."

Actually I noticed that Rosie had a bit of a lurker on her chin. She had been poking it about and I told her she shouldn't do that, she should try my special lurker eradicator. You squirt perfume on the lurker. Really loads and loads, and that dries it up. In theory. I used it on my nostril lurker and it worked a treat. Mind you, in the process I practically choked to death on Paloma (Mum's).

my bedroom

10.00 p.m. The sky is lit up with rockets from people's firework parties. And I am alone in my room. I'm very nearly a hermitess. SG's rehearsal has run on, so we can't meet up. Still, I'm not going to mope around, I'm going to do something creative with poster paints.

11.30 p.m. When Mutti and Vati came in I didn't speak to them, I just unfurled the CAT MOLESTERS banner I had made.

big red bottomosity

saturday november 6th

11.00 a.m.

The cat molesters went off shopping.

1.00 p.m.

I'd better start my make-up soon, it's only seven hours to the gig. But as I fully expect to be snogged to within an inch of my life, what about snog-proof make-up? To lippy or not to lippy, that is the question.

Rang Jas. Her mum called her and she eventually shambled to the phone. I said, "Oh, glad you could make it, Jas. My eyebrows have grown to the floor in the time it took you to get here."

Jas, as usual, took offence. "I was in my bedroom just working something out on the computer with Tom."

I laughed sarcastically. "Jas, you only snog in your room."

"We don't."

"You do. Anyway, lots of fun though this is, I want to ask you something of vital importance to the universe. Well, my universe, anyway. What do you think about lippy and snogging?"

"What?"

"Well, do you put lippy on and then wipe it off before lip contact, or do you let it go all over Tom's face and Devil take the hindmost?"

2.00 p.m. Results of lippy/snogging poll:
Jas only wears lip-gloss which she says gets absorbed in the general snogosity.

Rosie says she puts on lippy AND lip-gloss then just goes for full-frontal snogging with Sven. She also says that by the end of the night he is usually covered in lippy but he doesn't mind and wipes it off with his T-shirt.

Good Lord. We must remember however that he is not English.

The rest of the gang seemed pretty well to go along with the lip-gloss absorbed into the general snogosity theory.

So lip-gloss it is.

3.00 p.m. Surrounded by hair products.
My hair will not go right. It has no bounceability. It just lies there. Annoying me with its lack of bounceability.

Bloody *sacré bleu*. I won't be able to go out unless it starts bouncing a bit. I look like a Franciscan monk. Or Miss Wilson.

I'm going to stick some of Mum's hot rollers in it.

4.30 p.m. On my bed in rollers. V. attractive.
Reading my book *Don't Sweat the Small Stuff for Teens* to cheer me up and calm me down.

4.45 p.m. Hey, there is a chapter about hair! Honestly! How freaky-deaky is that?

It's called "Be OK With Your Bad Hair Day".

5.00 p.m. The short and short of it is that we are obsessed with our looks and imagine that other people really care about what our hair looks like. But they don't!!

So that is OK, then. Took out my rollers.

5.10 p.m. Vati ponced into my room (not knocking, of course) and said, "Tea is on the . . . what in the name of arse have you done to your head? You look like you have been electrocuted."

I hate my dad. Twice.

5.30 p.m. Time for my pore-tightening mask. (Because there is nothing worse than loose pores.)

Hmm. I lay there with my pores tightening.

In the book it recommends yoga for inner harmony. I must start doing it again.

5.35 p.m. Mind you, the author says he is "super glad" that he took up yoga at such a young age.

5.37 p.m. Perhaps he is a "super tosser"?

5.39 p.m. Or am I being "super critical"? Who knows?

Phoned Jools with my pore-tightening mask still on, trying not to crack it. Dad was pretending to be an orang-utan (not much pretending needed) as a "laugh". I ignored him.

I said to Jas, "Nyut nar nu naring?"

"Purple V-necked top. Purple hipsters."

Hmm.

Phoned Rosie. "Nut nar nu noing nid nor nhair?"

"Pigtails."

Crikey. We seem to be running the gamut of style from hippie to Little Bo Peep and beyond.

6.20 p.m. I've tried on every single thing in my wardrobe. Oh buggery, I am in a state of confusosity. I wish I had a style counsellor. I'm going to get one when I appear on record awards ceremonies with the Sex God. It won't be Elton John's style counsellor. It will be someone normal. And stylish. And a good counsellor.

6.30 p.m. I have decided to go for the radically sophisticated look for the gig, i.e. all black. With for special effect, black accessories (providing I can sneak out with Mum's Chanel bag without her noticing).

6.35 p.m. I'm wearing a V-necked black leather vest, short skirt and boots.

What does that say about me? Casual sophisticate? Inner vixen struggling to get out? Girlfriend of a Sex God? Or twit?

6.38 p.m. I wonder what SG will be wearing? What does it matter? We are all in the nuddy-pants under our clothes.

I LOVE his mouth. It's so yummy and sort of curly and sexy. And it's mine all mine!!! Mind you, I love his hair, so black and gorgey. And his eyes . . . that deep deep blue . . . mmmmm . . . dreamsville. And his eyelashes. And his arms. And his tongue . . . In fact, there isn't one bit of him I don't like. Of all the bits I've seen, anyway.

I wonder what his favourite bit of me is? I should emphasise it. My eyes are quite nice. My nose, yes well, we'll just skip over that. Mouth . . . mmm, a bit on the generous side, but that can be a good thing.

6.45 p.m. Phoned Jas.

"Jas, what do you think is my best feature? Lips? Smile? Casual sophisticosity?"

"Well, I don't know what to say now, because I was going to say your cheeks."

Good grief.

6.50 p.m. Phoned Jas again.

"What do you think on the basooma front? You know, emphasise them, do the, 'Yes, I've got big nunga-nungas but I'm proud of them!' or strap them down and don't breathe out much all night?"

That's when Vati went ballisticisimus about me being on the phone.

"Why the hell do you talk rubbish to Jas on the phone when she is coming round here in a minute and you can talk rubbish to her without it costing me a fortune?!!!!"

It's not me that talks rubbish. It's him. He just shouts rubbish at me. He's like Hawkeye with a beard.

I said to Mutti, "Why doesn't the man you live with go for

407

a job as a combination cat molester and teacher?"

beautosity headquarters

7.00 p.m. Jas came round to my house for us to walk to the clock tower together. Also I needed her for a cosmetic emergency. I had forgotten to paint my toenails and my skirt was so tight I couldn't bend my leg up far enough to get to my toes. I suppose I could have taken my skirt off but what are friends for?

I am too giddy and girlish with excitement to paint straight anyway. We went into the front room, which is warmer than my room – mind you, so is Siberia (probably). Vati was watching the news. Huh. Jas started on nail duty. I thought a subtle metallic purple would be nice. Robbie would think that was cool if my tights fell off for some reason. Anyway, then it said on the news, "And tonight the Prime Minister has got to Number Ten."

I looked down at Jas and said, "Oo-er. (Meaning he'd got to Number Ten on the snogging scale.) And then we both laughed like loons.

Vati just looked at us like we were mad.

clock tower

8.00 p.m. Met the rest of the Ace Gang and we ambled off to the gig. This was my first official outing as girlfriend of a Sex God. I wasn't going to let it go to my head though.

Lalalalalalalalala. Fabbity fab fab. Eat dirt, Earth creatures.

When we got to the Marquee club the first "person" I saw

was . . . Wet Lindsay, Robbie's ex. There is always a wet fish in every ointment. Every cloud has got a slimy lining. She has got the tiniest forehead known to humanity. She is quite literally fringe and then eyebrow. She was talking to her equally sad mates, Dismal Sandra and Tragic Kate. Every time I look at Wet Lindsay I am reminded that underneath her T-shirt lurk breast enhancers.

I said to Jas, "Do you think that Robbie knows about her false nunga-nungas?" but she was too busy waving at Tom with a soppy smile on her face.

The club was packed. I wondered if I should go find Robbie and say hello. Maybe that wasn't very cool. Better do a bit of make-up adjusting first. Because if the talent scout was there he might be looking for girls to form a band as well. I said that to Jas.

"Maybe we could be discovered, as a new girl band."

"We can't sing or play any instruments, and we are not in a band."

She is so ludicrously picky.

It was mayhem in the loos. You couldn't get near the mirrors for love nor money. The Bummers were in there, of course, larding on the foundation. Alison must use at least four pounds of it trying to conceal her huge lurkers . . . Or am I being a bit harsh? No . . . I am being accurate. And factual.

I came out of the loos into the club. It was bloody dark; you needed to be half bat to find your way around. And then, shining like a shining Sex God in trousers, I saw him. Tuning his guitar. He looked up and saw me and smiled. I went over and he grabbed me and dragged me into a room. ("Oh stop it, stop it!" I yelled . . . not.) It was The Stiff Dylans' dressing-room. I'd never been backstage before. I suppose I will have to get used to it.

We did some excellent snogging (six and a half) but then he had to go and tune up with the rest of the band. He said, "See you in my break."

When I went back to the loos my lip-gloss had completely gone!!! Absorbed in the snogosity.

9.00 p.m. Yeah! What a dance fest! I was so shattered after being thrown around by Sven that I had to go and have a sit down in an alcove with Rosie.

I could see Wet Lindsay and her wet mates dancing right in front of the stage. How desperate was that? In fact, it was all girls at the front, most of them dancing around in front of my Sex God. Smiling up at him and shaking their bums around. But he only had eyes for me. Well he would have done had he had a sniffer dog that could have come round and found me sitting in the dark behind a pillar, and gone back and told SG where I was. There was an older bloke in a suit standing by the side of the stage. I bet he was the talent scout.

Phew, it was hot and sweaty. I nipped off to the loos to make sure my glaciosity was still in place and I didn't look like a red-faced loon. My waterproof eyeliner seemed to be holding its own.

Rosie was readjusting her piggies next to me in the mirror so I asked her, "Do you get jealous of Sven?"

"No, not really. He's sort of quite grown-up in his own way."

As we came out of the loos we could see Sven almost immediately . . . he was in the middle of a big group, balancing a drink on his head and doing Russian dancing. It's a mystery to me how he manages to get down so low his jeans are so tight. I mentioned this to Ro-ro and she said, "I know, he always wears very snug trouser snake holders."

410

That made us laugh A LOT. We got up to join in with him and did fast dancing to a really slow record. All the gang came and joined in, in a big circle, so we did the trouser snake dance. Very hilarious, but cool too, I like to think. Sort of shows that although I know how to be a really cool dancer I can do individualosity as well as the next man.

The Bummers were talking to some really lardy-looking blokes in leather jackets. They were all smoking fags. In fact, you could hardly see their heads for smoke. Which was a plus. I did make out that one of the lard-heads had a moustache. I shouted to Jools, "Imagine snogging someone with a moustache!"

She said, "What . . . like Miss Stamp?"

The Bummers sloped off outside with the lard-heads, probably to go do Number Eight in some shed somewhere. Ugh.

9.30 p.m. Jools had been looking at Rollo for about a million centuries and moaning and droning on about him. He was hanging out with a bunch of lads round the bar. I was trying to concentrate on looking at the Sex God. He is sooooo cool. He's by far the coolest in the band. Dom, Chris and Ben are all quite groovy-looking but they don't have that certain *je ne sais quoi* that the Sex God has. That extra snogosity. That puckery gorgeosity combined with fabulosity. That sexgoderosity.

Jools didn't seem to know I was in Snog Heaven because she was rambling on. "He's quite fit, isn't he?"

"Yeah, he's gorgeous and he's all mine mine miney."

"Gee, I mean Rollo, you banana."

I was less than interested but she went on and on. "Should I go across?"

411

Pause.

"Or is that too pushy?"

Pause.

"I think it's always best to play a bit hard to get, don't you? Yeah, that's how I'll play it. He'll have to beg to get my attention."

5 minutes later

9.35 p.m. Rollo came across to Jools and pulled her to her feet. Jools went incredibly red. In fact she was beyond redness and into the Valley of the Boiled Lobster. Anyway at least now they were dancing. And she wasn't going on and on about him.

15 minutes later

9.50 p.m. Jools sitting on Rollo's knee and snogging for England. Oh well, as I said to Ellen, "She's obviously gone for the 'playing it hard to get' ticket."

Ellen didn't seem very interested. She has been waiting for Dave the Laugh to show up. I must have been to the loo with her about a hundred times just in case she has missed him in the dark somewhere.

I am without doubt a great mate. You wouldn't get Jas trailing backwards and forwards to the loo. Mostly because she seems to be glued to Tom. She has very little pride.

Quite a few lads have asked me to dance. Well, their idea of asking me to dance, which means they hang around showing off when I'm dancing with my mates. I must have that thing that you can get. You know, like baboons. When female

412

baboons are "in the mood" they get a big red bottom and then the male baboons know they are "in the mood" and gather round. Yes, that must be it – I must have the metaphorical red bottom because of the Sex God.

10.00 p.m. In his break Robbie came off stage and he looked over at me. This was it, this was the moment that everyone knew I was his girlfriend!! At last all my dreams were beginning to come true, I was going to be the official SP (snogging partner)!! No more hiding our love from the world. Just snogging a-gogo and Devil take the hind-most. I couldn't wait to see Wet Lindsay's face when Robbie came over to me. Tee hee. Yessss!!!!

In the meantime I lived in Cool City. I was sipping my drink and pretending to talk to Jas and Tom although every time Jas said anything it really annoyed me. I'd say, "OhmyGodohmyGod, I think he's coming over . . . oh that absolutely useless tart Sammy Mason is thrusting herself at him now."

And Jas would say, "She's actually quite a nice person, really good at Blodge."

Ludicrous, stupid, pointless things she was saying. In the end I said, "Jas, can you just pretend to talk to me but don't say anything in case I have to hit you."

Now there was a whole group of girls around Robbie, giggling and jiggling about in front of him! Then Wet Lindsay slimed up. And actually touched his cheek. My boyfriend's cheek she touched. With her slimy hand. Tom said, "Leave it, Gee, just be cool. Honestly, he'll like it better if you don't make a fuss."

Huh. What did Hunky know about it? Then he said,

413

"Besides which, you're not long off your stick and she will definitely kill you."

Fair point. She had deliberately and viciously whacked me round the ankles in a hockey match last term and I didn't want to be hobbling around for another two weeks.

I couldn't bear the tension of waiting for the SG to come over, it made me really need to go to the piddly diddly department. I nipped off to the loos. A minute or two later Rosie came in and she wasn't alone, she had Sven with her. He said, "Oh *ja*, here *ve* is in the girlie piddly diddlys." He scared four girls who went screeching out.

He is a very odd Norwegian-type person. Perhaps they have whatsits in Norwayland? You know, bisexual lavatories. Do I mean that or unicycle lavatories? No . . . unisex lavs, I mean. Rosie was completely unfazed by him being there, but as we all know she is not entirely normal herself. She said, "Robbie says he will see you in the dressing room."

Oh hell's biscuits. Pucker alert, pucker alert!! After an emergency reapplication of lip-gloss I made my way to the dressing-room. I just got near when I saw Lindsay was there again! This time fiddling around with his shirt collar.

Unbelievable.

Robbie caught my eye and raised his eyebrows to me and then behind her back gave me like a "wait five minutes" sign with his hand.

I was as livid as an earwig on livid pills.

Wait five minutes because of her . . .

Unbelievable.

Back on the dance floor all my so-called mates were too busy snogging their boyfriends to listen to me complain. OK, I would have to take action on my own. I said to Jas over Tom's shoulder because they were slow dancing, "I will not, definitely not, play second fiddle to a stick insect."

She said, "What are you going to do, then?"

I had to sort of dance along with them in order to keep up with where her head was. "I'm going to be absent. Upstairs. Don't tell him where I am if he asks you."

Then I hid upstairs in the club. I got a few funny looks from the snoggers up there as I crouched down by the stairs, but I didn't care. I could look down and see Robbie looking for me. He even sent Jas into the loos to see if I was in there. She did a ludicrous comedy wink up at me as she went. What is she like? If she had been a spy in the war German high command would have only had to get on the blower to her and say "*Vat haf* you been told never to divulge?" and she would tell them everything, probably including the Queen's bra size (sixty-four double D-cup).

Anyway I could see Robbie getting more and more worked up about not finding me. Ha and triple ha. Ahahahaha, in fact. So Mr Sex God, the worm is for once on the other foot.

On the downside I had made myself a snog-free zone.

10.20 p.m. After the SG had gone back on stage to play another set I went into the loos. Ellen was in there looking all mournful. She said, "I'm going to go. Dave the L. hasn't turned up. He said he would see me here and he hasn't come."

I tried wisdomosity about elastic bands, and when a boy says "See you", who knows what that means, etc. etc., but she wasn't interested. She went off home all miserable.

I made sure that Robbie could see how miffed I was. He tried his heartbreaking smile on me but I ignored him with a

415

firm hand and pretended to be laughing with my mates. I said to Rosie, "Wet Lindsay is a crap dancer, and her hair has no bounceability." Neither incidentally, despite all her efforts, have her basoomas. They just lie there. I think a bit of bounce in a basooma is a good thing.

I wondered what level of bounceability mine had when I was dancing? I went to a dark corner at the back of the bar where no one was to inspect them whilst I danced. Well, they certainly did jiggle, not always in time to the music either. Perhaps if I kept my shoulders rigid they would keep still. As I was trying rigid shoulder dancing Dave the Laugh turned up. I was so shocked I went, "Where have you been?"

He grinned. He looked very cool in black. He said, "Why? Did you miss me? Mrs Dumper." But he didn't seem bitter or anything. Perhaps he had forgiven me. He said, "God it's hot in here. Do you fancy a cold drink?"

Well, no harm in a cold drink with an old dumpee, is there?

Jas ogled me as I went off to the bar with him, but I just ogled back. Honestly, she acts like she's fifty. She'll start wearing headscarves soon and discussing the price of potatoes with anyone who will listen (i.e. no one).

Anyway, if the Sex God could hang out with his exes, so could I.

Dave the L. and me took our drinks outside for a breath of fresh air. I sort of said awkwardly, "Dave, I'm really sorry for, you know, using you like a red herring."

He said, "Yes, well . . . I was pretty upset at the time."

He seemed unnaturally serious. Oh God's pyjamas. I was meant to be having a laugh. Why was he called Dave the Laugh if he was not a laugh? He should have been called Dave the Unlaugh. Shut up, brain.

I said, "Well, you know, I just . . ."

He interrupted me. "Georgia, there is something you should know – I . . ."

Oh God. Oh Goddy God God. He sounded like he was going to cry. What should I do? I hadn't been to boy crying classes, I only went to snogging ones. I looked down at my drink and I could sort of sense him putting his head in his hands. I was just staring at my drink and avoiding looking at him. Then he said in a low sort of broken voice, "I haven't been able to get over you . . . I think, I think I'm in love with you."

Oh *sacré* bloody *bleu* and triple *merde*. I mumbled, "Dave, I don't know what to say. I, well . . . I . . ."

He said, "Perhaps if you could give me just one last kiss."

I looked round at him. And he looked at me.

And I noticed he was wearing a big false red clown's nose. And just gazing at me.

Actually it was really, really funny, even though the joke was on me. He just looked hilarious!! Both of us were falling about.

But then this awful thing happened. I accidentally found myself attached to his mouth. (He took the red nose off first though . . .)

midnight I was in such a tizz of a spaz that I was on time outside for when Vati turned up. Is it really necessary for him to wear a balaclava? And also it's like being on a quiz show; he kept asking me things. "So did you have fun, then? Did any lads ask you to dance?"

Why does he want to know everything? I'm not interested in him, why is he so interested in me? I would tell him what a complete fiasco he is making of himself, but I'm not speaking to him, so I can't.

1.00 a.m. I didn't say goodnight or anything to Robbie. I just couldn't. I didn't say anything to Dave the Laugh either. After the accidental snog I was in a sort of a daze. Dave the Laugh seemed a bit surprised too. He said, "Er . . . right . . . well . . . I think, I'll just like . . . er . . . at . . . go to the . . ."

And I said, "Yes, er, I think . . . I'll like, you know . . . just er . . . you know, go and . . . er . . . go . . ." But neither of us knew what we were talking about.

This time my big red bottom has taken things too far.

2.00 a.m. Am I a scarlet-bottomed vixen?
What will I say to Robbie?

2.30 a.m. For heaven's sake, it was just a little kiss! I am a teenager, I've got whatsit . . . lust for life. Also it was probably my hormones made me do it (officer).

3.00 a.m. What's a little kiss between exes?

3.01 a.m. And a tiny bit of tongues.

3.03 a.m. And nip libbling.

3.04 a.m. NIP LIBBLING??? What in the name of Jas's commodious panties am I talking about? You see, I am so upset I have got internal dyslexia

418

. . . I mean lip nibbling not nip libbling.

Anyway, I am not alone on The Guilt Train because Dave the Laugh is also on it. He is a two-timer with Ellen.

3.05 a.m. Oh God, she is my mate. I am bad bad baddy bad bad.

Jesus would never snog his mate's boyfriend.

3.15 a.m. I will probably never be able to sleep again.

Zzzzzzzzzzzzz.

sunday november 7th

9.00 a.m. The phone rang. Libby answered it.

"Heggo? Yes yes yes yes yes yes yes yes, listen."

I could hear her singing her version of "Dancing Queen" and there was a sort of banging noise as well – she would be doing the accompanying dance. God help the poor sod who was on the other end of the phone.

"Dancing bean . . . dancing bean . . . feel the touch of my tangerine . . . ine . . ."

It was so loud that even Mutti was forced to get up to try to shut her up. She said, "Libby, let Mummy talk."

There was the sound of a struggle and spitting and then I heard Mum say, "Hello? Oh yes, well hang on, I'll see if she's up." She shouted up the stairs, "Georgia, it's Robbie for you."

I shot out of bed and downstairs. Checking in the mirror to make sure I didn't have idiot hair. Although that meant the Sex God would have X-ray vision if he could see down the telephone.

Perhaps he did have extra sensory whatsit and he would sense my red bottomosity? Oh God. The Sex God!!! As she handed over the phone Mum winked at me. Shutupshutup winking.

I tried not to sound like a scarlet minx. I wanted to achieve casualosity with a hint of maturiosity. With no suggestion of red bottomosity. "Hi." (How cool, is that? V. cool, that's how.)

"Georgia? What happened last night? Where were you? Jas said that you got in trouble with your dad and had to leave."

Phew, for once in her life Jas had actually done something right. I said, "Er . . . yes, he got the mega hump like he always does and er . . . well, actually if I hadn't have gone he would have come in and danced and no one wants to see him doing the twist." What in the name of Beelzebub was I talking about?

Robbie seemed to relax then. He said, "Listen, I'm really sorry about last night. I really wanted to be around you and then there was the Lindsay thing . . . and the bloke from the record company being there, he wanted to speak to us after the gig."

Anyway, it was really dreamy talking to him. The record bloke wants to sign up The Stiff Dylans.

Wow!!

Robbie said he would meet me at the bottom of the hill at lunch-time.

Mutti followed me into my bedroom. She said, "So, Robbie then, eh? The really fit-looking one? He's gorgeous, isn't he?"

I went on applying my natural-looking make-up (just a hint of daytime glitter). I'm not officially speaking to her either (as she is the cat molester's handmaiden) except to ask for my pocket money.

Mum went raving on. "Look, come on, love, it was the only

420

thing to do. It's cruel to keep a wild animal cooped up all the time."

I said, "Well let Vati go and have a sniff around in the garden, then."

She went all parenty. "It's not funny to be so rude. We are only trying to do our best."

She looked like she was going to cry as she went out. Oh poo. Poo and *merde*.

10.00 p.m. It was fab!!! Being with my BOYFRIEND. It was cool actually, because we bumped into a couple of Robbie's mates and went round to their house. Dom was there from The Stiff Dylans. No one else I knew – they were mostly much older than me. How cool is that? And Robbie was holding my hand!!! In front of them!!!

One of them asked me what I was going to do at university. Er. I said, "Backing dancing." I don't know why.

I didn't say anything else after that, I just smiled like an imbecile a lot.

Dom and Robbie talked about their record deal. They're all really nice. Then John asked me if I smoked and I said only if my hair is on fire, and they just looked at me.

11.30 p.m. SG said he really rated me. He did the neck kissing stuff and ear snogging.

It was so dreamy. My only slight worry is Rosie's theory of things growing if they get snogged (like your lips). If he goes on snogging my ears will I get elephant ears?

midnight Lalalalalalalalalalala.

421

1.00 a.m. It's a bit weird being with people older than me.

1.15 a.m. Still, I have put my red bottom to bed; it will not be rearing its ugly head again. My nip libbling days are over.

I am and always will be the girlfriend of a Sex God.

The End.

trouser
snakes-a-gogo

monday november 8th

7.45 a.m. Woken at the crack of dawn by Vati yelling and carrying on downstairs. He was singing, "The boys are back in town, the boys are back in town. Yesssssss!! Owzat!!!!!!!! The boy's a genius!!!!!!"

It turns out some fool has offered him a job. He is going to be in charge of waterworks or something. I said, "We'd better dig a well, then." But M and V were too busy snogging each other to hear me. Erlack a-pongoes. Also they seem to be failing to notice that they do not exist for me.

Vati was UNBEARABLE at breakfast, wearing his dressing-gown slung round his shoulders like a sort of prize fighter and lifting Libby above his head with one hand. Actually that bit was quite funny because she clung on to the overhead lamp and wouldn't let go, and he very nearly lost his temper. I think he must be in some sort of hormonal middle-age thing because his moods are very unpredictable. One minute it's all jokes, the next minute you ask him for a measly fiver and he goes ballistic. Weird.

8.15 a.m. Met Jas. She said, "I told Robbie what you told me to, but I still don't under-

423

stand why you had to rush off."

"Dad had got his balaclava on."

"Oh right, I see. Yes."

And alarmingly she seemed quite satisfied. That is the trouble with telling people porkies – it is so easy. Should I confess about Dave the Laugh? Jas was my best friend. We knew everything about each other. I, for instance, had seen her knickers. But on the other hand she could be a terrible pain about morals and stuff. She might say it wasn't very nice of me as Ellen was my friend, etc. etc.

Hmmm. I'll think about it later. In the next life.

french

1.30 p.m. The whole school has gone bonkers!!! Our new substitute French teacher turns out to be a David Ginola look-alike!!! Honestly. He's bloody gorgeous. When he walked in even Rosie stopped plucking her eyebrows. Monsieur "Pliss call me Henri" has got sort of longish hair and really tight blue jeans. We are keen as *le moutarde* on French now. Any time he asks anything everyone puts up their hand. I can't remember the last time I saw anyone put up their hand in French. Usually we put our heads on our desks for a little snooze and just let our arms flop over if we are supposed to be answering anything. It's our little way of letting Madame Slack know how interested we are in Patapouf and Cliquot. Or whatever sad French people she is talking about.

break

2.30 p.m. And it isn't just us, you should see the teachers. I even saw Hawkeye giggling when she was talking to "Pliss call me Henri"!

The saddest of all is Herr Kamyer, who has gone completely giddy at having another man in the building. Unfortunately his idea of bonding involves a lot of spasmodic dithering about and saying "Oh *ja*. Oh *ja*, *sehr interestink*, Henri."

When Monsieur Henri opened the staffroom door for Miss Wilson her tragic 70s bob nearly fell off. They are all being pathetic, pretending to be interested in garlic and Edith Piaf and so on. Sad.

I, of course, as anyone who knows me will tell you, have always loved *la belle France*.

4.10 p.m. I said to Jas on the way home, "I have always *aimed la belle France*."

"You said you didn't like it because it was full of French people."

"Well, there is that, but apart from that I *aime* it very much."

dinner-time

6.00 p.m. I said to Mutti, "Can we have wine with our fishfingers like they do in *la belle France*?"

She just said, "Don't be ridiculous."

6.20 p.m. Vati is bringing Angus home from the vet tonight. Libby and me have made a hospital bed sort of thing out of his cat basket and some old blankets. Libby put one-eyed Teddy in it as well.

He'll be so sad and probably in agony. He will be a facsimile of a sham of his former cathood. He will just be like other cats now. Not the magnificent half-cat half-Labrador that he used to be.

I said to Mutti, "I hope it will not put you off your beauty regime, having Angus's trouser snake addendas on your conscience."

7.30 p.m. Hahahahahaha. Angus leaped out of his cat cage and immediately attacked Vati's trousers. When Dad went to put the car in the garage Angus shot out into the garden and over the wall.

I heard Snowy and Whitey yapping and Mr Next Door yelling.

Happy days!

my bedroom

7.50 p.m. Although it's a laugh having the French heart-throb around it hasn't quite taken my mind off my unfaithfulness with Dave the L. I don't know what to do. Am I the only person who has a secret red bottom? Oh, I have such guiltosity.

8.00 p.m. How can I concentrate on my French homework? Even if I had remembered to bring it home from school with me.

In my book about not sweating the small stuff it says "Don't keep your pain a secret".

Rang Jas. Even she is quite swoony about Henri.

"He's quite, you know . . . handsome, isn't he? In a French way."

I said, *"Mais oui. Très sportif.* Er . . . but lots of *les garçons* are, aren't they? It's natural at our age to be attracted to good-looking guys."

Jas was raving on, unaware of my secret pain. "No, I don't think so. It's only Tom for me. He is my one and only Hunky."

Good Lord. I went on, "Yes, but you said Henri was quite handsome."

"I know, but that is just fantasy, isn't it? I wouldn't dream of doing anything about it."

"Yes, but what if, for instance, it was hot and you thought he was going to say he loved you and then you noticed he was wearing a false red nose? What then?"

She pretended to not know what I was talking about. I must bear my secret burden of pain alone. *Quel dommage.*

One thing is for sure, I must never speak to Dave the Laugh again. I must eschew him with a firm hand.

9.00 p.m. Dave the Laugh rang!

Uh-oh. He said, "Georgia. I just rang to say don't worry about anything. I know how weird you can get. But it's OK. We just had a laugh. No one needs to know anything about it, we can be mates. Don't worry, Mrs Mad."

Crikey. How grown-up is that? Scarily grown-up.

He's right, though. I am just too sensitive for my own good. I should relax. It was just a little kiss.

9.05 p.m. And lip nibble. With a hint of tongues. But that is all.

11.05 p.m. I wonder what number on the snogging scale nip libbling should be?

11.10 p.m. Emergency snogging scale update:

1 holding hands;
2 arm around;
3 goodnight kiss;
4 kiss lasting over three minutes without a breath;
5 open mouth kissing;
6 tongues;
6¼ nip libbling;
6½ ear snogging;
7 upper body fondling – outdoors;
8 upper body fondling – indoors (in bed);
9 below waist activity (b.w.a.), and
10 the full monty.

midnight I wonder if it is possible to have two boyfriends? I mean, times are changing. Relationships are more complicated. In France men always have mistresses and wives and so on. Henri probably has two girlfriends. He would laugh if you told him you just had the one. He would say,

"C'est très, très tragic."

So if he can have two I could have two. What is good for le gander must be bon for le goose aussi. Je pense. Oh merde.

But would I want Robbie to have another girlfriend? No!!!!!

tuesday november 9th

7.50 a.m. Angus is amusing himself by ambushing the postman. Och-aye, they may have taken his trouser snake addendums but they cannae tak' his freedom!!

walking to school with jas

8.30 a.m. Jas was having a bit of fringe trouble (i.e. she had cut it herself and made herself look like Richard II) so she was even more vague than normal. She just went fringe fiddle, fringe fiddle. I was going to have to kill her. In a caring way. Oh the burden of guilt. I wanted to shout out, "OK!! I have nip libbled with Dave the Laugh. Kill me now." But I didn't.

german

10.20 a.m. In the spirit of European whatsit and also because I had finished painting my nails, I asked Herr Kamyer what was German for snogging. He went amazingly dithery and red. At first he pretended not to know what snogging meant but when Rosie and Jools started puckering up and blowing kisses at him he got the message. Anyway, it's called *Frontal Knutschen*.

As we left class I said to Rosie, "I rest my case *vis-à-vis* the German people. I will never *Knutsch* any of them."

french

1.30 p.m. When Jackie Bummer went up to collect her homework (!) she stood so close to Henri that she was practically resting her nunga-nungas on his head. If he had had the misfortune to have seen her in her sports knickers as I have, he would have been away laughing on a fast camel. (Or, as Henri would say, "away laughing on le *vite* camel.")

Uh-oh, I am thinking about Dave the Laugh again.

Merde.

6.00 p.m. Robbie phoned to say he really likes me. (Yeah!!!) He is going down to London (booo) for his meeting *vis-à-vis* becoming a HUGE star. (Hurrah!)

A HUGE star with a really great girlfriend.

6.10 p.m. I went into the kitchen to have a cheesy snack to celebrate. Angus was having a zizz in his basket. Even though he is no longer fully intact trouser-snake wise he is very cheerful. He was purring like a bulldozer. When I gave him one of his kitty treats he almost decapitated my hand. Libby wanted a kitty treat as well. I said, "They are not for human beings, Libby."

"I like human beans."

"Yes, but . . ."

"Give me human beans as well!!!!"

I had to give her one. Then the Loonleader came in and said, "Who are all these mystery boys, then, that keep phoning you?"

I went, "Hnyunk." Which in anybody except an absolute

fool's language means, "It is none of your business and I will be sick on your slippers if you go on."

Vati, of course, didn't get it. He raved on. "Why don't you bring them round here for us to meet?" On and on and ON about it.

I said, "As I have said many many times, I have to be going now."

my bedroom

8.00 p.m. Everyone gone out. I've got so much revision and so on it will be a relief to really get down to it.

8.05 p.m. Oh Blimey O'Reilly's pantyhose . . . What is the point of Shakespeare? I know he is a genius and so on, but he does rave on.

"What light doth through yonder window break?"

It's the bloody moon for God's sake, Will, get a grip!!

Phoned Rosie. "The Sex God has to go to London to see the record company people and discuss making an album. I don't mean to boast but I have to . . . not only am I the girlfriend of a Sex God, I am now going to be fantastically rich."

"Fab. Groovesville Arizona. Are you going to be living in an all-white penthouse with parrots?"

Sometimes I really worry about my friends. Parrots?

Then I could hear in the background, "Parrots, parrots? Oh ja." Sven seemed really interested in these bloody parrots, my new flatmates.

Rosie said, "Hang on a minute."

Her massive Norwegian boyfriend always seems to be

round her house: that is because she has very very nice parents who go out a lot. I could hear kissing noises and giggling and a sort of Norwegian parrot thing.

When she came back Rosie said, "Sven says can we come and live with you in your groovy London pad?"

"No."

"Fair enough."

11.00 p.m. I won't let my new-found happiness with a famous popstar spoil me though, and I definitely want my own career. Using one of my many talents. Hmmm . . .

What career combines being able to apply make-up and innovative trouser-snake dancing?

I could be a heavily made-up girl backing dancer!

wednesday november 10th

biology

1.30 p.m. I can do a magnificent impression of a bolus of food being passed along the alimentary canal. Mrs Hawkins said it was "terrifyingly realistic". So I'll probably get top marks in Blodge and become, erm, what is it you become when you do Biology? . . . A bloke with a beard ferretting around in swamps. Maybe I'll stick with the backing dancer idea.

10.00 p.m. I had to go to bed because Vati was singing "I Will Always Love Youuuuuuuuuuuuuuu-uuuuuuuuuuuuuuuuuuuuuuuuuuuuuuuuuu" by Whitney Useless.

11.00 p.m. Just nodding off when I heard this noise at my window. I opened it and looked out and there below me was the Sex God!! He'd got Angus in his arms as well. Aahhhhh. He blew me a kiss when I opened the window and said, "Come down."

I put on my coat over my jimjams and had just a second to remember my emergency Sex God drill . . . lip-gloss, comb idiot hair, suck in nostrils, before I crept downstairs and opened the door. The Olds were all still up in the front room, singing the national anthem, only to a reggae beat . . . I suspect a few barrels of Vino Tinto had been drunk.

Robbie gave me a really dreamy long kiss when I came out. Then Angus started yowling so I quickly shoved him into the kitchen and went out into the night again. I whispered, "Brrr, it's very nippy noodles, isn't it?"

Robbie looked at me like I was half insane (and half bonkers). Which I am so he is not wrong there. SHUT UP, BRAIN!!!

We went down to the bottom of the garden. It was lovely, all quiet and the stars out above us. We snogged under the stars for ages. It was weird actually, because after a while I couldn't tell where I ended and he began. Which you would think was a bit confusing (especially if you were trying to get dressed) but I liked it. A LOT.

midnight In bed.

He has gone.

To London.

Without me.

433

8.30 a.m. Still, life carries on. Tests to be done. Serious things to be thingied.

Today we have decided on Operation *La Belle France*. The whole gang went to school wearing our berets like *les françaises* and also with our collars on our coats turned up. Rosie even brought a bunch of onions for Henri, which in my personal opinion is taking things just that little bit too far. He was all groovy and smiley and said, "*Merci, mademoiselle*, I will make the *delicieusement soupe à l'oignon ce soir* and I will think of you when I eat it." Which is a plus and a minus in my book. *Très bon* to be thought of by Henri but not so *bon* to be associated with onions. He said it all in *la française* and I knew what it meant. I smiled at him to let him know that I knew what it meant.

11.00 a.m. The French test didn't seem all that difficult.

We have got Henri fever. Badly. All this morning we wandered around going "Haw he haw he haw" in a French accent. I wish I knew why. We just had to.

p e

1.30 p.m. I think even Miss Stamp might be on the turn because of Henri. I could have sworn she has had a shave.

break

Ellen and me were sitting on the radiator near the vending machine. In these cold autumn days it's quite pleasant having toastie knickers. I said to Ellen with great casualosity, "How's it going with you and Dave the Laugh?"

She said, "Quite cool."

What does that mean? I tell you what it means, it means that he hasn't told her about our accidental snog.

I may live to snog another day.

fish party

11.00 a.m. Very very bad snogging and Sex God withdrawal.

midday Even though I am not in the mood for shopping because I am so sad and aloney I forced myself to ask Mum for a fiver and made an effort to go out. Rosie, Jools, Ellen and Jas and me met in Luigi's as normal and then went off to Miss Selfridge. On the way there we had to go through the town centre and we were just walking along all linked up when we saw Dave the Laugh with Rollo and a couple of other mates. Uh-oh.

Dave the Laugh said, "Hi, dream chicks."

He is a very fit-looking boy. It's funny that even though of course I was really sorry (honestly, Jesus) about the red bottom business, it was always nice to see him. I never feel like such a stupid loon around him as I do with the Sex God. We were close to Jennings the greengrocer's where Tom works, so Jas HAD to pop in to see her so-called boyfriend.

I said, "Ask him if he has got any firm *légumes*." But she didn't pay any attention to me.

Ellen was being really girlie round Dave and flicking her hair

436

about. They were chatting and I was pretending to be looking at things with Rosie. But really I wanted to know what Dave the L. was saying to Ellen. I still didn't know if they were official snogging partners.

The lads went off and Dave gave Ellen a little kiss on her cheek. It made me feel a bit funny actually. I don't know why.

3.00 p.m. Ellen was all stupid for the rest of the afternoon. She is going to the cinema tonight so she said she had to go home to get ready. I said to Rosie, "So are they an item, then?"

Rosie said, "I know that she thinks he's really cool, but she won't tell me what number they have got up to . . . she says it's private."

I said, "That's pathetic."

And Rosie said, "I know, but I'll keep my beadies on them tonight at the cinema and see if I can tell."

It turns out that everyone – Jas, Tom, Rosie, Sven, Ellen and Dave, Jools and Rollo and a few more couples – is going out together tonight. Everyone, that is, besides me. *Merde*.

I am a goosegog in my own country.

3.30 p.m. Phoned Jas.
"I am a goosegog in my own country."
"Well come along tonight, then."
"I can't. You'll all be having a snogging fest. Don't worry, I'll just stay in whilst my best mates all go out together."
She said, "Oh OK, then. See you later."
Charming. And typico.

8.00 p.m. SG phoned. OOOOhhhhh. The record company wants to sign them up!!! They are going along to this big music industry party tonight at some trendy club.

midnight I am a pop widow.

sunday november 14th

lunch-time

1.10 p.m. Phoned Rosie. She said, "*Bonjour, ma petite pal.*"

"What are you doing?"

"Having an Abba afternoon. I am wearing my mum's old crochet bikini and . . . Sven! Careful of that glass chandelier!!"

In the background I could hear all this clattering and "*Oh ja oh ja oh ja!!*"

I said, "What is Sven doing?"

"He's juggling."

Of course he is. Why do I ask?

2.00 p.m. Jas is swotting with her boyfriend AGAIN. No one will play with me, they are all doing their homework. Huh.

8.00 p.m. Alarmingly I found myself in my room doing some French homework!!! Even Dad came to the door to look. This is a new sign of my maturiosity. Also I must make sure I can order things in Paris when

I am travelling over there with the band. I would feel like a fool if I didn't even know how to order mascara.

monday november 15th

french

1.30 p.m. Hmmm. Henri gave us back our test papers and I had come top!!! All the Ace Crew looked at me in amazement.

Jools said, "*Sacré* bloody *bleu.*"

But Henri gave me a really dishy smile. He said, "This is vair, vair well done, *M'mselle.*"

Blimey O'Reilly's trousers. He is quite literally GORGEOUS! If I wasn't the girlfriend of a Sex God and also dying to go to the piddly diddly department I would have snogged him on the spot.

break

As we left French and went to the canteen Henri was ahead of **2.30 p.m.** us. He has got excellent bottomosity. Herr Kamyer came bounding and dithering along the corridor. He looked delighted to see Henri.

"*Guten tag*, Henri. Vould you like a cup of coffee?" And they went off to the staffroom.

I said, "Herr Kamyer is making an absolute arse of himself, isn't he? Drooling around after Henri. Like a homosexualist."

Jas went all politically correct. "Well, there is nothing wrong with that. He might be gay, you know. He might be looking for happiness with the right man."

"Jas, don't be ridiculous . . . he wears tartan socks."

at home

4.30 p.m. Yesss!!! I came top in French! That will teach Madame Slack. In fact, I will tell her when she gets back, possibly in French, that instead of the stick she should have used *le* carrot. Like Henri. Oo-er.

7.00 p.m. To celebrate Vati's fabulous new job at the waterworks (!) I was forced to go out to a family meal at Pizza Express. Libby brought scuba-diving Barbie, Pantalitzer, Charlie Horse and a *Pingu* comic so we had to have a table for eight because she wanted them all to have seats of their own. (Yes, even the comic.) She tried to order them their own pizzas as well but Vati put his foot down with a firm hand. Even when she cried real tears. He said, "There are children starving in Africa."

I nearly said, "Well why don't you send your bottom off to them? That should keep them going through the winter."

But I didn't want to spoil a beautiful evening.

10.00 p.m. Sex God phoned. Yummmmmm!

The Sex God is relanding on Sunday. Actually he is coming back on Saturday and going to a family party; it's his mum's birthday. Jas is going with Tom. I sort of waited for him to ask me.

He said, "It would be great if you could come, Georgia, but maybe we should wait and introduce you to them first before you just turn up? What do you think?"

"Er . . ."

What do I think? What does he mean, what do I think? How should I know? If anyone knows what I think it won't be me. I, of course, will be the last to know. Hmmm, I wish me and the Sex God could see more of each other and, you know, do normal things like . . . Abba afternoons . . . and . . . snogging and trouser-snake dancing and so on.

Maybe when we live in our penthouse flat in London.

1.00 a.m. How many hours is it till the Sex God returns? Twenty-four times five plus the difference between . . . oh God, I don't know. Nauseating P. Green is really good at Maths. Perhaps, as she loves me so much, she could become like my human calculator. With glasses on.

1.15 a.m. No, she'd never fit in my bag.

tuesday november 16th

maths

2.45 p.m. Didn't those Greek-type people have anything to do but loll around in baths going "Eureka!!"? And also, I'll just say this about Pythagoras . . . Didn't he have any mates? Mates that would say, "Hey, Pythy baby . . . SHUT UP!!!!"

4.01 p.m. We were just pinning on our ears to do glove animal on the way home when we spotted Dave the Laugh and Rollo and Steve and a few others, hanging around . . . Ooo-er. Lad alert, lad alert!!! Damn, I didn't have any lippy on, but at least I could quickly rip my ears off. Ellen was patheticisimus – she ran back into the cloakrooms, going, "Oops! Forgot my fags!"

Oh yeah!

She came out five minutes later with just the merest hint of make-up on . . . lip-gloss, concealer, glossy eyeshadow, mascara . . . skirt rolled over, hair tousled . . . really natural.

I said, "Found your fags, then?" But she didn't get it.

Dave *is* cool-looking. In a someone else's boyfriend sort of a way. He gave Ellen a kiss on the cheek. Then he looked at me. I hadn't noticed how long his eyelashes are before. Probably because he had been a red herring and then he had been wearing a big red false nose. He said, "Hi, Georgia. Still grooving?"

I said, "Yeah, grooving like two grooving . . . er . . . groovers." And he laughed.

Ellen said, "Are you walking home?" And we all set off together.

Dave has been banned from school for a week. Hmm . . . my kind of guy . . . I asked him why.

"Well, you know that methylated spirit just burns and doesn't burn anything else?"

Ellen (space rocket scientist . . . not) said, "Oh yeah . . . it's to do with its low combustion point, isn't it?" And she was being all girlie and sort of hanging on his arm. I wondered what number they had got up to? Rosie said she thought Number Five (open mouth kissing). She couldn't really tell in the dark at the cinema. Also had he done that nip libbling thing?

Shut up. Shut up! Remember I am the girlfriend of a Sex God.

Dave said, "Anyway, in Science I put some meths on my

hand and set fire to it, then when Mr Martin asked a question I put up my hand. On fire. It was hilarious in the extreme, even if I do say so myself. Which I just did, because I heard myself."

It really made me laugh.

Rosie has asked them all to go to her house on Saturday because her parents are out for the night. After we split up at the bottom of the hill I said, "It was a laugh about the hand on fire thing, wasn't it?" and Ellen said, "Don't you think it was a bit dangerous?"

I have my doubts about whether she is quite laugh enough for Dave the Laugh.

6.30 p.m. Oh dear *Gott in Himmel*. Libby has snared a poor little boy that she calls her "boyfin". She dragged him home after kindy today. They are supposed to be playing at drawing in her room but it doesn't sound like that. I can hear her saying, "Now you lie here, Josh, me be nursey."

6.38 p.m. I suppose I had better go see what she is up to as her so-called mother is too busy being out to bother.

6.40 p.m. Libby was teaching Josh to snog! When I walked in she had got poor little Josh in a sort of stranglehold and had her lips puckered up. Josh didn't seem keen. In fact, he was crying. That didn't stop Libbs. I said, "Let Josh go now, Libbs, he doesn't like it."

She said, "Shhh Ginger. Mmmmmmmmmmmmmm. Smack smack yummmm."

Goodness knows where she has learned all this. I blame

Mutti and Vati for their exhibitionist porn evenings. I had to drag her off PLJ (Poor Little Josh) and put his glasses back on for him. He looked like a startled earwig in dungarees.

11.00 p.m. I told Mum about it but she just laughed.

thursday november 18th

physics

10.20 a.m. The Bummer Twins cut off half of Nauseating P. Green's tie.

lunch-time

12.30 p.m. Nippy noodles. I'm sure Elvis Attwood turns the heating down when it gets cold.

We all huddled on the radiator in the Science block. We were safe because it was Tragic Kate and Melanie Griffiths on prefect duty and neither of them are in peak physical condition (due to extreme breastiness in Melanie's case and general fatness in Kate's). They can never be arsed to check beyond the second floor. If Wet Lindsay or Hawkeye are on duty there is quite literally no hiding place. Once I had the unfortunate experience of hiding in the loo with my legs up against the door, pretending there was no one in there. (As you do.) Then, when I thought it was all clear, I looked down to see Hawkeye's beady eyes looking up at me from underneath the door. Scary bananas.

The madwoman from Tampax is coming tomorrow to tell us

all about sex and stuff. I said, "I will be wearing my earplugs. I cannot bear to have grown-ups discuss sex. It's unnatural."

Jas said, "Haven't your mum and dad told you the facts of life thing?"

I looked at her. "Erlack."

Actually Mutti did once ramble on about eggs and ovaries when my periods started. I didn't happen to have my earplugs with me so I had to hum a little tune in my head.

I said to the gang, "All we can hope for is that we get some free sanitary towels from Mrs Tampax."

Jas (the sanitaryware expert) said, "Don't you use tampons? They're so much more convenient. Why don't you use them?"

Resisting my natural urge to shove her off the radiator, I explained, "Because if I use them, Libby finds them, takes them out of their little holder and calls them "Georgia's mice". She trails them around for Angus to hunt. You have no idea what it is like in my house."

friday november 19th

11.00 a.m. Another reprimand! Just because Hawkeye heard me say "Schiessen-hausen" when I tripped over Jas's rucky strap. *Gott in Himmel*, you can't even say lavatory in German without some fascist taking offence.

re

1.30 p.m. Mrs Tampax came today. To tell us the facts of life. And to talk about sanitary-ware. It was when we normally have RE, so Miss Wilson was

445

the hostess (not with the mostest). It was EXCRUCIATING! Mrs Tampax raved on about eggs and trouser snakes. Miss Wilson was sadly hovering around at the back being "enthusiastic" (which means she smiles like a loon and her bob goes mental). She kept saying, "Um, very interesting point," and "How true," and "Yes, that's a complex issue, isn't it, girls?" whilst we tried to get under our desks. Why didn't she and Mrs Tampax (who, incidentally, looked like Meat-loaf) go off somewhere and talk about it together and leave us alone? It was really giving me the mega droop. To pass the idle hours Rosie sent round a note:

> *To whom it may concern,*
>
> *You have to choose one of these. Which would you rather?*
>
> ***1*** *Elvis Attwood gets to Number 7 with you. Heavy tongues are involved. He is in the nuddy-pants.*
>
> *or*
>
> ***2*** *No snogging ever again.*
>
> *Pass it on.*

We all had to put one or two. Everyone put two. The thought of Elvis getting to Number Seven (upper body fondling – outdoors) in the nuddy-pants made me feel sick. Get out of my brain, get out of my brain!

The next note was:

> *Which would you rather?*
>
> ***1*** *Miss Stamp rubs you down with a towel in the showers.*
>
> *or*
>
> ***2*** *No snogging ever again.*

I was very alarmed to see that Jas put number one.

break

2.30 p.m. I said to Jas, "What kind of snacks have you got, lezzie?"

saturday november 20th

saturday night is party night

7.00 p.m. The Ace Gang are going to be there. (Well apart from Jas, who is going to her so-called boyfriend's house to celebrate with her so-called boyfriend's parents.)

Robbie said he would come round to Rosie's if he could after the family "do". I feel sheer desperadoes to see him again. It's been ages since I saw him. Oh well. I wonder who will turn up tonight? Rosie and Sven, of course, Mabs and Steve, Jools and Rollo, Ellen and Dave the Laugh . . . Sara, Patty and me . . . and maybe some of Dave the Laugh's mates.

I'm sort of looking forward to it. It will take my mind off my jelloidness about the SG. Even though I will be, as per usual, the goosegog in the manger.

rosie's house

8.20 p.m. Sven opened the door wearing a Durex on his head like a hat . . . er . . .

"Ello, welcome to the fish party!"

What was he going on about?

When we went into the living room it was all full of netting and paper fish hanging up.

Rosie was wearing a really crap mermaid's outfit (her legs down one leg of her blue trousers and hobbling around). She said, "Cod evening."

Good grief.

Actually it was quite funny. There were fishfingers as snacks. Dave the Laugh arrived with his mates. Ellen was really giddy but I was cool as a mackerel. Sven said, "Let's dance," and we had to dance to fish-type music. Like the music from *Jaws*. And *Titanic*. Like fish. Which is not as easy as you would think because fish aren't big dancers. Dave was making me laugh because he really did look like a fish dancing! He even said, "This dancing is playing haddock with my jeans."

Then we played sardines – well, we played Sven's version of it, which meant that essentially we all got into the wardrobe and some people snogged. Although I am not naming names. But it was Rollo and Jools and Sven and Rosie. I was a bit too close to Dave the Laugh for my liking. He had to put his arm around me to stop falling over . . . It almost made me pucker up in the dark . . .

Oh stop it, stop it. I can feel my bottom getting redder and redder and bigger. I must not, must not get the big red bottom.

9.20 p.m. Back in the living room the gang were playing Truth, Dare, Kiss or Promise. Then the doorbell rang. It was Mrs Big Knickers herself and Tom. No Sex God though. I said to Jas confidentially, "Where is Robbie?"

"Who?"

God she is annoying. She went off to help herself to snacks. I followed her and said, "Jas, what did he say?"

Then, in front of the whole room, she said, "You know

448

when you did ear snogging with him? Well, what number is that officially?"

What is the matter with her?!! If anyone wants to know anything about my life all they have to do is to tune in to Radio Jas.

9.30 p.m. Hahahaha. Jas got "Dare" from me and I dared her to fill her knickers up with all the *légumes* in the vegetable basket. She was grumbling but in the end she had to do it and she went off to the kitchen.

I almost died with laughing when she came back. She had two pounds of potatoes, four carrots and a swede down her knick-nacks. And they were not full!!!

Rosie had to tell the truth about what number she and Sven had got up to . . . It was eight!!!! They had got up to upper body fondling – indoors. Honestly!!! It gave me quite a turn. Rosie wasn't a bit embarrassed or anything. Then Steve got "Dare" and had to eat a raw egg. Which is no yolk. As I pointed out.

Uh-oh. My turn.

Jas got her own back for the vegetable knicker extravaganza in a really horrible way. I got "Truth", and she said, "Do you fancy anyone besides the Sex God?"

Dave the Laugh looked at me. Everyone looked at me.

What was I? A looking at thing?

I said, "Er . . . well, I quite fancy . . . er, Henri." Phew.

That got them talking about Henri and his trousers. The game went on and then . . . Dave the Laugh got "Kiss". Jools said, "OK, Dave, you have to kiss . . ."

Ellen went all pink and incredibly girlish. But then Jools said, "You have to kiss . . . Georgia . . ."

449

Why did she say that? What did she know? Was my big red bottom showing under my skirt????

Whilst everyone went "Snog! Snog! Snog!" I went into the kitchen to get myself a drink.

I was in a state of confusiosity. I wish I knew what I wanted. I wanted everything.

I wanted the Sex God and Dave the Laugh, and also possibly Henri. Good Lord. I really was a nymphowhatsit.

That is when Dave the Laugh came out.

"Georgia."

"What?"

"You owe me a snog."

Oh God's pyjamas!!! He was my best pal's boyfriend. I was the girlfriend of a Sex God.

I would just have to say "No, Dave, the game is over."

And that is when I accidentally snogged him. AGAIN!!!

Oh, my lips had no discipline!! They were bad, bad lips!!!

Then he stopped, mid nip libbling, and said, "Georgia, we shouldn't be doing this."

That was what I was going to say!

He said, "Look, I really really like you. I always have, you know that. But I am not an idiot, and you know, other girls like me. They are only human; you have seen my dancing . . ."

That made me laugh even amongst the dramatosity.

He went on, because I seemed to be paralysed from the nose downwards. Well from the neck upwards and the nose downwards.

"You have to choose. You go for a Sex God or you go for me who really likes you and you could have a great time with."

Then he gave me a little soft kiss on the mouth and went back into the living room.

my bed

midnight I am beyond the Valley of the Confused and treading lightly in the Universe of the Severely Deranged. *Sacré* bloody *bleu*. I am supposed to be thinking about make-up and my nunga-nungas. Not life-changing decisions.

Sex God or a Laugh? Jelloid knickers or strange dancing? Nip libbling or ear snogging?

It is a stark choice.

sunday november 21st

breakfast

11.20 a.m. I was so bonkers that I was driven to ask advice from my mutti. I began to say, "Mutti, I have a . . ." when Vati came bursting through the door and said, "Christ on a bike . . . Naomi is pregnant!!!"

DANCING IN MY NUDDY-PANTS

More confessions of Georgia Nicolson

she who laughs last laughs the laughingest

my bedroom
midday as the crow flies
throwing it down

I've just seen a sparrow be quite literally washed off its perch on a tree. It should have had its umbrella up. But even if it had had its umbrella up it might have slipped on a bit of wet leaf and crashed into a passing squirrel. That is what life is like. Well it's what my life is like.

Once more I am beyond the Valley of the Confused and treading lightly in the Universe of the Huge Red Bottom. What is the matter with me? I love the Sex God and he is my only one and only, but try telling that to my lips. Dave the Laugh only has to say, "You owe me a snog," and they start puckering up. Well, they can go out on their own in future.

12.30 p.m. I wonder why the Sex God hasn't phoned me? The Stiff Dylans got back yesterday from their recording shennanigan. Maybe he got van lag from travelling from London? Or maybe he has spoken to Tom and Tom has just happened to say, "Oh Robbie, we all went to a fish party last night and when we were playing Truth, Dare, Kiss or Promise your new girlfriend Georgia accidentally snogged Dave the Laugh. You should have been there, it was a brilliant display of red bottomosity. You would have loved it!"

Oh God. Oh Goddy God God. I am a red-bottomed minx.

12.35 p.m. On the other foot, no one saw me accidentally snog Dave the Laugh, so maybe it can be a secret that I will never tell. Even in my grave.

12.45 p.m. But what if Jas has accidentally thought about something else besides her fringe and put two and two together *vis-à-vis* Dave the Laugh, and blabbed to her so-called boyfriend Tom.

She is, after all, Radio Jas.

1.00 p.m. I would phone Jas but I am avoiding going downstairs because it's sheer bonkerosity down there. Mr and Mrs Across the Road have been over at least a trillion times saying, "Why? Oh why???" and, "How?" and occasionally, "I ask you, *why?* And *how?*"

At least I am not the only red-bottomed minx in the universe, or even in our street, actually. Naomi, their pedigree sex kitten is pregnant, even though she has been under house arrest for ages. Well, as I have pointed out to anyone who can understand the simplest thing (i.e. me and . . . er . . . that's it), Angus cannot be blamed this time. He is merely an innocent stander-by in furry trousers.

I was forced to go downstairs in the end to see if I could find a bit of old Weetabix to eat. Fortunately Mr and Mrs Across the Road had gone home. However, the Loonleader (Dad) was huffing and puffing about trying to be grown-up, twirling his ridiculous beard and adjusting his trousers and so on.

I said, "Vati, people might take you more seriously if you didn't have a tiny badger living on the end of your chin."

I said it in a light-hearted and *très amusant* way, but as usual he went sensationally ballistic. He shouted, "If you can't be sensible, BE QUIET!"

Honestly, the amount of times I am told to be quiet I might as well have not wasted my time learning to speak.

I could have been a mime artist.

2.15 p.m. I mimed wanting to borrow a fiver but Mutti pretended she didn't know what I wanted.

back in my bedroom

2.45 p.m. Mr and Mrs Across the Road came around again with the back-up loons (Mr and Mrs Next Door). I thought I had better sneak down and see what was going on. No sign of Angus, thank the Lord. I don't think this is his sort of party (i.e. a cat-lynching party).

Mr Across the Road (Colin) is a bit like Vati, all shouty and trousery and unreasonable. He said, "Look, she's definitely, you know, in the . . . er, family way. The question is, who is the father?"

Dad (the well-known cat molester) said, "Well, Colin, as

you know, we took Angus to the vet and had him . . . er, seen to. So there is no question in that department."

Mr Across the Road said, "And they were . . . dealt with, were they? His . . . well . . . I mean they were quite clearly . . . er, snipped?"

This was disgusting! They were talking about Angus's trouser snake addendums, which should remain in the privacy of his trousers. They rambled on for ages, but as Gorgey Henri, our French student teacher, would say, it is *"le grand mystère de les pantaloons"*.

Which reminds me, I should do some French homework so that I stay top girl in French.

2.55 p.m. This is my froggy homework: "Unfortunately whilst staying in a *gîte*, you discover that your bicycle has been stolen. You decide to put an advert in the local paper. In French, write what your advert would say."

3.00 p.m. My advert reads, *"Merci beaucoup."*

4.00 p.m. I cheered up a bit because Granddad came round and set fire to himself with his pipe. He didn't put it out properly and then put it in his trouser pocket. It was only my quick thinking with the soda siphon that prevented an elderly inferno.

4.05 p.m. Still no call from SG. I am once more on the rack of love.

4.10 p.m. Phoned Jas.

"Jas."

"What?"

"Why did you say 'what' like that?"

"Like what?"

"You know sort of . . . funny."

"I always say 'what' like that, unless I'm speaking French; then I say '*quoi*?' or if it's German I say . . ."

"Jas, be quiet."

"What?"

"Don't start again, let me get to my nub."

"Oo-er."

"Jas."

"Sorry, go on then, get to your nub."

"Well, you know when we were playing Truth, Dare, Kiss or Promise . . ."

She started laughing in an unusually annoying way, even for her – sort of snorting. Eventually she said, "It was a laugh, wasn't it? Well, apart from when you made me put all those vegetables down my knickers. There's still some soil in them."

"Jas, now, or any other time is not the time to discuss your knickers. This is a situation of sheer desperadoes, possibly."

"Why?"

"Well, I haven't heard from the Sex God and I thought maybe . . ."

"Oh, didn't I tell you last night? He told me to tell you to meet him by the clock tower. He has to help his olds unpack some stuff for the shop this afternoon. Apparently they are going to sell an exciting new range of Mediterranean vine tomatoes that . . ."

459

"Jas, Jas. You are obsessed by tomatoes, that is the sadnosity of your life, but what I want to know is this: WHAT TIME did Robbie say to meet him at the clock tower???"

She was a bit huffy with me, but said, "Six o'clock."

Oh, thank you, thank you. "Jas, you know I have always loved you."

She got a bit nervous then. "What do you want now? I've got my homework to do and . . ."

"Jas, Jas my *petite amie* do not *avez-vous une* spas attack, I'm just saying that you are my number-one and tip-top pal of all time."

"Am I?"

"*Mais oui.*"

"Thanks."

"And what do you want to say to me?"

"Er . . . goodbye?"

"No, you want to say how much you love me *aussi.*"

"Er . . . yes."

"Yes what?"

"Er . . . I do."

"Say it, then."

There was a really long silence.

"Jas, are you there?"

"Hmm."

"Come on, ours is the love that dares speak its name."

"Do I have to say it?"

"*Oui.*"

"I . . . love you."

"Thanks. See you later, lezzie." And I put down the phone. I am without a shadow of doubtosity VAIR *amusant*!!!

4.30 p.m. Just enough time for a beauty mask to discourage any lurking lurkers from rearing their ugly heads, then in with the heated rollers for maximum bounceability hairwise. And finally, a body inspection for any sign of orang-utanness.

4.45 p.m. Now, then, a few soothing yoga postures to put me in the right frame of mind for snogging. (Although I bet Mr Yoga says, "Avoid headstands whilst using hair rollers, as this causes pain and crashing into the wardrobe." Only he would say it in Yogese, obviously.)

Uh-oh, I feel a bit of stupid brain coming on. Think calmosity.

5.00 p.m. Fat chance. I was just doing 'down dog' when Libby burst in and started playing the drums on my bottom, singing her latest favourite, 'Baa Baa Bag Sheet', that well-known nursery rhyme. About a bag sheet that baas. 'Baa Baa Bag Sheet' has replaced 'Mary Had a Little Lard Its Teats Was White Azno', which she used to love best.

5.05 p.m. No sign of Angus. The loons are still having a world summit cat meeting downstairs. I heard clinking from the kitchen, which means that the *vino tinto* is coming out, so there will probably be fisticuffs later when they get drunk.

Usual dithering attack about what to wear. It's officially dark by five o'clock so I need to go from day to evening wear. Also it's a bit nippy noodles.

5.10 p.m. So I think black polo-neck and leather boots . . . (and trousers of course). And for that essential hint of sophisticosity I might just have to borrow Mum's Paloma perfume. She won't mind. Unless she finds out, of course, in which case she will kill me.

5.15 p.m. Mum has got a plastic rainhat in her bag! How sad it would be to see her in it.

Still, on the plus side it means that she is taking a more reasonable attitude towards her age. Hopefully it means that she will be throwing away her short skirts and getting sensible underwear.

Oh, hang on, it's not a rainhat it's a pair of emergency plastic knick-knacks for Libbs. Fair enough, you can never be too careful *vis-à-vis* emergency botty trouble and my darling sister.

5.30 p.m. Sex God, here I come!!!

I didn't bother to interrupt the loon party; I just left a note on the telephone table:

Dear M and V,

I hope the cat-lynching party is going well. I have found a bit of old toast for my tea and a Jammy Dodger to avert scurvy and gone out. Remember me when you get a moment.

Your daughter,

Georgia

P.S. Gone to meet Jas about froggy homework back about 9 p.m.

Hahahaha *très amusant* (ish).

6.00 p.m. As I came into the main street I could see the Sex God was waiting for me by the clock tower. I ducked into a shop doorway for a bit of basooma adjusting and lip-gloss application. Also, I thought I should practise saying something normal so that even if my brain fell out (as it normally does when I see him) my mouth could carry on regardless. I thought a simple approach was best. Something like, "Hi," (pause, and a bit of a sexy smile, lips parted, nostrils not flaring wildly), and then, "long time no dig."

Cool – a bit on the eccentric side, but with no hint of brain gone on holiday to Cyprus.

I came out of my shop doorway and walked towards him. Then he saw me. Oh heavens to Betsy, Mr Gorgeous has landed.

He said, "Hi Georgia" in his Sex-Goddy voice and I said, "Hi Dig."

Dig???

He laughed. "Always a bit of a tricky thing knowing what you are talking about at first, Georgia. This usually makes it better . . ." And he got hold of my hand and pulled me towards him. Quick visit to Number Four on the snogging scale (kiss lasting three minutes without a breath). Yummy scrumboes and marvelloso. If I could just stay attached to his mouth for ever I would be happy. Dead, obviously, from starvation, but happy. Dead happy. Shut up, shut up!! Brain to mouth, brain to mouth: do not under any circumstances mention being attached to his mouth for ever.

The Sex God looked at me when he stopped his excellent snogging. "Did you miss me?"

"Is the Pope a vicar?" I laughed like a loon at a loon party (i.e. A LOT).

He said, "Er no, he's not."

463

What are we talking about? I've lost my grip already.

Luckily SG wanted to tell me all about London and The Stiff Dylans. We went and had a cappuccino at Luigi's. As I have said many times, I don't really get cappuccinos. It's the Santa Claus moustache effect I particularly want to avoid. Actually, I have perfected a way of avoiding the foam moustache; what you do is drink the coffee like a hamster. You purse your lips really tightly and then only suck through the middle bit. Imagine you are a hamster having a cup of coffee at Hammy's, the famous hamster coffee shop. Shut up, shut up!!!

The Sex God told me all about an agent-type person offering them a record deal and them staying in this groovy hotel with room service and looking around London.

I said, in between sips of hamster coffee, "Did you see the Changing of the Gourds?"

He said, "Changing of the Gourds?"

Oh no . . . I had forgotten to unpurse my hamster lips.

"Guards. The Changing of the *Guards*."

He really didn't seem to mind that he had a complete idiot for a girlfriend because he leaned over the table and kissed me. In public!!! In the café!! Like in a French film. Everyone was looking. Of course then it meant that I had to nip off to the loos for emergency lip-gloss application. It's very hard work being the girlfriend of a Sex God; that is what some people might not know.

We left Luigi's and walked towards my house hand in hand. Thank goodness Robbie is tall enough for me. I don't have to do the orang-utan lolloping along that I had to do with Mark Big Gob. I think that must mean that we are perfect partners, because our arms are the same length.

10.05 p.m. When we reached the bottom of my street I said to the Sex God that it would be better if he wasn't exposed to my parents because of the Angus fandango.

He asked me what had happened and I said, "Well, in a nutshell, Naomi is pregnant and the finger of shame is pointing towards Angus, even though he is well, you know . . . not as other men in the trouser addendum department."

When I eventually managed to tear myself away SG gave me a really amazing Number Six with a dash of Six and a quarter (tongues with lip-nibbling). I managed to not fall over and I very nearly waved at him like a normal person when he went home. I like to think I handled the whole incident with sophisticosity.

That is what I like to think.

SG is meeting me on Tuesday after Stalag 14. Hurrah!!!

Everything is going to be fabbity fab fab and also possibly *bon*. For evermore.

10.32 p.m. Wrong. Vati had his usual outburst of insanity when I let myself in.

"You treat this house like a bloody hotel."

As if. The sanitary inspectors would close the place down if they saw the state of my room. What decent hotel has a toddler pooing in its wardrobes?

kitchen

Mutti was wearing what I think she imagines is a sexy negligée. I tried to ignore it and said, "What happened at the cat-lynching party?"

"Well, even though Mr and Mrs Across the Road think in principle Angus should be made into a fur handbag, they had to admit that he must be innocent of Naomi's pregnancy."

She seems to think it was all quite funny. But then this is the same woman who, when I asked if she had ever two-timed anyone, said, "Yes, it was great."

Poor Angus is an innocent victim of Naomi's red bottomosity. This is a lesson for me about where blatant and rampant red bottomosity can lead. I have had a lucky escape.

10.45 p.m. I'm so exhausted by the tension of life that I barely have the energy to cleanse, tone and moisturise, let alone tape down my fringe. I am so looking forward to lying down to rest in my boudoir of love.

11.00 p.m. Libby has got all her toys in my bed AGAIN! All their heads are lined up on my pillow. And some of her toys are quite literally just heads. I don't know exactly how beheading is going to be useful in her future career but she is bloody good at it.

Libbs popped out from my wardrobe in the nuddy-pants, but wearing A LOT of mum's eyeshadow, and not on her eyes.

"Heggo, Ginger, it's me!!!"

"I know it's you, Libbs – look, sweetheart, wouldn't you like to go in your own snuggly, cosy bed and . . ."

"Shut up, bad boy. Snuggle."

"Libby, I can't snuggle; you've got too many things in my bed."

"No."

"Yes."

"Get in."

"Look, let me just take something out to make a bit of room . . . look, I'll just take this old potato . . ."

"Grrr . . ."

"Don't bite!!!"

midnight If I have to sing 'Winnie Bag Pool' to Mr Potato one more time I may have to kill myself.

I went to my so-called parents' bedroom door and talked to them from outside in the hall. I've seen Dad in his pyjamas before and it's not a sight for someone as artistic and sensitive as *moi*.

"Hello . . . it's me. Georgia. Remember me? Your daughter. And your other daughter, Libby, do you remember her? Two foot six, blonde, senselessly violent?? Ring any bells?"

Vati yelled, "Georgia, what is it now? Why aren't you in bed? You've got school tomorrow."

"Hello, Father, how marvellous to speak with you once again . . ."

"Georgia, if I have to get out of bed and listen to more rubbish from you . . . well, you're not too old to smack, you know!"

Smack? Has he finally snapped? He's never smacked anyone in his life. The last time he lost his rag with me, he threw his slipper and it missed me and broke his hilarious (not) mug in the shape of a bottom.

Mutti opened the bedroom door unexpectedly as I was leaning against it and I nearly fell into her basoomas.

She finally persuaded Libby to go into her and Dad's bed. So thankfully Libbs clanked off with Mr Potato, Pantalitzer, Charlie Horse, Scuba-Diving Barbie and the rest of her "fwends".

I was just snuggling down to go off into boboland when I heard her pitter-pattering back into my room. Oh dear God, she hadn't left something disgusting lurking in the bottom of my bed, had she?

She came right up to me and whispered in my ear, "I lobe you, Ginger. You are my very own big sister."

Awww. I put my hand on her little head. Sometimes I love her so much I feel like I would plunge into a vat of eels to save her. If she fell in one, which in her case is not as unlikely as you might think.

As a lovely goodnight treat, she sucked my ear, which was not pleasant, especially as she was breathing very heavily. It was like a big slug snoring in your ear. Still, very sweet.

Ish.

12.10 a.m. I've accidentally got to Six and a Half on the snogging scale with my little sister.

12.12 a.m. The Sex God does varying pressure, like Rosie says foreign boys do. Soft, then hard, then soft. Yummy scrumboes.

Oh Robbie, how could I ever have doubted our love?

12.15 a.m. Dave the Laugh is a bit full of himself, anyway. What was it he said at the fish party? "You have to choose: a Sex God or me, who you can really have a laugh with."

Yes, well, I have chosen. And I have not chosen you, Mr Dave the Laughylaugh. She who laughs last laughs the laughingest.

12.20 a.m. He *has* got fantastic lip nibbling technique, though.

12.25 a.m. I have gone all feverish now. I wonder where Angus is? I've not heard any wildlife being slaughtered for ages. Or the Next Doors' poodles Snowy and Whitey (also known as the Prat Brothers) yapping. He must be feeling really depressed. In a cat way.

Haunted by his lost love.

Half the cat he was, and only fading memories of his trouser-snake days.

12.29 a.m. What is it with my bed? Angus has got a perfectly cosy cat basket, but *oh* no, he has to come in with me.

12.37 a.m. And why does he like my head so much? It's like having a huge fur hat on.

Why does he do that?

Why?

monday november 22nd

8.25 a.m. Everyone late for everything. When Mutti took Libby to kindy, both had hair sticking on end like they had been electrocuted. They should try the cat hat method – it keeps your hair very flat.

Run, run, pant, pant.

Jas and I panted up the hill to Stalag 14, past the usual assortment of Foxwood lads. They are so weird. Two passed us and started doing impressions of gorillas. Why? Then another group went by, and the biggest one, no stranger to all-over-head acne, said, "Have you got a light?"

Jas said, "No, I don't smoke," and he said, "No chance of a shag, then, I suppose?" And he and his mates went off slapping and shoving each other.

I said to Jas, "They show a distinct lack of maturiosity, but never fear, that is where I come in. I have thought of something *très très amusant* to do with glove animal if it snows this winter."

Jas didn't say anything.

"Jas."

"What?"

"I said something *très amusant* and you *ignorez-voused* me. You do remember good old glove animal, don't you?"

"I know I got three bad conduct marks because you made me wear my gloves pinned over my ears like a big doggy with a beret on top."

"*Voilà*, glove animal. Anyway, I think he should make a comeback this term and liven up the stiffs."

She was pretending not to listen to me but I knew she wanted to really. She was doing fringe fiddling; however, I resisted the temptation to slap her hand, and said, slowly so that she could understand me, "Glove animals have to wear sunglasses when it snows."

"What?"

"Is that all you can say?"

"What?"

"You are doing it to annoy me, *mon petit* pal, but I love you."

"Don't start."

"Anyway, we will have to wear sunglasses with glove animal

if it snows, to prevent . . . snow blindness!!"

She didn't get it, though. I have to keep the comedy levels up at school all by myself.

assembly

9.20 a.m. I told the rest of the Ace Gang about the glove animal and snow blindness hilariosity and they gave me the special Klingon salute. Then I got the ferret-eye from Hawkeye and had to pretend to listen to our large and glorious leader, Slim. Her feet are so fat that you can't actually see any shoe at all. It is only a question of time before she explodes.

Slim was rambling on about the splendour of Shakespeare's *Hamlet* as an allegory for modern times.

For once she is right. Shakespeare is not just some really old boring bloke in tights, because after all it was he who said, "To snog or not to snog, that is the question."

How true, Bill.

break

Our new pastime to fill in the long hours before we are allowed to go home is called 'Let's go down the disco'. Anytime any one of the Ace Gang says it, we all have to do manic disco dancing from the 70s (excess head shaking and arm waggling). Even if I do say it myself, it is a piece of resistance.

german

We disco danced at our desks pretty much all the way through

471

German whilst Herr Kamyer wrote ludicrous things on the board about Herr Koch. As I said to him when we were leaving class, "*Vas is der* point?"

lunch-time

Very nippy noodles shivering around outside. What harm have we ever done to anyone?

I said that to the gang. "What harm have we ever done to anyone that we are made to go outside in Antarctic conditions?"

Rosie, Ellen, Jools and Mabs all said, "None, we have never done anything."

But Jas, who seems to have turned into Wise Woman of the Forest, said, "Well, there was the locust thing, and the dropping of the Blodge lab skeleton on to Mr Attwood's head and . . ."

Honestly, if I wasn't the girlfriend of a Sex God I would have had to duff Jas up, she is so ludicrously 'thoughtful' these days. I think I liked her better when she was all depressed and didn't have a boyfriend. Regular snogging has brought out the worst in her.

The Bummers came by all tarted up. Jackie wears even more make-up than those scary circus people. You know when you go to the circus and you accidentally see a trapeze artist close up and they are orange.

Alison Bummer, unusually spot free, just the one gigantic boil on her neck, shouted over to us as they headed for the back fields and town. "Bye, bye, little girls, have a nice time doing your lessons."

I said, "Honestly, I don't know how they get away with it. They turn up for register, hang around torturing P. Green for a bit, have fifty fags in the loos and then bog off to town at lunchtime, to see their lardy boyfriends."

We had a tutting outbreak as we shared our last snacks.

Rosie was shivering. "It is vair vair nippy noodles. I think I have got frostbite of the bum-oley."

Eventually, in between Nazi patrols led by Wet Lindsay (who may be head girl, but is still: a) wet and b) boyfriendless), we managed to sneak into the Science block.

science block
on our usual radiator

Ellen said, "It was a groovy fish party, wasn't it?"

Rosie said, "*Magnifique*. I found bits of fishfinger everywhere, though. Sven got a bit carried away."

I said, "He should be."

Jas said to Ellen, "What happened at the end? With you and Dave the Laugh, you know, when he walked you home?"

Ellen went all red and girlish. "Oh, you know."

I was prepared to leave it at that, but not old Nosey Knickers. She rambled on. "Did you and Dave the Laugh . . . do anything?"

Ellen shifted around on the knicker toasting-rack (radiator) and said, "Well . . ."

I said, "Look, if Ellen wants to have some personal space, well . . ."

But Ellen was keen as *le moutarde* (keener) to talk about my dumpee. "He did, er, walk me home and . . ."

The Ace Gang were all agog as two gogs, apart from me. I was ungogged. In fact, I was doing my impression of a cucumber (and no, I do not mean I was lying on some

473

salad . . . I mean I was being cool).

They all said, "Yes . . . AND???"

"Well, he, you know, well he, well . . ."

God's shortie pyjamas, I was going to be a hundred and fifty at this rate.

Ellen went red and started playing with her piggies (very annoying) and went on. "It was cool, actually. We got, well, we sort of got to Number Three and a bit."

What is "sort of Number Three and a bit" on the snogging scale? Perhaps I should "sort of" give her a good slapping to make her talk some sense. But no, no, no, why did I care? I was a mirage of glaciosity.

As the bell went for resumption of abnormal cruelty (Maths), Ellen said to me, "Dave does this really groovy thing, it's like, er . . . lip nibbling."

He had nip libbled with her!! The bloody snake in the tight blue jeans had nip libbled her. How dare he??

Ellen was rambling on. "We should add lip nibbling to our snogging scale."

Jas said, "We already have, it's Six and a Quarter."

Ellen said to Jas, "Oh, have you done lip nibbling, then? With Tom?"

Jas went off into the dreamworld that she calls her brain. "No, because Tom really respects me and knows that I want to be a prefect, but Georgia has done it. And she's done ear snogging."

Then they all started. "Is that what the Sex God does?" "Does it make you go deaf?" and so on. Triple *merde*.

As we went into Maths, Ellen said, "You know when we played that game and you were supposed to snog Dave, well . . . did you?"

474

I went, "Hahahahahahahahahahaha." Like a hyena in a skirt. And that seemed to satisfy her.

Once again I am in a state of confusiosity. In fact, I can feel my bottom throbbing again when I get a picture of Dave the Laugh nibbling my lips.

And now Ellen's.

He is a serial nip libbler. I am better off without him.

french

Mon Dieu. Fabulosity all round. We are going on a school trip to *le* gay Paree next term. We were yelling, "*Zut alors!*" and "*Mon Dieu!*" and "*Magnifique!!!*" until Madame Slack threw a complete nervy strop. The fabby news is that Gorgey Henri is going to take us. The unfabby news is that Madame Slack and Herr Kamyer, dithering champion for the German nation, are also going. Still, that will be a bit of light relief. Herr Kamyer is almost bound to fall in the Seine at some time over the weekend.

I wrote a note to Rosie: "How much do you bet we can do the famous 'Taking a souvenir photograph' of Herr Kamyer on the banks of the Seine and he falls in when we say, 'Just step back a bit, Herr Kamyer, I haven't quite got your *lederhosen* in yet.'"?

4.20 p.m. Walking home with Jas. I was trying to use her as a windbreak, but she kept dodging away from me. She is unusually full of selfishosity for someone who loves me.

I said, "Thank Cliff Richard's Y-fronts that nobody knows about my accidental snogging incident."

"What snogging incident?"

"I can't tell you. It's a secret I'm taking to my grave."

Oh *sacré bleu*. What is the matter with Jas (besides the obvious)?

When I accidentally told her my secret that I will never tell, even in my grave, she went on and on about how I should be ashamed. She is so annoyingly good, like Mother Teresa with a crap fringe.

home

Mutti in an unusually good mood. She had even bought a pie for us on the way home. Scarily like a real mum – apart from the ludicrously short skirt. She's not going to tell me that I'm going to have another little brother or sister, is she?

Still, I can't think of everyone else. I am not God, I have enough to worry about thinking about myself.

8.00 p.m. I am so worried about school tomorrow. I have so much to do.

8.10 p.m. I can do my nails and foundation and eye stuff during RE – Miss Wilson won't notice, as she will be sadly rambling on about the Dalai Lama or yaks or whatever it is she does talk about. But I suppose even she might notice if I took my curling tongs into class. I'll have to do my hair at lunchtime and hope the Bummers don't decide to put their chewing gum in it for a laugh.

looking out of my bedroom window

I'm amazed to see Naomi the sex kitten lounging around on the roof of our shed, showing off her fat tummy. She has got very little shame to say she is an illegitimate bride. Angus is in the garden below her, blinded by his love. Well, actually he's mostly blinded by the dirt he's digging up. He's got a huge bone from somewhere and he's burying it. Maybe as a midnight snack. He doesn't really seem to understand that he is not a dog. I may have to do some diagrams of mice for him and explain.

I went downstairs to the kitchen to find M and V absolutely all over each other. It's like living in a porn movie living in our house. Honestly, isn't she sick of him yet? (I am). He's been back about a month; surely by now they must be discussing divorce.

I said, "Erlack," in a caring way to let them know I was there. But my finer feelings make no difference to the elderly snoggers. They just started giggling, like . . . giggling elderly snoggers.

I said, "Vati, I don't want to be the person responsible for one of your unreasonable outbursts of rage, but . . ."

He said, "OK, as I am in a good mood you can have a fiver, because you did so well on your French test."

I was quite literally gobsmacked. For a second. Then I grabbed the fiver.

"Er, thanks . . . but, erm, I feel, in all fairness to you, I should let you know that Naomi is on our shed roof and that Angus is not a million miles away from her. In fact, as I left my room, he was licking her bottom."

No one went ballisticisimus, because apparently Mr and Mrs Across the Road have worked out that the pedigree boy cat they had over to visit with Naomi must have had more than a few fishy snacks with her.

Vati said, "Either that or she is having a virgin birth."

Hey, she might be! She might be having a little furry Baby Jesus (lots of them, in fact). She is due to give birth at

477

Christmas, after all. And God works in mysterious ways, as everyone knows.

I said to Jas on the phone, "It makes you think, doesn't it?"

She was all weird and huffy. "No, what makes me think is this: how come some people, naming no names, but you, Georgia, can tell such porkies to their so-called friends?"

She was rambling on about Ellen and Dave the Laugh, of course.

I said with deep meaningosity, "Jas, she who casts the first stone has to cast the logs out of her own knickers first."

That made her think. Then she said, "What in the name of frankincense are you talking about?"

I had to admit she had me there.

Her trouble is that she has never done anything adventurous, her bottom has never glowed with the red light of . . . er . . . red bottomosity.

I said to her, "Jas, Jas, my little nincompoop, I didn't MEAN to snog Dave the Laugh. It was an accident. I am a teenager and I can't always control my bits and pieces."

"What bits and pieces?"

"Well, you know, I have very little control over my nunga-nungas; for instance . . . and at the fish party with Dave my lips just sort of puckered up."

"I'm a teenager and I *can* control my bits and pieces."

"What about your fringe?"

"That is not the same as snogging someone else's boyfriend."

"You are getting very set in your ways, Jas."

"I am not."

"Well, name an interesting thing that you and Tom have done lately."

"We've done loads of really interesting, crazy things."

478

"Like what? And don't tell me about collecting frog spawn."

"Well, Tom is going to do ecology and so on . . . do you know we found some badger footprints in the park near . . ."

"Jas, I said name an interesting thing that you and Tom have done lately, not something about badgers."

But she had gone off into the twilight world of her brain. "Tom gave me a love bite."

"*Non.*"

"*Oui.*"

"I've never seen it."

"I know."

"Where is it?"

"On my big toe."

9.00 p.m. I am worried that in my capacity as the Sex God's girlfriend I may have to give a celebrity interview about my life and Jas will have to come on it. And she will talk rubbish. And perhaps show her love bite. Or pants.

9.15 p.m. Still, it has taken her mind off the Dave the Laugh fiasco.

I will have an early night to prepare myself for heavy snogging duties. I want to look all gorgey and marvy for SG and not have those weird little piggy eyes that I get sometimes when I have been kept awake all night by loons (Angus and Libby). Mutti has let Libbs sleep in the cat basket with Angus tonight, so I am safe.

9.35 p.m. Ah . . . very nice and cosy in bed, although I am having to sleep sitting up because I have rollers in my hair for optimum bounceability.

Phone rang. Vati yelled, "Georgia, another one of your little mates on the phone. You'd better hurry, I think it's an emergency. She might have run out of lip-gloss."

Vair vair vair *amusant,* Vati.

As I came down the stairs, he said, "We mean no harm, take us to your leader," because of my hair rollers. He really is in an alarmingly good mood.

It was Ellen. Uh-oh. I hoped she couldn't detect my red minxiness.

"Georgia, can I ask you something?"

"Er, like what?"

"Well, you know Dave the Laugh?"

DID I KNOW DAVE THE LAUGH????!!!!!!

I sounded a bit vague. "I know Dave the woman, but Dave the Laugh . . . ? Oh er, Dave the Laugh . . . yes, what about him?"

"Well, you know I really think he's groovy and so on and he did the lip nibbling thing, and that was, you know, quite groovy and not, you know, ungroovy . . . and how I have thought he is quite groovy for a long time and lip nibbling would, like, mean he thought I was groovy as well . . ."

(It was going to be the twenty-second century at this rate by the time she got round to telling me what in the name of Father Christmas's elfin mates Nobby and Les she was on about.)

She was still rambling on for England. "Well, anyway, it's nearly Tuesday."

"Yes and . . . ?"

"Well, he hasn't called me yet," she went on. "Well, what should I do?"

"Did he say he'd call?" (Not that I am remotely interested in what my ex-snoggees say. I am just being a great pal.)

"Not exactly."

"What did he say exactly?"

"He said, 'I'm away laughing on a fast camel – see you later.'"

"Oh."

"What?"

"It's the old 'see you later' thing, isn't it?"

"You mean it might be see you later, as in see you *later* not see you later?"

"*Exactamondo.*"

She went on and on about Dave the L. and about how surely he wouldn't nip libble her if he didn't like her, etc., etc. . . . I was so tired I tried to lie down on the floor, but couldn't because of my rollers. Good Lord, what am I? The Oracle of Delphinium?

Eventually she rang off.

10.00 p.m. What if Ellen finds out about me and Dave the Laugh? Will she still like me and realise that it is just one of those things? Or will she beat me to within an inch of my life?

How would I feel if the boot was on the other cheek?

I wish I wasn't so caring and empathetic. As Hawkeye said in English, I have a very vivid imagination.

10.15 p.m. Actually what she said was that I had a "hideous" imagination. But she is just

481

jealous because she has no life to speak of (apart from torturing us).

10.40 p.m. My nose feels very heavy. I'd better have a look at it in case there is a lurking lurker situation.

10.47 p.m. Hmm. I can't see anything. It doesn't get any smaller, though. I must make sure I always suck it in when I see the Sex God full on.

10.55 p.m. On the plus side, my nungas don't seem anymore sticky out than they are normally. Perhaps they have stopped growing. Or maybe they are on Christmas vacation, before they burst (quite literally) into life in spring.

11.00 p.m. I'll just give them a quick measure.

11.05 p.m. *Sacré* bloody *bleu* and also *mon Dieu*!! They measure thirty-eight inches!! That is more than a yard. There must be something wrong with the tape measure.

11.10 p.m. I've done it again and it's still the same. It amazes me that I can lumber around at all. It's like carrying two small people around with me.

I'm really worried now. I wish there was someone I could talk to about this sort of thing. I know there is an unseen power at work of which we have little comprehension, but I don't really feel I can consult with Jesus about my basoomas.

Or Buddha.

Anyway, I don't want to offend Buddha and so on, just in case He exists, which I am sure He does . . . but . . . I have seen some statues of Buddha and frankly his nunga-nungas are not small either.

midnight When I was in M&S the other Saturday, I saw a sign that said they had a breast measuring service (top job . . . not). Maybe I should get properly measured by a basooma professional and learn the truth about my condition(s).

_1.00 a.m._ Angus is on the road to recovery. I can hear him serenading the prat poodles with a medley of his latest hits: 'Yowl!' and 'Yowl 2 the remix'.

I got up to look. He is so brave in the face of his pain. I really love him, even if he has destroyed half my tights. He could have just given in, but no, there he was, biffing the Prat Brothers like normal. Naomi was parading up and down on the Next Doors' window sill, sticking her bottom in the air and so on. She is an awful minx. She is making a mockery of a sham of her so-called love for Angus. It's like in that old crap song where the bloke is wounded in the Vietnam War and his wife goes off with other men because he can't get out of his wheelchair. He sings, "Ru-beeee, don't take your love to town."

That is what Angus would sing. "Naom-eeeee, don't take your love to town." If he could sing. Or speak. And had a wheelchair.

school panto fiasco (a.k.a. complete twats in tights)

breakfast

Dad was singing, "Sex bomb, sex bomb, I'm a sex bomb," and doing hip thrusts round the kitchen. He'll end up in Casualty again if he's not careful. He was being all interested in me as well. Red alert, red alert!

He gave me a hug (!) and said, "I thought we'd all go to the cinema tonight. My treat."

I said, "Fantastic!!!" He thought I meant it and went off happily to flood people's homes or whatever it is he does at the Water Board.

I said to Mum, who was trying to get all the porridge out of Libby's hair before she went off to kindergarten,

"Mum, I can't go to the cinema tonight, I . . . I've got to stay behind and help with . . . the school panto."

She didn't even look up. "I didn't know you were in it."

"I'm not, I'm just, er, helping backstage. Bye, Mutti, Byeeee, Bibbet."

"Bye bye, Gingey, kiss Mr Cheese bye bye."

484

It was disgusting kissing Mr Cheese. (Mr Cheese is a bit of old Edam in a hat.) Not as disgusting as it will be at the end of the day when Libby brings him home again from playschool. With a bit of luck Mr Cheese will have been eaten by one of Libby's little pals.

I had a look at my pocket mirror as I walked round to Jas's place. Eight out of ten on the hair bounceability front. I am sooo excited. I love the Sex God and it will be beyond fabulosity and into the Valley of Marv when we go on tour to America. I think I could easily write song lyrics myself.

I said that to Jas as we walked to school. "Thank you, ladies and gentlemen, this one is called 'Sex God' and it goes like this: 'Oh, Robbie, you're the one for me, with your dark blue eyes and your . . .'"

I had a bit of writer's block then and I said to Jas, "What rhymes with 'me'?"

"What about 'two-timer'? Or 'crap mate'?"

"Jas, don't start again . . . oh hang on, I know: 'You're the one for me, with your dark blue eyes and your . . . snogability!!!' I am clearly a genius."

I put my arm round Jas in my happinosity and said, "You can show me your love bite when we get to Stalag 14."

She went a bit red and said, "OK, but don't tell anyone else about it." Which is ironic coming from Radio Jas.

assembly

Slim really on tip-top boring form this morning.

She bored us beyond the Valley of the Dim and into the twilight world of the Elderly Mad.

485

Speaking of which, we saw Elvis Attwood tapping at pipes with his hammer as we went out.

I said to him, "I think you should receive a knighthood, Mr Attwood, for your services to caretaking. Surely you of all people deserve to be hit over the shoulders with an old sword."

10.00 a.m. What IS it with this place????!!! Rosie and I have got bad conduct marks AND have to stay behind and help with *Peter Pan* every night this week after school. I cannot believe it! Just because we have naturally high spirits and *joie de vivre*. (And also got caught doing our 'Let's go down the disco' dance to 'There Is a Green Hill Faraway' in Assembly.)

It is so obviously hilarious. And not at all "indicative of stupendous childishness", as Hawkeye said.

10.30 a.m. Perhaps I am Spawn of the Devil in a skirt and have the third eye. No, I mean the second whatsit . . . sight. Because I told Mum that I was staying behind to help with *Peter Pan*, even though I wasn't, and now I am. I may have special powers.

No, I haven't got special powers. I tried for about a million years to make the wall clock fall on to Hawkeye's head, but it just gave me a very bad headache.

in the loos

11.00 a.m. I said to Jas, "For once in the entire existence of humankind my hair has got bounceability and whatsit and I am on detention."

She said, "Well you shouldn't be so silly."

What is silly about disco dancing?

She wanted to show me her love bite, but I couldn't summon up any interest.

_re_

Miss Wilson has written on the board: "Relationships – what are the ingredients?"

Good Lord, she would be the last to know, and also I don't think I have ever seen anyone over the age of six months wearing a pink smock, apart from her. Has she really not got one single mate who would have said to her, "Put the smock in the bin and we will never mention it again"?

I wonder if I should make Naomi a little pregnancy smock. In the spirit of Christmas?

Rosie has made some dreadlocks for her pencil and stuck them on to the end of it. She wrote me a note: "As a Rastafarian he has strong views on religious freedom."

I wrote back: "It's a pencil, you fool."

And she wrote: "That is what makes it even more remarkable."

But we are only trying to cheer ourselves up because of the _Peter Pan_ fiasco.

What am I going to do about the Sex God? He is supposed to meet me after school. I wrote to Jas: "If I tell SG I have been given detention duties helping complete twats into tights he will think I am a silly little schoolgirl."

She wrote back: "You ARE a silly little schoolgirl."

Cheers, thanks a lot. Goodnight.

last bell

3.50 p.m. I ran down the corridor to the cloak-rooms and threw myself in front of the mirror. This was my plan: emergency make-up, dash to the school gates, quick snog, explain to Robbie about my unfair incarceration by the Nazis (but not exactly mention the 'Let's go down the disco' incident, in case it was construed as a bit on the childish side), another quick snog, possibly Number Four, then quick as a bunny back to the main hall before ten past four.

Pant, pant. *Alors, alors*. Mascara, lippy, lip-gloss, rolly-over skirt, bouncey hair, bouncey hair.

Right. Ready for the Sex God in five minutes and thirty seconds. A new world record.

When I stepped out into the corridor, I walked straight into Hawkeye lurking like a piranha. Oh *Scheissenhausen*.

She loomed over me. "Georgia, you are helping with the Christmas entertainment, why does that require mascara? Remove it and go along to the main hall NOW!"

I slunk back in the loos. This called for the famous 'Getting out through the loo window and jumping on to the back field' routine. I almost decapitated two first years getting out of the window, but I made it. I ran along the back field and then down fag-ash alleyway (so called, because it is where the Bummers hang out) that runs between the Science block and . . . there he was, waiting for me. Sex God unleashed. He looked amazingly groovy. All the girls streaming out of the gates were eyeballing him as they went by. He said hi to Ali King and she practically evaporated on the spot.

After a quick suck in of the nostrils I sauntered out with

488

an attractive air of casualosity and said, "Hi."

Blimey, I'd managed to say something normal to him. That was a turn up for *les livres*. He smiled his smile and said, "Hi."

He put his hand through my hair (feeling its incredible bounceability, probably) and leaned down and kissed me. Wow. I knew that everyone walking past us was looking, but I had my eyes closed. I did try slightly opening my eyes, but I could only see a big sort of blurry pink thing, which gave me a bit of a turn, until I realised it was my nose really close up.

4.15 p.m. Probably because I am such a kind and caring person, Jesus has decided to take me for His sunbeam by letting me off the hook. The Sex God told me that he had to go and have a 'conference call' with some record people from Hamburger-a-gogo land and so he couldn't see me tonight.

I feel a mixture of sadnosity and reliefosity, with just a hint of peckishness.

4.30 p.m. Rosie and I have the ridiculously sad task of helping the 'cast' of *Peter Pan* into their costumes and sorting out the props. We are in charge of the 'dressing room', or PE changing room, as the normal might call it. We have to hang everything up in order and on different pegs, whilst Miss Stamp dashes about 'supervising'.

Wet Lindsay has got the leading part of Peter in *Peter Pan*, which I think is unfortunate casting, because she has to wear a green tunic and tights. She has got astonishingly stick-like legs. Also, for no good reason (other than I stole her boyfriend), she has taken against me. She wouldn't have me as her little helper, so Rosie has to help her into her tights and so on. (Erlack.) Tragic Kate is Wendy in the show and I have to help her into her duff wig with plaits.

Hours of boredom stretch ahead. Will I never be free of this hellhole?

5.10 p.m. The SG will be talking to people in Hamburger-a-gogo land now.

6.00 p.m. I said to Rosie, "Do you and Sven talk a lot?"

Rosie thought a bit. "Sven talks a lot."

"What about?"

"I haven't got the faintest idea. He's not, as, you know, English. Reindeer, possibly."

"Don't you mind that all you do is snog?"

"No."

8.00 p.m. Home again, in the sanctity of my luurve boudoir.

Mon Dieu, how boring was the rehearsal? It was almost as boring as Dad's stories about Kiwi-a-gogo land. Still, home at last and my bedroom is a Libby-free zone!

I haven't listened to my dolphin CD for a bit. I think I will put it on and meditate on my inner me.

8.10 p.m. I don't know who it is that thinks dolphins are soothing. It's just squeak squeaky squeak.

8.15 p.m. I do feel a bit sorry for them, though, because they get all those depressed people insisting on swimming with them. It might cheer up the depressed people, but I bet it depresses the arse off the dolphins. They just want to go out with their mates for a laugh and no sooner do they start playing Chase the Cod or whatever, than all these miserable types come and hang around stroking their snouts and crying.

Or am I being a bit harsh?

8.35 p.m. Everyone out as usual, round at Uncle Eddie's. God it's boring being by yourself. I may be forced to do my Blodge homework.

9.00 p.m. Rang Jas.
"Jas."

"*Quoi?*"

"What are you doing?"

"Blodge homework."

"*Moi aussi.* Are you drawing a hydra?"

"*Oui.*"

"Have you drawn its wafting tentacles yet?"

"*Non.*"

"I have. Also I have drawn in some cheesy whatsits being wafted in by its tentacles."

"Hydras don't eat cheesy whatsits. They are pond life."

"That's bit rude, Jas."

"It isn't – it's a biological fact."

"OK, Jas, but have you considered this? Perhaps hydras don't eat cheesy whatsits because no one has had the GOOD MANNERS to go down to the pond and offer them around!

491

Don't hydras deserve to be treated like human beings?"

9.15 p.m. Oh, I am so bored!!

In my *Don't Sweat the Small Stuff for Teens* it says: "Do something interesting and useful for others."

9.30 p.m. I can get 48 little plaits in my hair.

9.35 p.m. It makes me look like a complete twat, though.

9.40 p.m. Phone rang!!

"Georgia."

Yes and three times yes!!! It was Robbie.

The record company has done a deal with a big American company and they want The Stiff Dylans to go over there on tour and stuff. Wow.

Rang Jas and told her.

"What do you think I should wear to go on tour? You can never go wrong in black, can you?"

"Your dad will never in a million trillion years let you go to America on tour with a band."

"You will see, my little pal."

10.00 p.m. I will miss my Ace Gang when I go off with the Sex God.

Mutti, Vati and Libbs all came home. Libbs said, "Heggo, Gingey," and put her little arms up for me to lift her up. There was the usual wrestling match trying to get her into her own bed but no spitting, thank goodness.

I will really miss her when I go on tour.

10.15 p.m. I went into the living room to talk to my dear old vati. I feel quite fond of him now I won't be seeing him for much longer. He was lolling on the sofa watching TV, twirling his beard.

"Dad."

"Hmm."

"Er . . . you know . . . if I had a really good, life changing experience offered to me well . . . would you let me go?"

He said, "What fool has offered to adopt you?" And laughed like a bearded loon (which he is).

I went on with great dignosity. "Yes, very funny, Dad, Anyway, say I was invited to America – could I go?"

"No."

"Well, could I go to Paris on the school trip, then?"

"I thought you hated Edith Piaf."

"I do, but I *aime* very very much the other French people."

Anyway, the long and the long of it is that I can go on the Paris trip. I gave Dad a little kiss on his cheek when he said yes, and he looked like his head was going to fall off with surprise. But I can be a very kind and caring person, especially if I am about three thousand miles away in a different country.

midnight But this is only one string in my mistress plan. First Paris, France, and then Paris, Texas!!!

Howdy Hamburger-a-gogo types!!

friday november 26th

french

We've all signed up to go on the French trip to *le* gay Paree, apart from the Bummers (hurrah) and Nauseating P. Green and ADM (Astonishingly Dim Monica). P. Green and ADM are not allowed to go because their mums are worried about the drinking water being polluted in France, and also that they might lose their glasses. Which I think would be a plus.

Gorgey Henri was talking about the trip and sitting on his desk. Phwoar. I know that I am putting my red bottom aside with a firm hand but he is very groovy-looking.

When Gorgey Henri said, "I will show you . . . how you say . . . my EVERYTHING in Paris," I said, "Oo-er," which made Rosie laugh uncontrollably for about five minutes.

4.20 p.m. Forced to stay behind again to help with the *Peter Pan* fiasco. I think it's a crime against humanity to have to look at Wet Lindsay's stick legs night after night. But can I explain that to lesbian of the modern world Miss Stamp? No. She is in a fever of excitement, adjusting costumes, and sending Nana the dog (a.k.a. Pamela Green) scampering around. P. Green is alarmingly good as a dog. I may teach her some amusing tricks.

backstage

6.00 p.m. Backstage, rifling through the props box, because Tinkerbell (played by Melanie Andrews, 48DD in the basooma department) broke her wand when Nana leapt up at her by mistake.

I said to Rosie, as we rummaged around trying to find another one, "Do you think it's awfully wise to let Melanie Andrews loose on stage . . . ?"

Rosie said, "No, I don't. She's not small, is she? What if her enormous basoomas make her topple over and she kills a first former?"

I said, "I think in our capacity of backstage staff we should ban her on health and safety grounds."

tuesday november 30th

The Stiff Dylans are rehearsing every night. Robbie said I should come along and listen at the weekend when they are doing their new set. I think I should take an interest in my new life. I could make some suggestions about lyrics and so on.

saturday december 4th

Sven and the lads have organised a nature ramble tomorrow afternoon. I asked Rosie, "What does that mean?"

"Well, you know, we ramble off to the park and then we snog."

I can't go, though, because I am going to go to rehearsal with The Stiff Dylans. They have a 'mini-tour' of Scotland and Wales just after Chrimbo. Then they will be cutting their new album. Man. That is not what the album is called. That is just what pop-type people say.

I rang Jas to tell her. "The Stiff Dylans are cutting a new album, man."

"Why is it called 'Man'?"

Sometimes when I talk to Jas I can feel the will to live ebbing away.

sunday december 5th

Remind me never to go to a band rehearsal again. It is soooooo boring watching other people doing stuff. And talking about themselves. And me not being in it. I just sat at the back and nodded my head for about a million years.

Also, I think the rest of the lads think I'm a bit weird. I don't know why. I have always been the height of sophisticosity around them. Well apart from when Dom, the drummer, asked me what I was going to do at college and I said, "Backing dancing".

Oh and also when I danced around at a gig in front of Dom's dad because I thought he was an American talent spotter, but he wasn't. He was just Dom's dad waiting to help them pack up. And he thought that I was trying to get off with him.

But apart from those two minor hiccups I have been sophisi-cosity all round, I like to think.

Anyway, here is a brief resume of my glorious night:

    a) nodded my head for a million years

    b) sat on a drum kit in the van on the way home

    c) lost my balance and put my foot through the
       bass drum

    d) had to be dropped off first because I had to be
       in by ten o'clock on a school night

Double *merde*.

At least when I have to do the boring old panto stuff I can have a bit of artistic licence with Rosie.

I wonder how the nature snog went. I suppose Dave the

Laugh went with Ellen.

I don't think that The Stiff Dylans think I am full of maturiosity. I think they think I am the Yoko Ono of the band and that I will split them up.

monday december 6th

I can't believe the poo-osity of my life. Hawkeye said that as "a special treat" Rosie and I could help backstage at the panto again.

Hawkeye is without a doubt a sadist and ex-prison warder. And probably a man.

panto rehearsals

I taught Nauseating P. Green to catch a mini Mars in her mouth from four foot. She is taking this dog business alarmingly seriously. She even brought me a stick, but as I said to Rosie, "I draw the line at tickling her tummy."

Wet Lindsay was trying to take her tights off by herself when she lost her balance and nearly crashed into the sanitary towel dispenser. It really cheered me up. She got the mega-hump when I was laughing and doing my impression of her crashing about stuck in a pair of tights. Which was vair vair amusing but old Tiny Forehead didn't think so. After calling me "a pathetic little twit" she stomped off into a cubicle to get changed.

However, as any fool knows, I am the mistress of invention and with the aid of my compact mirror I was able to look under the door of the cubicle. I made Rosie come and have a look in the mirror because she didn't believe that Wet Lindsay wears a thong in real life. But she had to believe the evidence of her own peepers when she saw the thong nestling in Wet Lindsay's bum-oley. RoRo had to have a reviving chewy fruit before she could speak again then she said, "I am very sensitive, you know. That sort of thing may ruin my chances of becoming a vet."

So all is well that ends well.

10.00 p.m. Our house had been a relatively loon-free zone, but it was too good to last. Uncle Eddie was round tonight. As usual, he came balding into my room with one of his hilarious 'jokes'. He said, "Can a cross-eyed teacher control her pupils?" And looned off laughing like a bald loon.

10.15 p.m. Robbie phoned and he didn't mention the bass drum incident, which is a plus. He said, "What have you been up to, sex kitty?"

Prrrrrrrrrrrrrrr!!!!

midnight I do feel like a bit of a French resistance person, though, because I only see Robbie sort of in secret. There is no normal stuff with him. I said that to Rosie and she said, "What do you call normal?"

"Well, you and Sven, you see each other all the time and you must do normal stuff."

She just looked at me. "Have you met Sven?"

Hmmm, she has a point. Jas and Tom do normal stuff, though. In fact, they act like they have been married for about a trillion years. I'm not saying I want to be as boring as Jas and Tom – collecting frog spawn and doing homework together is too tragic for words. But what do you do with Sex Gods? Besides snog and worship them, I mean.

Opening night of the panto. When the audience started clapping to prove they believed in fairies, Tinkerbell flew out of control and crashed against the back piece of scenery, which fell over to reveal Miss Stamp having a fag. Very funny indeed, I thought.

And much less boring than watching Peter Pan poncing around in green tights.

9.50 p.m. Something quite alarming happened tonight. I was just sneaking off from the dressing room when Nauseating P. Green came bounding along, still with her dog ears on. And she had her mum, who is not unblessed in the huge glasses department, with her. They were both blinking at me and following me out of the door. Like two giant goldfish in skirts.

P. Green said, "I told mum that you were the one who really helped me with my dog tricks."

What is the matter with her???

Mrs Nauseating P. Green said, "It's really nice that Pamela and you are such good friends. Would you like to come round to our house on Christmas Eve? We do round robin story-telling and dress up."

I said, "Hrrmmmmm . . . Oh, is that the time, I must dash!" And made a desperate bid for freedom.

As we walked home, Rosie said, "She loves you very very much. You are her bestest pal." Good grief.

friday december 10th

Christmas frenzy mounting. I put some tinsel around my sports knickers for that little festive touch in PE. Miss Stamp for once did not have a nervy spas, which was a bit scary. Things soon got back to normal in Latin, though, because Hawkeye made us take the false snow (cottonwool) off our heads.

wednesday december 15th

last day of term

Hurrah!!! Thank you, thank you, Baby Jesus!!! Free, free at last!

last german lesson

We were all a bit on the hysterical side. I think the teachers must have been out for a pre-Christmas beverage, if you know what I mean, because Herr Kamyer told us an incomprehensible joke about a Swiss cheese (please don't even ask) and then laughed for about forty years. AND as we were going down the corridor we bumped into Gorgey Henri.

"Merry *Noël*," I said to him and he kissed my cheek and said, "*Merci, au revoir.* I look forward to 'aving you all again in the New Year."

Which made us apopletic with laughter. I thought I might have to throw a bucket of cold water over Rosie and Jools.

Henri smiled at us and said, "You are so crazee." Then he walked off in his groovy gravy jeans.

"Gorgey Henri is quite literally . . . gorgey,' I said. 'He is yummy scrumboes and also . . ."

Rosie said, "Scrummy yumboes?"

"*Mais oui.*"

6.30 p.m. Last night of the panto. *Mucho excite-mondo* (not).

Miss Stamp bought Coca-Cola and cakes for the cast as an end-of-show party thing. Unfortunately the little cakes were saying, "Eat me, eat me, you know you want to," and so Rosie and I were enticed by them. We only ate a few, but Hawkeye noticed and now we are banned from the party. *Quel dommage* (not).

8.00 p.m. Peter and the rest of the ridiculous Lost Boys are poncing around on stage. I may have to eat myself soon, I am so bored. I wonder where the Sex God is now? And if he is thinking about me. I wonder if he thinks about me as many times a minute as I think about him.

I've had to pretend that I am in training for hockey every night this week. Somehow, even though I believe that the only good relationship is an open and honest one, I can't bring myself to tell him that I am helping people into tights.

8.10 p.m. Rosie found something *très très magnifique* in a props basket at the back of the store cupboard – theatrical fur. Fake fur that you stick on with a special glue and you can make beards and sideburns and so on with it.

8.25 p.m. Rosie and I have to be on duty at the side of the stage, handing things over to Wendy and Peter and Captain Hook and so on when they come off. They are all sooo excited. And theatrical. Wet Lindsay just shouts orders like "Sword!" or "Panstick!" if she has to have her stupid shiny forehead touched up. It's VERY annoying, and boring beyond even the Valley of Boredom.

But now we have introduced the theatrical fur into the proceedings. Every time one of us has to go and get something from backstage we stick on a bit of theatrical fur, but just carry on doing our tasks as normal.

8.45 p.m. At first we had a sort of six o'clock shadow effect, but by the final curtain we had entered properly into the spirit of hairiness. Rosie had big furry hands and sideburns and I had one huge eyebrow right across my forehead. And no one noticed!!! Too busy admiring themselves to notice that two teenage werewolves were handing them their props. Very very funny.

Rosie and I were nearly dead from laughing by the time the curtain came down. The cast went out front to talk to their parents, still in their ridiculous outfits, even Nana. In fact, if I was P. Green's mum I would be worried about ever getting her out of her dog costume.

Whilst they did that we sneaked off home. I have rarely seen anything as funny as Rosie in her school uniform and beret with HUGE sidies and furry hands.

Luckily I managed to skedaddle home without seeing anyone I knew.

bed

It took me about a year to get my eyebrow off. In the end I had to use nail varnish remover. I've practically removed my forehead.

I must get plenty of beauty sleep and regrow my forehead because I am seeing my boyfriend this weekend. It's only one hundred and eighty hours until he leaves for the Isle of Man with his family for Christmas. And fifty-six of those will be spent sleeping. Unless Libby visits my bed.

saturday december 18th

churchill square

Out with the Ace Gang shopping for Chrimbo presents and lurking around hoping to bump into lads. We were just having a rest on a wall when the Bummers came sauntering past. Jackie Bummer was dressed completely in leather. Leather skirt, jacket, boots, coat . . . all of it nicked, I bet. She is like a walking crime wave. As a decent citizen I should turn her over to the Old Bill; however, I have my principles and I will never be a snitcher. Especially as snitchers can end up on the wrong end of a duffing incident.

Jackie looked at us like we were snot on legs and said, "Have to dash, little girls, only six shoplifting days to Christmas."

God, they are soooo common and tarty.

4.00 p.m. At home with my thoughtful Chrimboli gift. I hope Dad appreciates the ENORMOUS lengths I went to to get him some new socks. I had to wander around very old people's shops for ages to find anything suitable.

5.00 p.m. I wonder why I haven't heard from SG yet? I've got eight outfits on standby duty

503

and have applied undercoat foundation but it's very tense-making not knowing what is going on.

living room

Mutti and Vati wrestling about tickling each other. Vati had a very alarming pair of jogging trousers on. I suppose it's nice that they are so affectionate, but I don't like to think of certain people snogging. The Queen, for instance. Imagine the Queen getting to Number Seven with Prince Philip . . . erlack. Or Herr Kamyer with Hawkeye . . . erlack, erlack!!! Or Mr and Mrs Next Door in the nuddy-pants.

I must stop this and think of something normal. I might have to go and rub myself with salt to get myself clean again.

Mutti said, "Oh, by the way, when you were in town that really good-looking boy came round. What's his name?"

My face had gone all rigid.

Mutti went on. "You know, the older Jennings boy . . . he's in that band you go to see . . . is it the Bob Wilsons or something?"

The Bob Wilsons!!! OhmyGod, ohmyGod. I must go to my room immediately.

As I left the room Mutti said, "I thought he was really tasty. He said would you ring him."

Then Vati got hold of her and he was sort of tickling her with his beard and growling like a lion in jogging trousers.

bedroom

The Sex God has seen my dad's beard and trousers. He has been exposed to my family. He might even have spoken to Libby. She may have mentioned poo. Will he ever forgive me?

Phoned the Sex God.

"Hi."

"Er, Robbie, I'm really, really, really sorry about my parents, they're just . . . you know . . . I'm really sorry."

He laughed. "Your dad is quite cool."

"Pardon?"

sunday december 19th

Went to band rehearsal again. I have perfected the art of head-nodding and doing my nails at the same time. Dom was looking at me a bit funny, especially as he caught me nodding along to the music when they weren't actually playing any. But at least he has been able to mend his drum. You can still see a slight foot shape in it, though, which in my opinion adds a hint of *je ne sais quoi* to an otherwise ordinary drum kit. At the end the other lads' girlfriends turned up. Mia said hi to me and then, "We're going to the Phoenix bar, are you coming?"

Robbie said, "Well, I'm a bit shattered so we won't." But I knew he really meant that I was officially too young to go.

Pooo!!!

It's a shame that my internal maturiosity is not recognised by the constabulary.

monday december 20th

I haven't had much time to see the Ace Gang as I have been hanging out with Robbie. How cool is that? Double cool with knobs, that is how cool. Sometimes we talk in between snogging.

Well, mostly he talks because I think it is safer that way, and besides I have lots of other things to worry about whilst he is chatting on about The Stiff Dylans and world peace and so on. Things like avoiding nostril flair, or nip nip eruption, or even, as happened the other night, uncontrollable desires to start 'Let's go down the disco' dancing when he put some classical music on.

Rang Jas to catch up. "Hey. What has the Ace Gang been up to?"

"We only saw you yesterday, Georgia."

9.35 p.m. But I know the Ace Gang had a group outing to the cinema last night because Ellen came round to show me her Instamatic photos. How keen is that? To take photos at the cinema. They got thrown out and I'm not surprised. No one would have been able to see the screen with Sven and Dave the Laugh wearing their Christmas antlers.

The gang have probably missed me A LOT, even though they haven't said so.

Ellen said it was "fun" and "a laugh". I didn't ask her about Dave the Laugh, but she told me anyway, about a zillion times . . . that they are "an item". Huh. Who cares?

midnight I noticed in the photos that in addition to his antlers, Dave the L. was wearing the comedy red nose that he wore when he told me he loved me and I accidentally fell over and kissed him. But accidental snogging and red bottomosity are yesterday's news.

furry baby jesuses

wednesday december 22nd

11.00 a.m. The Sex God has gone off to the Isle of Man with Tom and the rest of his family. Then he goes straight off on tour of Och-aye land and Prestan-a-gogogogogo land (Wales).

We spent our last night together at his house because his parents were away. It was really groovy with *mucho* ear nibbling and snogging *extraordinaire*. I'm getting the hang of hands now (mine, I mean). I don't just let them dangle about, I give them lots to do. Hair stroking and back stroking and so on. (His hair and his back, not mine.) I think that snogging keeps me in tip-top physical condition. I may suggest to Ms Stamp that she put it into the training schedule for games. Hang on a minute, though . . . she might want to join in . . .

When the Sex God and I had to part (which took about an hour and a half because I kept coming out of my door after he had said goodbye and we would do all the goodbye stuff again), he handed me a small package and said, "Don't do anything too loony while I am away, gorgeous. Here is something for you for Christmas. I'll get you something else from Scotland or Wales." Which is nice.

Unless he gets me a sporran. Or a tartan bikini. Shut up, shut up, brain. It's only because I am full of sadnosity, probably.

I told Jas and she said, "Tom gave me a locket that has a photo of me and him in it that we took at a booth in Seaworld. It's got a backdrop of sea creatures and so on."

I said, "I hope you didn't make any dolphins be in it, because they have hard enough lives as it is, without being made to get into photo booths with you and Tom."

I was quite tearful after SG left. I hope he will like the identity bracelet I got him with my name on. Jas said I should have had *his* name engraved on it, which is what she did with Tom's.

Phoned Jas again. "Jas, why have you put Tom's name on his identity bracelet? Doesn't he already know who he is?"

She sighed like someone who is incredibly full of wisdomosity, which is ironic, and said, "What if he was unconscious or something and no one knew who he was?"

"And you think 'Tom' would do the trick, then?"

She said, "I have to go now." But I don't think she really did have to go.

I will put the little package that SG gave me for a Chrimboli gift under my bed.

12.30 p.m. Poo. I suppose I will have to get used to being a pop widow. I have to develop my own interests. I must use the time he is away usefully and wisely. I hope it snows early next term and then I can try out the hilariosity of my new idea *vis-à-vis* glove animal and snow blindness.

508

1.00 p.m. I wonder how much money I will need to go to America? I've got some money saved up, if I can find my bank book.

1.20 p.m. Hmm. £15.50.

1.30 p.m. If I am saving up for Hamburger-a-gogo I can't use money to buy any more Chrimboli prezzies. I will have to be creative.

Luckily I'm very artistic, as everyone knows. Miss Berry, the Art teacher, thinks I have a special talent. Not for art, though, sadly. She said I had a special talent for wasting everyone's time. Which is a bit harsh.

I am going to start making my Christmas gifts out of colourful materials and a needle and cotton.

10.00 p.m. I made some carrot twins for Libby. Two nicely carved carrots with rather attractive gingham headscarves and cloaks on. And for Mutti, a pair of sleep glasses. I cut the spectacle shape out of some fun fur fabric and attached an elastic band. I think she will love and appreciate them, but you can never tell.

As a thoughtful and forgiving gift at this special time of year, I took Naomi's pregnancy smock that I had spent many, many minutes making over to Mr and Mrs Across the Road's house. It has got tiny bows on it and four leg holes, which is unusual in a pregnancy smock. I left it on the doorstep with a note saying, "Best wishes from one who only wishes there to be love and peace in the world."

christmas day

Woke up to quite a few prezzies. Libbs climbed in my bed and we opened things together. I am very nearly quite fond of my Mutti and Vati. Vati gave me some CDs I actually wanted!!! Libby LOBED her carrot twins and dumped Mr Potato into the dustbin of life. (Which is just as well, as he was all crinkled and green.)

Mum, in a rare moment of sanity, has bought me a really good bra . . . which fits and is actually quite nice. Not too thrusting and not too shopping-baggy. Even when I jump up and down, there is very little adhoc jiggling. Perhaps now I will be able to dance free and wild, with no danger of knocking anyone out with my nunga-nungas.

No sign of snow yet, although it is very very nippy noodles.

1.00 p.m. M and D and Libbs have gone to visit miscellaneous loons, so I have a private moment to open SG's gift.

It's a compilation tape of songs that he has recorded solo, and it's got "For Georgia, with love, Robbie" written on the little cover thing. In years to come I will be on TV saying, "Yes, Robbie did write the track 'Oh Gorgeous One' for me. Likewise 'Cor, What a Smasher' and 'Phwoar'."

1.30 p.m. Hmm. There isn't a track called 'Oh Gorgeous One' or 'Cor, What a Smasher'. There are tracks about endangered species and one about Vincent van Gogh. Not exactly dance extravaganza music, more, it has to be said, music for slitting your wrists to.

510

2.00 p.m. I love him for his seriosity.

3.30 p.m. Big, big news breaking. And no, it is not that Father Christmas is just Dad in a crap white beard (even though that bit is true too). After Christmas lunch, Mr Across the Road dashed over and had a brandy with Dad because . . . Naomi is in labour!

I said, "Quickly, we must get her on a donkey and head for Bethlehem!" But they all looked at me in that looking-at way that adults have when they do not comprehend the enormity of my hilariosity.

I phoned Jas to let her know the joyful good news. "Naomi is having some furry Baby Jesuses."

"*Non.*"

"*Mais oui.*"

"What shall we do?"

I said, "You get the donkey and I'll sort out the snacks."

4.00 p.m. Angus is in (even for him) a very bad mood. He's been doing slam dancing in the kitchen to Christmas carols playing on the radio (i.e. he just throws himself against things for no reason). When 'Away in a Manger' came on he leaped out of the sink and up on to the plate rack, and then just sort of tap-danced his way along. Four plates and a soup tureen bit the dust.

4.30 p.m. Decided to take Angus out for a Christmas walk to help him work off his frustration and also ensure that we have something to eat our dinner from. I'm under orders to keep him on his lead in case his inner cat pain drives him to beat up little dogs.

4.35 p.m. As I was leaving Libby said, "I want to come."

Auntie Kath in Blackpool sent her an all-in-one leopard costume jumpsuit. It's got a tail and ears and whiskers and so on. Libby has had it on all day. Cute.

5.00 p.m. We had to turn back and get Angus's spare lead because Libby is a cat as well. I hope I don't bump into anyone I know.

5.30 p.m. It takes over half an hour to get out of the garden. Libby goes so slowly on her hands and knees.

Once I got her to move on, Angus found something disgusting to dig up. What sort of people bury manky old bits of clothing in other people's gardens?

5.45 p.m. So that is where Dad's fishing socks went. I remember Dad saying to Mum, "Have you seen my fishing socks?" and Mum saying, "They've probably gone out for a bit of a walk." Because they were so pingy pongees. Even Angus has reburied them.

6.00 p.m. Angus managed to shake me off the end of his lead by heading straight for a lamp post at eighty miles an hour and swerving at the last minute. Now he is prancing around on Mr Next Door's wall. The prat poodles are going berserk trying to leap up at him. Now and again he lies down and dangles a paw near them.

Snowy and Whitey have gone completely loopy now. Whitey leapt up and missed Angus's paw and crashed into the wall, but Snowy kept leaping and leaping and Angus was raising his paw slightly higher and higher.

In the end, Angus biffed Snowy mid-leap, right over on to his back. You'd think that Angus would be a bit miserable, or quiet even, as his beloved sex kitten gives birth to another man's kittens. But no, he is an example to us all. I don't know what of.

6.05 p.m.   Sheer stupidity leaps to mind.

in my bedroom

7.00 p.m.   Uh-oh, Mr Across the Road came and banged on our door. I looked down the stairs as Vati answered. It was weird, actually, because usually Mr Across the Road can rave on for England but he didn't seem to be able to speak. He just gestured with his hand for us to follow him. Perhaps he has taken up mime as a Christmas hobby.

We all trailed over to his house. I don't know why I am supposed to be interested. In fact, I thought as a mark of solidarity with Angus I would refuse to go. But I quite wanted to see the kittens.

Angus was on the wall and tapped my head with a paw as I went by. I said, "I'm sorry about this, Angus."

He just yawned and lay on his back chewing his lead.

7.10 p.m. When we got into his kitchen, Mr Next Door took us to Naomi. He didn't say a word. And Mrs Next Door was just staring down at the cat basket like there was something horrible in it.

Naomi was lying in the basket like the Queen of Sheba, surrounded by kittens. Seven of them . . .

All of them look like miniature Anguses!!!! Honestly! They all have his markings and everything. This is quite literally a bloody miracle!

10.00 p.m. A long, long night of Mr and Mrs Across the Road coming across and saying, "Why? Oh why??" and "How?" and occasionally, "*Why? And how?*"

In the end they worked out that Angus must have sneaked into Naomi's love parlour before his trouser snake addendums were, you know . . . adjusted. Super-Cat!!! He is without doubt the 007 of the cat world.

sunday december 26th

boxing day

The tiny (ish) kittykats are so gorgey. Jas came over and Libby and Jas and I went to visit. Mr and Mrs Across the Road let us in, but were very grumpy about it and were tutting and carrying on. Mr Next Door kept calling Angus "that thing". Which was a bit uncalled for.

And Mrs Next Door said, "Two hundred guineas, she cost us, and for this to happen with a . . . with a . . ."

"Proud, heroic Scottish wildcat?" I asked.

"No, with an out of control . . . *beast!*"

They're just a bit overcome with joy at the moment, but I am sure they will come round in a few thousand years.

Even though they are only a few hours old Angus and Naomi's kittykats are not what you would call the usual sort of kittykat. They haven't even opened their eyes yet, but they are already biting each other and spitting.

I used my womanly charms (which Jas rather meanly said made me look like an axe murderer), and begged Mr and Mrs Next Door to let Angus at least lick his offspring.

3.00 p.m. Eventually they said he could if he was kept on his lead at all times.

He strutted around purring like a tank (two tanks) biffing the kittykats with his head and licking Naomi. Awww.

That is what I want me and the Sex God to be like. Not necessarily including the bottom-exposing thing that Angus and Naomi go in for A LOT.

tuesday december 28th

Robbie has phoned me eight times!!!

It's a bit weird because there is always someone around ear-wigging. Dad's got ears like a bat. (I'll surprise him one day by walking into the front room whilst he is hanging upside down from the light fitting.) When I was talking to Rosie about how to put your tongue behind your back teeth when you smile because it makes you look sexier he came bursting out of the kitchen and said, "Are you going to be talking rubbish on the phone for much longer, because I want to make a call myself this century."

515

I said, patiently, "Vati, as I have pointed out many, many times, if you would have the decency to buy me my own mobile phone in keeping with the rest of the universe, then I wouldn't have to use this prehistoric one in the hall." But he just ignored me as usual.

wednesday december 29th

I arranged with Robbie that he would call me at four o'clock today (as opposed to Isle of Man time, which is about 1948, according to Robbie. I think they still have steam trains). This is the cunning plan we made, in order to be able to say what we like to each other (for example, "You are the most Sex-Goddy thing on legs, I want to suck your shirt, etc., etc."). I told Robbie the telephone number of the phone box down the road and he is going to ring me there.

in the phone box

4.00 p.m. Mark Big Gob went by with his midget girlfriend. Rosie didn't believe me when I told her how very very tiny Mark's girlfriend is, but she is. You could quite easily strap a bowl of peanuts to her tiny head and use her as a sort of snacks table at parties. That is how small she is.

Mark Big Gob gave me a hideous wink as he went by. It's hard to believe that he actually dumped me before I was going to dump him for being so thick. How annoying is that? Vair vair annoying, but . . . then the phone rang and my beloved Sex God of the Universe and beyond spoke to me.

at jas's

5.00 p.m. Jas's mutti and vati are out and we are practising for our trip to Froggyland by eating a typico French peasant meal: *pomme de terre* and *les* baked beans *avec le* sauce *de* tomato. Oh, and of course, de rigueur . . . we wore our berets and stripey T-shirts.

I said, "I 'ope that Gorgey Henri can control his passion for me when we reach Paree."

Jas was also wearing what she imagines are sexy shades. She's wrong, though – they don't make her look French, they make her look blind.

She said, "Gorgey Henri does not have *la* passion for you, he thinks you are *la* stupid schoolgirl."

"Oh, *mais non, ma* idiot, *au contraire* he thinks I am *le* genius."

We both had a lot of frustrated snogging energy so we had to do 'Let's go down the disco' dancing on Jas's bed for about an hour. We were pretending we were in a French disco inferno, which means we yelled, *"Mon Dieu!"* *"Zut alors!!!"* and *"Merde!"* A LOT.

midnight I think I may actually have broken my neck from doing too much head banging.

thursday december 30th

Woke up this morning and there was a sort of weird light in the bedroom. When I opened the curtains I discovered that it had snowed overnight!!!

Mr Next Door was already up wearing ludicrous snow wear

– bobble hat, duffle coat and rubber trousers, clearing his path with a shovel. He got to the end of the path near the gate and then had a breather to survey his handiwork. He probably imagines he is like Nanuk of the North.

It's a shame if he does, because as he walked back up his newly cleared path, he went flying on a slippy bit and ended up skidding along on his rubber trousers.

Happy days!!

11.45 a.m. Oh *très sportif*. We are going to have the Winter Olympics! All the gang are going to meet up on the back fields for snow fun and frolics.

"What are you going to wear?" I asked Rosie.

"Short black leather skirt, new knee-boots and a LOT of lip-gloss."

"That is not exactly sensible winter wear."

"I know," she said. "I may freeze to death, but I will look fabbity fab fab."

She is not wrong. I may have to rifle through my wardrobe for glamorous *après-ski* wear.

I don't know why I am bothering, really, as the Sex God is not here, but you have to keep up appearances for good humourosity and fashionosability's sake.

Phoned Jas. "Jas, what are you wearing for the sledging and snow sports extravaganza?"

"Well, I was thinking snug and warm."

"Well, you can't just wear your huge winter knickers, Jas."

"Hahahaha-di-haha. What are you wearing?"

"Hmmm . . . ski pants, ankle boots and I think roll-neck top and leather jacket. Oh, and waterproof eye make-up in case of a sudden snowstorm."

12.00 p.m. I think snow wear quite suits me. My hat de-emphasises on the conk front which is always a good thing. Lashings and lashings of mascara and lip-gloss for extra warmth and I am just about ready.

I managed to sneak out of the house without Libby hearing me. I love her, but she is being a pain about this cat costume thing – she won't take it off and it is beginning to be a bit on the pingy pongo side.

1.00 p.m. I was a bit late because Angus kept following me and I had to chuck snowballs at him to dodge him.

Dave the Laugh, Ellen, Jools, Rollo, Mabs, Sam, Rosie, Sven, Jas and some lads I didn't know were sledging down a hill on the back fields. Well, apart from Ellen, who was in a ditherama at the top of the hill. She was not exactly dressed for downhill sledging (her skirt was about half an inch short and she was wearing false eyelashes). But neither was anybody else exactly dressed for downhill sledging, and that wasn't stopping *them*. As the rest of them whizzed down the hill in a sledge sandwich – boy-girl-boy-girl sledge – Ellen was fiddling with her hair and gazing down the hillside.

She said, "I've been going out with him for nearly three weeks now. In hours, that is . . . er . . . a lot."

I didn't say anything.

"Do you think he likes me as much as I like him?"

I didn't say anything. I am keeping my wisdomosity to myself.

"Do you think I should ask him?"

"What?"

"Ask him how much he likes me?"

"Er . . . I don't know . . . I mean, boys are, you know, not girls with trousers on, are they?" I astonished even myself with my outburst of extreme wisdomosity. Ellen looked at me all blinky and expectant, like I was a fortune-teller or something. I felt a bit like that bloke in *Julius Caesar*, the one who says, "Beware the idle of March."

Ellen asked me why she shouldn't ask him. Good question. Good. "Er . . . because Dave might feel like you are putting pressure on his individualosity."

"His individualosity?"

"Yes."

"What, by asking him if he likes me as much as I like him?"

"That's the one."

"Well, what should I do instead, then?"

"Be cool, and, you know . . . er, funny and relaxed . . . and fun and happening and . . . er . . . so on." What am I talking about? Alarmingly, Ellen seemed to think I made sense.

By this time, Dave and the gang had struggled back up the hill with the sledge. Dave said, "Nippy noodles, isn't it?" He was smiling at me. He's got a really cool, sort of naughty, smile. It makes you think of lip nibbling. "Look, girls, I couldn't put my hands down the front of your jumpers, could I? To warm them up? There would be nothing rudey-dudey in it, you understand. To me your nunga-nungas are just a pair of giant mittens."

Ellen looked a bit puzzled. As I have said many times, I wonder if Ellen is quite a good enough laugh for Dave the Laugh?

friday december 31st

new year's eve

2.00 p.m. The Ace Gang are going to SEVEN parties, but as a mark of respect Jas and I have decided not to go with them. We are having our own widows' celebration.

Actually, I would rather go out than be cooped up with Jas, but I know that Dave the Laugh will be there and I don't want to entice my bottom into another display of redness. Especially as I have got snogging withdrawal VERY badly.

11.00 p.m. This is the glorious start to my New Year . . .

Jas and I stayed in and watched people on television kissing each other and waving their kilts around. Jas is staying over and my so-called parents and Libby have gone out to some sad party. They actually asked if I would like to go with them. When I indicated that I would rather set fire to myself they left me alone. However, as a special treat Mum got us some food. I said to Dad, "Jas is more of a champagne, girl, really, so if you could just get a few bottles. I think that would make our fabulous evening go with a swing."

He didn't even bother to reply.

On the stroke of midnight, Jas said, "Shall we?"

And I said, "Jas, don't even think about asking me to snog you."

She got all huffy. "No, I wasn't going to. I was going to say, shall we have a celebratory disco inferno dancing experience with the aid of soft toys?"

12.30 a.m. And a happy New Year to one and all!!!

Our New Year 'Let's go down the disco' experience, with the aid of Charlie Horse and Teddy as partners, was actually quite good fun on the funosity scale. Although I was slightly worried about Jas because she did actually snog Teddy.

She said, "I'm pretending it's Tom."

I said, "Teddy is very very like Tom in many ways – his furry ears, for instance."

We were just biffing each other with Charlie and Teddy when the phone rang.

It was SG and Tom phoning from the Isle of Man. Yeahhhhhhh!!!

The Sex God said, "Happy New Year, gorgeous, see you soon." Then he had to go and toss dwarfs or whatever it is they do in the Isle of Man to celebrate. I read that they still have birching there, so anything could happen.

Jas was Mrs Moony Knickers after talking to Hunky, and we just went to watch people snogging and singing on TV.

1.15 a.m. Ho hum pig's bum.

When my 'family' got home, as a hilarious treat, Dad had brought home a bit of coal. He said, "It's called 'first footing.'" It should be called 'first loon in'. He burst in like the original red-faced loon and said, "Happy New Year." Then he tried to hug me and Jas. We beat him off with Teddy and Charlie Horse and then Libby joined in and hung on to his beard, as Jas and I made a bid for freedom to my room.

sunday january 2nd

11.30 a.m. To keep our spirits up, Jas and I made a list of things to take to Froggyland with us.

"We are going to have to hire an extra ferry to take our hair products over," I told her.

monday january 3rd

2.00 p.m. Moped around at Jas's. We are united in widow sadness. We listened to sad songs and practised being interviewed on Michael Parkinson. Jas is hopeless at it. When I (as Parky) asked her what her hopes for the future were, she said, "World peace and more freely available organic vegetables." How interesting is that?

Not, is the correct answer.

Ooooh, I am soooo bored and lonely. NOTHING happens around here.

I lolloped home up our street. At least Angus is happy, though. He is lolling around on the wall overlooking Mr and Mrs Across the Road. He is a very proud dad. I wonder how long it will be before we are allowed to name the kittykats? Mr and Mrs Across the Road are being very unreasonable about it all, and won't discuss it.

When I got back to the house Mum said, "Robbie rang you. The number's beside the phone."

I got the usual jelloid knickers (and added leg tremblers and a quick spasm of quivering-a-gogo).

Should I phone him back or just wait for him to phone again? I must think.

Perhaps if I ate some chocolate orange egg it would calm me down. There was one left under the tree.

The front room was a nightmare of beardosity. Vati had some of his mates from work and Uncle Eddie round watching the football. He was slurping beer and being all jolly. "Georgia, this is Mike, Nick, Paul and Bingo . . . the lads!"

Lads? Since when were lads eighty-five? And a half.

The great tragedy is that the 'lads' are going to be forming a football team. I was about to say, "Should men in your physical condition hurl themselves around a football pitch?" But then Dad dropped his bombshell.

"Georgia, what is this with Robbie? Why is he phoning you all the time and coming round? How old is he?"

I said with great dignosity, "Father, I am afraid I can't discuss my private life with you as I have a date with *Lord of the Flies*."

He said, "Who's he, then?" And the 'lads' all laughed.

I said, "It is a book by William Golding that I have to study for my homework."

I got out of the room fast. As I went up the stairs I could hear the 'lads' raving on. "They don't know they're born these days, do they? Reading books . . . French . . . In my day any kid in the street with two ears was a sissy . . ."

I heard Dad say, "Our school still had capital punishment." And they all laughed like bearded loons. Which they are.

10.30 p.m. I can't phone Robbie because then Dad will know that I am phoning him and that will make him even more full of suspiciosity.

11.00 p.m. *Lord of the Flies* is so boring . . . and so weird. I always thought boys were very very strange, but I didn't think they would start eating each other. Bloody hell, I must make sure I never end up on an island with a bunch of boys!

wednesday january 5th

Tom arrived back from the family Chrimboli. Jas was ridiculously excited. She is a fairweather pal, because I know I will be dumped now that her so-called boyfriend is back. And SG isn't back until next Tuesday.

friday january 7th

Snowed like billio overnight. Angus leaped out of the front door like he normally does and completely disappeared from view, the snow was so deep. He loves it and is leaping and sneezing about in the back garden.

Rosie and the gang are going sledging down the back fields. But I am not in the mood for winter sports until my beloved returns. I explained this to Rosie and she said, "Make love, not war." What is she talking about?

Besides, I saw Ellen and Dave the Laugh holding hands down at Churchill Square yesterday and it made me feel a bit funny. I don't know why.

saturday january 8th

10.00 a.m. Robbie phoned from East Jesus (or Prestan-a-gogogogoch . . . anyway, somewhere in Welsh country). The gigs are going really well,

525

but he is shattered and can't talk much because his throat is sore from singing. He said, "I miss you, gorgeous."

Boo hoo, this is so sad.

Still, he is back on Tuesday. I may distract myself by doing snogging exercises to limber up.

sunday january 9th

6.00 p.m. My exercise regime: doing my yoga sun salute ten times and then pucker-ups (like Mick Jagger) forty times.

8.00 p.m. Stalag 14 starts again tomorrow. Shall we never be free? On the bright side, the snow gives a very good comedy opportunity for an outing of glove animal.

Rang around the Ace Gang.

"Rosie."

"*D'accord*. It's me."

"Is it you?"

"Yes."

"Goodbye."

"Goodbye."

Rang back. "I'll just say this: Operation Glove Animal and Snow Blindness."

"Pip, pip."

Phoned Jools and Mabs and Ellen, who are all prepared. Then I phoned Mrs Useless Knickers. "Jas, it's snowing. Prepare glove animal."

"Oh no, we'll only get bad conduct marks immediately."

"Yes, but think of the hilariosity of it, Jas."

"But . . ."

"Jas, if you can't think of the hilariosity, think of the severe duffing you will get if you don't do it."

monday january 10th

Rendez-voused at the bottom of the hill, where we all clipped on our glove ears under our berets and put on sunglasses. As we bobbled up the hill, Rosie was nearly going to the piddly-diddly department on the spot as she was laughing so much.

8.55 a.m. Mabs did actually walk into a tree because she couldn't see through her sunglasses. Oh, how we laughed.

As we approached the school gate, we could see Hawkeye lurking. We tucked our ears up under our berets, but kept our sunglasses on.

Hawkeye tutted and ferreted at us as we walked by. She said, "What is this nonsense?"

I said, "It's to prevent snow blindness, Mrs Heaton."

She said, "It's a pity there's no way to prevent stupidity." Which I think is quite bad manners for someone who is teaching the youth of today, but I didn't say so.

tuesday january 11th

8.25 a.m. Sex God back today AND the kittykats have opened their eyes!!! They are sooooooo sweet and, as I explained to Jas, "Now they can see to fight properly."

Robbie came round to see me as soon as he got back. How cool is that?

When he arrived at the door, Dad called me and then he and Mum spent about a million years raising their eyebrows and looking 'wise'. And trying to be modern and to get on with the youth, which is ludicrous.

Vati started to talk about Kiwi-a-gogo land. I said, "Fancy going for a walk, Robbie? I'm a bit . . . er . . . hot."

And Dad said, "It's pitch black and about minus seven outside." He was going to go on and on, but then I saw Mutti give him a 'look', a 'modern, understanding mum look,' that said, "Come on, Bob, remember when you were that age?" Which is a physical impossibility for my dad. How very very embarrassing. Shut up, stop looking, shut up, shut up.

Vati said, "Be back by eleven."

Oh, how sad and embarrassing.

Robbie took my hand and once we got away from our house into the dark street he snogged me. Yipppppeeeee!

Cor, bloody nippy noodles out there. But I have my love to keep me warm (that and the extra pair of knickers I put on).

I must say, I think my puckering exercises have paid off, because I haven't got any aches or pains. Robbie told me about being on tour. He said he wasn't sure that he really liked it. But I'm sure that is just a phase he is going through. Once we are squillionaires he will change his mind.

I wonder why he asked me if I liked the countryside? Maybe he wants us to go and snog in the great outdoors?

wednesday january 12th

8.15 a.m. Dad brought me a cup of tea in bed this morning! I said, "Vati, why are you waking me up in the middle of the night? Are you on fire?"

I had to pull the sheets up really quickly in case he could see any bits of my body. He hung around after he had put the cup down. He was sort of all red and beardy.

"Georgia, I'm not trying to . . . well, I know you have your own mind . . . and Robbie seems like a really, you know, great bloke . . . but he's, you know, a big lad and well . . . well, it's just that . . . well, don't get too serious too soon."

What in the name of Buddha's bra is he going on about now?

Then he ruffled my hair (very, very annoying) and went out. Robbie's a "big lad". What does that mean?

I really will have to break the news soon that I am going off on tour to Hamburger-a-gogo land with The Stiff Dylans. Vati obviously doesn't think I am capable of maturiosity. But he is wrong.

Wrongy wrong wrong.

I wonder how much money I will need for *le* gay Paree weekend, for essentials and so on? I might test the water *vis-à-vis* spondulicks for my trip to Hamburger-a-gogo land with a simple enquiry about available finance for Froggyland.

front room

7.30 p.m. Vati was actually doing a press-up when I came in. I hope he is insured.

"Vati."

"Urgh."

"Can I have £220 for my weekend in Paris, please?"

I thought I was going to have to use my first aid skills on Vati. Which would have been a shame as I only know how to force a boiled sweet out of someone if they are choking to death.

saturday january 15th

The snow has melted, thank the Lord. It is so hard on the elderly. However, they can be quite suspicious, the elderly. I offered to go shopping for Mr and Mrs Next Door yesterday in case they were frightened of going out. And they were quite surly about it. I said to Mr Next Door, "I couldn't help noticing that you are even more unsteady than usual on your feet in this kind of weather." And he told me to go annoy someone else, which is a bit rude, I think.

2.00 p.m. As everyone is out, SG came round. We snogged for thirty-five minutes without stopping (I timed it because I could see the clock over Robbie's shoulder). Rosie rang whilst he was here and said they were having an indoor(!) barbecue at her house tonight. The theme is 'sausages'. Robbie couldn't make it, though, because he is busy.

Bye bye, dreamboat.

8.30 p.m. I didn't go to the sausage extravaganza. Heaven only knows what sausages would bring out in me; I was bad enough at the fish party. I will concentrate on my French vocabulary instead so that I can ask for things in Paris.

9.00 p.m. Sausage is *saucisson* in French. Shut up, brain.

I am a bit worried because Robbie turned up this afternoon not in his groovy mini, but on a secondhand bike.

11.30 p.m. I hope he doesn't suggest we go for bike rides together. It is minus a hundred and eighty degrees, and the last time I rode a bike my skirt got caught in the back wheel and I had to walk home in my knickers.

frogland extravaganza

monday january 17th

stalag 14
quatre days to our frogland extravaganza
french

M'sieur "call me Henri" really is sooo cool and gorgey. He told us what we are going to do on our school trip to *la belle France* and what we should bring. We're going to stay in Hôtel Gare du Nord and visit the Champs Elysées and the Pompidou Centre. Loads of *très bon* stuff. Madame Slack came in and took all our forms that we had to take home for signing – the forms saying that even if we were set fire to by raving French people, the staff are not responsible, etc. She also said, "Girls, on Saturday there will be a choice of excursion in the morning. You can go on a grand tour of the sewage system of Paris with me, go up the Eiffel Tower with M'sieur Hilbert or to the Louvre with Herr Kamyer. Please come and sign up for your choice."

As we queued up we argued about which trip to go on as a gang. Jas was the only one who wanted to go down into the sewers. I said to Jas, "What is the point of going down the sewers?"

"Because it is historical and we might learn a lot of stuff we don't know."

I said, "*Au contraire*, we will learn a lot of things we DO know. We will learn that French sewers are like English sewers, only French."

Jas looked like a goggle-eyed ferret.

I explained. "It is just tunnels full of French poo – how different can French poo be from English poo?"

So we are all going up the Eiffel Tower with Gorgey Henri.

Ellen said, "I'm looking forward to going and everything, but I will really miss Dave the Laugh . . . he's such a . . ."

I said, "Laugh?"

"Yes," she said, and went all red. Good Lord.

I am, of course, used to being away from the Sex God. He's only been back a week and I'm off to Frogland.

I sometimes wish he was more of a laugh, though. There is a slight danger that underneath his Sex God exterior there lurks a sensible person. He has just bought a bike to save the environment. And it might not stop there . . . he might possibly buy some waterproofs.

thursday january 20th

Slim gave us her world famous (not) 'Representatives of Great Britain abroad' speech. Apparently we have the weight of the reputation of the British Isles on our shoulders.

I said to Jools; "I'm already tired, and we haven't even got on the coach yet."

midnight I've managed to whittle down my necessities to one haversack full. Jas and I are doing sharesies on some things to save space. For instance, I am supplying our hair gel for the weekend and she is supplying moisturiser. I will not be sharing knickers with her, though.

I said *au revoir* to *mon amour*. He came round on his bike AGAIN, and also (this is the worst bit), he talked to my dad about Kiwi-a-gogo land . . . and he didn't shoot himself with boredom. In fact, he even asked questions, which proved he had been listening to Vati raving on about Maoris. *Très* weird.

friday january 21st

aboard l'esprit

midday On our way to *la belle* France at last. If we ever get there it will be *le miracle*, because: a) it is a French ferry and b) we have a madman at the helm. When we set off from Newhaven we went in and out of the quay three times, because the captain forgot to cast off.

1.00 p.m. *Zut alors*, we are being tossed about like *les corks*. I may complain to the captain (if he has not been airlifted home to a secure unit) and suggest he stops driving us into eighty-foot waves. Herr Kamyer, dithering champion for the German nation and part-time fool, has just lost his footing and fallen into the ladies' loos.

1.15 p.m. In the restaurant there is a notice that says, "*Soupe du jour*", so Rosie said to the

534

French waiter, "Can I have *le soupe du* yesterday, please?" But no one got it.

1.30 p.m. Staggering around on the decks in gale-force winds.

I could see Captain Mad up in his wheelhouse thing.

1.32 p.m. The only way to stay upright is to hold the flagpole at the back of the boat.

1.35 p.m. Why does he keep staring at me? I'm just clinging on to this French flag because I want to live to see Frogland.

Just then the boat lurched violently, and that's when it came off in my hand.

2.30 p.m. Madame Slack, who until then had been attached to Gorgey Henri for most of the voyage (like a Slack limpet), decided to make a big international thing out of the flag removing incident.

She gibbered in *le* Frog to Captain Mad, who had come down to the deck (hopefully leaving someone who could drive in his place). They did a lot of pointing and shouting and shrugging.

Incidentally, why has Madame Slack got two huge handbags? She keeps sellotape and a ruler in one and a hankie in the other. Should someone like that be in charge of the youth of today? Is France a nation of handbag fetishists, I wonder? As I said to Jas, "Even Henri has got a little handbag."

Rosie said, "You are definitely going to have to walk the gangplank. *Au revoir, mon amie.*"

"What makes you think Captain Mad could find a gangplank – I'll be amazed if he can find France." But I said it quietly. I didn't want to start the shrugging again.

In the end, Madame Slack called me stupid about a zillion times, which could have upset me, but I know I am really full of geniosity.

I had to apologise to Captain Mad. In French.

4.45 p.m. Still in this sodding boat, bobbing up and down in the Atlantic or wherever it is we are now.

Suddenly Rosie said, "Land!!! I can see land, thank the Lord!" and got down on her knees. Which was quite funny. It could be Iceland, though, for all we know.

Captain Mad came on the PA system and said, "Ladeez and Jentlemen, ve are now approaching Dieppe."

I said to the gang, "With a bit of luck, he'll manage to dock by tomorrow evening."

9.00 p.m. Miraculously survived the ferry journey and caught the train to Paris. I think the driver might have been wearing a beret, but we still managed to arrive at Hôtel Gare du Nord in *le* gay Paree!! Right in the middle of everything.

The lady behind the desk said, "Welcome, I will show you to your rrruuuuuuums." I thought French people were actually being funny when they put on their accent, but they aren't being funny, they are being French. That, as I said to Jas, is why I *aime* them so much.

Gorgey Henri has let the Ace Gang be in the same room together!!! How fab is he? Usually we get split up in class, but the six of us are back together again. Yes!!! *Les* girls have arrived. It's a really groovy room as well. I have a bed by the window. I lay down on it and said, "Aaahhh, this is the sort of life I will be leading from now on."

Rosie said, "What? Sharing a room with five other women? Are you setting up a lezzie farm?" I had to duff her rather savagely over the head with my pillow.

Jas had brought the photo of Tom and her at Seaworld and she put on the table by the side of her bed. Ellen tried to sneak a book under her pillow, but I saw it. "What's that?" I asked.

"Oh, it's just a bit of homework I brought with me."

Rosie fished it out and read out the title. "It's called *Black Lace Shoulder*, a story of passion on the high seas." Now we know what sort of homework she is doing: snogging research. It was a semi-naughty book. I flicked through it and found a bit to read to the rest of the Gang.

"He captivated women with his fierce, proud face, his lean, well exercised body and his aura of sexuality, wild as that of a stallion."

Rosie said, "That's like Sven."

Jas said, "What, he's like a stallion?"

"Yes."

I said, "A stallion in loons."

Rosie said, "*Mais oui.*'

"*Quel* number have you got up to now with *le* stallion in loons on the scoring system?" I asked.

"Eight." Upper-body fondling indoors. All our eyes drifted towards Rosie's basoomas, which, it has to be said, are not gigantic.

Ellen said, "Is it, does it . . . I mean, are your, erm, nungas . . . getting bigger?"

Rosie looked down the front of her T-shirt. "I think they are a bit. Not as much as Georgia's, though."

Oh no, here we go. I thought my new nunga-nunga holder had stopped this sort of talk. To change the subject I said to Ellen, "What number have you got up to with Dave?"

She went all red. "Oh, well, you know, he's like really a good, well, kisser."

Yes, as it happens, I do know that he's a really good kisser.

Rosie was all interested now. "Has he touched anything?"

Ellen was about to explode from redness. "Well, he stroked my hair."

We haven't even bothered to put hair-stroking on our snogging scale. If we had, it would have been Minus One.

Out of our bedroom window we can see the streets of Paris and the French-type *garçons*. Some of them look quite groovy, but their trousers are a bit too short. Perhaps this is the French way. I said, "Look, people are wearing berets and they're not even going to school. Unless they still go to school at ninety-four."

saturday january 22nd

saturday in paris

9.30 a.m. Oh *j'aime* Paris muchly. For brekkie we had hot chocolate and croissant. All the French kids dipped their croissant into their hot chocolate. How cool is that? Yummy scrumboes.

We set off with Gorgey Henri for the Eiffel Tower. I was

singing "Fallink in luff again, never vanted to . . ." until Rosie pointed out that Marlene Dietrich sang that and she was by no means a French person.

up the eiffel tower

11.00 a.m. Jas and I got split up somehow from the rest of the gang. Well, mainly because Jas was dithering around making me take a photo of her with some French pigeons. How anyone would know they were French pigeons, I don't know. I said to her, "We will have to draw little stripey T-shirts on them when we get the prints back."

Anyway, the others had gone on ahead and we got trapped just in front of a group of French schoolboys of about nine years old. They spent the million years it took climbing the steps looking up our skirts.

Jas was OK because she had her holiday knickers on (same gigantic ones as her daywear in England, but with a frilly bit round the gusset). I, however, had normals on, and so I tried to walk up the stairs with my legs together, which is not easy. Every time I looked behind me I could see the little boys ogling like ogles on ogle tablets.

When we eventually got to the top, Jas said, "It's your fault. You should have worn sensible knickers."

"Jas, *fermez la bouche* or I will *fermer* it for you."

oh la la la gay Paree

2.00 p.m. We walked along the banks of the Seine in the winter sunshine. There were musicians and so on playing and a bird market. I wanted to take a chaffinch or some lovebirds home with me, but I knew that they'd only last two minutes if Angus got a snack-attack in the middle of the night. As we passed a bloke playing a saxophone underneath one of the arches, he put down the sax and started doing a juggling thing with his hands. It was a bit peculiar, though, because, as I said to Jas, "He hasn't got any balls."

Rosie said, "Oo-er . . ." which set us off on the uncontrollable laughing fandango.

Jas said, "He must be doing a sort of mime thing." Mime juggling? In the end, unfortunately, we realised that he was actually pretending to juggle my breasts. I am the first to admit that I can be paranoid about my nungas, but in this case it was clear even to Jas that he was a perv. He pointed at my nungas and made a sort of leering, licking smile and then continued his pretend juggling. How disgusting!!

Am I never to be free from the tyranny of my basoomas? I buttoned my coat up as tightly as possible.

la nuit extravaganza

Henri took us down rue St Denis in the evening and said, "Zis is where the ladeez of the night ply their trade."

Jas said, "I can't see any ladies of the night, all I can see are a load of prostitutes." She astonishes me with her hilarious stupidosity sometimes.

Actually, it should have been called "rue de Bummer", because all the prozzies looked exactly like the Bummer twins. Only less spotty.

It isn't even just Henri who has a handbag, lots of les français men have little handbags. And no one laughs. Weird. I may buy one for Dad, as a souvenir.

sunday january 23rd

Herr Kamyer has reached dizzying heights of giddiness since he's been in Paris, even going so far as to wear leisure slacks and a jumper with a koala on it. Jas said kindly, "Perhaps it's a Christmas gift from his mum." But I don't think so. I think he knitted it himself. And I think he is proud of it.

1.00 p.m. Jas and Rosie keep nipping off to phone Tom and Sven every five minutes.

I would phone Robbie, but I don't really know what to say to him. What if he asks me what I have been doing? What would I say? "I pulled off a French flag, some boys looked up my skirt and finally a bloke with a saxophone juggled my breasts." I wouldn't mean to say any of that, but I know I would blurt it out.

2.15 p.m. Herr Kamyer has been showing us how to ask for things in shops. I know how to do this already: all you do is ask Gorgey Henri to go and ask for whatever it is you want in the shop. He does, after all, know the language. However, Herr Kamyer thinks we should learn stuff, so he keeps going up to French people and asking for things, which is hilarious in the extreme as: a) no one has a clue what he talking about and b) they wouldn't give him anything any-way, because he is not French.

Oh, I tell a lie. He did manage to get something. He went into the tourist information centre for a map. "I vill be back in a moment, girls, *mit der* map and ve vill proceed to the Champs Elysées."

He came out ten minutes later dithering like a loon with a souvenir walking stick but no map. As I pointed out to Jools, "The tragic thing is that they speak English in the tourist information centre."

plunging into the seine photo opportunity

We tried the 'Just step back a bit, Herr Kamyer, I can't get all your jumper in' tactic on the banks of the Seine. But Herr Kamyer looked back before he moved so he did not plunge into the Seine. And now we really do have a photo of Herr Kamyer in his jumper.

nôtre dame

4.00 p.m. Very gothic. No sign of hunchbacks, though. So . . . with a marvellous display of imaginosity (and also after Herr Kamyer, Henri and Madame Slack had gone into the cathedral) the Ace Gang got into their hunchback gear (haversacks under coats). We were getting ready shuffling around and yelling, "The bells, the bells," but then Jas and I stepped on to a bit of green grass verge to take a photo of the Ace Gang being hunchbacks against the romantic backdrop of Notre Dame (*très* historic). Suddenly all hell broke loose. Whistles went and some absolute loon started yelling through a loudspeaker in French at us. Then we were surrounded by blokes in uniforms. I thought we were going to be taken to the Bastille.

I said to Jas, "What have we done? Ask one of them."

She said, "You came top in French, you ask." Unfortunately, I had come top in French only to annoy Madame Slack. I had learned twenty-five words and then made sure I answered every question using only those words.

Just then Henri came running back to save us. He started yelling and shrugging his shoulders and soon everyone was shrugging shoulders. Even the bloke selling birdfood. I don't know what he had to do with it.

I turned to the gang. "Wait for a big group shrug and then run like the wind for sanctuary into Notre Dame. We must beg the priests to save us."

It all got sorted out in the end. The French loon patrol turned out to be park keepers. Sort of like park Elvises. Apparently you are not allowed to step on their grass, because it drives them insane.

Madame Slack gave her world famous 'Once again a few bad apples have spoilt the reputation of England' lecture and gave us all bad conduct medals. I mean marks.

I said to Jas, "You would think that she would encourage us to bring history to life, but oh no, *au contraire*, we are pilloried on the spike of . . . er . . . life."

9.30 p.m. Henri took us out to a restaurant tonight. It was really groovy, apart from some old drunk at the piano who kept moaning on about "*Je ne regrette rien*". Ellen asked, "What is he going on about?"

I said, "He's saying in French, that he doesn't regret a thing, which he quite clearly should. He should regret having started this song, for one thing."

Henri said he was a famous French singer. Good Lord.

Very, very funny evening. There was a notice on our table

543

saying what you could have to eat. It said "Frogs' legs" at the top. When the waiter came he spoke English (sort of). "Good evening, Mademoiselle, what can I get you?"

I said, "*S'cuse moi*, have you got frogs' legs?"

He smiled. "Yes, M'selle."

So I said, "Well, hop off and get me a sandwich, then."

We laughed for about a million years. Even the waiter thought it was funny (ish). However, Madame Slack heard what had happened and said we were "giddy".

monday january 24th

last morning in gay paree

Sitting by myself in a café because the Ace Gang have gone off to look at some French boys. I even ordered a cup of coffee for myself. And a croissant. Well, actually, it looks more like an egg sandwich (because it is an egg sandwich), but at least it's not a walking stick.

pompidou centre

midday You can't move for white-faced loons in the area around the centre. Some of them just stand still for ages and ages, painted all white like a statue. Then when you are really bored from looking at them, they slowly move a finger, or lift a leg, and then go back to being still. And people throw coins in their hats for that. I said to Rosie, "What is the point of mime artists? Why don't they just tell you what they want?"

Then I noticed that a gorgey *garçon* was watching me watching the white-faced loons. I kept catching him looking at me. He was cute. *Très* cute. And his trousers were relatively normal. And he wasn't wearing a beret. And he was handbag-free.

He caught my eye and smiled quite a dreamy smile. He was very intense-looking, with incredibly dark curly hair. However, I am a red bottom-free zone and I was just about to ignore him when he went off.

Ah well. *C'est la guerre,* as they say here, although what the railway station has to do with anything, I don't know. (Or is that *gare*? Oh, I don't know. As I say to Madame Slack, French is a foreign language to me.)

5 minutes later

The gorgey French boy came back and brought me a red rose!! He said, "For the most beeootiful girl," kissed my hand and then went off into the crowd.

Honestly.

The Ace Gang were dead impressed. We discussed it for ages. It didn't fit into the snogging scale anywhere. And it wasn't a "see you later". Was I supposed to follow him? Should I have done something erotic with the rose?

As I have said with huge wisdomosity many times, boys the world over are a bloody mystery.

au revoir

We got on the train and said *"Auf Wiedersehen"* to the city of romance. We have our memories to take home with us. More importantly, we also have our HUGE comedy berets.

We found them in a souvenir shop in the station that sold

musical Eiffel Towers, nuddy-pants cancan dancers and other sophisticated gifts. The berets are gigantic and they are wired around the rim, so that they stick out about a foot from your head. Excellent!!! They are quite hilarious in the extreme. We each got one. I can't wait to wear them to school. They make the lunchpack berets seem traditional by comparison.

When we got on the train, Madame Slack went off to the teachers' compartment, probably to chat with Gorgey Henri about handbags they had known and loved. We took the opportunity to try on our new berets. All six of us leaned out of our carriage window wearing our gigantic berets as the train pulled out. We were yelling "*AU REVOIR, PARIS! WE LOVE YOU ALL!!!*"

And guess what? The people on the platform all waved and cheered. They were shouting, "*Bonne chance!*" I think.

I asked Jas, as we tucked into our cheesy snacks for the journey, "Do you think that the French-type people think we really like our berets?"

She said, "No, I think they think we are English people and therefore not normal."

"How could they think that?" asked Rosie.

Then I noticed that Rosie was wearing a false moustache as well as her beret.

Oh, how we laughed.

on the ferry heading home

Uneventful trip home because we had a normal captain (i.e. English).

Also we had chips. A LOT.

I was quite overcome when we saw the white cliffs of Dover,

until I realised we aren't going to Dover and they are just some crappy old white cliffs of somewhere else.

midnight Arrived home to my loving family. As I came up the drive, Angus shot over the wall and gave me a playful bite on the ankle as he passed. I opened the door and yelled, "*C'est moi!* Your daughter is home again, crack open the fatted calf and . . ."

Angus had pushed his way in first and Dad started yelling. "Get that bloody cat out! This house is full of fleas."

I said sternly to Angus, "Angus, stay out of the house, it is full of fleas!" But the Loonleader didn't think it was funny. Even though it is.

12.10 a.m. Libby was pleased to see me, at least. She woke up when I came in and said, "Heggo Gingey."

She made me a card with a drawing of a cat band on the front. Angus is the lead singer, although why he is upside down, I don't know. The audience is little mice and voles in disco wear.

By the time I had unpacked my bag, Libby had fallen back to sleep in my bed with her "fwends". She is so lovely when she is sleeping and I gave her a kiss on her cheek. I wonder how I will get on without her when I go to America. It made me feel a bit weepy, actually. I must have boat lag.

Just as I was dropping off into snoozeland, Mutti came in. I think she might have had a couple of glasses of *vino tinto*, because she looked a bit flushed.

"Hello darling, welcome back. How was France?'

"*Fantastique.*"

"This came for you." And she handed me a letter. In the Sex God's handwriting!! Wow and wowzee wow!

Mutti came and sat on my bed.

"So, did you have a fab time?"

"*Oui. Très sportif*. Night, night."

"Did you see the Eiffel Tower? It's amazing at night, isn't it? Was it all lit up?"

Oh, good grief. I know she was being a nice mutti and everything, but I wanted to read my Sex God notelet. I said kindly, "Mum, I'm a bit boat-lagged, I'll tell you all about it in the morning."

She touched Libby's cheek and then she touched mine.

"Don't grow up too fast, love." She looked all tearful.

What is the matter with grown-ups? They are always banging on about how childish you are and telling you to grow up and so on, and then when you do, they start blubbing.

After she'd left I ripped open my letter.

> *Dear Georgia,*
>
> *Welcome home, snog queen. I'm really looking forward to seeing you. I've thought about you all weekend and I wanted to tell you that I like everything about you. Your hair, your gorgeous mouth. The way I say "goodbye" and you say "I'm away laughing on a fast camel".*
>
> *See you Tuesday.*
>
> *Lots of love,*
>
> *Robbie*

Phwoar. I put the letter under my pillow. My very first love letter.

1.00 a.m. Well, unless you count that one that Mark Big Gob sent me, which looked like he had written it with a stick.

1.05 a.m. Dave the Laugh sent me quite a nice letter when Wet Lindsay deliberately hit me on the ankle with her hockey stick. Actually, the reason I say "I'm away laughing on a fast camel" instead of "goodbye" is because of him.

And "nippy noodles".

1.10 a.m. And "poo parlour division" instead of "loo".

the cosmic horn

tuesday january 25th

Exhausted, but up like a startled earwig at 8.15 a.m., thanks to Libby blowing her new bugle in my ear. What complete fool has bought her that? Dad, obviously.

school

I wore my beret proudly this morning (not the huge one, as I didn't want to get a reprimand first thing). I wore my beret *à la française* on the side of my head. When I saw Hawkeye, I said, "*Bonjour Madame*, I *aime* a lot your *très bonne* outfit *ce matin*."

"Just get in to Assembly and try to be normal for once." That's nice, isn't it? You try to add a little bit of beautosity and humourosity into a dull world and that is the thanks you get.

As we slouched past Elvis's hut, I nudged Jas. "Elvis has got a bell! How ludicrously sad is that?" He has a bell on the outside of his hut and a sign above it that says: "Ring the bell for the caretaker". Hahahahahaha.

assembly

Slim in tip-top jelly form this morning, in her attractive

elephant-tent dress. We were all still in *la belle France* mood, saying "Ah, *bonjour*" and nodding at each other a lot and shrugging.

Slim ordered, "Silence, at once. And stop shuffling around like silly geese. I have something very serious to tell you. I am sorry to say that the whole school has been very badly let down by a few bad apples. Girls from this school have been involved in a criminal act. And I intend to make an example of them by punishing them in the severest manner."

All of the Ace Gang looked at each other. God's slippers, what had we done now? Surely Madame Slack hadn't told Slim about the hunchback incident? Or the accidental French flag fiasco?

Hawkeye was glaring at us as we shuffled around. Slim went on. "Two girls have been arrested for shoplifting in town. Charges are to be made."

All of us went "Yessssss!" (inwardly). The Bummers had finally come to the end of their reign of terror. Yesss!!!

But then we noticed a dog in the ointment. The Bummers were in the row in front of us, looking as tarty and spotty as normal, and also . . . not bothered.

Slim continued. "The two girls are Monica Dickens and Pamela Green. They are, as of today, expelled from school. I trust this will be a warning to any girl who imagines that crime has no consequence."

We were all amazed at the news. I kept saying to the others, "Nauseating P. Green? And ADM? Shoplifting?"

Jools said, "Nauseating P. Green can hardly see the end of her nose. She would be a crap shoplifter. She'd have to ask a shop assistant to point things out to her."

She is not wrong.

Weird to think that behind those huge glasses lurked a mistress criminal.

I said, "And ADM?? She came to a school dance in ankle socks once. That is not shoplifting wear."

break

Behind the sports hall we all huddled together under our coats discussing the scandalosa.

Rosie said, "I can't believe Nauseating P. Green actually went shoplifting in a gang with ADM."

I said, "Do you remember when ADM owned up to Miss Stamp about not having had a shower after games last term? And no one had even noticed that she hadn't. Miss Stamp didn't notice. In fact, I don't think she had actually noticed that ADM had even been doing games. That is not the attitude of a mistress criminal, that is the attitude of an astonishingly dim person. Which is what she is."

"I was never very nice to them," said Jas. I feel bad now. I wonder if we can visit them in jail and maybe take them things . . . you know, knitted things and so on. Oranges."

I said, "Jas, they are not in the Crimean War. They don't need you to knit balaclavas. They won't go to jail."

Jas was rambling on, "Well, Slim said they were expelled and bad apples and so forth and . . ."

"Jas, can I say something?"

"What?"

"Shut up."

"Well, I . . ."

"That is not shutting up, Jas, that is keeping on talking rubbish."

"But . . ."

We could have kept that up for centuries, but then the Bummers walked around the corner. Jackie Bummer said, "Clear off, tiny tots, we want to have a fag and you are sitting in our ashtray."

Jools (bravely, but stupidly) said, "This is just ground, anyone's ground, it's not . . ."

Alison came over and got hold of her hair, "You are *in* our ashtray, so why don't you get *out* of our ashtray."

We grumbled and groaned as we collected our things. I hate them, I hate them. As the Bummers lit up their fags, Jackie said, "Sad about the criminal element in this school, isn't it?"

In a fit of stupidosity, I said, "Yes, well, why don't you leave, then?" To which Jackie answered, "Careful, Big Nose, as a severe duffing often offends." Then she flicked her cigarette ash on to my head and said, "Oh, woops."

I had to wash my hair with soap in the loos and then dry it upside down under the hand dryer. Fortunately, I had my mega-duty hair gel with me. Otherwise there would have been a Coco the Clown incident.

maths

It's a bit funny not having P. Green's head bobbing around at the front of the class. "I miss her," said Rosie. "It's not the same firing elastic bands with no target." She is all heart.

Still, I can't spend any more time thinking about other people. It's only two hours until I meet the Sex God. It's double Blodge after this, so providing I don't have to do anything disgusting with pond life, I will be able to get my nails done and foundation on, and possibly mascara, if I crouch down at the back.

double blodge

I thought of an hilarious biology joke (which is not easy). I wrote to the gang in a gang note: "Lockjaw means never having to say you're sorry."

They did their famous cross-eyed sign of approval.

Also, I have made a lovely new furry friend (no, not Jas). It's a pickled vole. There are all kinds of disgusting things pickled in jars in the Blodge lab, but this is a really cute vole that has its little paws up so that it looks like it is waving at you.

I wave back. I may call it Rover. Rover the vole.

last bell
in the loos

Mucho excitemondo. My hand was shaking when I was doing my eyeshadow. I very nearly put 'sex shimmer' all over my face, which is not attractive. I made Jas wait for me to walk out to the gate. I said, "So, Jazzy Knickers, what are you up to tonight? Whilst I am seeing my boyfriend?"

She was sitting on the sink looking at her sideways reflection. "I've got quite nice cheeks, haven't I?"

"Jas, you've got adorable cheeks. One on each side of your nose. Couldn't be better."

She thought I meant it. "Tom is doing his irrigation project and I'm doing my German homework tonight. It's due in. You should do yours – Herr Kamyer will have a nervy spas if you don't."

"Jas, as I have said many, many times . . . never put off

until tomorrow what you can avoid altogether."

Jas was still admiring her cheeks. "Well, you say that, but what will you feel like when you go to Germany and you can't say anything?"

"I'm not going to go to Germany."

"You might, though."

"Well, I won't."

That shut her up for a minute.

"But say you had to."

"Why, what for? I don't like pickled cabbage."

"What if Robbie had to go there for a gig? You'd feel like a *dumschnitzel.*"

Actually she did have a point.

4.20 p.m. We walked out across the yard to the gates. I made Jas shield me, just in case any of the *Oberführers* were around and noticed that I was all made up. Since the shoplifting fiasco all the staff and prefects are on high alert. Miss Stamp even told Melanie Andrews off because she didn't have a name tag in her sports knickers. I really, really don't want to imagine how she found that out.

Rosie, Jools and Ellen were loitering without intent near Mr Attwood's hut, so we all linked up. Robbie was leaning on the gate. Phwoar!! I could feel his Sex-Goddy vibes even by Mr Attwood's special bell. But then I noticed that he was not alone, he was talking to Tom and Dave the Laugh and Rollo! Ellen, Jas and Jools nearly fell over with shock. They had no make-up on. Also Ellen had mistakenly put her beret on because she couldn't be arsed to open up her haversack. Emergency, emergency!!!

Ellen snatched off her beret and said, "OhmyGod, ohmyGod, what shall I do??"

In the end Rosie and I formed a sort of defensive wall behind which Ellen and Jas and Jools applied emergency lippy and rolled over their skirts. Rosie and I had to pretend to be swapping books. I was laughing attractively and so was Rosie, as if we were casually unaware that we had three mates crouching behind us. Jas said from near my ankles, "What are they doing? Can they see us?"

"They're just talking."

Rosie said, "We're going to have to pretend to notice them in a minute, are you ready?" Then the three of them leaped up like leaping things and we all walked up to the gates in a state of casualosity (and lip-glossiness).

Robbie looked marvy. He gave me his dreamy smile and pushed his hair back. "Hello."

I was in Ditherland. It's bad enough when it's just me and him, but in front of the lads and, in particular, in front of Dave the Laugh, I turn into Herr Kamyer in a skirt (i.e. a twat).

I was completely out-dithered by Ellen, however, who I thought might start doing highland dancing, she was hopping about so much. Tom was nuzzling Jas and she was all red and smiley and dim. How come boys don't go spazoid? They all seemed very cool. I noticed (even though I didn't care) that although Dave the Laugh said hi to Ellen and kissed her cheek, he didn't do any nuzzling. In fact he gave me a look.

It was an 'Hello, red-bottomed minx, we meet again'-type look.

my bedroom

9.00 p.m. I had a dreamy time hanging around with the Sex God. I made all kinds of excuses about wanting to get things from all the shops so that people would see us together. I waved at loads of people, even if I didn't know them very well. I even waved at Mr Across the Road as he staggered out of the pet shop with two tons of kitty litter. He was so surprised, his bottom nearly dropped off.

Robbie said, "Shopping is over, now it's time for snogging." Then we went and had *le* snog *par excellence* by the racecourse.

My lips are quite tired, actually. They may have to have an early night.

midnight I wonder if Jas is right for once. Maybe Nauseating P. Green will have to go to the naughty girls' prison. Like in *Prisoner: Cell Block H*. She might get duffed up every day by sadists. Much the same as school, really.

Shut up, brain.

I care too much for people. I am a bit like Jesus. Only not so heavily bearded.

wednesday january 26th

school

On our way to the art room we had a quick burst of 'Let's go down the disco' in the corridor until we nearly crashed into Nauseating P. Green's mum. She was crying as she went into Slim's office.

Oh, poo.

break

Hiding in the games cupboard. It's full of hockey sticks, but at least it is not minus fifteen degrees like it is outside.

Kate Richardson told me that Jackie Bummer has got ten leather coats, all different colours. And Jackie was also showing off and saying that she and Alison made Nauseating P. Green and ADM go and do their shoplifting for them. Like in *Oliver Twist* . . . or is it *David Copperfield*? Anyway, one of those really depressing stories about tiny orphans with Fagin in it. They frightened P. Green and ADM into going into shops and putting leather coats on under their own coats and walking out of the shop and then handing them over to the Bummers. They said that if they didn't get six each they would do something horrible to P. Green's hamsters. They even gave them a special tool to get the security labels off.

Rosie said, "Well, why did they get caught, then?"

I explained, "Because P. Green tried to steal six coats at once. She put them all on under her own coat and then got trapped in the revolving door as she tried to get out."

1.00 a.m. On the bright side, Mutti says I can have some new boots. To wear to the gig that my boyfriend is playing at on Saturday at the Buddha Lounge.

1.10 a.m. Did I mention that there is a gig on Saturday that my boyfriend is playing at? Once again I can expose myself as girlfriend of a Sex God? Oo-er.

thursday january 27th

Herr Kamyer was telling us about the Müller family from our German textbook – about Klaus going camping and getting his *kocher* out. Klaus always uses his *kocher* to *koch* his *spanferkel* (suckling pig). Jas was annoying me by doing a quiz in *Cosmo*. Not an interesting quiz about what kind of skin you have or whether you are a sex bomb or not. It's to find out what your natural body clock is. Whether you should stay up late, and get up late or whether you should get up early and go to bed early.

Who cares? Jas does. She wrote me a note: "I like to get up early and that makes me a Lark-type person. Tom likes to get up early as well, so he's a Lark and not an Owl, and that makes us get on really well. I wonder what the German for 'lark' is?"

I wrote back: "*Larken*." But she doesn't believe me.

I ended up doing the stupid boring quiz because it insinuated itself into my brain. I am very impressionable, which is why people should be very careful about what they bother me with. For instance, when we did *Treasure Island* I developed a limp. Anyway, it turns out that I am a moderate Owl. On our way to Maths I said to Jas, "That means that, although I like to go to bed late and get up late, I am not very fond of fieldmice."

She said, "Your eyes are a bit owly, sort of bulgey."

"Oh dear, now the little lark is going to get a duffing from the moderate owl." And then I biffed her over the head with my Science overall. She said I had to stop, because I was making her fringe go all wonky. And no one wants that.

559

break

I have been made hockey captain!!! Honestly, at this rate I will become a regular citizen and possibly start doing voluntary work with the elderly mad! Er no, forget that bit. I've just remembered the last time I went round to Granddad's and accidentally went into his secret money drawer to borrow a few pounds for essentials. Chewing gum and so on. He had set his false teeth open as a trap. When I opened the drawer they slammed shut.

Even though he is supposed to be deaf, Granddad heard his false teeth bang shut from the bottom of his garden. He laughed so much I thought I might have to call the emergency services. But I contented myself by hiding his pipe.

Anyway, back to my triumph on the pitch. Miss Stamp announced that I would be captain. The Ace Gang were all doing the 'Let's go down the disco' dance as celebration, until Miss Stamp told them to pull themselves together and get into the showers. Which quite literally put a dampener on things . . .

When we were dressed and going off to English, Miss Stamp took me to one side and said, "You have the makings of quite a good captain, Georgia. Make sure your attitude matches your hockey skills."

I haven't the faintest idea what she is on about. I said to Rosie, "Is she implying that I have insufficient maturiosity?"

Rosie said, "I don't know . . . but . . . let's go down the disco!!!!"

We did our special disco inferno dancing across the playing fields. Elvis was lurching around in his overalls. "What are you doing now? Messing about, playing the giddy goat."

I tried to explain pleasantly to the old maniac that we were in girlish high spirits. Pointless, though. He just went mumbling off.

"In my new capacity as hockey captain," I said, "I may have him confined to his hut for the foreseeable future."

in the front room

7.00 p.m. Vati said, "I'm going to start going to the gym three times a week to get in peak physical condition for our football matches." I didn't laugh. He started doing a sit-up in the front room. Good grief.

I went off into the kitchen in search of something to eat. Oh yummy, a yoghurt without mould on it! Mum does not take her nurturing role very seriously. But if I complain she'll only say something ridiculous, like, "I'm at work all day. Why don't *you* make something?"

When I went back into the front room, Dad was back lying on the sofa watching TV. I asked him, "How many sit-ups did you do?"

"Well, I think it's a mistake to rush into things."

"Just the one, then?"

He pretended to be interested in some gardening programme.

7.30 p.m. Mum came in from her girls' aerobics all red and giddy. She said to Vati, "Don't get up, Bob, try and rest yourself." But I don't think she meant it. I followed her into the kitchen in the hope that she might have some food hidden in her leotard. She did have a tin of beans, as it happens, so we tucked in.

"It's very very like Paris in our home," I told her.

She wasn't paying any attention – just being red and adjusting her bra. Then she burbled on. "We had such a laugh tonight, Gee. Prue and Sandy went to this singles bar the other night and got off with a couple of Russian sailors. Sandy said Ivan could only say *"Niet"* but that he was a really good snogger."

I just looked at her.

"Mum, that is disgusting"

"Why?"

"Because, well, they are mothers."

"I know, but they haven't got husbands anymore. They are single women again who have children."

"I know, but . . ."

She'd gone off on one, though. "Do you think that anyone over twenty-five should just stay in for ever?"

"Yes."

"You're being ridiculous."

"I am not."

"You're a teenage prude."

I was thinking, "A prude, am I? You wouldn't say that if you knew the amount of lip nibbling I had done. I have been practically eaten alive by boys!!" But I didn't say it.

8.30 p.m. In the bath, contemplating my life as the girlfriend of a Sex God and also tip-top hockey captain.

And also why nunga-nungas float. What is the point of that? Perhaps in prehistoric days they were used as lifebelts in times of flood. But if that was the case, why did they bother with Noah's Ark? Mrs Noah and all the women could have just floated about and everyone else could have climbed on board.

Then I heard raised voices. Libby started shouting, "Fight, fight!!"

Vati was yelling. "I don't watch television all the time . . . and what if I did, what's wrong with that?"

Mum yelled back, "It's boring – that's what's wrong with it!"

"Well let's talk about bloody aerobics, then. Go on, tell me how many times you wiggled your arse in time to the music!"

"Boring pig!"

And then Libby started yelling, "Bad piggy, bad piggy!!"

Sacré bloody *bleu*. I am going to be an orphan soon. Ah well.

friday january 28th

breakfast

This not talking to each other thing is driving me to the brink of bonkerosity. How am I supposed to experience growing up if the so-called grown-ups are making *me* be the most grown-up?

Mum said to me, "Would you ask your father if he would mind looking after his daughter Liberty tomorrow evening, as I have a pressing social engagement?"

Oh, good Lord. I said to Dad, who was half an inch away fiddling with his beard, "Dad, would you mind looking after your daughter Liberty tomorrow evening, which is, incidentally, when I shall be at a pressing social engagement myself, because Mutti also has a pressing social engagement, apparently."

Dad went all red and trousery. He said, "This is ballocks."

I said to Mum, "He said this is ballocks."

And Dad said, "Don't bloody swear. It's not clever."

And I said, "And he said, don't bloody swear it's not clever."

Dad started to say, "Don't be so bl–" and then he stopped and I looked at him in a helpful way and said, "And he said, don't be so bl–" But he walked out and slammed the door.

Mum said, "He's so childish." Which is true, but I think it's ironic that she should say it when she is wearing a T-shirt that says "Go girl" and fluffy mules.

saturday january 29th

Up at the crack of 8.00 a.m. for pre-gig preparations.

Vati was up as well in his ludicrous football shorts. He was being all 'masculine'. Mum was still ignoring him, but I said, "Goodbye, Vati, this may be the last time I see you fully limbed."

He chucked me under my chin (!) and said, "I'm in my prime, Georgia, they won't know what hit them." Then he strode off like he thought he was David Beckham. Which I think he does.

I said to Mum, "Vati is very very like David Beckham, isn't he? Apart from being porky, heavily bearded and crap at football."

She just tutted and did that basooma adjusting thing she does.

10.00 a.m. When I came out of the bathroom wrapped in a towel Mum was staring at me. Sort of inspecting me. Surely she couldn't tell that I had used her strictly forbidden skin stuff?

"What?" I said.

"Your elbows stick out a lot."

What??? What fresh hell? Sticky-out elbows??? I said, "What are you talking about?"

She was prodding my arms. "Well they do, don't they? I've never noticed them sticking out like that before. Look at mine. They aren't like yours. Do you think you've dislocated them playing hockey or something?"

Dislocated my elbows? I stormed off to my room to inspect them. Perfectly ordinary elbows. Maybe a bit sticky-outy, though.

Phoned Jas. "Jas, do you think my elbows stick out?"

She was, as usual, chewing something, probably her fringe. "They've always been a bit odd-looking."

Thank you, Nurse Jas. She's too self-obsessed to bother with my elbows. She just raved on about how she and Tom have joined The Ramblers' Association. She's not kidding. She could ramble on for England. I didn't know there was a special association for it.

lunch-time
in my bedroom

I am having some relaxing 'me' time. And 'me' time means groovy music and an eye mask. Libby is making some ear-muffs for the kittykats, out of some cottonwool, I think.

1.30 p.m. Mum came in and went ballisticisimus. The cottonwool ear-muffs for the kitty-kats are made from her new packet of tampons. She huffed off with what was left and accused me of selfishosity for not notic-ing. I yelled after her, "Mum, it is very hard to notice anything when you have tea bags on your eyes."

She came back in again to take Libby down for her bath and said, "I think we should get those elbows looked at."

What is she rambling on about? Get them looked at by whom? An elbowologist, no doubt.

On the funny side, I have just looked up 'elbow' in German and it is *Ellbogen*.

Campingfahrt means not, as you might imagine, an unfortunate incident with Libby in a tent . . . it means 'camping trip'. I think I have a natural talent for languages.

6.30 p.m. *Mucho excitemondo* and jelly knickers activity. I am a vision in black, wearing my new and groovoid boots.

7.00 p.m. Met the gang at the usual place to go to the gig. Sven had his special flares on. They have a battery in them and little lightbulbs all the way down the seams. When he presses the battery his trousers light up. He really is bonkers. And huge.

When we got to the door of the Buddha Lounge he said to the door guy, "Got evening, I am Sven and these are my chicks. Let us in, my trousers want to boogie." And Rosie isn't a bit embarrassed.

We all went immediately to the loos. It was the usual scrum in there. Ellen was sooooo nervous (again), like a jellybean on a trampoline. She kept going into a ditherspaz saying, "I really, really rate Dave, you know."

We said, "We know."

"But I really, you know, like him."

"WE KNOW!!!"

Out in the club it was heaving. We found a little corner to

566

use as gang headquarters and had a good eyeball around. All the lads were by the bar, Dave the L. (hmmm, cool shirt), Rollo, Tom, and a bunch of their friends. Oh, and Mark Big Gob was there with his rough mates. I hadn't seen him since the telephone box incident. He deliberately looked at my nungas and licked his lips. How disgusting he is!!! I pity his poor tiny midget girlfriend. At least my basoomas are nicely protected in their Christmas holder. Mutti said she got it specially because it had 'extra-firm control'.

Then, from behind the stage, The Stiff Dylans came out to start their set. Groovy pyjamas. Everyone went wild. The Sex God looked around and saw me (just casually flicking my hair back and exuding sophisticosity). He smiled at me and then blew me a kiss. Oh, yes! In front of everyone. Oh, yes and *bon*!

10.00 p.m. Dancefest *extraordinaire*. Top fun all night. As I may have said before, Dave the Laugh is . . . er . . . a laugh. And also quite a cool dancer. Ellen doesn't really like dancing, so when she had gone off to the ladies' he made me do the conga with him. He made me do it to 'Oh No, It's Me Again', which is one the Sex God composed that's on my Chrimbo compilation tape. It's a slow number and really serious about someone (van Gogh, I think) who wakes up and looks at himself in the mirror and says, "Oh no, it's me again," which is depressing. But not to Dave the Laugh, who thought it was a conga opportunity. Robbie was singing with his eyes closed (hmmm, very moody), but then during the slow guitar break he looked up and I think he caught sight of me and Dave conga dancing. He didn't look full of happinosity. In fact, he looked a bit miffed.

I stopped doing the conga then, but Dave shouted at me,

"Don't stop mid-conga; it's very bad for my cong."

What in the name of Elton John's codpiece is he on about? He's naughty, though. When we were dancing he let his hands sort of drift on to my bottom. I could feel it slightly flushing. Down, bottom, down.

Ellen still wasn't back from the loo, so we went across to the bar to get a cold drink. He said, "I think I have got the General Horn."

I said, "What is that?"

He explained that 'having the horn' means fancying people. And it's got various stages. "You can have Specific Horn, when you fancy one person. Then if it gets worse you get the General Horn, which is when you fancy loads of people. But worst of all is the Cosmic Horn."

He was really making me laugh and feel funny at the same time, but I couldn't help asking, "What in the name of Lucifer's bottom is the Cosmic Horn?"

"That is when you fancy everything and everyone in the universe."

Blimey.

Ellen came over then and grabbed Dave's arm. She said, all girlie, "Dave, do you fancy going outside? I'm a bit hot."

Dave sort of hesitated and looked at me in a peculiar way and then said, "Me too." And they went off. Ellen is sooo keen on him, it's ridiculous.

I said to Jas (and Tom, as they are like Siamese twins. I wonder what happens when she goes to the loo?), "Honestly, Ellen is really uncool about Dave. She practically stalks him."

Jas said, "You stalked Robbie."

I laughed in an attractive way. "Oh Jas, I did not stalk him . . ."

Jas rambled on like an unstoppable loon. "And you made me assistant stalker. Also, do you remember when you made me go round to Wet Lindsay's house and we went and looked in her bedroom window and saw her in her thong?"

Tom said, "You went round to Lindsay's house and looked in her window? I didn't know that! Does Robbie know?"

I quickly said, "Tom, have you ever had the Cosmic Horn?"

Just then The Stiff Dylans finished their set and came off stage. I went off to find Robbie for the snog break, but it was hopeless. There were loads of girls all crowded around him in the dressing room, and I couldn't get near.

He said over the top of their heads, "I'll walk you home at the end, don't leave."

midnight Outside the Buddha Lounge. Jas asked, "Is your vati picking you up?"

"No," I told her. "I've got a special prison pass, which means that I am allowed to get home by myself. Mostly because Mum is out and Dad can't walk after playing football with the 'lads'. They only lost by 13–0."

The gang set off, a band of merry snoggers and I was left outside by myself.

12.15 a.m. Brr, quite nippy noodles. Where is he?

I went and looked in through the doors, Robbie was talking to six girls: the rest of the band's girl-friends, Sam, Mia and India, and another three. I recognised a couple of them because they used to be in the Sixth Form and had gone off to London to fashion college or something. Perhaps that explained why one (Petra) was wearing a Tibetan bonnet with ear flaps. Petra had long blond hair that poked

569

out of her bonnet (very Tibetan . . . not). She was swishing it about like, er, a swishing thing. Robbie was laughing with them. But as I always say, "She who laughs last . . . er . . . doesn't always get the joke."

Why was he talking to them? Perhaps he was doing PR for his career. Or perhaps they were like those groupies I read about that used to hang around boys in groups and make little statues of their manly parts out of plaster of Paris. I didn't see any bags of plaster, though. Although one of them did have a haversack. The plaster might be in there. Just then Robbie saw me and said, "Georgia, hi."

Petra looked round and said (in a bonnetty way), "Oh hi, Georgia. Long time no dig. How are you? How's Stalag 14? Not wearing your beret?" And she laughed in a common way.

Robbie looked a bit uncomfortable and said quite quickly, "Well, nice to see you all again, see you later. Come on, Georgia."

Hahahaha and double hahaha. That shut Petra up. She looked amazed to see me and Robbie walk off together.

Robbie was a bit quiet on the way home, but when we walked through the park he got hold of me and kissed me for a really long time. I only remembered to start breathing half way through, so nearly passed out.

It was like a snoggers' rave in the park. Every bush was full of them. Mark Big Gob was there with his tiny little girlfriend. And it was very dark, but I am almost sure that he picked her up and put her on a tree stump to snog her. Either that or her legs get very fat towards the ankles.

When we got to my gate, Robbie said, "Petra and Kate have just come back from backpacking round India and Nepal."

I said, "Oh, that explains the ear flaps."

The Sex God pinched my nose. "What am I going to do with you?"

"Take me to Hamburger-a-gogo land with you."

"Hmm, I wonder what your dad would say to that."

"He'd say bye and God bless all who sail in you." SG didn't look like he believed me. Or knew what in the name of arse I was talking about.

1.00 a.m. Libby was still up when I got in. She had her pyjama top on but her bottom was flowing free and wild. She is not what you would call inhibited, which is a pity. She was giving Teddy a late-night haircut. Mum said when I came in, "Come on, Libbs, it's very late and your big sister is home now. Time for bed."

Libby didn't even look up, she just said, in an alarmingly grown up voice, "Not now, dear, I'm busy."

2.00 a.m. Kissed the back of my hand goodnight. I think I am becoming a champion snogger. As Peter Dyer said when I went for snogging lessons, I apply just the right sort of pressure, not too pressing and not too giving. Much like my nature, I like to think.

In a way, it's a shame not to share my special snogging talents far and wide.

3.00 a.m. What am I talking about? I love the Sex God, end of bottom. I mean end of story.

3.15 a.m. Looked out my window. Angus and Naomi are on the wall . . . Do cats snog? Perhaps they have a cat snogging scale.

3.30 a.m. Do owls snog?
SHUT UP, SHUT UP. This is all Dave the Laugh's fault with his Cosmic Horn talk.

monday january 31st

Met Jas at her gate. She showed me her Ramblers' Association badge. Honestly. Apparently you go off with other half-wits and wander around the countryside looking at things. I said to her, "The gig was groovy bananas, wasn't it?"

"Yeah, fabby."

"Jas, don't you ever, you know . . . get the horn for anyone else besides Tom?"

"No. I am not like you. Promiscuous."

"Jas, I'm not promiscuous."

"Well, you flirt with Dave the Laugh."

"Well, I . . ."

"In fact, you snog Dave the Laugh . . . and I bet you would snog Gorgey Henri if he asked you."

"Well . . . I . . ." For once she had a sort of point.

The Ace Gang all wore enormous berets this morning to remind us of our visit to *la belle France*. It seems about six hundred years ago. We have decided to commemorate the occasion by having a National Hunchback Day. Maybe we will wait till things cool down a bit at Stalag 14 first, though.

When we got near the school gates we took the comedy

berets off and had our ordinary ones underneath. (From comedy to tragedy in one movement!) So hahahaha to the *Oberführers*. We are too full of cleverosity for them.

As we were walking past Hawkeye something really horriblimus happened. Nauseating P. Green was standing near the gates! She looked like she had been blubbing for about a million years. I smiled at her and she started to come over to us. Oh, good grief. Then Hawkeye saw her and said, "Pamela Green, you are not to come anywhere near this school again. You are a complete disgrace."

P. Green started blinking and stuttering. "But Mrs Heaton, I . . . I didn't . . . it wasn't me, I . . ."

Hawkeye just snapped at us. "Come on, you girls, get into school NOW!" I wonder if she was a doberman in a previous life.

cloakroom

I said to Jas, "Nauseating P. Green is obviously a twat of the first water but I do feel sorry for her."

Jas said; "I wonder if we should . . . er . . . go and see someone about it."

Rosie said, "And then get the duffing-up of a lifetime from the Bummers?"

Hmm, she had a point.

Still.

games

Brrrrrrrrrrrrr. Miss Stamp has had us doing hockey manoeuvres in minus five hundred and forty.

As we shivered I said to Jas, "Even seals would stay in their little seal homes on days like this. They would stay snuggly tucked up knitting and chatting."

Jas got interested in the seals. She's a bit obsessed with sea creatures, I think. "Do you think they have their own language? I wonder what sort of thing they talk about?"

"They talk about the great seal package holidays they had been on. Greenland by night, Antarctica weekend breaks, two nights on a top-class iceberg and as much krill as you can eat."

This is the life. Charging around on a frozen pitch, whacking concrete balls at each other with sticks. Once you got the feeling back in your bum it was quite good fun, actually. I was tearing up and down the pitch like David Beckham (without the shaved head and manly parts, of course, but with the consummate ball skills). Well, until I accidentally whacked Jas on the knee (above the shin pad) with a ball.

It was her fault, really. I whacked a really good goal in the net but Mrs Slow Knickers didn't get out of the way in time (probably because she was weighed down by her enormous sports pantibus). As she hobbled off she was moaning and groaning and blaming me. "You're mad, Georgia, hitting balls around like . . . like . . ."

I said, helpfully, "Like a brilliant hockey captain?"

"No, not like that"

"Well, like what?"

She was red as a loon. I gave her my famous world-renowned affectionate hug, but she pushed me off and said "Like . . . a promiscuous HOOLIGAN."

Oooooooh. Now she had really upset me.

lunch-time

Lad alert!!! Lad alert!!! Dave the Laugh was at the school gates. He looked in a bit of a funny mood. Normally he is all smiley and sort of cocky (oo-er), but he wasn't smiling. And he looked a bit tense. He is really nice-looking. If I didn't have the Sex God I would definitely want to go out with him. Especially as Tom told me that Dave made a huge banner and hung it on top of their school, and it said, "For sale". Which anyone can see is vair vair funny. By the time I got to gang headquarters (first floor loos), Ellen was being Dithering Queen *extraordinaire*. She was saying, "Oh, oh, what shall I do? What shall I do?"

Jas said, "Just go and talk to him. He's come to see you. That's really nice." Then she went all dreamy and dim. "Tom sometimes just gets an urge to see me and he comes to meet me on the . . ."

I said, "Veggie van?"

She didn't even look at me. She just continued to talk to Ellen as if I hadn't said anything vair vair hilarious. "He comes to see me on the spur of the moment." Then she gave me her worst look (scary bananas) and limped off.

I called after her, "You know I love you, Jas. Why are you not touching me with a barge pole? And eschewing me with a firm hand? And *ignorez-vousing* me?" She still didn't pay any attention.

After about a million years applying lip-gloss, Ellen went out to meet Dave the L.

We all watched from the loo windows whilst they talked. I said to Jools, "He didn't snog her when he saw her, did he?"

Rosie was doing her toenails; she had bits of soap in

between each toe to stop the polish going smeary. I must remember not to use the soap ever again.

Anyway, Rosie said, "Sven always snogs me when he first sees me. In fact he snogs me pretty much all the time. Even when he is eating."

We all said, "Erlack!"

Dave and Ellen went behind the bike shed and we couldn't see what was happening. I was sort of glad about that somehow, because even though I had a boyfriend, was ecstatic, in seventh heaven, couldn't be happier, never thought about another boy for a second, had set aside my red bottom with a firm hand, only had the Specific Horn with no sign of the General Horn at all, I didn't really like to see Dave the Laugh snogging other people. I don't know why.

maths

Ellen was blubbing in Maths. She was sniffling next to Jas and I could see that she was telling her what had happened, but as Jas is even *ignorez-vousing* my notes, I couldn't find out anything. Then Ellen put her hand up and said she felt ill and could she go to sick bay.

I know I often feel like blubbing during Maths, but I thought she was being a bit over the top having to go to sick bay. Mind you we were doing pi, and I may have said this many times before, but didn't the ancient Greeks have anything better to do than measure things? Or leap out of baths, yelling *"Eureka!"*

When Miss Stamp (quarter lesbian, quarter sports *Oberführer* and also quarter Maths teacher . . . hang on, that only makes her a three-quarter person . . . ah well) asked

us why Archimedes shouted *"Eureka!"* when his bath over-
flowed, I said it was because *eureka* is Greek for "Bloody hell,
this bath is hot!!!" Which may well be the first ancient
Greek joke.

afternoon break

World news breaking! Dave has dumped Ellen!! And Ellen is
not a happy dumpee. In the Chemistry lab loos Ellen was
nearly hysterical. Her eyes were all swollen like mice eyes. She
was gulping and trying to talk, and then blubbing again. Nurse
Jas was hugging her.

Finally Ellen managed to say, "He, he, said he first realised
at the . . . at the . . . fish party that he . . . that he . . . that he
. . ." Sniffle, sniffle, gulp.

I thought, I'm ever so peckish. I wonder if it would be
really unfeeling if I just nibbled on my Mars bar?

But then Ellen managed to go on. "I mean, I said to him
. . . 'Is it something I've done?' And he said . . . he said . . .
'No, you're a great girl, it's something I've done, not you.
It's a sort of General Horn-type thing.' What does he mean??
What has he done? What General Horn thing?"

Oh God. Oh Goddy God God.

The others were nodding, but Jas was nodding and looking
at me. Like a wise old owl in a skirt. But with arms instead of
wings. And no beak.

Then the bell went. Phew.

4.30 p.m. On the way home, Jas walked really
quickly ahead of me, like she had some-
thing stuck up her bottom. I nearly had to jog to get alongside

her. I put my arm around her and she sped up even more, so that we were both jogging along.

I said, "Jas, Jas, my little pal, I'm sorry about bonking you on your knee. Do you want me to kiss it? Or carry you home? I will. I will do anything if you will be my little pal again."

Jas stopped. "All right, don't drop me, though." So I had to carry her home. All the way home. And she is not light – her knickers alone must weigh about half a stone.

I was nearly dead by the time we reached her gate. I tried to put her down, but she said, "This is the gate, not my bed." So I had to carry her right to the door. She unlocked the door still in my arms, whilst my head practically fell off with redness, and then I had to carry her upstairs to her bedroom.

It did make us laugh, though. As we were lying on her bed with a squillion of her soft toys, I said, "Jas, have you forgiven me now?"

"Polish my Ramblers' badge." So I had to polish the badge. Then she said, "I might be preparing myself to forgive you."

I fed her a cheesy whatsit and she munched on it. Then she said, "But will Ellen forgive you?"

"What do you mean? For what?"

"For snogging her boyfriend and . . . for . . . for allowing your red bottom to rule the roost."

"Jas, my bottom is not a chicken."

"You know what I mean."

"Don't start all that 'you know what I mean' business."

"Yes, but you do know what I mean."

my room

Jas thinks that I should tell Ellen what happened *vis-à-vis* Dave the Laugh, because then she will know that he is a serial snogger and lib nippler . . . or whatever . . . and then she will not pine for him.

Hmmm. She might not pine for him, but she might pull my head off.

Mum came bustling in. "Are you ready?"

"For what? Nuclear war? World peace? Tea? A surprise inheritance?"

"Dr Clooney . . . er, I mean Dr Gilhooley."

"Gorgey though he is, Mum, why would I be ready for him?"

5.00 p.m. I had a quick look at my *Ellbogen*. I haven't thought about them much lately because of all the other emergencies that have been happening. They are a bit odd-looking, actually, when you get them naked. And I won't be able to go around wearing long sleeves for the rest of my life, especially in California. And what about the press when I go to premieres and stuff with Robbie? I don't want headlines pointing my elbows out to the world: "*Sex God and weird girl with sticky-out elbows go to top restaurant.*"

As we entered the Valley of the Unwell (Dr Clooney's waiting room), I said to Mum quietly, "What can he do about them anyway?" I said it quietly because the room was, as usual, full of the mentally deranged.

Dr Clooney is quite gorgeous. Blue-eyed, dark and sort of sexy. He makes Mum go in a terrible tizz, all flushed and basoomy. He said, "How can I help?"

Mum pulled up my sleeves exposing my elbows and said, "Her elbows stick out."

Dr Clooney laughed for about a million years. He said,

579

"Honestly, I would pay you two girls to come to my surgery every day." Then he walked over to examine my elbows.

Dr Clooney smiled at me. Phwoar!! "Georgia is a racehorse."

What in the name of Miss Stamp's moustache and matching eyebrows is he talking about?

He went on. "She's got long limbs and not much fat on her body, so her elbows seem to be more bony and exposed than someone who has a different body shape. As she grows they'll be less noticeable."

I thought Mum was going to snog him on the spot. "Oh, thank you, Doctor, it was such a worry. Anyway, how have you been doing? Done any dancing lately?"

On the way home I said to Mum, "What did you mean, done any dancing lately?"

Mum went all red and delirious. "Well, I've just, you know, seen him out sometimes, when I've been with the girls . . . dancing, and . . ."

"Yes . . . and . . . ?"

"Well, he's very fit." Oh, dear God. My own mother is displaying alarming signs of the General Horn.

9.00 p.m. On the plus side, the *Ellbogen* mystery is solved . . . I am a racehorse.

10.00 p.m. Rosie phoned. "Georgia. Something really awful has happened."

"Has your hair gone all sticky up? I think mine has."

"No, it's not that."

"Lurker alert?"

"No, worse."

"Blimey. You're not having a baby Sven, are you?"

"Sven is being sent back to Swedenland. He has to help out with his family farm, or whatever they have over there."

"Is it a reindeer farm?"

"GEORGIA, I DON'T KNOW and I don't care!!!"

Rosie is sheer desperadoes. She says if Sven goes to Swedenland, she goes too. I said, "Well you'd better find out where it is first. You drew the wheat belt across the Irish Sea in our last Geoggers test."

tuesday february 1st

breakfast

8.05 a.m. This is ridiculous – Mum and Dad are still not speaking. Normally I would be glad of the silence, except it means they both speak to me and ask me things. Like, "So, what's number one this week in the pop charts?" How sad is that?

school

It's like the Valley of the Damned. Rosie is moping around, Jools has had a fight with Rollo and Ellen is sniffling around the place like a sniffler *extraordinaire*. You only have to say to her, "Do you fancy one of my cheesy whatsits?" and she runs off to the loos blubbing. And Jas keeps looking at me. Looking and looking.

I said to her, "You should be careful, Jas, one of the first formers was in a staring competition last week and she stared for so long that her eyes went dry and she had to go to hospital to have them watered."

She just sniffed. It is a very very good job that I am full of cheeriosity, also a tip-top hockey captain.

re

Rosie sent me a note. "I've found out where Swedenland is. I'm going to go after Sven and get a job and make new Sweden-type friends."

I wrote back: "Is there much call for fifteen-year-old snoggers in Swedenland?"

She looked at me when she got the note and did her famous impression of a cross-eyed loon. Then she wrote: "Anyway, what will YOU do in Hamburger-a-gogo land for a job? Your very amusing impression of a lockjaw germ, or . . . er . . . that's it."

evening

Same bat time. Same bat place.

Libby was applying some of Mutti's face powder and lipstick to Angus whilst he sat on my bed. And he didn't seem to mind. In fact, he was purring. Becoming a furry vati has made him alarmingly mellow. Or a homosexualist.

Robbie has gone off for some interview thing. He didn't really explain what it was about. Popstar stuff, I suppose. Rosie is very very wrong if she thinks I will not be able to do anything in Hamburger-a-gogo land. I could form a girlfriends' hockey eleven and play my way across America.

wednesday february 2nd

6.30 p.m. Hockey tournament today with me at the helm. But more to the point, Wet Lindsay has resigned from the team. HURRAH! She says it is a protest against me being hockey captain, because I am a facsimile of a sham and have the attitude of a juvenile pea. Useless stick insect ankle molester.

Cracking victory!!! The most amazing day. We played six matches and won all six! I scored in each match, and even though I do say it myself . . . I AM A HOCKEY GENIUS!!!

I had to give a speech when I accepted the cup for our school. It was my chance to show the world and, in particular, the heavily moustachioed Miss Stamp that I am full of wisdomosity and maturiosity and gravitas (not gravy ass, as Rosie thought). I said, "I would just like to say that I owe this victory to many people. To my team, to my school, to my mum and dad for having me, to the ancient Britons for giving me my proud heritage, to the early cavemen, without whom none of us would have got here, as they invented the wheel . . ."

Miss Stamp was about to implode but she couldn't do anything because the head of All Saints school seemed to think I was being *très amusant* and clapped A LOT at the end of my speech.

thursday february 3rd

school

Hahahahaha. Slim had to mention my name in Assembly and congratulate me!!!

Hawkeye looked like she had poo in her mouth (which she probably did). Slim, as usual, was in a ludicrously bad mood. Her chins were trembling in time to the hymns. She said, "Despite what I have said before, certain elements in this school continue to think they can carry on flouting school rules. Mr Attwood misplaced his cap a day or two ago and found it today, burnt to a cinder. This is my final warning to you all: Be very, very careful of your behaviour, as all misdemeanours will be treated very seriously."

As we ambled off to English, I said, "Mr Attwood probably set fire to his own hat on purpose. He hates us because we are young and lively."

Jas said, "And because we drop skeletons on him."

"Well, yes . . ."

"And the locusts ate his overalls . . ."

"Yes, well there is . . ."

"And he tripped over his . . ."

"Jas, shut up."

re

Rosie has been living in Glum City all day since her beloved Sven got in his Viking boat (Olau Lines ferry) and went off to Swedenland today. He has only gone for one month, but she insists that she is going to go and live in Swedenland with him for that month. Miss Wilson was telling us about her unhappy childhood, so I took the opportunity to draw some fashion items for Rosie to take with her to the Nordic wastes. I drew her wearing furry glasses and a nose warmer. I even did a vair vair funny drawing of her in a fur bikini, but she could hardly

584

be bothered to join in, even when we started our traditional RE humming. (We all start humming really softly and at the same time carry on as normal so that you can't tell we are humming. Or where the humming is coming from.) Miss Wilson thought it might be the radiators. It drives Miss Wilson round the proverbial bend . . . not so far to go in her case.

break

In sheer desperadoes to cheer Rosie up, I had a moment of my usual geniosity. We were slouching along past Elvis's hut with its stupid sign that says: "Ring the bell for the caretaker." I said to RoRo, "*Un moment, mon* pally." Then I went and rang his bell.

He came looning to his door, like the grumpiest, most mad man in the universe, which he is. He glared at me and then said, "What do you want?"

I said, pointing to his sign, "What I want to know, Mr Attwood, is why you can't ring your own bell."

Anyway, he didn't get it. He was rambling on and I was just about to slope politely off, when Wet Lindsay came round the corner. She was ogling us like an ogler with stick legs, which she is.

Elvis was so red I thought his head might explode, but sadly, it didn't. He was shouting, "It's always you, messing about, coming in my hut. You let those bloody locusts eat my spare overalls . . ."

I tried to be reasonable with the old maniac. "Mr Attwood, Elvis, I wasn't to know that the locusts would eat your overalls. I merely thought they would like a little fly around in the Blodge lab after being cooped up in their cage."

Mr Attwood was still yelling. ". . . and I bet it was you who burnt my cap!"

Oh, for heaven's sake.

maths

I was just peacefully buffing my half-moons, when Hawkeye put her head round the door. She barked, "My office, now!!!"

hawkeye's office

Oh *sacré* bloody *bleu*. Hawkeye was livid as a loon. She was all rigid with indignosity. "I am sick to death of this, Georgia Nicolson. You have a perfectly good brain and a few talents, and you INSIST on squandering them in silly, childish pranks and unkindnesses. When Miss Stamp told me that she had chosen you as hockey captain, I had grave doubts. I still some-times get headaches from your ridiculous display at the tennis championships last year."

Oh Blimey O'Reilly's vest and pants, what is it with teachers? Do they make lists of things that happened ages and ages ago and just hang around waiting for something else to add to them? Why doesn't she read some of the books I read? Let things go . . . relax, don't sweat the small stuff, talk to dolphins, go with the flow . . . etc.

Hawkeye hadn't finished. "However, these latest so-called jokes have confirmed what I said to her; that you have a silly attitude and are a poor example to both your peers and, more especially, the young and impressionable girls in this school. You are relieved of your duties as hockey captain forthwith."

I started to try to say something, but I felt a funny prickling feeling in my throat. I had to hand back my captain's badge. And what is more, I am on gardening duty with Mr Attwood for a month!

When I came out of Hawkeye's interrogation room, Wet Lindsay was smirking around. I bet she snitched on me. I didn't dignify her by saying anything. I have more pridosity than that.

Rosie was waiting for me around the corner. "Was it the forty lashes or has she just cut your basoomas off as a warning to others?"

"She's sacked me from being hockey captain."

RoRo put her arm around me.

my bedroom

11.17 p.m. I wanted to phone the Sex God and tell him about the hockey captain fiasco and I was going to. But I wasn't sure whether he would think that the 'Ring the bell for the caretaker' thing was *très amusant* or the act of a twat.

midnight I bet Dave the Laugh would think it was . . . er . . . a laugh.

Why am I thinking about him?

friday february 4th

lunch

I didn't feel much like talking and the gang kept being nice to me, which was a bit strange. So I went off by myself to think.

What was it Billy Shakespeare said? "And as we walk on down the road, our shadow taller than our souls . . ." Oh no, that was Rolf Harris doing his version of 'Stairway to Heaven'.

How crap was that?

The gang were following me around at a distance. Like stalkers in school uniforms.

I really loved being captain, though. Oh, double poo.

Even when you are the girlfriend of a Sex God things can go wrong. And anyway, what is the point of being the girlfriend of someone if every time you want to tell him something you can't? That is like being the ungirlfriend of someone. That is what I am: an ungirlfriend.

And not hockey captain. And with quite sticky-out elbows.

I moped around to the back of the tennis courts and a voice shouted out, "Has naughty Big Nose been in trouble with the scary teacher?" The Bummers were sitting having a fag on a pile of coats.

Oh, joy. The *pièce de résistance*. *Merde*, poo and triple bum.

Alison Bummer had a draw on her fag and then went off into a sort of hacking coughing fit.

I said, "Still in tip-top physical condition then, Alison, I'm pleased to see."

Alison gave me a very unattractive look (which is actually the only look she has). And I was just walking off when I heard a little voice say, "Can I get out now? It's almost end of break and my knees are really hurting."

Jackie said, "I'd like to let you out, but I haven't finished my fag yet." And I realised the Bummers had some poor little first formers underneath the coats on 'chair duty'.

I turned back. "Let them out, you two."

Jackie pretended to be really scared. "Oh, OK then, Georgia, because we are sooooooo very very frightened of you."

Alison joined in. "Yes, you might hurt us with your enormous nose."

I looked at them and I thought, Right, that is it. I have been pushed to the brink of my tether. My hockey career might be over, but there is still something I can do for England. (And no I did not mean leave it.)

I marched back so quickly to school that the stalkers had to almost run to keep up with me.

They did catch me just as I was going into Slim's outer sanctum. "Gee, what are you doing?" Jas asked.

I said, "I'm going to tell Slim about Nauseating P. Green and the Bummers."

Everyone said, "OhmyGod!!!"

Jools said, "They will kill you if they find out."

Rosie said, "Slim might not trust you because of all the trouble you've been in."

I said, with great dignosity, "I will have to take my chance, then."

Then this really weird thing happened. Jas said, "I'm going to come in with you and tell what I know as well." So I hugged her. She tried to get away from me and spoiled the moment by saying, "Well . . . you know . . . erm . . . I mean, I am a member of the Ramblers' Association and . . ."

She would have rambled on, but Rosie said, "Yes, I'll come in as well. I will be on a reindeer farm by summer anyway, so what do I have to lose?"

All the Ace Gang said they would come to tell Slim with me. Even Ellen stopped sniffling long enough to join us. We were like the Six Samurai or whatever it is. We could ride around the countryside wronging rights and so on.

Then Slim appeared like a wardrobe in a dress and I slightly changed my mind.

4.30 p.m. Well, we did it. We snitched on the Bummers and they have been immediately suspended from school and the police went straight round to their houses. God knows what will happen next.

6.00 p.m. I'll tell you what happened next. Nauseating P. Green and her mum came round to my house. OhmyGod, they know where I live!!! They were blubbing and carrying on in an alarming way.

Nauseating P. Green brought Hammy, her hamster, around to celebrate, which was a bit of a mistake because Angus took him off to play hide and seek with Naomi and the kids. But we managed to find Hammy in the end and I think his fur may grow back in time.

The P. Greens left after several centuries of excruciating boredom and goldfishiness. But sadly it didn't end there. I have become a heroine in my own lunchtime.

Vati said, "I am really, really proud of you, my love." I thought he was going to start blubbing.

Mum was hugging me. In fact, they both forgot they were not speaking to each other and they were BOTH hugging me. Then Libby joined in with Teddy and Scuba-Diving Barbie. I never thought the day would dawn when I would be victim of a group hug.

I may never do another nice thing in my life – it really isn't worth it.

Robbie rang. I started to tell him about my day. "Hi Robbie, honestly, WHAT a day I've had. Well, guess what happened. The Bummers were sitting on some first formers and . . ."

Robbie interrupted me. "Georgia, look, I have to see you tomorrow, it's quite serious."

I said, "Have you broken a plectrum?"

But he didn't laugh.

Oh God. What now? What fresh hell?

go forth, georgia, and use your red bottom wisely

saturday february 5th

I am meeting the Sex God at the bottom of the clock tower. Libby wanted to come with me and ran off with my make-up bag. She ran in to the bathroom and held my bag over the loo, saying, "Me come."

I had no time to negotiate, so . . . I just lied. "OK, go and get your welligogs on."

She ambled off to get them and I snatched my make-up bag and escaped through the door. There will be hell to pay when I get home. In fact, I will be surprised if there is a home left by the time I get back.

I had to apply my make-up crouching behind our garden wall. I could see Mr Across the Road looking at me. He should do some voluntary work – perhaps he could be a seeing-eye dog or something.

11.00 a.m. Robbie was already at the clock tower when I got there. As soon as I arrived he pulled me to him, which was a bit of a shame as he was wearing a coat with quite big buttons and one went right up my nose. I didn't say anything, though.

He said, "Let's walk to the park. I want to go to that place where we first sat together. Do you remember?"

Oooh, how *romantico*. He sang his first song to me there with my head on his knees. (He was sitting down at the time, otherwise I would have looked ridiculous.)

On the way there Robbie didn't say anything. It makes me really nervy when people don't speak. Dad says it's because I don't have much going on in my own head, which is hilarious coming from someone who knows all the words to 'New York, New York'.

When we got to the exact spot where we first kissed, Robbie looked at me. "Georgia, there isn't an easy way of saying this, but I'm going to have to go away."

I said, "Hahahahaha . . . I know, to Hamburger-a-gogo . . . and I'm coming too. I've been practising saying 'Have a nice day', and I can very nearly say it without throwing up." I rambled on, but he stopped me.

"Georgia, love, I'm not going to Los Angeles. That interview I went to was for a placement on an ecological farm in New Zealand. And I've got it. I'm going to go live there for a year. It will be really, really hard to leave you, but I know it's the right thing to do."

"A placement . . . a . . . in . . . a . . . Kiwi-a-gogo . . . Maoris . . . sheep . . . the . . . it . . . I . . ."

in bed
crying
a lot

How can this be happening to me? After all I've been through. The Sex God said he realised it was a shallow, hollow facsimile of a sham to be a popstar.

I said, "We could recycle our caviar tins."

But he was serious. I should have known when he turned up on his bike that something had gone horribly wrong.

1.30 p.m. Kiwi-a-gogo land, though . . . Loads of sheep and bearded loons. And I am sure that the men would be just as bad.

Robbie flies off to Whakatane next week.

Next week.

Perhaps I am being paid back for having the Cosmic Horn.

1.35 p.m. Robbie said maybe I could come over for a holiday when he was settled in. I cried and cried and tried to persuade him not to go, but he said this weird thing. He said, "Georgia, you know how much I like you, but you are only young, and I'm only young and we have to have some time to grow up before we settle down." And even though I was really really blubby, I felt a funny kind of reliefiosity.

4.00 p.m. Phoned Jas and told her. She said "OhmyGod" about a million times. Then she came round and stayed overnight with me. She said I could wear her Ramblers' badge, but I said no, thank you.

In the middle of the night, in the dark, I said to her, "Jas, do you know what is weird?"

"What?"

"Well, you know I am on the brink of tragicosity and everything, but . . . well, I've got this sort of weird . . . weird . . ."

"What?"

594

"I'll tell you if you stop saying 'what'."

I could hear her chewing in the dark. What had she found to chew?

"I've got this weird feeling of reliefiosity."

And she said, "What, like when you need a poo and then you have a poo?"

sunday february 6th

5.30 p.m. I've spoken to Robbie. He is upset, but he is definitely going.

He cried on the telephone.

I am absolutely full of tragicosity. I went for a walk down to the square where the gang usually hangs out. I feel lonely as a clud.

Not lonely as a clud for long, because I bumped into Dave the Laugh, on his way to play snooker. He said, "Hello, groovster. How are you?"

I said, "A bit on the poo and *merde* side, to be honest."

"Yeah, me too. Do you fancy going down to the park and hanging out for a bit?"

He's really nice actually, almost normal, in fact, for a boy. He is upset that Ellen is upset, but he says it wouldn't be right to keep going out with her just because he felt sorry for her.

I said, "You are quite literally full of wisdomosity."

I told him about the Robbie fandango.

He smiled at me, "So then, Sex Queen, you are not going to go to Los Angeles, you are going to go to Whakatane and raise elks with Robbie?"

in my room

10.00 p.m. Everyone is out. Mutti and Vati have gone out on a 'date' and Libby is staying at her friend Josh's for the night.

Dave the Laugh and I talked for ages. About life and the universe and everything. Yes, we did. And then . . . we SNOGGED again!!! I can't believe it!!! I am like Jekyll and Whatsit in babydoll pyjamas.

10.05 p.m. I must have the Cosmic Horn because of spring (even though it is February).

Dave the Laugh said we are only teenagers and we haven't been teenagers before, so how can we know what we are supposed to do.

He's right, although, I haven't a clue what he is talking about. He said we should just live live live for the moment!!! Blow our Cosmic Horn and be done with it.

I must do something. I feel like I am going to explode.

10.10 p.m. Phoned Jas. "Jas."

"Oui."

"Do you ever get the urge?"

"Pardon?"

"You know, to flow free and wild."

She was thinking. "Well, sometimes when Tom and I are alone in the house together."

"Yes . . ."

"We flick each other with flannels."

"Jas, you keep talking on the telephone and I will send out for help."

"It's good fun . . . what you do is . . ."

"Jas, Jas, guess what I am doing now."

"Are you dancing?"

"Yes I am, my strange little pal. But what am I dancing in?"

"A bowl?"

"Jas, don't be silly. Concentrate. Try to get an image of me flowing wild and free."

"Are you dancing in . . . your PE knickers?"

"*Non* . . . I am DANCING IN MY NUDDY-PANTS!!!!"

And we both laughed like loons on loon tablets.

I danced for ages around the house in my nuddy-pants. Also, I did this brilliant thing – I danced in the front window just for a second whilst Mr Across the Road was drawing his curtains. He will never be sure if he saw a mirage or not.

That is the kind of person I am.

Not really the kind of person who goes and raises elks in Whakatane.

the end

midnight Looking out of my bedroom window. (Partially dressed.)

I can see Angus, with a few of his sons and daughters, making an escape tunnel through Mr and Mrs Next Door's hedge. He's still blowing his horn, even though he has no horn to blow.

Surely God wouldn't have invented red bottomosity unless he was trying to tell me something. He is, as we all know, impotent. Or do I mean omnipotent? Anyway, He is some kind of potent. Perhaps He is saying, "Go forth, Georgia, and use your red bottom wisely."

That will be it. So I can snuggle down now, safe in the sanctity of my own unique bottomosity.

Hang on a minute, who is that? By the lamp post? Oh, it's Mark Big Gob with his latest girlfriend, walking home. He must have dumped the midget and moved on to bigger things, because this one at least reaches his waist. Still, I cannot point the finger of shame at him. None of us is perfect. Although I don't think it's entirely necessary for his mouth to be as big as it is. He is like part bloke, part blue whale.

1.00 a.m. Still looking out the window.

Perhaps I could have Dave the Laugh as an unserious boyfriend, and for diplomatic world relations-type stuff, also have that gorgey French boy who gave me the rose in gay Paree.

Hmmm. Here come Mutti and Vati, back from their night out.

So, I could have the Cosmic Horn for now. And I could save the Sex God for later!!

Perfect. Providing he doesn't get a Kiwi accent and start snogging sheep.

So all's well that ends well in God's land.

I'll just say goodnight to the stars. Goodnight stars.

And the moon. Goodnight moon, you gorgeous, big, round, yellow, sexy thing.

Phew, I really have got the Cosmic Horn badly.

Mutti and Vati have got out of their car and although they

are holding each other up, they are still not fighting, so all is still well with the world.

Hang on a minute. They're not holding each other up, they are snogging.

That is so sad. And disgusting.

THE OFFICIAL AND PROPER END.
PROBABLY.

If you would like more information about books available from Piccadilly Press and how to order them, please contact us at:

Piccadilly Press Ltd.
5 Castle Road
London
NW1 8PR

Tel: 020 7267 4492
Fax: 020 7267 4493

Feel free to visit our website at:
www.piccadillypress.co.uk